MOCKYMEN

IAN WATSON

GOLDEN GRYPHON PRESS • 2003

This is a work of fiction. All the characters and events portrayed in this novel are either fictitious or are used fictitiously.

The first section of this novel first appeared in *Interzone*, October 1997, as a story entitled "Secrets."

A leatherbound signed first edition of this book has been published by the Easton Press of Norwalk, Connecticut.

LIBRARY OF CONGRESS CATALOGING–IN–PUBLICATION DATA

Watson, Ian, 1943–
    Mockymen / Ian Watson. — 1st ed.
      p.   cm.
    ISBN 1-930846-21-5
      1. Human-alien encounters—Fiction.   2. British—Norway—
    Fiction.   3. Reincarnation—Fiction.   4. Adoptees—Fiction.
    5. Norway—Fiction. I. Title.
    PR6073.A863   M63   2003
    823'.914—dc21   2003003612

First Edition.

MOCKYMEN

For Kris

PAST

Chapter 1

July had been a wretched month so far. When it wasn't raining, it was drizzling. This ought to have been good news for the reservoirs, but the water companies were whining that England needed weeks of sustained downpour. Those greedy privatized utilities hadn't re-invested enough of their profits. While umbrellas were bumping into one another, water was being imported by tanker all the way from Portugal, where there were floods of the stuff. Apparently there was a genuine drought in Scandinavia, but Scandinavians probably organized their affairs more sensibly.

The persistent precipitation was not good for profits at the Fern-hill Farm Craft Centre. Steve and I were selling a reasonable number of jigsaws by mail order, but we also relied on visitors. A silvery-haired old gent, who arrived in a black Mercedes on a quiet Monday morning, piqued our interest.

The gravelled car park was always at least half full, but the vehi-cles belonged either to our fellow craftsfolk or to God's Legion which owned Fernhill. Steve had just fetched a couple of mugs of coffee from the tearoom in the former milking parlour, back to our unit in a converted byre. Usually we saw to our own drinks, but our autojug had quit the day before, and we had forgotten to bring its twin from home. Shuttling an essential piece of domestic equipment to and fro was obviously a non-starter. We would need to buy a replacement.

"Look," I said, "a rich customer."

The well-heeled gent might wish to have a book expensively bound in tooled leather by Nigel, next door to us. No: an umbrella occupied one of the gent's hands, and a walking stick, the other. Forget any book, unless it was pocket-sized. Maybe he was interested in commissioning a hand-engraved goblet from Charlotte, on our other side?

The man looked to be in his late seventies. Leaning on his stick, he glowered at a God's Legion mini-bus, which was painted in luridly clashing blue and green and yellow. Eye-catching, was the idea. A prominent Day-Glo scarlet slogan proclaimed salvation through Jesus.

As a rule God's Legion refrained from parking any of their distinctive "troop transports" at Fernhill in case the sight was off-putting to visitors who were only interested in a collector's doll house or a souvenir Victorian-style glass paperweight. What we would generally see here would be one or other of the Legion's more anonymous builder's vans. Big in the building trade, the Legion was. The former farmyard here at Fernhill showcased hundreds of pieces of reclaimed architecture: convoluted old chimney pots several feet tall, marble fireplaces, towering iron gateways.

"He can drive," I said hopefully, "but most of the time he's sedentary. So he's a jigsaw addict. Big tray on his rug-covered lap. His housekeeper bringing a mug of hot chocolate."

In addition to house repairs, God's Legion was also into health food, grown on Glory Farm ten miles away. Many of the legionnaires, male and female, lived communally in a manor house renamed Salvation Hall, and worked for bed and board and pocket money, under the eye of their leader, a schismatic Baptist minister named Hugh Ellison. Charismatic, vain, and autocratic, Ellison banned the fifty residents of Salvation Hall and the similar cohorts at Glory Farm from watching any television, so I'd heard.

The aim of the Legion was to rescue young folk who had gone astray in London, runways from broken homes or refugees from abuse. To rehabilitate those vulnerable orphans of the streets, train them, bring Christ back into their lives, and also fruitful labour. The Legion was steadily expanding its business and property interests to fund its good works. Legion workers had converted the derelict farmhouse and outbuildings of Fernhill into the workshops and showrooms of the present craft centre. Legion girls ran the tearooms, selling glory-food. However, no obtrusive propaganda was on show, nor were any of us craftspeople interested in being born again. Rents for the units just happened to be very moderate. Maybe us craftspersons were window dressing, proof that the Legion was no doctrinaire cult but a broad-minded, benevolent body.

The silver-haired man began to walk slowly towards the yard, around which were the majority of our workshops and showrooms. He paused to look into Ben and Barbara Ackroyd's ceramics studio (specialists in signs and plaques, handmade, painted to order, world-wide mail-order service).

"He wants a nameplate for his house."

"No, Steve, he's just resting."

A ceramic nameplate featuring daffodils or bunny rabbits might be a bit naff for our dignified gent. You might well say that what Steve and I produced at Majig Mementoes was naff. Yet you had to find a commercial gimmick, a vacant niche in the craft world. When we applied for the unit, the name of our enterprise had provoked suspicion from Hugh Ellison, who had vetted us personally. What was this about *magic?* Here at Fernhill we would find no New Age craftspeople peddling pagan symbolism!

Majig Mementoes is merely a catchy name, we explained. Jig, from jigsaw—plus magic moments, treasured memories, as in the song. We would turn any photograph into a special personalised jigsaw. Wedding photograph, holiday photo, baby or pet portrait, pic of your house or your garden at its best, or your classic car. The jigsaw could be a surprise present for someone. It might serve as a promotional ploy, advertising your business. Rectangle or circle or star-shape: you name it. Your initials linked together. Car-shaped, yacht-shaped, cat-shaped. If a client had no suitable photo available, I could take excellent pictures with my digi-camera. We also imported speciality collector-jigsaws from America and Sweden, mostly for sale by mail order.

"What kind of *specialties*," demanded Ellison, "does Sweden offerR?" He had this knack of echoing the final sound in each sentence—a trick to avoid the usual "ums" or "ers." No hesitations figured in his speech.

Craggy and patriarchal he looked—someone who would roll up his sleeves (after first removing the well-tailored jacket and the chunky cufflinks) and plunge rescued souls into a tub of water to cleanse them. Alas, he was losing his hair, and wore what remained rather absurdly long in the camouflage style of a vain bloke who cannot admit to reality.

"SwedenN—?"

"Nothing naughty," Steve hastened to reassure him. "A company in Helsingborg makes the most difficult jigsaws in the world. Forty thousand unique pieces to the square metre. That's over twenty-five pieces to the square inch."

"That ought to keep Swedes out of mischiefF." As if Swedes were forever romping in the nude, feeding each other wild strawberries.

We would undertake any reasonable jigsaw commission. Steve, with his woodworking skills, and some accountancy courtesy of a training course offered by the Council for Small Industries in Rural Areas. Me, with my qualifications in photography and graphic design, and some marketing know-how, thanks again to COSIRA, which had oiled the wheels for us to take out a bank loan for working capital.

Ellison's next question was, "Is a unit at Fernhill *big* enough for you to manufacture jigsawsZ?" Now he had his financial hat on. (Let not a mischievous gust of wind blow into the little office behind the tearooms, where he interviewed us, and expose his comb-over!) Steve explained how the colour separation, lithoprinting, spray-mounting, and lamination would be carried out by a printing firm in Blanchester, our county town nearby, which would also produce the cardboard boxes. Our main expense had been the computer and software for editing and tweaking electronic pictures, and the scanner for digitizing customers' own photos.

The silver-haired gent had moved on, to pause outside Donald and Daisy Dale's Chess Yes! (Handmade, hand-painted sets, characters out of Arthurian Legend to Star Trek; unusual commissions welcomed.) Still, the brolly did not go down—not until the old man reached our own unit, and proceeded to step inside. We were in luck. Calling out a cheery greeting, we busied ourselves so he would feel at ease while he looked around, though we did sneak glances.

A framed oval jigsaw held him spellbound. Two lovely twin sisters, early teenage, with blond pigtails, were leaning laughing against the basin of the Fountain of Trevi in Rome. Both girls wore polka-dot frocks, one of yellow spots on red, the other of red spots on yellow. Photo by proud Daddy, who lived in our own village of Preston Priors and who ran a Jaguar dealership in Blanchester. Daddy had sent out our jigsaws of his girls as Christmas presents to relatives at home and abroad. He had been only too happy to let us to keep one on permanent show at Fernhill. Whether all the recipients would be enchanted by the proud gift ("See what lovely children *I* have!") was, perhaps, another matter.

In his younger years our visitor must have been handsome in a Germanic way—him driving a Mercedes directed my mind along these lines. Lofty brow, aquiline nose, blue eyes, jutting chin, and no doubt a flaxen mop of hair in times gone by. His broad shoulders had shrunken in. He no longer stood so straight and tall in his posh suit, as once he must.

"May I ask some questions?"

I would have put his accent as educated Tyneside, if it had not been subtly foreign. Steve and I were all attention.

That van: did all of us here belong to God's Legion?

Definitely not. I explained the situation.

Who had paid for the special advertising feature in the county newspaper on Saturday, profiling the craft centre? It was the four-page spread which had brought us to his attention.

Why, that had been Hugh Ellison's notion to promote the place. God's Legion bore half the cost. Collectively, us craftspeople paid the rest. Nowhere in the profile was there any mention of glory or redemption.

He consulted our brochure. "You are Chrissy Clarke. Chrissy is short for Christine. I suppose you sympathize with the aims of these evangelists."

"Not especially! It's only a business arrangement. The rents are cheap."

Our visitor probed our background a bit more, which I thought was rather impertinent, but he *was* a potential client.

Steve and I had met as students at art college in Loughborough. Both of us were keen on jigsaw puzzles. Photography and graphics; woodworking; blah blah. I did not go into details about how we were only renting our cottage, or how on Earth we would ever find a chance to have kids.

Changing tack abruptly: how tiny could the pieces of a jigsaw be made? As soon as I mentioned that company in Sweden: could we show him an example of their products right now?

Of course we could.

The miniature intricacy delighted him. "This is very fortunate. *Majig*, I do like that name."

Steve chuckled. "God's Legion was a bit suspicious of it at first."

Those blue eyes twinkled. "I can guess why."

"We had thought about calling ourselves Jiggery-Pokery."

"What does that mean? I do not know the words."

"It means something crafty," I intervened. "It's from a Scots word for trick, which probably comes from the French for game. But really, it suggests deceitfulness."

"You explain well to a foreigner."

"That's because I had a German boyfriend for a little while before I met Steve." Heinz had been studying graphics at Loughborough. I had thought he was sweet.

"A German boyfriend? That's good."

"Because *you* are a German?" My tone was a touch tart.

"Because it broadens the mind. In fact, Miss Clarke, I am Norwegian. My name is Knut Alver, and I have a proposal. . . ."

What a proposal it was, certainly as regards the fee he offered, and the fringe benefits—a quick trip to Norway at his expense, returning via Sweden and Copenhagen.

To give Mr Alver his due, he made the commission sound as *normal* as he could. He felt very nostalgic, so he explained, for the land of his birth. Unfortunately, he was terrified of air travel. Boat trips made him seasick. A car journey to Norway would be too gruelling at his age, even if a chauffeur was at the wheel.

In Oslo, he went on, there is a sculpture park—the creation of a certain Gustav Vigeland. This park and its statues epitomize the spirit of Norway. Mr Alver wanted majig mementoes of the place, to assemble at his leisure. By so doing, he would be putting his own life in order metaphorically, before the grim reaper came for him.

He wished us to go to Oslo and take pictures of various sculptures in the park by moonlight. We should carry our film to that Swedish firm, for them to produce four custom-made jigsaws with as many thousands of pieces as they could pack into each. He would pay the Swedes in advance on our behalf. Mr Alver tapped the Swedish box we had shown him.

"Keep Publishing: that is what the name of the company means."

Steve grinned. "Persistent people, eh?"

Mr Alver regarded him oddly, then chuckled.

What's more, Alver went on, we must *drive* with our film the three hundred or so miles from Oslo to Helsingborg in Sweden in a hire-car, for which he would pay.

"It is good to keep in touch with the ground. Even railway trains are somewhat detached from the landscape. I have never liked trains—"

There seemed to be few forms of transport of which he did approve! Ours not to reason why. A drive through Sweden could be lovely and fascinating. I did correct him on one point.

"No films are involved, Mr Alver. I use a digital still camera. The images store electronically on a pop-out cartridge."

"Oh . . . These pictures must be taken late at night, by moonlight. Is it technically possible with such a camera—as regards exposure?"

Simpler and faster. Camera on a tripod. Half a minute or so by moonlight should be fine. Bight and early next morning, we would return to take the same pictures by daylight. The Swedish company's computer would tweak the digi-pictures to enhance and smooth out grain and add in extra detail.

"This is excellent—better than I hoped." Then Mr Alver proceeded to broach the slightly bizarre aspect of the commission.

"That park is most magical by moonlight. It is open all round the clock, and perfectly safe for a stroll at any hour—"

One good reason for taking the pictures at midnight was that we should have the place pretty much to ourselves. During daylight hours tourists, particularly Japanese, infested the Vigeland Park, so he had heard.

"All of the granite sculptures in the park are nude figures—of men and women, young and middle-aged and old, and of boys and girls and babies. The park is a celebration of the cycle of life—"

Here came the delicate part of the commission. The Norwegian gent insisted that Steve and I in turn must press our own naked flesh against the sculptures he specified, embracing those granite nudes. Two photos of Steve doing so; two photos of myself. Resulting in four jigsaws. Circular ones, each half a metre across. In black and white.

Steve is skinny. Rabbit-skinny, is the way he refers to it. Imagine a rabbit dangling, skinned, in a butcher's shop. He's redheaded—curly-haired—and covered in freckles. I'm plumper. Frankly I'm a little plumper than I ought to be, though my breasts are petite. Good childbearing hips, and never mind about the milk supply. Usually I wear my long dark hair tied up. Neither of us were pinups, but of course that is true of most people.

"I require nothing frontal. I am an old man. Nudity is not titillating to most Norwegians. This is a . . . symbolic thing. You will understand when you see the sculptures. Adopt whatever pose is most comfortable."

I nodded reassuringly at Steve. Free trip to Scandinavia. Nice fat fee for a little work.

"And there'll be nobody in the park but us?" Steve asked.

"There will be a few people, but it is a big place. I want you to take the photographs on the central elevated platform. From there you can see all around. The sculptures provide cover—"

For our exposure, ho.

"I imagine you will wear clothing which you can remove quickly—"

Quite, a dress without knickers underneath. I could forgo a bra. Steve should wear underpants in case he zipped himself.

After the jigsaws were produced in Helsingborg, we should take the ferry across to Denmark and fly back with the four boxes of jumbled pieces from Copenhagen, where we would leave our rent-a-car. On our return, we would phone Mr Alver so that he could come to Fernhill to collect the goods. He would not confide his address to us because, frankly, he was something of a recluse, who feared being burgled now that he was frail. This was another quirk I could easily live with. He would book our flights and a hotel room in Oslo near the park, and a hotel in Helsingborg. Tickets and such would arrive in the post. Half of our fee he would pay in advance right now, and in cash.

And so it was agreed. And shaken upon. Mr Alver insisted on clasping my hand, and Steve's too. He hung on to us for about five times longer than your average handshake. Maybe this was a Norwegian expression of sincerity.

Chapter 2

At the top of the fifty-mile-long fjord, the Scandinavian Airline Service jet commenced its turn towards the airport. What a compact city Oslo seemed, hemmed in by hills. A wilderness of more hills rolled far into the distance. The same landscape stretched for a distance equal to about half the length of Europe, with only a few million Norwegians to stipple the empty spaces.

The plane banked westward, past the stocky twin-towered city hall of red brick on the waterfront. Probably we overflew the sculpture park, but without spotting it.

A taxi took us from the airport to a street of shops and businesses, called Bogstadveien, and decanted us at a certain Comfort Hotel. This sounded suspiciously like a sex establishment, but proved to be patronised by Norwegian families on holiday. Our room was tastefully mock art nouveau, recently revamped. One oddity was that each landing of the Comfort Hotel boasted a communal trouser press. During our stay I never saw any of these presses in use. What if, overnight, someone stole a guest's pants? Maybe no one would dream of such a prank in Norway.

People might be too busy guarding their trouser pockets!—in view of the sky-high price of a beer in the hotel bar, and anywhere else—not to mention the cost of meals, clothes, books, and all else. Norway was a seriously costly country.

We had arrived around six in the evening. A glance at the bar and restaurant tariff sent us out along the street, past shops and a few other hotels and bars, in search of somewhere more reasonable — until we wised up and returned. Beer at six pounds a glass was the norm. We would eat and drink in the hotel, and not feel guilty that we were exploiting Mr Alver.

We booked a coach tour of Oslo for the next day, picking up from our hotel early on. National Gallery (for a gape at *The Scream* by Munch), Viking longships, Kon-Tiki, et cetera, ending up at the Vigeland Park. Clear sky permitting, we could return to the park late the same night simply by walking from Bogstadveien, no great distance, according to the hotel receptionist.

Our fellow sightseers proved to be a mixed bag of Americans and Europeans. Japanese tourists rated entire coaches to themselves. The day was balmy, clouds few and fluffy in a blue sky. Those Viking boats in the museum at Bygdøy — we were getting our bearings — were larger than I had expected. Likewise, the crowds of visitors. This was also true at the Vigeland Park, at least by day.

"God, it's *so* Teutonic — "

Steve was right.

A monumental sevenfold row of wrought-iron gates topped by huge square lamps led to a grassy avenue lined with maple trees. This sward led to the powerful central axis of the park, which was crisscrossed by geometrical paths. We crossed a long bridge, many pale, grey, granite physiques young and old upon its parapets. A few figures were grappling with a dragon of mortality, which eventually sapped its victim. Likewise, at the gates, lizards had been gripping young children.

From the bridge, upward and upward the park rose, stage by stage, flight of steps by flight of steps, towards a distant monolith. The impression was of a hugely elongated, flattened ziggurat, a Nordic Aztec temple.

A mosaic labyrinth enclosed a great fountain. Around the fountain's rim, muscular bodies were entwined with sculpted trees resembling giant stone broccoli, infants dangling from the branches. Over-sized nude men bore the weight of the massive basin. Struggle. Growth. Sexuality. Death.

Ascending past stone bodies (and many camera-toting Japanese), we came to an oval plateau. So many tourists milled about here that we might have been negotiating an open-air dance floor.

On rising plinths a zodiac of hulking figures, young and old, embraced and wrestled and clung to one another. It was four of those groups to which Steve and I must attach ourselves that night, when the place was quiet. Those plinths and their burdens partitioned circular stairs leading to the summit, where a monolith soared thirty or forty feet high.

So phallic, that fountaining column of bodies! Those at the base looked like corpses. Higher up, frozen movement began—a yearning ascendance skyward. The tip was a swarm of small children suggestive of cherubs or magnified sperms.

"It's like some sort of nature-worshipping Nuremberg rally! The Nazis must have loved this place when they were here."

Quite, Steve. The park was still being finished during the Second World War, when Norway was occupied—so the tour guide on the coach had explained.

My idea of the history of Norway consisted of the Vikings followed after a giant void by Ibsen, then by Resistance heroes being parachuted into forests to sabotage Nazi U-boat bases and heavy water factories. (Not everyone was a Resistance hero—a certain Mr Quisling, whose name became a byword for treachery, had headed a puppet government of collaborators.) Stonecarvers did not complete work on the monolith in the park until 1943. I imagined black-clad SS officers strolling by, blond fräuleins on their arms, psyching themselves up to breed more of the master race to replace losses at Stalingrad.

Those various lizards and dragons in the park might be a mordant echo of the way Norwegian life was being strangled by tyranny, as well as a perennial image of the way death finally defeats life—but not before new children are spawned.

"It isn't my cup of tea, either," I admitted. "It's all so *heavy*. I'll feel like a human slug pressing myself up against the figures . . ."

Tonight, tonight. If the sky stayed clear. Clouds were in short supply over Scandinavia.

"You'll look great."

Would Mr Älver think so too? And likewise of Steve, draped against granite? Such puny physiques, ours, compared with the adamantine anatomy on show. Evidently this did not matter, compared with the symbolism. When we had checked the positions of the groups we were supposed to interact with—to the north, south, east, and west—we retraced our steps, a thousand of them, so it seemed, before we regained the vast wrought-iron gateway. We said goodbye to the coach courier and walked back to the hotel to be sure of the distance. The journey only took fifteen minutes.

Viewed from the monolith plateau by the light of the moon, this park could have designed to summon aliens from the sky, to be their landing site.

Or to summon *something*, at any rate.

Pompeii-like, a race of giants was petrified in the midst of life's yearnings and raptures and struggle, or melancholy acceptance.

Far away down below a tall, beaming, granite mother ran, child in her outstretched arms, her long, stone hair blown back. We had passed her earlier; and also a grinning father hoisting a lad up by the wrists high above his own head. By contrast, up top all adults were kneeling or bending or sitting bunched up, or they only came into existence at the knee. An elderly seated couple consoled each other. A kneeling wrestler hurled a woman over his shoulder. Only children stood upright.

The exaggeration of the figures—the massive, sleek stylization —banished any notion that these bodies might momentarily come to life. Yet to run my hand over the smooth granite surfaces was to discover, by touch alone, sinews and muscles which had been invisible even in bright daylight. Only physical contact revealed the hidden dimension.

The moon was full. Clouds were few. Some people were loitering on the bridge of statues, but that was far away. With a wax crayon I marked the position of the tripod's legs for reference in the morning. Steve stripped and leaned against that stone man hurling a woman away from him. He held still, skinned rabbit against moonlit granite.

We had finished with three of the groups. Hair hanging loose, I was about to shuck off my dress and sandals and mount a plinth to join a tight cluster of chunky stone girls. Bums outward, pigtailed heads bowed, these recent graduates from childhood appeared to be absorbed in comparing their presumably burgeoning genitals. What was within their charmed circle was solid rock, of course.

Which was when The Drunk arrived.

His short fair hair was tousled, his face, even by moonlight, weatherbeaten. Checked shirt, jeans, workman's boots. God knows if he had been spying, blending in ghostlike behind other sculptures. He addressed us in English. We were from Britain? Photographers? Midnight is the best time of day for photographs here! Himself, he comes to this place whenever he is in Oslo when the moon is full.

Although his voice was slurred, vocabulary and grammar were commendable for a drunk—and a feather in the cap of the local educational system. With the tipsy care of someone treading a line between obstacles, he chose his words.

"Like a fish on a hook I come here. Like a whale being winched."

"Do you work on a whale-ship?"

The drunk shook his head.

"You're a trawlerman?"

No, his job is to drive a giant bulldozer. Right now, he is employed in the construction of Oslo's new international airport, forty kilometres away from the city in empty countryside. Do we know about it? Fornebu Airport (where we had landed) is to shut. Too many flights over the city. Hide the airport where nobody lives. Previously he worked building dams. Norway needs many new dams because of climate change, did we follow him?

Tugging a wallet from his back pocket, the man fumbled out a laminated card illustrated with his photo. This, we must inspect by the light of the moon.

"My permit to drive heavy engineering vehicles. Carl Olsson: my name. Actually it is not my name. I was adopted, do you understand?"

"Adopted, yes."

"I would like to buy you a drink. Good open-air restaurant over there. Great view. But it is closed."

Of course a café would be closed at half-past midnight.

The construction site, up-country, is dry in the alcohol sense. Nothing to do there at night but watch television in huts. Monotonous! However, he's well paid, so he can afford a binge in town. What else to do with his money?

We agreed about the hideous cost of alcohol.

Olsson showed his teeth, grinning. "If Norwegians drink, they knife each other—personally I do not." He was a well-controlled drunk. "People believe this will happen. So it is illegal to carry even a little penknife. In the village where I was raised, dancing is banned. The people think it is the devil's doing, dancing. That is near Bergen."

"Do you go home much?" *Why don't you go back home right now?*

"Nothing for me there. I come here. When I am drunk, it feels better. Tomorrow afternoon I catch the bus back to the new airport. By then I will be sober."

To come to this park, he needed to dull his senses? Mr Olsson seemed to have a screw loose.

"Please, will you take my photograph beside these stone girls and send it to me?"

I agreed—provided that he would go away afterwards.

"I don't mean to be rude but we have a job to do here. We can't do it if someone's watching."

Norwegians might not care a fig leaf about nudity—according to Mr Alver—but Carl Olsson was more muscular than Steve. I worried about arousing the man.

"Yes, you want to be alone. I respect that." Burrowing in a pocket, he found crumpled paper and a ballpoint pen. Resting paper on plinth, he printed. "This is the address of the construction site—"

Steve stuffed the paper into his jeans. Mounting the plinth, Olsson draped an arm around the shoulders of those clustering closeted girls. My camera was already in position. The Drunk held still with total concentration until I told him, "It's done."

He jumped down, but then he lingered by the granite group, leering at us.

"There is somewhere deeper than this, somewhere no tourists ever see, hidden away in darkness where no daylight reaches. It is the *other side* of this park. I do not mean where that café is—I mean the under-side, the black side. Vigeland had a younger brother, you see. The younger brother built a private death-house for himself. It is in the hills where the rich people live, the Slemdal district. If you tell me your hotel and we go in a taxi I will show it to you."

Thanks but no thanks. "You have your bus to catch tomorrow," I reminded him.

"Will you be sure to send me the photograph?"

"Yes, yes." *Just go.*

Out came that wallet again. "I pay you for the printing and postage."

"No, no, this is a gift. Be happy, Mr Olsson. Goodbye, Mr Olsson."

Blessedly he did depart. Intent upon walking straight, he did not look back. By now the time was creeping towards one o'clock. I stripped. Steve operated the digi-cam.

On our way back to the hotel, we kept an eye out for Olsson. No sign of him. We set our travel alarm clock and caught some sleep before our return to the park at dawn. Then we went back to bed until lunchtime.

Steve made arrangements for an Avis car to be delivered bright and early next day, to be left in Helsingborg in Sweden for a surcharge. This done, we caught a tram downtown to spend the afternoon roaming and goggling at prices.

A Serb (or so he said) accosted us. Fanning out photos of cute naked black children and mud huts, he solicited money to fund him to join an aid project in Mozambique.

A lone Scottish piper in full tartan was playing a wailing lament, his woollen bonnet on the pavement for kroner. I'm sure he was the same fellow we had seen in the market square in Blanchester just before Christmas.

Oops, and further along Karl Johan Street where Munch and Ibsen used to stroll, were Bolivians in ponchos and bowler hats playing their wooden pipes, with the begging bowler set out.

When we finally reached Helsingborg after traversing much lush farming landscape, the town proved to be a nondescript one of medium size which seemed to owe its existence mainly to its harbour with ferry terminal leading over the water to fabled Elsinore; but the hotel where Mr Alver had reserved a room for us was rather splendid. The Grand boasted special rose-coloured rooms for women guests, though since I was with Steve I did not qualify for the rose-carpet treatment, nor would I have wished to.

Mr Alver had also recommended that we treat our contact at the Swedish company to a slap-up lunch in the hotel restaurant, to grease the wheels. Next noon, we hosted Per Larsen. Slim and blond, Larsen wore a shiny dark blue suit which had seen long service—leather patches protected the elbows. The Swede seemed a bit snooty about our mission, though this had nothing to do with the fact that nude photos of our backsides were involved.

"I suppose," he said presently, "this whim is not exorbitant by the standards of jet-set people who squander thousands of dollars on a party dress . . ." He raised his glass of wine. "Who am I to complain?"

Fairly soon I gathered that people in this part of Sweden were thrifty to the point of meanness. Larsen probably had accepted our invitation to lunch so as to save on sandwiches. This gave a new meaning to eating wild strawberries—food for free.

Steve teased him. "You might say that all jigsaw puzzles are frivolous."

Larsen would not countenance this. "Oh no! You must realize that poverty forced many people from this area to emigrate to America. Those who remained were ingenious in setting up small industries. Speciality jigsaws are a part of this."

So jigsaws were virtuous. It turned out that this region of

Sweden also boasted the highest concentration of splendid manor houses and castles. I guess this figured. Rich nobles, poor peasants. "Mr Alver must have no family," mused Larsen, "to wish to spend his last days assembling these jigsaws. He will be assembling images of you as well. Seeing your bodies take shape slowly."

"Our backs are turned. We are merely symbolic."

"Your backs are turned, Miss Clarke. You hand him those jigsaws, then you have nothing more to do with him." Hard to tell whether this was advice, or a statement of fact.

Previously we had planned on taking a taxi to the company premises. In the thrifty circumstances the three of us caught a bus—to a building near a public park which housed all that remained of Helsingborg Castle, namely the *Keep*. At last the penny dropped. Keep Publishing. Resolute persistence had nothing to do with it. Mr Alver must have been amused by our naive assumption.

Larsen screened our digi-cartridge pictures. We had a technical pow-wow. Circular jigsaws, yes. Half a metre across. Since the photo of our drunken acquaintance embracing those granite girls was also on the cartridge, we asked Larsen to make a couple of ordinary prints of it. Whether we would actually mail one to Carl Olsson remained a moot point.

We spent three days in Helsingborg, and visited that Keep a couple of times. A fairly impressive relic, its top gave a scenic view over the sound busy with shipping. Meanwhile the namesake company was producing those four *keepsakes* for Mr Alver, those majig mementoes.

When Mr Alver came to Fernhill to finalize the business he seemed entirely satisfied, even though he had no immediate proof of the quality of the work. This was because he had insisted that there should be no illustrations on the box lids. Steve carried four blank boxes to the black Merc, and our benefactor departed, to begin the painstaking task of assembling those jigsaws without any guide other than his own memories of the Vigeland Park from goodness knows how long ago. We popped the photo of Olsson into an envelope, but did not attach any sticker giving our address—behaving rather like Mr Alver, come to think of it. After our brief flurry of foreign travel normal life resumed.

It was not until early the following summer that the bad dreams began.

Chapter 3

At first, the details of what we dreamt eluded us like some monster disappearing underwater, though we both felt we were being involved in some terrible activity, evil and powerful. At school I once knew a girl called Donna who saw a therapist because she was plagued by "night terrors." Poor Donna would awake from deeply scary dreams in a state of sheer panic. Similar misbehaviour of the mind could not suddenly be afflicting both Steve and me. Becoming a bit hollow-eyed, we visited Doctor Ross, our GP, who deduced that we were stressed out by worries about our business, bank loan, et cetera. Ross prescribed sleeping pills. We only took those pills once—and found ourselves locked into a nightmare, from which we could not escape for ages.

My nightmare came in swirling fragments, as if I had acquired the kaleidoscopic eye of an insect, or was watching a jumble of jigsaw pieces undergoing assembly. If the jigsaw succeeded in assembling itself, so much the worse for me! All the pieces were aspects of the Vigeland Park by night—and by flaming torchlight. Glimpses of stone figures, of geometrical patterns, of uniforms and fanatical faces. And of a naked woman—of flesh, not granite. Curly flaxen hair and full thighs—she was nude in spite of a dusting of snow on the paving stones. A long knife caught the light. Something vile was about to happen. The monolith of sculpted bodies reared high, towards a full moon.

These images seemed scattered across the inside of a balloon, constantly shifting around upon the inner surface. My dream consciousness was within the balloon, at the empty centre. Outside of the balloon, birds were diving, their beaks like spearheads. Whenever they neared the balloon they veered away as if space itself twisted to repel them.

And then I was outside the balloon. The images within beat against their confines, hideously patterned moths trying to burst free. The balloon's transparent skin imprisoned them, for the moment. No birds were attacking now—the birds had become those moths, inside. Hawk Moths, Death's Head Moths.

Pressure was mounting inside the balloon. The tip of the monolith, its glans knobbled with naked young bodies like some droll condom designed to arouse, was pressing up against the outer skin. If the skin ruptured, the glans would spout blood and sperms and moths in an orgasm of evil vitality.

Steve and I had woken together to a dawn chorus. Early light seeped through our curtains. Steve floundered to the window to expose the world, and us. Quickly he took refuge in bed again. He held me. Five A.M., by the alarm clock.

"It's the park, isn't it? Something happening there once. It's building up again, Chrissy, because Alver is putting the pieces together—the pieces of the jigsaws!"

"We're part of it," I whispered, "because he touched us, and we pressed our own flesh against the sculptures—"

By stopping us from waking prematurely, Dr Ross's pills had forced us to register the dream in more detail, and remember it. We would scarcely wish for a repetition of such clarity—confused though it was. We would hardly wish to stay trapped so long inside that place, that mental space! The alternative was indefinable night terror, and the sense that something was gathering strength.

We lay there trying to define what might have happened in the sculpture park. The Death's Head Moths inside that balloonlike sheath, the birds attacking it in vain . . . The uniforms, the flaring torches, the nude woman, the knife . . . Nazis in Norway, no doubt of it. These images were emerging as if the photographs we had taken, to be divided into thousands of pieces, had captured much more than merely the surface of things.

If something atrocious happened in that park during the Second World War, why would Knut Alver be trying to conjure it up again so many years later? He had talked about putting his own life in order before the grim reaper came. Alver must be trying to atone for something hideous in which he had been involved, in Norway, when his country was occupied. He could not, he dared not, revisit his homeland. By some mental contagion, we were sensing his inner torments as he strove to confront and exorcise those. He had set himself a penance: to devote his remaining time on Earth to assembling images of the place where a great sin had been committed. When the pictures were complete, he could die at peace, with a sense of closure and absolution—liberated just as his motherland had been set free long since. The Spirit of Norway would accept him back into its bosom.

When Steve dialled Alver's number, shortly after eight o'clock, all he got was a continuous ringing tone. The number had been disconnected. Directory Enquiries told Steve that nobody by the name of Alver was listed anywhere in the whole county.

"He must live somewhere in this county or he wouldn't have seen the newspaper—!"

Alver had paid us in cash—tidy sums on both occasions, tempting us not to enter them in our accounts, a temptation to which we had yielded, as most people probably might. But the hotel bills —those had gone on to Alver's American Express Gold Card account. The hotels must have kept details . . . and Keep Publishing, as well.

From Fernhill later that morning I phoned Per Larsen in Helsingborg and told him that we had lost some of our records. When I called back in the afternoon: name on credit card: Knut Alver, card number blah blah—which I carefully copied down. After I had thanked the Swede, I phoned American Express in Brighton.

"I have to reach Mr Alver," I begged. "There has been a death." This made no difference to customer confidentiality.

"At least tell me, is the card still being used?"

My informant dithered, then conceded that the account had been cancelled the previous November.

"I don't think Alver was his real name," was Steve's opinion.

I imagined the phone books of the whole county in a pile— eight, ten of them? How many Norwegian-sounding names might we find listed?

"He may not use a Norwegian name, Chrissy. Not if he was a war criminal."

"Why is he living in England rather than Paraguay or somewhere?"

"Maybe he did hide in South America originally, Chrissy. But

Paraguay isn't very close to Norway. It's been a long time. More than fifty years—"

A while ago I had seen a piece in the Sunday *Observer* on the subject of elderly Ukrainians and Hungarians living in Britain, who might once have been members of SS units involved in exterminations. Living here undisturbed for the past half century! Had any Norwegians volunteered for the SS?

Would the police be any help? We only had dreams as evidence. We might be wrong. What had prompted the *Observer* story, I recalled, had been the *failure* of a prosecution of an eighty-year-old Ukrainian—because watertight proof was lacking. After half a century witnesses' memories were unreliable. We did not even know our suspect's real name.

"Perhaps we ought to ask Hugh Ellison for a spot of assistance."

"You can't be serious, Steve. He would only want to pray with us. Accept Jesus into your heart as your protector."

"I was thinking more along the lines of God's Legion buzzing around the county doing all those building jobs. Seeing all sorts of places. One of the Legion could have heard some gossip somewhere. Rich Norwegian recluse in the Old Rectory at Sod-Knows-Where, keeps to himself, he do."

This was grasping at straws. We may as well turn to our parents, or to book-binding Nigel. Such moments brought home to me how Steve and I did not actually have many close friends. Acquaintances, yes. Pals in whom we could confide: not really. Steve and I were each other's bosom friends, self-sufficient. Maybe this had something to do with our devotion to jigsaw puzzles rather than to, say, team sports. (Not that we ourselves did many jigsaws for fun these days!) At college we had courted by slotting pieces together over a can or two of beer, until we too slid together as a perfect match. If only we had time and money for a child, she or he would be our friend too. We would be a trio.

What was *Alver's* game? Penance and self-forgiveness, or something sick and sinister?

"Do you think Alver has any idea we might be affected like this?"

"Covered his tracks, didn't he?" said Steve.

Bright, breezy July day. Last week, there had been half a hurricane. A coach crowded with schoolkids lumbered into the car park. An educational outing: maximum nuisance, minimum gain— unless Tracey or Kevin went home and badgered their parents for a present of a very special jigsaw. I would need to act jolly.

*   *   *

The knife slashed my throat. Dream-pain was distant and blunted. I felt what a beast must feel in the slaughterhouse, restrained and stunned but still aware.

My lifeblood clogged my windpipe. Strong, gloved hands were dragging me upright, a dying animal, legs spasming uselessly, around the moonlit, torchlit monolith, thrusting my nakedness against hard granite figures so that my blood smeared the stone. Deep voices were chanting solemnly. Blut. Stein. Macht. Schild. Schutz. Odin. I had no voice. I was choking, drowning in my own blood.

Then my throat cleared and I screamed.

Of late, we had been leaving the curtains open while we slept.

I clutched Steve. "Do you think anybody heard?"

"What the hell does that matter?"

"The neighbours might think you're murdering me or hurting me. Did you dream?"

"Nothing—I don't think so. I don't remember. Did you take a sleeping pill without telling me?"

"No—" Words still echoed in my head.

"*Blut's* blood," Steve said. "*Stein* is what you drink out of in beer halls. It said *Macht* over the gate of Auschwitz."

"They weren't drinking my blood—they were spilling it on the paving, rubbing it on to the sculptures we took pictures of."

"*Odin's* a Norse god—"

"I know that. Those Nazis, they must have been sacrificing to Odin there in the Vigeland Park. They cut that woman's throat to mark the place with her blood. It was some sort of Nazi pagan rite—Alver must have taken part. There *is* someone we can ask about this, Steve! Olsson! Carl Olsson."

"The drunk?"

"Haunting that park when the moon's full. Obsessed with it. What did he say about an *other side* to the park? A black side. He wanted to take us somewhere, to show us . . . a death-house, he said. We sent him that photo. Him hugging the same granite girls the Nazis rubbed blood on. If fondling the sculpture made *us* dream, maybe it affected him too?"

"Olsson never took his clothes off."

"He can find out something for us—he's a Norwegian."

"A bulldozer driver, a part-time drunk."

"He was lonely. This'll give him a goal. We must do something, Steve!"

I decided that sending a letter to the new airport site was too slow.

We had the name of the civil engineering company. The international operator came up with the phone number and connected me to the company's office in Oslo. Bless foreigners for learning English so fluently. It's an emergency, I said. I must get in touch with an employee of yours.

I held, while a tape played Grieg at me. A brisk-sounding woman came on the line, and I must repeat my rigmarole, and hold again. Money ticking away.

"Miz Clarke, are you there?"

Yes, yes, all ears.

"I am sorry for the delay. Mr Carl Olsson is no longer employed by us—"

I was calling all the way from England. Carl Olsson was our friend. This was a matter of life and death.

Unfortunately, Mr Olsson was released from his contract the previous month because of a problem. Yes, Miz Clarke, you are right: a problem connected with alcohol. The company did not know where he had gone, though his address on record was a village near Bergen. She spelled the address for me, complete with slash through the letter "ø." I cradled the phone.

"That's the village he never goes back to," Steve said.

"He was proud of his license. He would only have got drunk on the job if dreams had been bothering him."

"That's a touching faith you have in him. Now he'll be working on dams again—in the middle of nowhere."

"He can't be, Steve! He won't have a clean reference. They may have endorsed his license. I don't know what their system is. He might only get another job after he attends a government alco clinic."

"Nothing stops him from getting a labouring job. Shelf-packing in a supermarket. Sign on a boat as a deckhand, sail to Australia."

"Don't try to steer me away from this, Steve! It was my throat they cut. We can't put up with this. He'll be in Oslo, Olsson will. He'll be getting drunk and going to the park at night, especially if the moon's full."

Oslo: back to that hotel on Bogstadveien? Paying our own fares, paying our own hotel bills, beer at six pounds a glass, lunch at fifteen quid a head, for a week, two weeks? We would use up all the profit we had made from Alver, aside from the fact that we had spent it months ago.

"We needn't both go, Steve."

"Don't be absurd."

Soon we were close to a quarrel.

*   *   *

Steve was my friend, my lover, my partner. I wanted him to father my child—she would be a daughter, of course—whenever we could afford this. Now he was baulking, rejecting my intuition, scared of the cost when we were already paying a hateful price. Despite him being the first to suggest that Alver may have committed war crimes, Steve was afraid to take this seriously—scared, finally, to commit himself, reluctant to put all the pieces together. He would rather those were all back safely in their box, with a blank lid closed upon them.

Although I accused him of this, at the same time I realized that I wished to go on my own to Norway. Alver had duped us, he had used us—because we were naive. As a pair, Steve and I would compromise and not be extreme. Because a woman had been killed in the park, not a man, I was ahead of Steve in my dreaming. Alone, I felt sure that I would be more focused.

A solo trip would cost half the price. One of us must stay to mind the shop. I seized upon these two pretexts, convinced that I would find Olsson waiting for me. I felt little need of Steve's "protection," which in any case he was not delivering—unfair and contradictory though that sounds.

A strained day passed. After we had eaten some lasagne that evening, Steve ferreted away to dislodge me from my position.

"A woman was killed with a knife in that park. When Norwegians get drunk they knife people."

"Not Olsson."

"He might see you as the cause of him losing his job."

"Women are stronger than men," I informed him. "Stronger than *nice* men," I added, to cushion his ego. Our relationship had altered. Damn Alver for this.

"How long will you give it before you quit looking?" Ah: my journey would be fruitless, so I could safely undertake it. Steve was vacillating, exonerating himself. Deep down, he was relieved that I was taking the initiative. I must not despise him for this, must not resent it. I should feel grateful, not betrayed.

"Ten days tops," I replied. A rational male answer, precisely timed, cut and dried.

"I ought to come—I'm part of this too."

Men have this way of talking emptily to justify themselves, and never being able to shut up.

"Next Saturday there's a full moon. I should leave on Friday. Ticket, hotel, traveller's cheques," I recited.

"Will you phone me each evening?"

"If possible. Mustn't run up bills." Oh the reproachful look in his eyes—this could lead to more empty, irritating words. "We'll need to compare our dreams by phone."

We would not be sharing the same bed, but if we continued to dream of the park in a sense we would still be together.

"In Duty Free," he suggested, "why don't you buy a bottle of rum and stock up on Coke in Oslo?"

Such a practical thought. Was it a trick question?

"I hadn't thought of that. Maybe I will. Good idea."

Chapter 4

When the plane banked and levelled out, this time I did spot the park: grey granite geometry and lines of trees bisecting lawns. From an altitude of a few thousand feet everything looked so flat except for the trees backed by their shadows.

A venue for Odin? The Vigeland Park was a far cry from Valhalla. No pagan gods down there; just the struggle of life enshrined in stone—Nordic spirit. A big bottle of Captain Morgan rum bulked my hand luggage.

On the map of Oslo spread out on my lap, ironically there *was* an Odin Street not too far from the park. And just a stone's throw from the Comfort Hotel was a Valkyrie Way.

Even if the Valkyries managed to avoid colliding with a tram, their ride would be brief along the short stretch of street named in their honour. Those female dispensers of destiny to warriors in battle, those issuers of entry visas to Valhalla, would be obliged to pass and re-pass a Burger King—for the presence of which I was thankful. My take-away dinner of a Whopper and fries was merely expensive, not out of this world. I phoned Steve to tell him I had arrived, and of my wonderful discovery of fast food so close by.

With mad cow and stodge digesting in my belly, it was along

non-heathen Church Way—Kirkeveien—that I walked late that night to revisit the park. The sky had clouded over. The moon coasted into sight, a spectral white yacht with a single full-bellying sail. Here was I, going to meet a drunk at a place where I had taken my clothes off, and he might not even be there. On this occasion I wore jeans, not a dress.

When I finally made my way up on to the granite plateau, there was Olsson, keeping a Vigeland vigil. A long scruffy raincoat hung open over checked shirt and Levis. As we gazed at one another he steadied himself against a granite buttock.

"You did not send me your name or address."

"I'm sorry about that. I'm sorry you lost your job. My name's Chrissy. Chrissy Clarke."

While the moon sailed into view and away again, I told him about the mysterious Mr Alver and the jigsaws and the dreams.

Dreams, oh yes, dreams. He had dreamed of me naked here among uniforms and torches. Sometimes me, sometimes a blond beauty. Before he accosted us that night, maybe he had been playing Peeping Tom and was now mixing up memory and dream, but I did not think so.

The chanting, the knife, the blood . . .

"*Blut. Stein. Macht,*" I recited.

He nodded. "*Schild. Schutz.*"

"And *Odin.* A toast to Odin, drunk in blood?"

"Toast?" he queried. And in Norwegian: "*Ristet brød?*" He mimed buttering and biting.

"No, no, I mean," and I raised an imaginary glass, "Skol!" Hardly the most sensible gesture to make to a man with a drink problem.

"Ah, *Skål!*" His brow furrowed. "They did not drink blood. They rubbed the blood on the stones. *Blut* is blood. *Stein* is stone. *Macht* means power, but is also a verb, makes."

Steve had been off-track.

"Blood-stone-makes-shield-defence." Carl's chant sounded like some strange version of the Stone-Scissors-Paper game. "Do you know of the SS?"

"Of course."

"They were the *Schutz-Staffel,* the defence squads. Actually, SS senior officers did not want to fight to the death in Norway. Some SS man must have been here, though. Some black magician."

"Stop, stop, you're losing me—!"

*   *   *

Carl had been supplementing his memories of history lessons in school by asking older people and looking in books.

Evidently Norway fascinated Hitler ever since the Führer took a Strength-Through-Joy cruise to the fjords in the 1930s; and Himmler, head of the SS, was obsessed with the mystical meaning of Nordic runes. Hitler saw Norway as the "field of destiny" of the war. Half a million German troops were to be stationed in this country. Big naval guns were stripped from battleships to be mounted in coastal forts.

Militarily this focus on Norway did not make much sense. Oh, there was a lot of coastline, controlling a vast swathe of sea, posing a threat to Allied convoys to Russia. Norway also owned a huge merchant fleet — the majority of those boats sought refuge in Allied ports. Due to shortages and sabotage and go-slows, Norwegian ship-yards only completed two or three new vessels during the entire occupation. Demonstrably, the outcome of the war hung on events in Central Europe, not off on the margin of the map.

"Your own Winston Churchill, he was hooked by Norway too — "

"My Winston Churchill? Mine? He must have died before I was born."

"Has what happened here *died?* Even if a million tourists take pretty photos?"

I suppose, but for Winston Churchill, the whole of Europe might be a fascist empire nowadays. Nazis on the Moon. No Israel. Moscow, a radioactive desert. A swastika embellishing the Union Jack.

"Listen to me, Mrs Clarke — "

When Steve and I finally had a kid, I might become Mrs *Bryant* but so far we had seen no need for a wedding ceremony. To correct Olsson could lead to complications. I simply listened.

Were it not for Norway, apparently Churchill might not have risen to the top as the war leader best able to defy Hitler. The fall of Norway, with losses of British planes and personnel, toppled Neville Chamberlain. In actual fact British intervention in Norway was Churchill's own fault, but Chamberlain bore all the blame for it. Because the debacle made Churchill Prime Minister, Norway loomed unduly large in his mind.

In Hitler's mind there were Wagnerian considerations. The god Wotan, in Wagner's *Ring*, equals Odin, kingpin of the Viking pan-theon. Several Nazi leaders, such as the racist Alfred Rosenberg, desired spiritual as well as political union with a Nordic Norway under its home-bred National Socialist, Vidkun Quisling. The high echelons of the German Nazis were already into paganism and the occult.

Churchill and Hitler: I was getting this strong sense of two megalomaniacs (one good, the other evil) confronting one another globally, while both of them were obsessed about a country on the fringe—to the detriment of wider strategy.

Tormented by his ambiguous affinity to the Vigeland Park —which had been reinforced recently by the dreams—Carl Olsson had found out rather a lot. I suppose he knew the general drift already, and only needed to dig a bit deeper. After all, he wasn't an ignorant man! Quite fluent in English; and in German too, so it seemed.

When Germany was on the brink of defeat, Fortress Norway— *Festung Norwegen*—beckoned as the final bastion for the embattled Nazis, a worthy stage for the twilight of Gods and supermen, the final bonfire or the ultimate victory. It was touch and go whether Nazi leaders would relocate to Bavaria—or to Norway.

"General Böhme commanded the huge army here," Carl explained to me. "Böhme was crazy for Norway. Norway could be defended. And the Reichscommissar for Norway, Josef Terboven, he was fanatical about this too. Hitler very nearly came here instead of dying in Berlin. He hoped that new super U-boats based in Norway would turn the tide even if Germany fell—"

"Super U-boats?" I had never heard of any such thing. Were those real or imaginary?

"They were ocean-going monsters, Mrs Clarke, berthed in Bergen and in Trondheim."

But oil was in short supply, and the first super U-boat only sailed from Bergen, futilely, a couple of days before Germany surrendered.

In mid-March of 1945, Reichscommissar Terboven had summoned General Böhme and the naval commander to ask if they could vouch for the loyalty of their men in the event of Hitler and Himmler and gang coming to Norway. Even the bombastic Böhme could not guarantee this. The SS bigwigs did not favour *Festung Norwegen*. After Germany fell, Terboven blew himself up with a hand grenade.

"But some time in March, Mrs Clarke, the event happened here because here is so powerful and Nordic a place, even if Gustav Vigeland was raised in a fanatically Christian home—"

Evidently the sculptor's dad was a Bible-thumper. The torments of hell were a daily refrain in the Vigeland household.

"Too much Satan," Carl quoted. "That's what Gustav Vigeland said about his childhood. Not enough Jesus. A whole lot of darkness, only a little light. My own upbringing was not quite as bad —always there were the sunny prayers for my soul! Because I was born under a cloud, a child of sin, illegitimate. A stained bastard—"

Vigeland's dad did loosen up eventually—because of alcohol and another woman, ill health, and the failure of his little furniture business.

"So genuine darkness came. Yet here in the park is vigour and power, the thrust of nature. The life force, a fierce power changing its shape as the god wills—the Odin force of old. Odin, that's what the Nazis saw here. A victory-force. Victory over enemies, over death . . ."

Carl clutched at the pocket of his raincoat. Hoping to find a bottle to dull himself. He must already have thrown the bottle away empty.

"Josef Terboven would have been here. And Quisling."

"And Knut Alver, whatever his real name is. Did Norwegians join the SS?"

"Oh yes, there was the Nordland regiment, of Scandinavians and Finns, but there were problems."

Though the Germans assured recruits that they were joining a pan-European force to bring a new order to the continent, training methods proved to be exceptionally brutal, so a lot of Norwegian volunteers deserted. Not Alver, obviously. He must have become an officer.

"And some magician was here. Some Nazis meddled with magic. Wotan-worship, Odin-worship. Blood-and-soil-worship. I hate all worship, Mrs Clarke! When I lost my job I went back to Bergen. This time I threatened. I really scared my fake parents. They must tell me why I was a scandal or I would burn the farm down. They thought I was going to kill them—that I would cut their pious psalm-singing throats."

Might he have clutched at his raincoat to see whether he had a knife in the pocket? A hideous vision came to me of butchered bodies in a farmhouse. If Carl Olsson was wanted by the police surely the construction company would have known and would have warned me. I must concentrate on him utterly, as if I was his sister and I loved him.

Gently I asked, "What did you learn, Carl?"

Why, he had discovered the shameful secret that his mother Christina—born late in 1944—was the offspring of eugenic mating between a German Waffen-SS officer and a young Norwegian woman named Liv Frisvold. Liv Frisvold's brother Olav was a fanatical pro-Nazi who had joined the SS.

Liv shared Olav's fascist beliefs. She had volunteered, or been persuaded by Olav, to take part in the Lebensborn project—the "Fount of Life" breeding programme, by which prime Aryan males of the SS would bestow their genes upon perfections of Aryan womanhood. Liv's child would be a splendid bonding of Nordic and Teutonic, of Germany and Norway.

The baby had ended up fostered in Stavanger, with the cleansing name Christina. (My own name, almost!) At eighteen years of age she disgraced herself by becoming pregnant by some American sailor. The foster parents packed her off to stay with relatives in Bergen, where she gave birth to a boy, who was Carl. Christina was unworthy to raise him—the boy must be separated from the stain of his past. So the Olssons had adopted him, to raise him on their farm as part of their family, a Christian duty. To them, the secret was confided, though they were ignorant of what became of Liv, or of Olav.

"When Christina was twenty-one she ran away from Stavanger. My adoptive parents say they think she went to America." Carl shuddered. "Do you know what I think? I think it was Liv Frisvold who was killed here in March 1945. My grandmother. In the blood-sacrifice."

He seemed calmer now.

"What were they hoping for, Carl? What were they trying to do?"

"Blood-stone-makes-shield," he said. "Whatever that means."

"What is Knut Alver trying to achieve now, half a century afterwards?"

Carl gazed at the monolith of naked bodies surging upward. "You came to find out, Mrs Clarke. It will come, it will come."

The orgasming come of a man. Or was he referring to some power gathering to erupt? The monolith was like a phallus. So rooted, so immobile.

"That other place—the dark place. Have you been there recently?"

"I cannot! Something stops me. Like a coat in a dream, wrapping me tight. A dream of myself and woman. The coat gets in the way. There is no way to take it off. Do you understand?"

"Maybe," I said.

He had not pressed his naked flesh against the granite girls when

I took his photograph. *Where do you sleep?* I nearly asked him. Meaning, in a hostel? In some rented room? *Do you have savings?* I might give him the wrong idea.

"Now that you are here, Mrs Clarke, we can go to the dark place together. I will take you there tomorrow. Really, it is you who will be taking me."

Relief flooded me. "Let's do that, Carl. Tomorrow."

"In the afternoon the mausoleum is open. We will meet at your hotel and go by taxi. Without a taxi, we have too far to walk from the bus route, you see, and it is all uphill. Let me walk you back to your hotel."

Yes: away from this place. Back to Comfort. The desk clerk of that respectable establishment would not admit a drunk along with me in the middle of the night.

Ought I to offer to buy Carl Olsson lunch the next day? I did not want to, not in the hotel restaurant, at any rate — and its rate was steep. As we walked back along Kirkeveien I told Carl, "I found a place where I can afford to eat. There's a Burger King in Valkyrie Way."

"Tomorrow I shall only eat breakfast," he said. "We do not waste time. We need to be at the mausoleum by two o'clock before other people arrive. Not many visitors go, but early we can be alone. I think before we go tomorrow I only need a drink."

In the hotel bar, of course. At six pounds a glass, if beer was his tipple. I could hardly refuse.

Myself, I packed in as much breakfast as I could. Cereal, cold meats and cheese and bread. I debated whether to phone Steve to tell him I had met up with Carl Olsson, just in case . . . in case what? The night before, I had been alone with Carl in the park without incident. My sleep had passed without disturbance too. No, I would wait.

At twelve-thirty I was in the bar, nursing a half of draught Guinness, three pounds worth. McEwan's Export was also available on draught, not to mention bottles of Newcastle Brown Ale. When I expressed surprise to the barman, he said that thousands of Norwegians go from Bergen to Tyneside for shopping because England is much cheaper. This could almost have been a pub in England, except that the job-lot of old books which served as décor on high shelves all had Norwegian or Swedish titles. Nobody else was using the bar yet. In came Carl, who had combed his hair and put on a Paisley tie that looked like a view down a microscope at swarming amoebas. He had cut himself shaving.

On impulse I told him, "I have a bottle of rum in my room."

"Ardour is of the earth," he said. At least, that's what I heard.

"Ardour?" I queried.

"Ar*ler*," he repeated, pointing to the bottles of Newcastle Brown.

"Oh, you mean *ale*. It rhymes with whale, in the sea."

"Ale," he resumed, "is of the earth, and spirit is of the sky. I think I need a drink of spirit."

The barman was hovering hopefully, polishing a glass, so I said to Carl, "Come up, then."

In the corridor upstairs, a North African was pushing a trolley of towels. A friendly, grinning, skinny fellow. As soon as we entered my room, protest burst from Carl.

"Fifteen per cent of our population today is Moslem, do you know? Here, in *Norway*. One and half people in ten. What does that tell you?"

I shrugged. I could guess what it might tell neo-Nazi nationalists.

"What it tells *me*," he said, "is that unskilled jobs go to Arabs, if I cannot drive again because I am not clear in my head."

In view of which, it may have seemed perverse of him to refuse any Coke to dilute the rum. Yet I understood when he poured a full glass of Captain Morgan and swigged it back neat.

"That tower of bodies!" he exclaimed. "The power dammed up, the climax delayed . . . birds, moths!"

"You dream about birds and moths, Carl—"

He glanced at his watch. "We must go to the dark place. You are my passport."

Chapter 5

When snow thawed in the spring, streams must froth through these hilly woodlands of Slemdal, spilling over the narrow winding roads. Leafy gardens screened substantial old wooden houses. Stainless steel sculptures stood on one lawn: a giant cockerel, a unicorn. The nameplate on the gatepost was that of some company office, blending with nature. Quite a little paradise, hereabouts.

"Near here," Carl said, "the leader of the traitor Quisling's personal guard is killed with machine-pistols by men of our Home Front."

Blood had flowed here, as well as melting snow.

"In revenge the Germans shoot fourteen men who are in jail for sabotage. Quisling is satisfied."

I sat in numb silence while Carl directed the taxi driver, who had never heard of the mausoleum. On a narrow lane, we pulled in beside a big red brick building hemmed by trees, a cross between a barn and a basilica. The taxi fare, we shared.

Heraldic creatures decorated the brickwork of the frontage. In a little lobby, behind a table bearing pamphlets, a bearded young man sat. This earnest, spiritual-looking custodian eyed Carl with disapproving recognition.

"I am bringing a visitor from England," Carl announced in English.

The custodian promptly addressed me in soft-spoken English. "You're very welcome. Are you an artist?"

"A photographer," I told him.

"Ah . . . I regret . . . It is dark inside, you see, and photography is forbidden by the family."

"I don't have a camera with me. Not today."

We couldn't stand around chatting. Other people might come. Carl opened a stout wooden door for me.

Entering this place was like stepping inside a cavern illuminated by infrared rather than natural light, as if here was the haunt of some nocturnal creature which remained invisible in the gloom. The lighting consisted of weak little spotlights focused on sections of the walls and the vault above. Nude figures were everywhere: babies and children, lovers, toiling adults, old folk on the verge of death. Copulation was in vigorous progress, and births — an umbilical cord the size of a hawser coiled between mother and newborn child. Dimly detectable figures caressed one another. They exchanged blows. They writhed in spasm. Such a surfeit of procreation and struggle and death.

Here was a Sistine Chapel frescoed by an artist who was definitely no Michelangelo. More like that Swiss fellow — rhymes with the radioactivity counter, Giger, that's him — with his monstrous biologies; although lacking Giger's artistic slickness. The subdued lighting seemed intended to hide the clumsiness of the obsessive work. Years this must have taken, years of crepuscular drawing and colouring. Mad, compulsive years brooding about the passions and mortality of the flesh.

Because of the utter dimness, figures emerged dreamlike, spectrally, and slid out of sight again. Hades, yes: a kind of Hades was here, full of dead shades re-enacting their lives, bodies stripped bare and overblown. The dark side of the Vigeland Park, indeed.

Each footstep gave rise to a thrumming reverberation. The echo was intensified by the next footfall, into a slurring, sloshing boom. If I screamed in here, the acoustics might deafen me. In such gloom, the entrance was almost lost to sight as Carl guided me deeper, hand on my elbow. Here was a dream place, sealed away hermetically, not part of the natural world despite all its depiction of natural functions.

When we came to the far wall, the noise of our approach rose up to dizzy me, and Carl caught hold of me.

His tongue and his rummy breath invaded my mouth. His

hands thrust under my jacket and sweater, and upward, but I had worn no bra for him to unclip. Turning me, he pressed my breasts to the frescoed wall. I felt his stiffness. This was insanity. At any moment the door might open. Visitors might enter. I did not cry out. The amplified echo would have shattered my skull.

"We must," he breathed in my ear. "We must." Must and lust and thrust and dust.

He unfastened my belt to release my jeans. Down to my knees he pulled the denim and my knickers. As his cock butted clumsily, I leaned numbly against the wall. Was this rape or necessity? Was it my recompense to him, or was it a way of unlocking secrets? His open zip was a rasp. Delving, his hands prised my legs apart. If I had not cooperated, he could never have cleaved me. Not last night in the park, not in the hotel room, but here and now in this perilous place, in this awkward stance, I adjusted my position as best I could to accommodate him. The thought of disease crossed my mind, of AIDS. Of Steve so far away. At least I was on the pill. Had I taken my pill last night before I went to the park? My routine was all cocked up. *Wait a moment while I take a pill.* The mad magnified hum of Carl's panting deafened me. I bit on my lower lip.

Like some slut in a back street—of my imagination!—I held my sweater up so that my bare tits stayed in touch with the painted plaster. Here was a red light district of the mind, an infrared light district.

Carl's weight squashed me against the wall, sandwiching me. A stranger coming into the huge mausoleum might fail to notice at first—then only vaguely spy a man in a long loose raincoat examining the furthest extreme of this place very closely. The circuit was complete: from Alver to me to the sculptures to Carl through Christina to Liv to the blood that was spilled to the monolith thrusting its shape in miniature into me. Images assaulted my mind, invading me.

Almost courteously, he had rearranged my clothing while I was still dazed by perceptions. What a gent this bulldozer driver was at heart. My nickers sat uncomfortably, twisted, clammy. I knew now that magic has laws—of affinity, analogy, contact, contagion, not the laws of logic but of primitive mentality.

"Those Nazis, they tried to make a magical barrier around Norway—"

"And Sweden too, because Sweden is joined to Norway like a Siamese twin—"

That had been the aim of the blood-sacrifice—to raise up an Odin force to resist attack, to repel invasion. The geometry of the sculpture park, the embodiment by the figures of lifelong struggle against death, of fertility, of willpower, that central surging phallus of bodies: these were perfect for this purpose.

"It *was* Liv Frisvold who died in the park. My mother's mother . . ."

Fanatical Nazi supporter, who had merged the Nordic and the Teutonic in the person of her daughter. Fertile mother. Valkyrie. She had volunteered; her brother had volunteered her. Either; both. Olav Frisvold had been there when she died, her throat cut.

"Olav Frisvold is Knut Alver, Carl! He wants the power—"

Germany surrendered. Fortress Norway failed as a scheme. Nazis fled. Those who could. With gold and loot, those who could. By secret routes, to Paraguay, to Brazil. The force stayed locked up all these years in the core of the sculpture park, on that plateau, in that monolith.

"The birds were planes, flying to attack the Germans in Norway—"

"The barrier worked, Mrs Clarke. Not against enemies of the Nazis—but against Olav Frisvold, who had fled, by denying him entry back again—"

"Stopping him from coming here in person—"

"To harvest the power—"

"To use it—"

We spoke as if wrapped in a *folie* for two, reinforcing each other's conviction, which few other people in the world would be able to share. Oh we were in duet.

"Because he is old—"

"Near death—"

"To use the power to delay death—"

"Take the energy into himself—"

"Make himself strong again—"

"Make himself *young* again—?"

"The way he was in 1945 when his sister died—!"

"Your photos smuggled out the images he needs, cut into thousands of tiny pieces, too small for the net to intercept what they carry—"

"The net around Norway, blocking him from linking with the power in the park—"

Just then, the door opened thirty metres or more away, and Carl released me. A middle-aged man and woman stepped respectfully into the obscure mausoleum as if into a church. The man removed his hat.

"I must come to England," Carl said. "Find my old uncle—"

"Great-uncle—"

"Yes, great-uncle. Stop this happening. If it happens . . ."

Would the tip of the monolith erupt before the astonished gaze of Japanese tourists, geysering upward a flare of light, a blazing flux? While, over in England, Alver stood naked in the little central space between the four circular jigsaws, each touching rim to rim, north, south, east and west . . . When that happened, nightmares would rage through my mind, and through Steve's mind, and through Carl's, roosting inside us, deranging us. We hurried past that middle-aged couple, who barely glanced at us.

In the lobby the custodian raised a hand. I suppose we were flushed and disarrayed. Did he have an inkling of what we had perpetrated in his temple of art?

"That lady who went inside," the bearded young man told me with quiet pride, "she is the professor from the University of Uppsala who has been researching the biography of Emanuel Vigeland for fifteen years." As if I should be filled with respect and reverence. "You must not miss the museum."

"I thought *this* is the museum."

"This is the Doomsday—the Last Judgement. Next door is the gallery annex, with framed oil paintings. They are so colourful. Do see them."

"Thank you," I said.

"It is a privilege."

We went outside, into fresh air.

"Those paintings next door are not very good."

I would take Carl's word for it. A Saab with Swedish plates was the only vehicle in sight. How few people came here. We returned up the leafy lane. I hitched at my clothes in vain. The long hike downhill to the nearest bus route was likely to be uncomfortable.

"I must come to England," Carl persisted. "I must stay at your home."

He seemed to have little sense of what was feasible, and what was not. On the other hand, did I? I had just had a fuck with him— of an entirely functional sort—in that awful parody of the Sistine Chapel.

"What will we tell your husband, Mrs Clarke?"

Undeniably Carl was tenacious, even if there was a huge warp in his temperament. He was like some tree, erect but twisted through ninety degrees half way up its height.

"You may as well use my first name—"

His hand jerked up, to snatch my very words from the air, and his fist closed.

"No! It is too much like the name they gave to my mother. Your first name is personal. If I use it, I may think we like each other. I must call you Mrs Clarke." Wham-bang, no thank you, Ma'am. He was right, of course. "What do we tell Mr Clarke?"

"That we had a vision in the mausoleum?"

"A vision . . . Vidkun Quisling's brother Jørgen saw visions of Vidkun after the traitor was shot. Jørgen took drink and drugs and went to spirit, spirit—"

"Spiritualists?"

"Yes. Say to Mr Clarke that I gave you some hash to eat, do you understand hash?"

"Cannabis. Resin."

"Say that you felt you must press your breasts against a fresco, in the darkness, the same way you touched the sculptures. This put you in touch with the truth."

"And what put you in touch with the truth?"

"I held your hand—the way Olav Frisvold held yours."

"We held hands." How sweet.

"Like spiritualists at a see-ainsey."

"Séance."

"A séance," he repeated.

Would Steve swallow this? At least until everything was over, and Carl had returned to his own country, and I could explain . . . or not need to explain at all.

"How do we find Olav Frisvold, Mr Olsson? Do we make big prints of the photographs—"

"Yes, make big prints!"

"And stand on them naked?" I mimed cutting my thumb. "Spill a little blood upon them? And see what happens?"

He nodded vigorously. "Maybe. We shall do something!"

An immediate something would consist of Carl catching a train to Bergen, the overnight boat to Tyneside, then a National Express coach to our own county—while I flew back home by air. Carl's route would cost less than mine. In another sense it had already cost him dearly. Me too, me too.

We proceeded downhill past foliage-screened gardens and serene rustic-looking homes.

*   *   *

He told me when to get off the bus. Himself, he stayed on board.
Bye-bye until England, Mr Olsson.
    Foremost, I craved a bath. Before I climbed into the tub in the
Comfort Hotel I drank a big glass of rum as if I was some girl in
trouble decades ago trying to induce a miscarriage. Light-headed
from the spirit and the hot water, afterwards I made my bleary way
to Burger King to take on much-needed ballast, a bacon double
cheeseburger which I ate then and there. When I got back to the
hotel, it was six o'clock, five o'clock in England. Steve would be
heading home. I only intended to snooze for an hour. It was ten,
and dark, when I woke up. What I ought to have done earlier, of
course, was phone Scandinavian Air Services before I resorted to
rum and soaking myself and eating and napping.
    I dialled home.

"Back *tomorrow?*"
    "So long as there's a seat free on the plane. I'll call you as early
as I can, tell you the arrival time so you can meet me. There's too
much to explain on the phone, Steve. I found Carl Olsson in the
park—as I said I would. Mr Olsson is Alver's great-nephew, and
Alver's real name is Olav Frisvold—"
    And Carl Olsson was only an adoptive name; and his mother
Christina had certainly not received that purifying name from *her*
own mother; and I was not exactly "Mrs Clarke." Identities were
haywire. Nothing was what it seemed, not least the sculpture park,
pride of Norway.
    "Listen, Steve: Mr Olsson is coming to England—by boat,
'cause that's cheaper. He'll need to stay with us till we can trace
Frisvold. Get big laminated prints made of the four photos we took
—same size as the jigsaws—"
    "You're starkers on two of the photos."
    The sheer irrelevance of this almost made me laugh. *Olsson
stuck his cock into me in the mausoleum.*
    "Norwegians don't bother about nudity. It's no big deal, remem-
ber? Mr Alver, unquote. So I'm hoping to see you tomorrow," I
ended brightly.
    "You've done *very* well. Hang on: do you want the prints land-
scape-style or cut to circles?"
    "Circles, exactly like the jigsaws. All in one piece, of course."
    "What do we *do* with them? What is Alver trying to do?"
    "When I get home, Steve."

*   *   *

That night the dream was terrible. Torchlight flickered. I was shivering convulsively. The intent thin face of a weasely man wearing a peaked braided cap and round, wire-rimmed glasses swam before my eyes while strong hands held me upright. Voices were chanting. *Blut. Stein. Macht. Schild. Schutz.* The knife cut into my throat and I choked in awful pain.

I had to drink a great volume of Coke direct from the plastic bottle, gasping between gulps. Most of it, I vomited into the wash basin.

Chapter 6

On the way back from Heathrow Airport I told Steve, who was driving, about the supernatural barrier around Norway and about Carl's grandmother and her brother Olav, who was Mr Alver, who was now trying to extract the power from the sculpture park to cheat death—presumably!

The four big laminated pictures would be ready by the next day. Steve would jig-cut them into circles. When Olsson arrived, we would try to mimic whatever Olav Frisvold was attempting, to give us some clue to where he was.

Steve fretted. "Olsson may be thinking of, well, trying to kill Frisvold—"

"He said no such thing."

"It can't be a family reunion he's hoping for!"

"These dreams have to end! Frisvold probably killed enough people while he was in the SS."

"Listen to what you're saying, Chrissy! Frisvold may be a criminal, but we can't take the law into our own hands."

We had reached the high cut through the last rampart of the Chiltern Hills, the microwave relay tower atop rising like a pale lighthouse. From here the motorway plunged down into Oxford-shire and a vast vale of farmland, misty with distance and heat. We were discussing a murderer, and murder, and magic, which had contaminated us.

"God's Legion might believe us now, Chrissy. Ellison might."

"If Ellison was a high Anglican or Catholic he might have some ideas about the occult and exorcism. But a Baptist evangelist? Jesus and tambourines?"

"He has the vans. He has the troops."

"Ex-addicts and muddled runaways who have been born again. Will Frisvold grow *younger*? Or will he—will he shift into someone else's body? Some younger body?"

"Whose? He doesn't know about Olsson."

"He might have dreamed about him. That can't have been his plan to begin with. I'm thinking about you and me."

"He wouldn't want your body, Chrissy."

"What's wrong with *my* body?"

My body, in which Carl Olsson had rooted . . .

"Nothing at all! What I mean is, he wouldn't want a woman's body—not a Norse Siegfried like him. He may have someone lined up at his home. A gardener or valet. It's just that I can't imagine someone becoming younger. Skin freshening, muscles toning up, bones growing strong again. It's easier to imagine him swapping minds with a younger person."

"Then the newly inhabited body kills the feeble old husk?"

We were becoming a bit unhinged. Steve drove carefully, taking me home.

On my initiative we made love that night. A reunion of our bodies in bed; and we slept peacefully.

Two mornings later at Fernhill, a phone call from Newcastle. Olsson had disembarked from the overnight boat. He was about to board a National Express coach for a seven-hour journey to Blanchester, changing at Birmingham. Of course we would meet him.

And we did so, that evening.

While we were driving back to Preston Priors, from the rear of our car Olsson said, "I have dreamed badly."

"We have beer in the house—"

Olsson rooted in a duffel bag and produced a bottle of rum.

"I am bringing you a present."

Politely Olsson praised the fields of sheep and wheat, and the rolling leafy land. He admired Preston Priors as we entered it. The ironstone cottages were mostly slate-roofed though some were thatched. Norman church; old vicarage and old school-house, no longer inhabited by either vicar or schoolma'am. Defunct pub, converted into a house. Big village green complete with genuine duck pond. Our own cottage was part of a terrace down less exalted Hog Lane.

And inside of Oak Cottage: exposed beams and joists in the kitchen-cum-dining room—also in the sitting room where the four big laminated photos lay on the carpet, rims touching. Steve had shifted furniture aside to make enough space. Olsson would be sleeping on the sofa, though only after the pictures had been stacked in the kitchen, covered with a tablecloth to hide them, neutralize them.

We ate noodles and meat balls and olive Ciabatta bread fresh from the oven and drank some red wine. At eight o'clock we adjourned to the sitting room. Hog Lane never caught any late sunshine. Perfectly reasonable to close the curtains and switch on a lamp. The low ceiling made any central light fitting impossible.

"Like a—séance." Olsson had remembered the word.

"Just wait till I bring the candles!"

We were used to power cuts in Preston Priors whenever there was a violent storm, so we kept a stock of candles. Candlelight would mimic the flicker of the torches in the sculpture park on that night years ago. While I fetched two packets and matches, Steve brought an assortment of saucers and egg-cups for the candles to stand in. Olsson was peering at the pictures of Steve and of me on the floor.

"Bring a sharp knife from the kitchen," he said. "To stick in the space in the middle. Like a . . ." The name eluded him. Maybe he meant like the gnomon of a sundial. A spindle. An axis.

Whatever were we doing here in our sitting room in cahoots with a Norwegian who wasn't quite right in the head? Steve frowned at me, but we must follow our instincts. When I brought a kitchen knife Olsson stabbed the point down hard, right into the floorboard below. What did a mere cut in the carpet matter? Twanging the handle, he made the knife quiver. After Steve and I had lit all the candles, I switched off the lamp.

"So," said Steve, "do we stand together in the middle holding hands?"

Do we take our clothes off? I wondered. I felt no instinct to do so. Quite the contrary.

"Did you bring hash, Mr Olsson?" Of course he hadn't.

"I think," said Olsson, "we kneel down and each cut our finger a little on the knife. Rub our blood together. Rub it on the pictures. I think so. We repeat the German words."

Blood. Stone. Makes. Shield.

"Maybe in reverse. To take us back . . ."

So we crowded together on our knees, upon the pictures. Slicing our thumbs just a little on the knife blade, we mingled our blood, and smeared those big nocturnal images of the Vigeland Park.

"*Schutz. Schild. Macht. Stein. Blut,*" we chorused. If Hugh Ellison should somehow be listening at the window. . . !

Two dozen candle-flames began to rock. The flames dipped then stretched up again as if they were being breathed in and out by some unseen presence.

"Uncle, where are you?" called Olsson. He said things in Norwegian and German. Soon he became frustrated.

"I need rum!" Rising, he stumbled to the kitchen.

"Christ," hissed Steve. "Rum and a knife—"

Returning with the bottle, Olsson knelt again. Squeezing the blade of the knife with his right hand, he jerked, then exposed his palm. Blood flowed from his life line and heart line. Gritting his teeth, he poured dark spirit over the bleeding wound. With a shudder, he drank from the bottle. Plunging his palm down upon the patch of exposed carpet, he screwed his hand around, chanting, "*Blut. Blut. Blut.*" Sounded as if great drips of liquid were plopping from a tap into a bucket of water. What was I supposed to put on that stain to get rid of it? White wine? Salt? Would he catch hold of me next, smearing my skin and my clothes? As the candle flames danced, highlights gleamed in the laminated pictures, and shadows lurched around our sitting room.

Then the flames were burning evenly. All was calm. Nothing whatever was happening. If anything had been on the point of happening, it had faded away.

I dressed Olsson's hand. We opened beers, and swigged, sitting together on the sofa.

"Tomorrow night," he vowed, "we will do it again, but I spill more blood. I felt it start to come, but we lost it. We must all spill blood. Maybe you buy a hen."

Poor hen. Poor carpet. Poor us.

When the doorbell rang insistently, the clock on the bedside table showed two in the morning. Steve lurched to the open curtains, and peered into Hog Lane.

"Come here," he whispered. Again, the summoning peal. In my pajamas, I joined Steve. Below: a black car, a Mercedes.

"It's Alver's car. Frisvold's—"

Up through the floor came noises of blunder. Olsson was up and about. Before either of us could decide what to do, we were hearing voices downstairs. Olsson must have opened our front door.

"Stay here, Chrissy—"

"*No!*"

The old gent had relapsed into one of the pine carver chairs in the kitchen. Olsson was leaning against our dresser crowded with plates and ornaments, the knife in his bandaged hand. On the red floor tiles, in a heap: the tablecloth.

"Both of you come in here now! Sit and put your hands on the table—" Frisvold's voice held a weary authority, and his liver-spotted hand, a nasty-looking pistol. I had never seen a gun before in real life, but the name Luger occurred to me.

No smartly tailored suit, tonight. Before driving here, he must have thrown on whatever came to hand. Old trousers and sweater, under an open overcoat. No socks on his feet, just brown leather slippers.

"Sit!"

Of course we obeyed. Frisvold spoke to Olsson in Norwegian. Carl retorted now and then. I could grasp not a word of what they were *snakking* about, which was about the only Norwegian word I knew apart from *skål*. *Snakker*, to speak. *Jai* don't *snak Norsk*. After a while, I interrupted:

"You gave us nightmares, Mr Frisvold. Your life's a nightmare."

"What do you know?" Was he asking me, or sneering?

Anger boiled in me. "How about you sacrificing your sister in that park in 1945?"

He winced. "My sister wished that, to buttress the Reich. So that there could be some strength left! So that Bolshevism would not wash over Europe the way it did. We have had to wait fifty years for the red tide to go away. She was no faint-heart like my countrymen. What I regret is the failure, the abject surrender. Your interference is making her die in vain once more."

"Excuse me, but *you* came to us—to use us."

Frisvold peered derisively at the bandage on Carl's hand. "Now I have found her grandson. My own blood, out for revenge—something we Norwegians seem to specialise in. Put that silly knife away, Carl Olsson. You hurt your own hand, you fool."

"My blood brought you here, Uncle."

Frisvold inclined his head, conceding. Having won his point,

Olsson placed the stained knife on the dresser next to a Delft milk jug, then subsided into a chair.

The old man tutted exasperatedly. "Revenge, revenge. Thousands of patriots persecuted for decades after our so-called liberation —and now me, to be thwarted. You don't know what I'm talking about, do you? You are ignorant. Your heads are full of lies."

"You'll be telling us next," Steve cried, "that the concentration camps were a lie!"

"I did not know about those. I never saw one."

No doubt my expression was jeering.

People often talk wildly to justify themselves, but the spin which Frisvold put on the Second World War and on his country's part in it soon had me reeling—and Carl as well. Before long Carl was sitting with one hand clutching his head, his eyes red with rum and beer and fatigue. Steve, too, was fairly pop-eyed.

Quisling, shot in 1945 for his betrayal of Norway? Quisling who had given his name to treachery just as Judas Iscariot had? According to Frisvold, Vidkun Quisling was one of the great humanitarian figures of the twentieth century, and one of the most perceptive.

What did anyone know about Quisling? Scarcely more than his despised, hated name! Yet during the early nineteen-twenties, apparently this very same Quisling had saved a fifth of a million people from starvation in the Ukraine, almost single-handedly. During 1922, with Soviet consent, he was running the Russian railway system to improve famine relief. So impressed was Trotsky, that he asked Quisling to reorganize the Red Army. A rival offer came from Imperial China, to reorganize their administration. To prepare for this task, Quisling learned Chinese—but the Chiang Kai-Shek revolution intervened. That was the sort of man we were talking about; not that Frisvold himself had personally been close to Quisling. Quisling was too fastidious.

In his youth Quisling had learned Hebrew because he was deeply religious. What's more, he was such a nifty mathematician that he understood quantum theory. He also understood what was going to happen to Norway, land of make-believe, when the great powers began brawling, unless his countrymen *did* something. Hence, his National Unification Party, *Nasjonal Samling*, NS. That was no Nazi party. Far from it. The NS aimed at putting some backbone into Norway and saving its independence, the way the Finns had saved themselves.

Blind, selfish, and lazy, the Norwegians possessed little more than a police force, even though Norway was one of the easiest countries in the world to defend with anything more than a microscopic army. Throughout the 1930s Quisling was the Churchill of Norway, the lone voice warning of national suicide, and being abused for his pains. Frisvold certainly had it in for his countrymen.

Did Quisling conspire with the Nazis? Not a bit of it. Quisling stepped in to frustrate the Germans and minimize the effects of an occupation. When the invasion started, the King of Norway and the General Staff had more important matters on their minds—would you believe they were enjoying a Roman-style banquet, accompanied by a lecture on Gastronomy in Ancient Rome?

Off his own bat, an elderly Norwegian officer did manage enterprisingly to sink the German flagship, sending all the occupation officials and their documents to the bottom of the Oslo Fjord.

"*His* reward after the war was to be prosecuted as a traitor, because he belonged to Quisling's *Nasjonal Samling!* This NS member was *sinking* the Nazi flagship, not cheering and saluting it—"

Sinking the flagship gained Oslo precious hours, which were squandered. Did the Norwegian government announce immediate mobilization over the radio? On the contrary, they sent out call-up papers by snail-mail.

And then the government and the King ran away, with not a word to the people, without making any arrangements for maintaining public services.

If Quisling had not stepped in, Norway might have been treated like Poland. By a ruse, Quisling managed to keep the home shipping fleet in Norwegian ownership. He kept the Norwegian flag flying over parliament, at least for a while. He was so obstinate. Ribbentrop loathed him. Quisling even obtained amnesties for former enemies of his, whom the Germans arrested. He was always at odds with Reichscommissar Terboven. Quisling did say a few silly things about Jews but the fact is that when roundups loomed, he delayed these for ten days so that Jews could get away. It was his own *Nasjonal Samling* members who helped Jews make their escape to Sweden. The only voice actually protesting about arrests of Jews was the *Nasjonal Samling* Bishop of Oslo—so he got ten years in jail after the war.

Topsy-turvy, indeed.

"Our nation could never come to terms with any of these truths," Frisvold ranted on, "or that a great debt of gratitude was

owing! Quisling's name was blackened. Vengeance was easier—
vindictive reprisals which went on for years. During the mockery of
a trial Quisling endured, the authorities were sticking wires in his
cranium like medieval inquisitors to test if he was sane. Or to send
him insane. This was while he was trying to conduct his own
defence on a starvation diet. Give him no more than a little herring
for lunch!—even though no Norwegians ever went hungry the way
the Dutch did during the war, thousands dying of starvation. Our
King even wanted Quisling's execution to be deliberately botched,
to torment him—"

If Frisvold was telling the truth, this was shocking. Though why
was he telling us at all? After decades of pretending to be somebody
else, at last he had an audience? One from whom he might win
sympathy? Whom he might convert to his point of view—so that
we would voluntarily step aside, instead of him shooting us? The
gun in his hand seemed so evil. Though if it were not for the gun,
would we be listening?

Olsson broke in. "Quisling got no amnesty for men who were
shot in reprisal after the Home Front killed the chief of his bodyguard!"

"Pah, he couldn't. If he did not agree to it, the Germans were
going to shoot even more prisoners. The Home Front's pig-headed
adventures only made the Reichscommissar and the Gestapo take
off the kid gloves."

"What are those gloves?" asked Olsson.

"The Home Front provoked Terboven and the Gestapo so they
stopped acting softly. Terboven was glad of any excuse."

"Why was that?" asked Steve.

"Because Josef Terboven was a spiteful bully. Inferiority complex cloaked in arrogance. Norway was the trial run for him becoming Reichscommissar of Britain if an invasion succeeded—did you
know that?"

Steve shook his head.

"Yes, Terboven would have been boss of Britain! You know
nothing, do you? Quisling warned the Home Front but they played
into Terboven's hands in his contest with Quisling. That's what use
the Home Front were."

Olsson moaned. "At home we had a *photo* on the wall, of a big
German general saluting a lad of the Home Front as he surrendered
to the boy."

"Oh that famous photo! It was staged, for public relations. No
German could *surrender* to any Norwegian. Thanks to Quisling,

Norway and Germany signed an armistice in 1940 so that they would not be at war. The government-in-exile knew nothing about this, because they had run away."

"What people know, is a lie?" cried Olsson. "And the real resistance was Quisling?"

"That's right. Such truths are unacceptable."

Frisvold was telling us that nothing was as it seemed—so therefore neither was he as he seemed. I could hardly square this with my dream.

"Is this supposed to clear you of blame? Blame for joining the SS? For the blood-sacrifice of your own *sister?* Were you and Quisling trying to *protect* Norway there in Vigeland Park?"

Frisvold uttered a croak of a laugh. "Quisling was no part of that! He was so religious he wanted to resign during the occupation to become a lay pastor. Josef Terboven was there in the park, the Reichscommissar—he worshipped Hitler."

"What did this Terboven look like?"

"Thin. Round spectacles with wire rims. Receding hair, parted on the left, oiled and combed back. He looked like a human rat, though he wore a fine uniform."

That was the man I had seen in my dream—but who was it who actually cut Liv Frisvold's throat?

"Some of the SS were there," Frisvold went on. "And Weiner, the Gestapo chief, who shot himself later on—"

"But *you* got away."

About this, he was willing to tell us too.

All along, the Nazi high command had been planning to retreat to Norway . . .

"Or Bavaria," I said, remembering.

Oops, pardon me. This was merely another example of my ignorance—of how I swallowed clichés like a lazy fish a pretty fly. The belief that the Nazis intended to hole up in the Bavarian Alps was a masterpiece of black propaganda, probably the only real jewel of German disinformation. On the strength of that Eisenhower diverted a whole army—regardless that the Allies had cracked the German codes and ought to have known better. Norway was always the real destination for the final showdown.

Yet by then there was too much chaos. The red tide, flooding from the east. Hitler had lost his marbles, too far gone in madness to issue sensible orders.

So: get out of Norway or else face the music.

In spite of personal animosities Josef Terboven had set aside a plane—a bomber—for Quisling to escape in. And for other people, of course. Frisvold would have been on that bomber, which would rendezvous with a long-distance U-boat, capable of reaching South America.

Naively and stubbornly, Quisling chose to remain in Norway. He thought that his faultless logic and patriotic service would be appreciated. Delay, delay.

And then, from Berlin via Denmark, arrived the *Belgian* fascist leader, Leon Degrelle.

"Who?" I asked.

Pardon our ignorance, again.

In cliché land Degrelle would be the Belgian counterpart of Quisling—if Quisling had ever been the collaborator he was slandered as being. This Degrelle—endowed with sublime good luck —was the only figure of such wicked prominence to survive and thrive anywhere in Europe after the war. He was The One Who Got Away—to Spain.

Leon Degrelle . . . Pay attention, Chrissy.

Frisvold was only acquainted with the Belgian for a very short time in Oslo, but it was an intense acquaintance. Both men had served in the Ukraine, in calamitous conditions. Degrelle loved hanging out with collaborationists, bragging and drinking and revelling in the trappings of Nazism. Germans themselves were never close mates of his. Even after fighting alongside them, he still never learned a word of German.

"*Mais moi, je parle Français,*" Frisvold confided. "Leon's life and exploits were poured into my ear. What a bond developed between us."

Because of both men's service in the SS. And because Frisvold could *snakke Norsk* and *sprechen Deutsch*, which was of invaluable help to a monolingual Belgian marooned in Oslo with just a few cronies.

Frisvold had served the Reich—and Degrelle had formed a Walloon storm-trooper brigade, which became part of the Waffen-SS. After the Allies overran Belgium, Degrelle and his Walloon Legion fought the advancing Russians in a last ditch attempt to save Berlin. Failing, he and a few associates left the Legion in the outskirts of Berlin and fled.

Degrelle had friends in Spain, and resources tucked away there, money and gold—as well as a lot of money in the south of France (but France was out of bounds). Always Degrelle was financially canny. He married money (though this never stopped him from cheating on his wife). He hit a jackpot when he borrowed money from his own Rexist Party's coffers to buy a big perfume company which the Germans sequestered from its Jewish owners.

Spain spelled sanctuary. It was with Frisvold's assistance that Degrelle and his now-tiny party were able to commandeer a light aircraft with long-range fuel tanks and the scarce fuel to fill them.

"Don't tell me you're a pilot too."

"No, Miss Clarke, the pilot was a Belgian, Robert Frank."

What a journey that was, flying almost fifteen hundred miles by night over Europe, variously embattled or liberated. Maybe Frisvold had been telling the truth when he said that aeroplanes terrified him. This plane only barely reached Spain, crash-landing out of fuel on the beach at San Sebastian just a few miles beyond the border. Degrelle hurt his foot. Into hospital he was whisked. Generalissimo Franco was not best pleased at his uninvited fascist guest, but being a fascist himself he prevaricated about extradition. Four months after the crash-landing Degrelle vanished from hospital. The Spanish government denied all knowledge. Ten years later Degrelle emerged in public from the protection of his Spanish friends. He prospered. A construction company owned by him built air bases for the Americans in Spain.

"He paid you well for the plane," Olsson said.

I was keenly interested in sources of wealth. Frisvold pursed his lips. He was evasive about what happened to him after San Sebastian, though obviously from wherever he went to he had kept tabs on what was happening in his homeland. I imagined the wily buccaneering Degrelle nursing a bag of diamonds, sequestered from Jewish dealers in Antwerp—or him entrusting his new buddy Frisvold with gold bars to take to Paraguay to establish a bolt-hole in case Spain let him down . . .

"Actually, Miss Clarke, many Norwegian families made a lot of money during the war by supplying the legitimate needs of the occupying authority. Selling trees, supplying construction material —this was perfectly proper under the terms of the Berne Convention."

Frisvold may have taken gold of his own on that plane, transmuted from some family forest by the alchemy of the occupation. .

"Perfectly proper and legal!"

"Are we supposed to think, Mr Frisvold, that you're more sinned against than sinning?"

Exasperatedly: "Norway almost went bankrupt after the war by punishing the so-called profiteering families, wrecking their businesses in an orgy of revenge! The Norwegian government asked the British what you intended to do about your own collaborators. The people of your Channel Islands: those were in the same situation. London told Oslo it was going to do nothing—forget about it. Norwegians could never take advice. If America had not stepped in with lavish aid, Norway would have gone down the drain—"

"Things seemed different during much of the war," Frisvold insisted. "Hitler looked set to win. Thousands of Norwegians fought the Red Army alongside the Germans. Not against Britain, never— only against Communism, which was to eat up half of Europe."

Only Quisling had the genius to see what eluded even the Germans, namely that the Hitler-Stalin pact would fall apart—and what would stem from this: *red tide*. Norwegians were glad to volunteer to strengthen Germany's muscle. They were the best fighters since the Vikings.

"They *deserted*," Olsson contradicted him.

"Rubbish! The Germans decorated many for gallantry. Fifty fought to the last defending the Reich Chancellery."

"It must have been crowded there, what with Belgians and Norwegians and goodness knows who else."

Frisvold glared at me. "Have you seen a trawler net being winched tighter and tighter?"

"A net with sharks in it," Steve said.

"And with holes in the net," retorted Frisvold. "All these Front Fighters from Norway could have been the nucleus of Norwegian defense after the war. Instead, they were imprisoned, then forced to be street-sweepers. Even now, Norway refuses its responsibilities in Europe and prefers to dream."

"*We* have been dreaming," I reminded him.

"May I have a drink of water?" he asked me.

One thing which Quisling did not favour was a special Germanic SS Norway Force, under the ultimate command of Himmler. Quisling even started a whispering campaign against this thousand-strong force, which was destined not only to fight Communism but also for other duties in the Greater Reich.

"Things seemed different," repeated Frisvold. "Events had an inevitability. I am haunted by certain brutalities, but at the time . . . The Americans committed atrocities in Vietnam, did they not?

No one knew about the Nazi death camps. My goal was Nordic-Teutonic union against Slavic-Asian Bolshevism. My sister's goal too. Odin power—"

Culminating in that occult ritual at the eleventh hour in the Vigeland Park . . .

"Do you understand now?" asked this old man with the gun. With his free hand, he stroked the uppermost picture of the park, of me in the buff embracing granite. "I have the right to use the energy because of my sister. She was a valkyrie! Her participation was voluntary. She would allow no one to take her life but me. Not Terboven, certainly! *Me*, her adored brother, her hero. Oh, Liv," he cried out. "*Life* is the meaning of her name!"

This was deeply sick.

"I have the right to become young again," Frisvold declared. "I have the right to live again."

"By stealing someone's body?" I shouted at him.

He looked amazed. "Of course not. How could *that* happen? I shall live again by reincarnation."

CHAPTER 7

Surely the old man was deeply mad.

Then he began to tell us about the Nazi scientific expedition to Tibet. Photos have appeared showing German scientists measuring the heads of grinning Tibetans with callipers, as if racist anthropology was the principal purpose of the trip; but it was otherwise . . .

Hitler believed in reincarnation. "The Soul and the mind migrate, just as the body returns to nature"—thus spake the Führer, though not in public.

The Gauleiter of Thuringia, Artur Dinter, said the same thing much more openly. An early Nazi recruit, Dinter published a book preaching reincarnation—and also demanding that the Bible should be reorganized. Get rid of the entire Old Testament with all its Jewish blather. Cut out all the Epistles of St. Paul and all of the Gospels except for that of mystical St. John. Even St. John's Gospel would need a touch of rewriting to remove Jewish taint. The resulting Bible would have been somewhat slim: from Word-made-Flesh to Apocalypse in a few quick steps. Politically this was embarrassing for Hitler. The Führer hoped to win the support of Evangelicals and Catholics. Banning most of the Bible was not a vote catcher. So this particular gauleiter was ousted from the Nazi

Party. However, on the subject of reincarnation, Adolf still saw eye to eye with Artur Dinter.

Heinrich Himmler also believed firmly in reincarnation—as well as in runic magic; the black twin lightning flash symbolizing Himmler's SS was the double Sig rune. Himmler adopted the ideas of a man called Karl Eckhart, author of a book titled *Temporal Immortality*.

"According to Eckhart, each man is reborn as one of his own blood-descendants—"

Himmler was on the verge of distributing a special printing of twenty thousand copies of Eckhart's book to the SS when Hitler put his foot down, again for political reasons. Heinrich, head of the SS, was sure that he himself was the reincarnation of a previous Heinrich who, a thousand years earlier, established the Saxon royal family and thrust the Poles eastward (not as in North and South Poles, but as in *untermensch* people). The SS were carrying on his ancestor's splendid work.

Where, oh where, might one discover the recipe for reincarnation? Where else but in Tibet, one of the secret places of the world where the rebirth of lamas and Dalai Lamas was routine! The result was the SS science outing of the late 30s in search of arcane wisdom. And the expedition did strike pay dirt, according to Frisvold.

The old man jawed on about mandalas, Tibetan meditation-mazes which were very like the runic maze in the Vigeland Park. He spoke about some Tibetan rite of "Cutting Off" involving a magic dagger, which stirred up occult forces, if any were in the vicinity. The Cutting Off of Norway from Allied attack, hmm? This would be a Nordic, Teutonic rite, not an Asian ritual; a rite from the land of Valhalla, where Odin chose slaughtered heroes for immortal struggle; a rite where blood played a central role. Yet behind it lurked . . .

"The power to reincarnate me, because my blood-sister gave her life in a wasted sacrifice." Frisvold's scowl challenged any of us to contradict him. "After you stop meddling and after I succeed, you will be free of your nightmares. After I am born again, carrying on the cycle of life with full self-awareness of who I was."

We were enmeshed in this now. "How can you do it?" Steve whispered.

By way of reply Frisvold touched the muzzle of the Luger to his lips.

The gun was not for *us*, although he used it to intimidate and control us. Shooting us might be bad *karma* immediately prior to a reincarnation. No, the pistol was meant for himself. While he knelt amongst the images of the Vigeland Park back in his house, wherever that was, he would stick the muzzle of the Luger in his mouth and fire a bullet into his brain. His soul and his mind would transfer into some embryo or foetus to be reborn elsewhere.

"You have money," Olsson shouted out suddenly. "I have no job."

Frisvold had not come here expecting to meet his great-nephew and to be asked for cash. But he delved in his coat pocket.

"Before I came out I picked up my wallet. Who knows, I might need petrol." How many miles had the Mercedes travelled tonight? Very likely that car was leased, not owned outright. Frisvold's house was probably rented. He would not be leaving any assets behind him.

"You can have whatever is in here. I shall not need it after tonight."

"Petrol money," sneered Olsson. "You have put your wealth in a Swiss bank, is that it? With a secret number which you will remember!"

A look of momentary alarm crossed Frisvold's face, to be replaced by smug triumph. Where else would his wealth be safe until he grew up again? It made perfect sense.

"What if you are reborn an *African* or an *Arab*, Uncle?"

"No, there will be some affinity. Racial affinity." Again, that croak of a laugh. "Maybe I will be born a Finn."

"What if you *are* born African and poor as shit?" I jeered at him.

A firm shake of the head. "My soul and mind will find a proper abode."

Steve could not contain himself. "What are you going to do when you're reborn? It's years and years from cradle to being able to stroll into some bank in Zurich!"

"What do you recommend, Mr Bryant?"

"Me?"

"Yes, what would you do? I'm interested."

"Well, I would . . ." Steve had spoken without thinking, and promptly ground to a halt.

"You are utterly helpless. Dependant. Suppose that you can make your newborn mouth shape words properly. Do you confide in your new parents? You risk being smothered as a devil-child—or becoming a media sensation! What benefit is there? Do you tell the truth about yourself? What you achieved is not easily repeatable by other people! You are a freak—and a sort of monster, because you cut your sister's throat. Do you invent a false past life?"

Steve was at a loss. Frisvold had had far longer to think through the implications.

"Will your new parents cooperate? Will they hurry to Switzerland, equipped with that magic number and password, and then surround you with luxury? A giant TV screen showing adult movies to wile away the boredom? A baby's mini-gym, to help you mature faster? You are a lottery ticket they have won! Once they have collected, they can tear up the ticket."

He had arranged some kind of password for identification in Zurich in whatever future year. Number plus password would give access to whoever turned up, white or black, young or even younger.

"You are a baby, Mr Bryant, who must follow a biological plan for growing up. What will you do?"

"I don't know," Steve admitted.

"The best strategy is to reveal *nothing*. It is to pretend to be a baby—to accept the boredom and the indignity. To become a young boy—and to grow older till you are a youth. You must try not to seem too strange to your parents. You can be precocious, something of a prodigy. When you are fifteen or sixteen you can escape— with a whole new lifetime ahead of you."

"And when you're old again you can't perform the trick a second time, because you used up the power?"

Frisvold sipped water. "I think physical immortality is around the corner, for the rich. Machines the size of molecules will repair the body."

"What if you're born crippled?" Steve persisted.

"I take the risk. It is better to be born than not be born."

"What if you *like* your new parents?" I asked him.

"I must certainly seem to like them. And maybe I will. Now," he said, "I want you to carry these pictures to my car."

"What about me, Uncle Olav?" clamoured Olsson.

A smile flitted. "You can try to find me again. The same way the Tibetan priests set out to find a reincarnated one. It can take them years of travel and prayer and divination. And, of course, the child must be willing to be recognized."

He had driven away, taking our pictures with him. Frailty notwithstanding, he still had reserves of stamina.

How long ago did he establish himself in this country, poised just across the North Sea from his homeland? Britain is an island, surrounded by a cordon of sea. Therefore it is similar to Fortress Norway with its invisible magical girdle. No doubt he waited as many years as he dared before setting events in motion—no point in premature suicide! Then opportunity presented itself in the form of Majig Mementoes. Without us what would he have done? Something, but I doubt he would have told us.

Olsson was counting the money in the old man's wallet—looked to me like a couple of hundred pounds. A bastardly inheritance.

"Will you go back home soon?" I asked.

Sourly: "To the land which is not as it seems—if Uncle Olav is accurate. Will we dream anything when he kills himself tonight?"

Would we have any proof of the event?

My dream had changed. I was a statue on a plinth, frozen in mid-stride. In my outstretched hands I held a naked child of granite, who stared at me by starlight. The child's knees were up in the air as if moments earlier I had snatched him from his potty. Chubby arms reached towards me, as I held him at arm's length.

And then I was running across grass, naked and barefoot, bearing the child ahead of me.

On the radio in the morning, the final news headline is sometimes a quirky piece, which then drops into oblivion.

"In Norway last night," said the news reader, "lightning struck a pillar of granite sculpture in the middle of Oslo's sculpture park—splitting the top open, according to reports. The sculpture park is one of the principal sights of the city, visited by as many tourists as the Viking longboats. Skies were totally clear at the time. Experts are investigating."

Agog, we sat in silence through the whole of the news but the oddity received no further coverage.

Olsson clapped his hands, and winced. "I shall go back today. I think I can visit the park now without drinking—and for the last time too. Soon I will be able to build a dam. Can you drive me to the bus station?"

Of course we could; and gladly.

A week later, the police called at Fernhill. By ill chance Hugh Ellison was in the car park, talking to a couple of young legionnaires. God's centurion intercepted the two occupants of the police car, and soon he was guiding them helpfully in our direction.

"These are the proprietors of Majig MementoesZ: Miss Chrissy Clarke and her partner Mr Steve BryantT."

As Ellison dallied, a chunky uniformed man in his mid-thirties

identified himself Detective-Sergeant Curry, and his younger brunette female colleague as Detective-Constable Carroll.

Curry produced photographs of the pictures of Steve and me in
the sculpture park by night. Each of the laminated circles was
propped against a background of striped wallpaper. In miniature
was my long dark hair and bare buttocks, and Steve's skinny
frame, splayed against granite nudes. Craning to see, Ellison sidled
forward. Oh of course, our business sticker had been attached to the
otherwise blank jigsaw boxes.

"Do you recognize these?" Curry asked.

A special commission for a Norwegian client, name of Mr Alver,
said I.

"*Special,*" Ellison echoed softly. Curry seemed content for him
to remain while we were being questioned.

Sculpture park in Oslo; sentimental journey on an old man's
behalf, et cetera. An eccentric old gentleman: he read about us in
the newspaper, in the special supplement featuring Fernhill last
year. We never found out where he lived.

"Did you do other poses for this client?" DS Curry asked.

"Poses? Of course not." The whole point of the commission was
the sculpture park. Norwegians thought nudity was normal. Anyway, Alver was an old man.

"*Was* an old man?"

"I cut those jigsaws last year," Steve explained.

The DS made a show of examining the photos. "Excuse me, but
these aren't jigsaws."

"Those are the pictures before being cut up."

"Before being jigged. I see." In the detective's mouth the word
jigged sounded suspect and dirty.

I could see the slope that we were about to slide down. How
could there be pristine versions of the pictures? What is the production method? Name of the printing company, if you please!
A call would prove that Steve had the copies made just over a
week ago. As yet, no mention had been made of Frisvold being
dead—assuming that he was. We—Steve mustn't—fall into the trap
of revealing that we thought so.

"You said you never knew his address," said DC Carroll. "How
could you do business with him?"

"Mr Alver always came here."

"Always?"

"Twice. Once to commission, once to collect."

"How did he pay?"

Oh not the unvealed income angle!

"What is this about?" I asked the woman detective. "I'm mystified."

"We're puzzled too," said Curry. "We hope you can cast some light."

"*On what?*"

"On Mr Alver's death. We entered his property yesterday evening following reports of curtains staying closed although his car was there."

"Where *is* his, er, property?"

Curry ignored my question. "Your Mr Alver had been dead for several days. Maybe a week." What response was he expecting? *Poor fellow!* Or: *Was it a heart attack?*

"How?" was what I said.

"He blew his brains out—all over your jigsaws. He had been kneeling among them, stark naked."

"Jesus Christ," I said, "that's awful!" *Beware, beware: Curry hadn't said what he used to blow his brains out.*

I choose my words carefully. "Last year he told us that he wanted to come to terms with his life—by doing those jigsaws of his beloved homeland—before the grim reaper came. That's what he said."

"Bit of an enigma, your Mr Alver. What else did he say?"

"Well, he couldn't travel much because he hated planes, and boats made him seasick—that's why we went to Oslo for him. What do his neighbours say? The people who reported about the curtains."

"You appear to have had more contact with him than his neighbours."

"Oh no, it was only business."

Shit, had anyone down Hog Lane seen the Mercedes at dead of night?

"I'm still puzzled," Curry continued, "about the, um, uncut versions of the jigsaws."

"You can't assemble a jigsaw without a picture to look at—"

The DS studied Steve. He scanned our little showroom, where all jigsaw boxes carried illustrations. "Your boxes, the ones in his house, those had no pictures on them."

"Ah: the pictures would have been too small for him to see clearly."

Do shut up, Steve.

"I see," Curry said. "And there's nothing more you can tell us about Mr Alver?"

Sensibly, Steve just shook his head.

"How about you, Miss Clarke?"

"Not that I can think of right now. Mr Alver wasn't very forthcoming. When he said that about the grim reaper I never realized!"

"But you were prepared to take nude photographs of yourselves for him?"

"That was art." Behind me, I heard Ellison sniff.

Curry regarded the framed jigsaw of the two pigtailed girls in polka-dot dresses beside the Fountain of Trevi. "Unlike your other jigsaws . . ."

"He paid us in cash, by the way," I told DC Carroll. She raised an eyebrow, but after all the police are not the tax authorities. "And oh, he used a credit card for our hotel bookings. American Express, I think."

"You think."

"Suicide, that's so terrible." As if this was only now fully registering on me.

"Especially," the woman detective said, "when you have to see a body in that state."

"We don't need to, do we? I mean, to identify him?"

The DC shook her head. "We have a problem with next of kin. Who to notify. Mr Alver burned a lot of documents."

Not the jigsaw boxes, damn him! At least the house must have been locked from the inside, so suicide was the only explanation.

"Why do you suppose he would burn documents?"

"I've no idea. The Norwegian embassy may be able to help you with identity and family."

"We do realize that."

"If we think of anything else," I promised, "we'll phone you right away."

Blessedly it was time for thanks for our assistance. Police are busy, and not always very bright. Fingers crossed that they didn't pop back and say "Oh, by the way . . ."

Hugh Ellison stayed.

"Nude picturesZ. You assured me that nothing of the sort was involvedD—"

I tried pleading, but we would not join Ellison in a heart-searching prayer. As of four weeks' time Majig Mementoes was evicted, banished from Eden.

Bad news number two came a fortnight later, when my period failed to arrive.

So here is another springtime, and we are still in Oak Cottage. We were forced to borrow money both from my parents and from Steve's. The arrival of a grandson prompts generosity.

James Douglas Clarke (Jamie) is named diplomatically after my own Dad and after Steve's Dad. My Mum and Dad would rather that we had married, even in a registry office. In my view money was better devoted to keeping us afloat than spent on any ceremony.

Babies often stay blond and blue-eyed for quite a while. Steve hasn't dropped any hints, but surely he must recognize the resemblance to Carl Olsson, minus thirty-odd years and booze-abuse. That's why he encourages that girl Caroline to help out at Majig Mementoes, particularly on days when I do not feel like going there with Jamie in his carry-cot—now that Majig Mementoes is part of the Canal Craft Centre in Blanchester, a converted warehouse, lousy location. I am not blind.

Skinny Caroline has brown dreadlocks, a dozen silver rings in her ears, one in her navel, a stud in her nose like a gleaming crystal of snot. She's one of the travelling people—not that she travels far from a tatty old narrowboat moored near the Craft Centre, shared with several kindred New Age souls, plus a baby and a mongrel. Most travellers rarely range further than the Social Security office and the pubs in town.

If I had my Carl, Steve will have his Caroline, it seems. On days when I stay home, I imagine Steve hanging up the "Back in an Hour" sign at Majig Mementoes and consorting with Caroline on the narrowboat, assuming that the others—and the baby in a sling, and the mongrel on its length of string—are roaming the streets, trying to score some splif to smoke. Caroline lowers the tone of Majig Mementoes, but she helps out usefully, for what is not much more than pocket money.

Steve must be *blind*—or banal—to have missed the main fact about my son, such a quiet and amenable baby. No sleepless nights for us, not a single one. Finance aside, there's no excuse for post-natal depression.

Here I am at home, on another afternoon of the blue-skied drought which has migrated here from Scandinavia. I know perfectly well that Steve is on the narrowboat with Caroline, sharing a splif before they peel their clothes off. Our Health Visitor, well-intentioned Mrs Wilson, has driven off in her blue Nissan Micra after weighing Jamie, filling in her chart, seeing how well this radiant Young Mum is coping. All is fine. Jamie is certainly not autistic. Flat on his back in the carry-cot he lies focusing on me precociously, while I sit alongside.

"I know you understand me," I croon at him. "I know you're Mr Frisvold. Nice Mrs Wilson won't be calling here for another month. We're on our own together, you and me. Steve doesn't really count —he isn't your Daddy, and he never bathes you. I want you to think very carefully about what I might do if you don't begin talking, Mr Frisvold—if you don't tell me the number of the Swiss account and the password. We can't afford the rent much longer.

"Tell me about Degrelle and gold and diamonds. Tell me about your gold—it's what fairy tales are all about.

"Are you to me listening, baby? Of course you are. Don't try to pretend you're only a baby. Or I might tickle you. I might tickle your foot with a lighted candle. I don't want to do that sort of thing. You have a whole life ahead of you, Mr Frisvold, I promise. After you tell me, there isn't going to be any cot-death—nothing of the sort, I swear. But you have to cooperate. Collaborate, eh, Mr Frisvold? I'm going to light a candle, just to show you. You never cried since you were born. Maybe you should have done."

I do hope he won't compel me to be a bit cruel. I don't know if I can bring myself to hurt a baby, even if its skin repairs quickly. I have bought such miniature socks from Mothercare. Today I shall merely show him the candle, maybe hold it close to the sole of his teeny-weeny foot for a little while—until he squeaks, "Stop!"

Identities may be false, history may be a lie, and my child is also a deceit. Yet I am filled with joy, awaiting baby's first word—for then life will expand like beautiful petals bursting open from a tight bud and become rich, abundant, luscious.

PRESENT

Chapter 8

WHO
AM
I?

Well me, I'm Anna Sharman, analyst for the M Department of the Combined Intelligence Service. No relation to Britain's first astronaut, Helen Sharman, if anyone remembers her name nowadays. The "M" stands for Mockymen. Here I sit in my office on the 30th floor of Centre Point in London while a gale howls outside and rain blurs the window. This great vertical waffle of a building at the junction of New Oxford Street and Charing Cross Road used to be the headquarters of the Confederation of British Industries. Now it's the Ministry of Alien Liaison.

More to the point, that cry of identity-crisis—*Who am I?*—fills the final page of Jamie Taylor's scrapbook, notebook, diary—call it what you will.

Adolescents such as Jamie often pose such questions, of seemingly supreme importance. Even though I'm in my mid-thirties I might well ask the same question of myself. But that's another matter.

The black-bound book, which I have before me, is bizarre. It's a lavishly illustrated history of the Waffen-SS, Adolf Hitler's ruthless racist warrior regiments, published in 1997, the same year Jamie was born.

Jamie tore out every other page. On to each side of the remaining pages he stuck white paper, restoring the ravaged book to its original bulk.

Upon some pages he wrote brooding thoughts. "Death will be just like dreams. You simply won't realize that you're dead. But what if you wake up?" That sort of thing. Glued to facing pages are jigsaws of news clippings about Mockymen and Bliss and dummies.

Other pages carry nonsense poems, smorbrods of random words of English, German, French, even for some reason Norwegian. If you recite the words aloud they have a weird resonance. Facing these are collages of magazine clippings about Mockymusic groups. Maybe Jamie was penning pan-European lyrics for some future Mockygroup which he might start up—even though he showed little interest in group activities in school, and had no close chums. Typical loner, bottled up, confiding in his peculiar book. Here and there photos of the Waffen-SS show through faintly, and ghosts of text about élites of Nordic warriors, Runic magic, invasion, racial purity, extermination. Jamie's hypothetical Mockygroup doubtless would have been a xenophobic, anti-alien one. The book fits the profile of a potential serial killer more than of a future Blisshead.

According to Ruth and Martin Taylor, Jamie's adoptive parents, around the age of ten their boy began asking, "Who am I?" The fact that he was blond (Ruth Taylor being a brunette and her husband's hair chestnut) had begun to nag at him.

With qualms, though fairly confident in their caring upbringing of a problematic child, the Taylors finally explained to their son that he was adopted. If he really wished to know who his birth-mother was he would be able to find out when he was eighteen, but they themselves were not allowed to know.

Nevertheless, Jamie *was* his original name. The Taylors had begun to foster him when he was five months old and felt that a change of identity might confuse him.

They also told him that he had been mistreated as a baby—that's why he was taken into care, though they knew no further details. Sometimes Jamie's feet hurt, making him limp. According to the podiatry department of the local hospital, the flexor tendon of his left foot was shorter than it ought to have been, as if permanently cramped.

That cry of "Who am I?"—written before he ran off to London to become a Blisshead—has a special importance for us when Jamie Taylor uniquely is the only dummy ever to recover his identity spontaneously, anywhere in the world, to the best of our knowledge. And we do try to make our knowledge the best, believe me.

So I turn over the pages of Jamie's big black book, hunting for any clues I may have missed.

Meanwhile my comp is tracking our mysterious young man, recording and scanning for key words in the noise-traffic transmitted from the transponder chip in his shoulder, about which he knows nothing. A trio of smart microcopters not much bigger than bumblebees navigate the gusts and squalls of the city in Jamie's general vicinity, picking up and rebroadcasting the signal, as if he is a criminal on parole.

We would love to chip all the dummies under Hyde Park and track the movements of all the alien Mockymen automatically instead of resorting to teams of Watchers, but the aliens specifically banned the bugging of the dummy bodies they use to get around in, and they have the know-how to detect infringements. We would not want the Mockymen to withdraw the blessing of their presence from Britain. BritGov readily agreed to the death penalty as punishment for serious assault on a dummy. Well, our seemingly permanent centrist government, in power for the past eighteen years, was becoming increasingly strict even before the civil unrest of the hardship decade!

True, we're still a democracy in name, but since the marginalization long ago of the Tories (whom I might otherwise have supported, as Daddy does) and the co-option of the Liberals, what we have is unchallengable mono-government under everlasting Mr Bee. Two years ago there was an endorsement referendum, ratifying the status quo by a fairly big margin. Humpties cried foul, but who could argue with results from the new securely encrypted electronic polling stations?

To try to chip dummies covertly is *not* a bright idea. And of course the watchers (that young couple window-shopping, that chap walking his dog) principally serve as protectors for itinerant Mockymen, even though we have interned all known agitators.

I remember H-S growling, "Bloody aliens could have been a *real focus* for intelligence work instead of BritGov tying our hands and suppressing every breath of dissent."

That's Jock Henderson-Smith, my chief along the corridor. Not quite a Highland chief, but almost. He's a big man with big hairy hands. Another couple of years and H-S will reach retirement age.

He and I generally address one another rather formally. I'm Miss Sharman to him. He's H-S, or Sir. This conceals the fact of us being fellow conspirators. Oh not conspirators in the sense of sympathizing with the Human Patriots—the Humpties' brand of anti-alien agitation was futile, and could only lead to activists being shut up in the big camp in Northumbria's Kielder Forest. Humpty Dumpty had a big fall.

But in the sense that certain of us within the security service have a chance of sussing out the aliens' real game, if things are not quite as they seem.

A bit of history (me being a historian, after all). Our two main branches of national security, MI5 and MI6, hotbeds of paranoia and rivalry and blunder, really lost their way when the Soviet Union collapsed a quarter of a century ago. Six, failing to spy the significance of the new nationalisms and then trying to latch on to international terrorism and crime. Five, behaving like an incompetent secret police. Leaks, scandals, whistle-blowers. More and more administrators instead of operatives; extravagance on the one hand, budget cuts on the other. The Government Communications Headquarters at Cheltenham basically becoming a wagging tail of the American bloodhound which owned the ears up in space.

Upshot: a supposedly leaner combined service, based at Vauxhall Cross—just in time for the awful decade, of apparently imminent global collapse. Economic, political, environmental; slump, regional wars, super-bug plagues, the whole rotten works. Human civilization about to go down the drain. And consequent domestic unrest. The suddenness of it all! Downfall of the house of cards.

I joined the combined security service either out of idealism or despair. Finger in the dike. Damage limitation by buttressing the tough-choice emergency measures of BritGov. Secret Service required to shore up society on the verge of collapse. Boat about to sink. Control and discipline needed. Stamp out any subversion.

Yes, *idealism!* I wanted history to *continue.* I didn't want anarchy and chaos, a new Dark Age lasting indefinitely (because resources would be gone, or unreachable ever again) or a new medievalism after a few hundred years of mess and death, a future of chickenshit and toil and superstitious tales of a previous golden age as tangled as the ruins of former cities would be.

But then, of course, the Mockymen arrived in 2010 with their bail-out package.

The thirtieth floor of Centre Point is the intelligence service's presence here at MAL, the alien liaison ministry. Monitoring of alien activity goes on here and at the transit station under Hyde Park and from Vauxhall Cross, but never real *snooping*. Never treating the aliens like Eastern Bloc "cultural attachés" from the grand old days of H-S's youth. BritGov expressly forbids this approach. Anybody who tries to spook our alien benefactors is for the high jump.

Directly and indirectly, ten thousand people may be involved in monitoring and assessing Mockymen matters, in scientific "analysis" of alien tech, in keeping Humpty-watch, and an ear to the ground abroad since we're in economic competition with other alien-blessed lands—excluding those Islamic countries which refused to deal with Mockymen.

Yet there is *no* department of covert activity. Admittedly, until now there has been nothing to hook on to—and maybe there *still* is nothing—so that H-S and I and others in his network have essentially been playing at conspiracy.

Espionage has always been a Great Game. In addition to idealism or despair maybe I should add to my motives a tendency to treat life as a game. A game I intended to win, maybe losing bits of my soul in the process.

So we may chip no dummies. As for chipping Jamie—why, he ceased being a dummy when he became himself again, didn't he? So the rule did not apply.

Might the diagnosis of Jamie's condition have been mistaken?

When the ambulance with police escort brought him into the complex under Hyde Park, could Jamie have been in a common-or-garden coma?

All the signs were that he was one of the small percentage of Bliss users whose year of pleasure ends not with routine numbness for the rest of their lives but with the deep nirvana state, flat-brain oblivion. A vacancy which an alien mind can fill.

For three days Jamie lay abed, attached to an intravenous feeding drip and catheter, pipettes leaking lachrymal lubricant into his open, unseeing eyes. Dummies are always stored naked, the better to spot any blemishing.

That storage hall at Hyde Park resembles some huge hospital ward during a plague of encephalitis lethargica which causes no visible physical harm but renders its victims zombies. Calm and cool, there, as a morgue. The rota of bored nurses at their desks wear sweaters under their whites, and leg-warmers, thermal underwear, and gloves. When not checking glucose and urine bags they read pop-fic or whatever. Surveillance is by a couple of panning CCTV cameras. No ranks of cameras are assigned to each individual bed. Where would be the point of that? Dummies never move except occasionally to blink their blankly staring eyes. Not all dummies are kept at Hyde Park, of course, only the best and most serviceable ones. Overspill is at well-guarded facilities in Pembrokeshire and Dumfries.

And on his third day at Hyde Park Jamie arose, tethered by catheter and IV tube and wires. A nurse pushed her doctor-beeper and hurried to stop him from harming himself. On a section of surveillance tape I can study Jamie standing by the bed looking confused, three nurses assisting.

Jamie was so flummoxed to find himself in such surroundings, obviously being stored as a host-body, meat for a Mockyman. If I had been in his shoes (or lack of them) I would have been terrified that a nurse might slide a needle into my arm to restore me to oblivion.

The doctor who came knew that anything out of the ordinary must be notified ASAP to an intelligence duty officer; and Max Adams acted promptly. Isolate Jamie in an examination room. Notify H-S, as per standing orders. Remind the witnesses of the Official Secrets Act.

A pair of Mockymen "advisers" are always on duty somewhere in the transit station—two by day, two by night, keeping an eye on things. Consultants, supervisors. They did not discover, and Jamie was whisked away to a private clinic. Already H-S was controlling who knew what.

After reassuring Jamie that he would *not* be restored to his former state and status (how could he be?), we kept him for a week for observation and tests.

Remarkably, Jamie had not lost his sense of taste and smell, as other Blissheads always did after their year of lotus-eating. This was *new*. Could it be that Jamie never was on Bliss at all, in spite of his avowal of this and the statement of the paramedics who brought him in? Those ambulance men were relying on Jamie's "friends" who phoned Oh-Oh-Oh, the flat-line, to report him comatose and collect the dummy-finders' fee; and of course Jamie's own zombie condition fitted the profile of dummy.

In line with use of Bliss, his resistance to injury was considerably enhanced. The benefit of seamless healing, which continues way beyond the twelve months of euphoria, was his. Cells behaving almost like a foetus's once again. Your post-Bliss body might be lacking in sensitivity to the pleasures of life—to the scent of a rose or the savour of a sausage—but it's resilient and repairs itself speedily. How useful for the Mockymen to inhabit reliable, sprightly post-Bliss dummies—and an added inducement to wannabe Blissheads, if such people think so far ahead. If they ignore the fact that cancers are an occasional side effect; over-enthusiasm by cells.

To test Jamie's powers of cell repair we asked his consent to make a few test cuts under general anaesthetic. His attitude to a few cuts seemed highly ambivalent! Really he had no choice but to agree. While he was anaesthetized we took the opportunity to have the tiny chip implanted in his shoulder.

We could hardly keep Jamie caged up. Well, we *could,* but this would have been bad for his morale and state of mind. Whatever made Jamie different must come from his life in the world-at-large, from his background, whatever. So: let him carry on with his life— whatever life he chose to carry on with—and keep tabs, while I delved into his roots. By now H-S had hived the matter off for super- vision by yours truly.

During the week of observation Jamie had answered all our questions with apparent truthfulness. When we released him would he go back to those adoptive parents in Stratford-upon-Avon? Or to the same casual acquaintances who had sold him to BritGov to be a dummy? He seemed genuinely unsure.

So we set Jamie loose, kitted out in fresh togs and with a chip not on but in his shoulder. The clothes he wore on admission to Hyde Park had been binned, too scruffy to reuse as part of the wardrobe for Mockymen. To tide him over: a hundred Euros in the pocket of a decent though not ostentatious black leather jacket.

Lo, off Jamie goes for sanctuary to the home of two of our longest-serving couriers, Zandra Wilde and Barnabas Mason—this certainly merited attention.

Evidently Jamie was not interested in telling the Taylors his whereabouts; or at least not right away. I was interested in them, though. So off I must go to Stratford-upon-Avon.

It's a Saturday when I make the trip, the weather mild and bois- terous, though not too squally. After phoning the Taylors, putting them rather on tenterhooks, I spend the morning in my office in a fairly deserted building listening in on highlights of Jamie. Lunch of a corned beef wholemeal sandwich in the office; then I'm off to the helipad.

I would not by preference go to Stratford by car, even a hover-car. Food factories, fusion power plants, desalinated water: fine and dandy. Mr Mockyman, next year please can we have a cheap inde-structible coating material, weatherproof, traffic-proof? No, I wish to arrive in Shakespeare's birthplace fast and fresh.

I have whistled up a couple of escorts from the security pool. Peters, whom I have seen before. And Rogers, a new face. I can look after myself well enough, but H-S wants no risk-taking now that we have gone operational, so to speak.

No town looks its best in late November, but Stratford weathered the grim years fairly well. Now that the arsoned Shakespeare Memorial Theatre has been rebuilt in red brick much as before, I gather that foreign tourists are reappearing in force. Visibly, the pop-ulation of swans and of pesky Canada geese has recovered now that the Avon has regained a fuller, cleaner flow thanks to the piping inland of desalinated, oxygenated water.

Our pilot sets us down—*whop-whop-whop*—on the grass flatland of the recreation grounds across the river from the new theatre. The Moscow State Circus has pitched a big top here, I'm delighted to see. The world resumes its amusements. Behind trucks and caravans a juggler practises in a stiff and mischievous breeze. Along the towpath, saplings raise willowy exclamation marks between the big full stops of sawn-off bases of dead trunks now dolled up as rustic seats.

A black Volvo waits for me. Peters stays with the pilot to mind the turbochopper. Rogers comes with me, though he will remain in the car. We're heading just a little way out of town along the Blan-chester Road.

To the adoption agency, Stratford must have seemed an ideal place to raise a child—offsetting the fact that the Taylors lacked experience of rearing any other kids. Low sperm count misfortune; all the gender-bending hormone-disruptors in the environment. Not that Stratford lacked its tally of crime and delinquency, but that was mostly on the other side of town. When the adoption took place, Martin Taylor, at thirty-six, was a prospering self-employed electrician, electricians being king pins of the building trade. Ruth was a primary school teacher, who would give up her job for a few years to care for the child whom Martin could not sire himself.

Soon enough, our Volvo pulls up outside a semi-detached mock-Tudor house, gravelled garden hedged by trim firethorn—a sort of natural barbed wire dense with red berries. Parked on the gravel:

a compact blue VW, a snail-shell iridescent and glassy. Open garage doors reveal AVON ELECTRICALS on the back of a white van.

Martin admits me. Fifty-three years old now, he's of medium height, stout in a robust way (not at all visibly feminized, but that is in the gonads), and he sports a fringe of grizzling chestnut beard. He barely glances at the identification card I offer: Anna Sharman, Bliss Research Trust. He and his wife have been waiting anxiously.

Ruth is more of a mouse. Her hair may have greyed rapidly after her boy ran off. They usher me through into the lounge with predictable questions:

"Is Jamie all right—?" Waving the wand at the wallscreen, imploding rugby players to a fast-fading point of light.

"He hasn't become a . . . Oh don't say that!"

A dummy. Quite. A smell of kippers lingers in the lounge. The Taylors must have eaten in here, plates balanced on their laps, to keep an eye on the street. I had told Martin on the phone that the Trust assisted Jamie very recently and that a certain matter needs discussion in confidence.

"You can set your mind at rest on that score, Mrs Taylor. Your son's in good shape."

"Where is he—?"

"Unfortunately he went off without telling us."

"You thought that *we* might know—?"

"No, Mr Taylor, I gathered that he had not kept in touch with you."

Bitterly: "A Blisshead wouldn't bother—so he did get hooked on that filth, chucking his life away."

"Unless," Ruth says forlornly, "he was helping in this Bliss Research of yours? You did say Research. Was Jamie some sort of volunteer? He left a scrapbook in his room with cuttings about Bliss and dummies—"

"Did he? I'd be very interested to see that."

I sidestep the matter of how he actually came to us (though he did depart with some cash in hand, rest assured).

No thank you, I will have nothing to drink. Discreetly I vent a petit burp, a bit sulphurous. Preservatives in the corned beef, probably. I love the stuff. Maybe I'm aftertasting bisphenol from the lining of the tin can, but I have no male embryos inside me to harm, and as for the breast cancer risk, some year soon the Mockymen may give us nanotech for gobbling tumours and repairing cells. Goodies come bit by bit, and getting the environment and economy back in kilter takes priority.

"Jamie told us he can still smell and taste things," I inform the Taylors. "We're wondering if there might be some new variety of Bliss, and what this implies. I realize that governments oversee the manufacture and distribution . . ."

And indeed Jamie obtained his dose of Bliss (three capsules, to be taken on three successive days) from an approved supplier, and no other such case has cropped up. Unique, he is. An utter oddity, a quirk.

"You realize how sensitive a matter this might be?"

"Bloody government," curses Martin, "selling us out, selling our kids. Condoning that damned brain-twisting drug. Death penalty for dummy bashers."

"To be perfectly frank, the Bliss Research Trust treads a narrow line between legality and, well, matters that the general public remains a bit in the dark about."

Martin nods.

"It might cause difficulties if you're indiscreet. We depend so much upon the Mockymen for our global recovery, don't we?"

"You mean that Big MAL might come down on you."

"And on Jamie too. And on you."

"In French," remarks Martin, "*mal* means evil."

"I suppose the acronym seemed chummy, like a big brother."

"Big MAL, Big Brother."

"Whereas the Paris counterpart is quite neutral—MRE, Ministère des Relations Extraterrestres. In my opinion putting MAL in Centre Point in London was hamfisted—an all-too-visible hub around which all revolves nowadays. They ought to have stuck the ministry in Pall Mall. Our alien pals, hmm?"

Martin eyes me carefully. "I'm not one of those Humpties."

Of course not. But the Bliss Research Trust *might* be a slightly subversive organisation. It would be nice not to need to misdirect these good and distressed people but obviously I have to.

"On the subject of sensitivity, Mr Taylor, was Jamie what you might call hypersensitive? Did he experience tastes and smells more intensely than other people? Did he suffer from hay fever, asthma, allergies?"

A frown on Ruth's face. "His left foot used to hurt him from time to time."

"It doesn't seem to now. Though you only said from time to time."

"Maybe," Martin snarls, "he spent his time as a Blisshead treading hot coals like a fakir! A fake fakir."

Ruth frowns. "Jamie was sensitive about his feet, Miss Sharman, but he didn't go into ecstasies over food or flowers."

"Not until he took Bliss!"

"Martin, she's trying to help."

"How did you get into this, Miss Sharman? Or is it Missus?" Martin's hand flexes. He would like a longer gander at my ID, but the etiquette of asking eludes him.

He sees a well-groomed woman, oval face, short black shingled hair, five-five in height, slim build, high eyebrows over almond eyes, pert little chin. Today I'm wearing a dark blue suit, white ruffled blouse, maroon silk scarf. No rings on my fingers, short nails varnished pearly. He could not imagine me in camouflage clobber on a firing range, or cradling a Heckler & Koch in a practice village. After graduating (unlike fifty per cent of the intake) from the Joint Services School of Intelligence at Ashford, I took supplementary weapons training, and it chuffed Daddy no end that my "postgraduate" course was with his former regiment. Daddy retired as a Major in need of a hip replacement, after hostage rescue during the chaos in North Africa in '07, the mass migration famine troubles.

At the JSSI down in Kent I was already a graduate in the everyday sense: Upper Second in History, Balliol, 2001, just before the grim time started. To Daddy's chagrin my brother Tony had no such spunk as me. Tony's dream (in the midst of impending global collapse) was to be a gourmet chef. Now he's nutrition supervisor at the big camp in Kielder Forest where the Humpties are dumptied out of harm's way; which pleases Daddy belatedly—the boy, doing his bit for the nation.

"We need to know more than we do about Bliss, Mr Taylor—because it's *alien*. But we need to tread carefully."

Oh indeed.

Chapter 9

At my flat in Bloomsbury the melodies are romantic (in the musicology sense). Brahms, Richard Strauss, Sibelius. Here in my office I have a large collection of Mockymusic on minidiscs, for analysis not for pleasure.

Youthful rebellion—or passionate acquiescence in the state of affairs—manifests itself in a ghastly wailing thumping noise which both mimics and derides (or celebrates) what people imagine alien music might be: the eerie skirling stridulation of giant grasshoppers, legs fiddling away, creaking shrilly, the pounding throb of froggish air-sacs in some swamp, the howl of otherworldly banshees.

I regularly give a lecture on Mockymusic to intelligence trainees. The Mockers, who were retro-Goth, gave rise to the Mochas, five brown-skinned Anglo-Caribbean lasses who relaunched themselves as the Dum-Girls—Dum, from dummies—swaying and gaping and crooning nonsense-syllables as if waiting for their bodies to be possessed and used; part of their appeal, I suppose. (Their nonsense was not unlike Jamie's polyglot lyrics.)

Mocassins was an Indian group (as in curries and Hindus) which in turn inspired the Mocassassins whose lyrics were virulently anti-alien, so we had to suppress them. Gigs in the Kielder Forest from now on, my lads! Likewise the Dum-Dums—dum, from bullets this time, put a dum-dum in a dummy, dum-dum-dum.

Into the Dum-Dums's shoes stepped the Dim-Sums, wailing in Cantonese in the style of Peking Opera. This sounded wonderfully alien to kids who weren't part of the considerable Chinese community here in England, but it decoded as similar Mockyphobia from the perspective of the oldest civilization of Earth. The Chinese know all about opium being imposed by outsiders to tame a population, not that China itself hasn't eagerly embraced Mockymen goodies, food factories especially. Consequently the Dim-Sums also must take a trip to Kielder, leaving the charts topped by infatuated Mockygroups such as the Zomb-Eyes, with their holographic contact lenses, stars twinkling in their eyes.

For me, Sibelius always evokes forests, millions of pine trees, freedom — dare I say it, the feeling of fulfilment you can enjoy when you're quite alone, as someone with a secret agenda essentially is. A sense, almost, of special destiny. My most recent lover, as of two years ago — Gerry Walsh — found Sibelius far too melancholy, not romantic at all.

Gerry was, and still is, with the Sleeping Beauty Unit. Special Bodies Unit is the correct designation. Backstairs bods, his biz. Dummies, which a family hangs on to in defiance of the law, loath for their beloved offspring to become a puppet used by an alien.

Looking after a dummy at home isn't easy. You need black-market IV equipment, big nappies in lieu of a catheter. Where's the benefit? Your lad or lass is never going to wake up. As a host body at least your ex-son or daughter can benefit from occasional exercise, an outing in the fresh air. Despite frequent public service announcements, some families persist in hiding their dummy for months — till the problems of coping become too much and they hand the body over to the state. Alternatively they make the grievous decision to let their dummy waste away, suffocate it, bribe a dodgy doctor, whatever.

Crime plays a role in a number of ways. With Bliss freely available, few kids become hooked on Crack or Fraz or Hop nowadays. Pushers can see no profit. Supplying IV kit and drip-bags and privacy for hapless parents is a new if minor string to crime's bow. Dummies can yield bootleg body organs. A gorgeous dummy can be exploited sexually. To me this seems like necophilia (minus the dead-cod coldness and whiff of corruption), but Gerry fleshed out cases for me which I only knew from in-house reports and media leaks. (*Deliberate* leaks: Save your daughter from being abused as a sex-doll! Register a dummy now!) No wonder Gerry craved romance in his spare time.

Of course, let's keep things in perspective. The growing number of dummies is out of proportion to the number needed as hosts for aliens—*not* a statistic that BritGov broadcasts—but it is still utterly trivial compared with, say, Alzheimer cases. Only snag, dummies will endure very much longer. In years to come we'll have a bit of a dummy mountain. No suggestion, as yet, of euthanasia for surplus dummies—as happens already in China, we believe. This is a problem BritGov is deferring, rather as the matter of future decommissioning was deferred in the heyday of building nuclear power stations. In fact, many dummies are never fitted with skull sockets, so they will never go anywhere.

My relationship with Gerry came to an end because I seemed too cool to him, too preoccupied. Too covert for him to covet. Sorry I can't tell you what I'm doing tomorrow; that's classified. By then H-S had entered the picture, becoming a sort of second father to me—a father whom one addressed as "Sir," like a Victorian daughter. From H-S at last I received my secret agenda, which he had divined I needed, even though it might yield no fruit. Distrust these alien Greeks bearing gifts! What's hiding inside their wooden horse? If only we can find a chink to peep through!

I was so relieved to find that there *is* a wheel within a wheel, and that some people in the intelligence service, if only on principle, suspect aliens of duping us. Oh I know that in the past Cold Warriors—of H-S's stripe—could not credit, for example, that the Soviet Union was coming to a speedy end. How wrong they were —but the alternative to scepticism, they would have said, is crass naïveté.

When Ruth brings Jamie's black book downstairs, on a quick scan I know that it contains vital clues, even if Jamie had no idea what those clues meant.

"Can we borrow this, Mrs Taylor?"

Martin butts in. "What does it have to do with Bliss research?"

"Oh you don't want this left in your home. Why was your son fascinated by Nazis and genocide? Killing off undesirable foreigners, if you take my meaning. Alien persons with alien attitudes."

Ruth is alarmed. "You mean his book could get us into trouble?"

"You, or Jamie. Yes, it might. If Big MAL cottons on to your son. If Jamie gets into difficulties."

"We've become a tyranny because of the bloody Mockymen," Martin fumes. "The whole world's a banana republic."

I incline my head. "Or in Britain's case, a can of worms."

He leans forward suddenly. "Do you think the Mockymen are really *worms?* Worms with huge mental powers! They tell us it's an alien mind as gets transferred into a dummy's head. What if it's really a worm? A physical worm putting feelers into the dummy's brain to move the arms and legs and march it around."

"I don't think that's so, Mr Taylor." Yet I make a mental note. Are some Humpties who have avoided internment starting a whispering campaign? Will a new Mockygroup wail about worms, infestation, parasites—pouring scorn on the whole system of transit stations such as Hyde Park, couriers such as Zandra and Barnabas, matter transmission to the two star-worlds?

"I suppose your son started writing and sticking things in this book soon after the pod-ship arrived?"

Ruth's reply surprises me. "No, he was twelve when he brought the book home. He swapped it at school for the wristwatch we'd given him for his birthday just the week before."

"Felt a bit cut up about that, I can tell you!" Even now, Martin looks pissed off. "Par for the course, I'd say, in retrospect."

"How do you mean?"

"Tossing his life away on Bliss a few years later."

"He's still alive and kicking, Mr Taylor."

Walking around, talking, doing his own thing instead of some Mockyman's thing: that is the mystery.

"Then for the little bugger to tear the book up! Ripped half of the pages out of it, he did, and threw them away. Bloody hell. Why didn't he simply take a hammer to his birthday watch?"

"Was he much of a problem, your son?" This question, directed to the former schoolteacher.

She replies judiciously. "In a lot of ways he was precocious—speaking and walking and understanding things. School work all seemed a breeze. But he was distant as well. Secluded, broody. Though well-behaved."

"Till he ran off," from Martin.

Ruth does not relish bitter remarks about Jamie. "Miss Sharman, it was a bit before his *thirteenth* birthday that the aliens came."

Turning to the back of the black book I read out, "*Who am I? That's what we wonder about them,* right? How would you say their arrival affected Jamie?"

"Affected everyone, didn't it?" growls Martin. "Knocked the world for six. Puppet people, puppet governments."

Ruth darts a warning glance at her husband. "Be fair, love. Without what happened there mightn't be electricity in this house by

now, or running water, or food in the larder—and we *are* in charge
of our own destinies."

Martin's expression remains unconvinced. Me, I am not here
to winkle out a closet Humpty who thinks of himself as part of a
resistance movement, fruitless and toothless and amateur. Jamie is
much more important than any petty subversive capers—perhaps.

What exactly are these beings from the stars who use human bodies
as hosts and couriers? The question lacks an answer and maybe it
always will.

When the pod-ship arrived in Earth orbit five years ago, the crew
which awoke from hibernation consisted of half a dozen Mocky-
Lemurs—furry bipeds with big eyes. Those were not the original
bodies of the controllers, masters of this neck of the universe. The
six Lemurs were all dummies, by-products of Bliss, each hosting the
mind of a Mockyman as its operator.

We call the operators Mocky*men* on the assumption that the
cryptic creatures are approximately humanoid. How else can they
operate humanoid and human dummies smoothly?

True, you can usually distinguish a human dummy from an
ordinary person by some quirks of speech and mannerisms, even if
hair style or hat hide the skull socket. During the early days several
lynchings occurred—although in many countries Mockymen
became quite the rage in a positive sense. Japan especially. In their
desire to ape a dummy controlled by an alien mind some Japanese
enthusiasts go so far as to have a phony socket implanted in their
craniums. Much Mockymusic pays similar homage, just so long as
we keep the extreme Humpty element purged.

The operators *might* be highly evolved spiders or crabs. They
may even be worms, I suppose, huge worms with big intellects.

Anyway, half a dozen dummy Lemurs arrived equipped with the
blueprints for instantaneous transit from Earth to two star-worlds.
Plus the promise of lots of other high tech know-how as inducement
to trade—an offer to be grabbed, a veritable lifeline just as the world
seemed set to go down the drain, up the spout, into the maelstrom.
And very quickly too. There's a branch of math, aptly named
Catastrophe Theory, which models such situations. The sudden flip
from life-more-or-less-as-usual to systems collapse for civilization.

Drain rhymes with pain. That slow boat (actually, damn fast
boat!) set out from the nearest of the worlds used by Mockymen
soon after Earth's radio output first reached it. For decades the pod-
ship had been travelling towards us. But as soon as transit-tech is in

place, *bingo*. One moment, Hyde Park (or the Tuileries, Paris, or New York's Central Park). Next moment, the transit stations on the worlds we call Passion and Melody.

One tiny snag. A living body in transit suffers excruciating pain. An agonized moment measureless to man, outside of time, so that it can seem to last forever. Or no time at all. Which is where couriers such as Zandra and Barnabas come in . . .

Never trust the supposedly known facts. My history tutor at Oxford, Richard Cornwallis, taught me that. Recount what is familiar time and again, and cracks appear in the fabric. Connections fray, new explanations emerge. Tell the story until it disintegrates and turns inside-out: that is my concept of intelligence analysis. My lack of trust alienated Gerry eventually, despite what we shared.

Jamie is someone who distrusted *his* identity. Is that merely because he was adopted and because his birth-parent mistreated him, causing deep insecurity?

What am I missing?

Every few weeks I visit the transit station buried under Hyde Park so as to keep my finger on the pulse, as it were.

MAL is in plain view for all to see, manifest evidence of openness; Centre Point is an ideal location. But as regards the vital transit station, British protesters were so steamed up about Bliss and dummies that an above-ground site might be a target for sabotage. A guarded stockade would be such an eyesore and focus for ill-feeling. Because the Mockymen insisted that all stations, for convenience, should be in the hearts of capital cities BritGov needed a hardened site, preferably invisible.

The greening of Park Lane was one of the last big items of civic improvement before the slump really set in. Bury all the traffic and roll the carpet of Hyde Park almost to the doors of the Dorchester Hotel and the Hilton. Restore six acres, and people-access from Mayfair. Let there be new fountains and shrubs and trees (which were to fare badly during the long Summer droughts).

From Marble Arch on its noble piazza, where Blissheads hang out nowadays oblivious to rain or shine, down I plunge in a hover-taxi into a multi-lane tunnel.

Half way along the tunnel, my taxi filters west into the former underground car park and coach park which was converted into the transit station.

Into the blast containment area we glide. No need to check each vehicle arriving, only those persons whose business leads them deeper within. Medical staff and technicians. Couriers and Mocky-men. Myself. I would be angry not to have my retina scanned—quickly and smoothly—even if my face is fairly familiar. The Moll from MAL.

Here is the medical zone where we process and store new dummies; where ex-people and new couriers receive their skull sockets.

Come this way, to an arrival lounge. An orderly is wheeling from storage a nude young dummy-woman on a gurney. Wardrobes occupy the length of one wall, stocking a wide range of male and female attire. A lady costumier presides. She's also in charge of cabinets of personal effects, cash, credit cards, combs, pocket computers, whatever the well-dressed Mockyman or Mockywoman might need during its sojourn on Earth.

Unsteadily, a courier walks in. He's a Chinese Brit, and he looks a bit yellow round the gills from his recent ordeal. He slumps on to a couch beside the gurney so that his head is close to the dummy's head. We try to keep about fifty people in the courier pool, though there is quite a high turnover.

The transfer-doctor pulls down the connector on its mobile boom. Into the courier's skull socket goes a white plug, linked to a black plug by a fat worm of flexible coaxial cable. The black plug connects with the young dummy-woman's head. Mockymen technology, all of this; blueprints and circuit diagrams provided for us, the resulting equipment rigorously checked by our alien advisers with tiny testing devices. Although we built to order, we do not understand the principles.

Us peasants can at least be trusted to distinguish between black and white. Sometimes one of the Mockymen advisers is present, though not on this occasion. It's all routine.

For about ten seconds the courier shivers. Looks like one of those spasms I have in bed when I'm about to fall asleep, a tiny fit, quite pleasurable. The brain, disconnecting itself from operating the limbs—otherwise, while dreaming, we would try to run and jump and seize hold of things. The dummy twitches too.

Then the naked young woman shifts her head, raises a hand. The doctor disconnects the pair. Transfer complete. The Mockywoman sits up and looks around. She swings her bare feet down on to the floor.

Now it's the costumier's turn to demonstrate the use of knickers and tights and bra, like some air hostess miming safety instructions.

But this Mockywoman has been here before. It dresses itself efficiently. Then it declares, "I must see Man-chester."

Some arrivals proceed to Centre Point in pursuance of ongoing trade deals. Others need to check on the functioning of food factories, or whatever. Many behave as tourists, heading off to wherever the fancy takes them. In London the War Museum is quite a hit, we've noticed. Bit of a security nightmare, but Mockymen insist on freedom of movement. Declared reason: to admire places. Maybe it's even the real reason.

You might expect language and sense of self to be fairly inextricable, but an effect of Bliss in the case of dummies is that they retain command of their native languages (Mockymen for the use of), even though their original personalities have departed. The alien user can latch on more or less fluently. We manufacture Bliss as per instructions, though once inside a body (human or monkey or guinea pig) its derivatives elude analysis, self-destructing if sampled.

Come this way, come this way: to a departure lounge.

Lionel Evans, a stocky, dark-haired Welshman, is about to leave, monitored by one of our dispatch officers and by a lanky-haired, gangly puppet-youth. The adviser looks too dippy and wet behind the ears for any responsibility—but just how old is the alien mind within?

A Mockyman is already installed in Evans, inaccessible to the courier's thoughts—just as the Mockyman will be oblivious to the courier's pain.

Wearing trainers and jeans and zipper jacket, and with a black plastic case gripped tightly between his knees, our well-paid Welsh volunteer sits hunched upon the dispatch disc. He's sweating a bit. Deep narrow vents in the disc correspond to daggers of Mockymetal jutting downward from the lid above.

Power hums. Abruptly the lid slams downward upon the disc. And Evans has vanished (though I imagine I hear a receding scream as those blades enter the receptors). Slowly the lid rises up again. Lo, the disc is perfectly clean. No squashed flesh, sprayed blood, or shattered bone soils it. Her presto, Evans is now light years away.

Us peasants do not understand this miracle, even though we carry it out routinely. As the jaws of the Iron Maiden slam shut, a living body disappears here and appears on another world. How, how?

Evans, I know, is fascinated by the history of torture. According to him there never was an authentic Iron Maiden of Nuremberg. In the 19th century some macabre German who owned a castle commissioned the notorious device as décor for his Schloss. Probably, according to Evans, the German got the idea from a punishment known as the Mantle. Drunks and promiscuous women were popped into a sort of slim barrel hinged in front, with a metal helmet on top, to be led hobbling around town or to stand stock-still in it. Gott in Himmel, vot if we add *spikes* and *blades* inside the device? A literal Iron Maiden would kill its victim quite quickly, which is hardly the point of torture. The machine is a historical fantasy, a lie.

"The really iffy thing about torture," Evans once told me, "is the way it produces lies instead of truth. Unless your victim is a fanatic or total idealist sooner or later he'll confess anything to stop the pain —and his tormentors will believe him. Pain blinds us to truth."

Personally I would not have said that was the most iffy thing about torture! Inflicting physical pain is disgusting, which I suppose means that I lack the mind-set of a courier. But in some deep philosophical sense, is what our couriers report about Passion and Melody vitiated by their ordeal en route and on return? Most couriers are preoccupied by pain, in one way or another. In the case of Zandra and Barnabas the obsession is scarification . . .

But come along with me: in another room a courier is about to arrive. About to arrive? Here I indulge in a touch of fantasy, since arrivals are always unpredictable. No bell rings to herald an impending arrival. Nothing can precede the event. A reception officer sits patiently, occupying himself with a book of crossword puzzles. Disc and lid are tight together. Of a sudden the lid flies upwards. There on the disc is a returned courier, tight-lipped and trembling, sometimes venting a shriek.

High-speed imaging and freeze-frame show the "suction into existence."

"It's as if," says Evans, "your body is sucked out of all those holes in the disc. It's as if you're dragged from a hundred light years away through a sieve of knives."

The passenger-mind entirely avoids the pain. Dummy-bodies operated by Mockymen could certainly transit from Earth to wherever—blanks, with the alien mind pulling the puppet strings as the governing consciousness, just as when they stroll around London or Tokyo or Brasilia. But then the Mockymen would experience the excruciation personally. They have no intention of doing so.

Does this fastidiousness signify their level of civilization, when other species must suffer pain on their behalf? A regrettable consequence of transit, alas alas! Only a very small number of volunteers need to be couriers. One in a million. Less than one in a million in the case of China. Us Mockymen cannot suffer this ordeal, lest we perturb our clarity of thought.

*   *   *

Transit to wherever, to wherever. A hundred light years away? Or twenty, or thirty? Or a thousand?

Mere humans do not know the location of the stars orbited by Passion and Melody, although we can reasonably guess that Passion is closer to us because the pod-ship came from there. Passion is a name of convenience, suggested by the big soulful eyes of the Lemurs—although the souls behind those eyes were not those of the Lemurs themselves. Our destinations are hermetically restricted, dedicated solely to the reception and despatch of human couriers and the upload and download of hitchhiking Mockymen. Couriers from Earth transit to the Melody Hilton and the Passion Hilton, reception centres without any windows or access to outside.

We do happen to know (hush hush) that an American courier smuggled a miniature TV set through to Melody on behalf of the National Security Agency. The set picked up no signals whatever, no images of Mocky-life on the Mocky-world. Just snow. Is the whole reception centre shielded? Does the home life of aliens not include TV?

The personnel whom couriers encounter are all Mocky-aliens. On the world we call Passion: dummy-Lemurs. On the world we call Melody: dummy-Ivorymen—the voices of the natives there are musical and their bodies seem like smooth flexible porcelain. Never do our couriers meet a genuine local. No sightseeing tours for the likes of Evans or Zandra or Barnabas. No alien pubs to hang out in with fascinating natives. Not even a window to peep out of.

Adjacent to those alien stations presumably there are similar facilities for despatching Ivoryman-couriers or Lemur-couriers to other worlds in the Mockymen empire, and for storage and processing of alien versions of Blissheads—all within a city of ordinary Ivorymen or Lemurs, forever unglimpsable.

"So why won't they let us set foot on those worlds, eh Miss Sharman?" I can hear H-S quizzing me a couple of years ago.

"They want to avoid embarrassing us—"

"Aye, the cultural quarantine excuse. Keep the full wonder of Mockymen culture from us so we don't feel belittled."

"Plus, to preserve the alien Lemurs and Ivorymen from human influence—"

"So that we don't get a chance to contaminate their civilizations with Shakespeare or Frank Sinatra. Bollocks, I say, Miss Sharman." H-S does have a colourful turn of phrase at times.

"They can't be worrying we'll spread diseases, not with all their bio-know-how."

"Och, isn't it wonderfully altruistic of them to bail us out? Just some weeds and worms from Earth in exchange for wonderfully helpful things, fair exchange, no robbery. Yon pair of star-worlds seem to me more like Eastern Europe of years ago, border posts policed by stooges with no minds of their own, foreign travellers restricted to the transit lounge. What's life like for your average native Ivoryman or Lemur?"

Thank God for H-S. He freshened my sense of purpose, and of course he was giving himself a metaphorical boost of monkey glands into the bargain.

While I was in the Taylors' home, Rogers and the driver were listening to Saturday afternoon sports coverage on the car radio. Nice quiet suburban street, no roaming Blissheads, no villains about, nothing to keep an eye on, not even me approaching. Arsenal nil, Wolves two. Rogers quickly changes wavelength as I open the rear door of the car, and a well-bred Scotswoman's voice is saying in stereo, ". . . call of the majority nationalist party in the Scottish Parliament for full sovereignty . . ."

"Keeping up on current affairs, eh? Top marks for diligence. No, don't switch off. Back to the chopper, driver."

". . . and independent Scottish control over the resources of the Rockall Trough has brought a speedy response at Westminster . . ."

As soon as I'm belted, the Volvo pulls away to return me to the banks of the Avon, bearing my prize, the obliterated history of the SS.

". . . the Prime Minister derided the demand as 'a quarrel about worms' and pointed out that Britain's alien associates established a transit station in London, not in Glasgow or Edinburgh . . ."

"Do you think it's a quarrel about worms, Rogers?" I feel I should pay more attention to him. I may be going to quite a few places in his company. He's a good-looking fellow. Sandy-haired, trim and tough. Nice blue eyes. Peters always seems to me stamped from some banal Action Man mould. Whereas Rogers . . .

Rogers shrugs, but I persist. "Do you think so?"

"If the Scots get total independence, Miss Sharman, the Mockymen may pull out of London."

"Would that be a bad thing?"

"Bad for our economy. A lot of Scots thought they were going to get independence ages ago. But, well, the hard years. Not such a good idea. I was in action against the Scotch Bonnets," he adds.

Ah, his credentials. Midway through the awful decade, as everything seemed to be falling apart, Scots-Nat terrorism—the Scotch

Bonnet is a very fiery chili shaped like a tam-o'-shanter. An unfortunate episode. Scotland's aspirations must go on the back burner, where they still remain during the alien-led renaissance.

The book I cradle on my lap is bound in a black laminate decorated with two big silver lightning flashes, the SS symbol. Nordic runes, I recall. The letter S in Viking writing: *Sig*, meaning victory, as in *Sieg Hiel*. Already we're approaching the roundabout where we'll turn off past the olde worlde Swan's Nest Hotel and boathouse to the parkland fronting the river. I must wait till I'm on my own before poring over the book in detail.

"It's a colonial situation, isn't it, Rogers?"

He's sharp. "Which one do you mean, Miss Sharman? Us and the Scots—or us and the Mockymen?"

Us and the aliens, of course, whose real faces we never see, only the faces of dummies.

CHAPTER 10

Worms, worms. A can of worms.

The majority of all animal species on Earth are not insects, as people used to imagine. No, they are worms—tiny worms which live in the ocean depths buried in mud. Nematodes. Millions of species of nematodes. The World of Worms, that's Planet Earth from a statistical viewpoint—at least as regards Britain's place in the scheme of things.

Oh, and let's not forget about marine viruses and bacteria. A million bacteria in every gram of ocean mud. Ten times that many viruses. Maybe a million viruses in a drop of seawater. Basically, the sea is a virus soup. When we think sea, we human beings think herrings and starfish, because those are more our own size. Regardless of pollution and overfishing, the seas could never be chock-a-block with fish; and that is because of all those viruses.

Not killing the fish off, no. The viruses target bacteria. This pushes bacteria to diversify, resist, evolve new tricks. Even so, almost half of all bacteria die from viruses. The virus-infected cell bursts and spills its substance into the water to feed other bacteria—instead of becoming a titbit for a protozoan which in turn is a snack for a bigger plankton, onward and upward to the herring. Take viruses away, and the sea could support many more herrings.

Basically, most diversity occurs down at the very humble level, with worms as the superstar giants.

From a host of newly discovered nematodes come unfamiliar enzymes and molecules of pharmacological value to the Mockymen. What nature has devised during billions of years of evolution is so much more prodigal and surprising than whatever biochemists —even superior alien ones—might try to build from scratch.

With the exception of Bliss, we have no idea what exotic drugs and elixirs the Mockymen make from such substances, or what use they put them to on their own worlds and on other worlds within their hegemony. Nice word, hegemony. From the Greek: to be in the forefront. Biology is the power-science, the control key.

In return for our worms and whatnot we gain fusion, desalination, food factories (even if we don't quite understand how they work). Next year please can we have everlasting tarmac? Quite a bargain. We were going down the drain. Now we aren't.

Not that marine worms are the whole of it! From Brasilia and Jakarta couriers carry samples of weeds and beetles from what still survives of the rain forests. Most countries can yield a tithe of something alive, with some natural magic ingredient lurking in it, undreamed of by us but of use to aliens—more prized than any works of Plato or Mozart or Leonardo.

What we do *not* gain is speedier access to the solar system or further beyond. As soon as the first human dummies became available, the six Mocky-Lemurs of the contact team transferred their minds into young human hosts. Flexing their new muscles (as it were), the Mockymen insisted that the vacated Lemur bodies be incinerated. We were not to autopsy any alien flesh. A signal sent the empty landing module back into orbit to rejoin the pod-ship. On autopilot the pod headed towards the sun, to burn itself up a few months later. We were not about to inherit a secondhand starship and hibernation technology.

In February, 2010, after negotiations by radio, the landing module of the pod-ship had descended right beside the ever-so-useful United Nations headquarters in New York. Appropriate place: not quite four hundred years earlier the Indians sold Manhattan Island to the Dutch for a measly sixty guilders. Selling one's birthright for a potage of lentils, hmm? The nations of Earth were getting much more than *that*.

Bliss crystals are a nano-mimetic drug, so called. Human understanding of nanobiotechnology is inadequate, but Bliss was part of the price, for priceless aid.

Qualms about allowing a radical new drug to circulate? Why,

Bliss would cleanse a heroin user of his habit, if he switched. Bliss would clean up a major social problem at the trifling cost of a percentage of users becoming dummies, serve them right. Nice to see euphoric faces on the streets instead of lawless addicts mugging you to pay the pusher-man.

Drug trials supervised by expert committees? Animal testing followed by human volunteers? Cut the cackle. Mockymen arrived in the nick of time to avert famine and chaos. Every plus has its price. Moreover, word was that the Brazilians and the French were about to deal with the Mockymen, so as to steal a march. Most of us shaky dominoes soon fell into line, with the exception of certain Islamic countries. Let Bliss abound. Build transit stations. Recruit couriers with a tolerance or a penchant for pain. Forget rocketry, think socketry.

Nothing that the Mockymen promised us has proved false (so far). Just, we don't need to know very much—ever—about who runs the cosmic show.

Here's a possible yardstick for a sapient civilization: drug use. The inclination to meddle with your brain chemistry and get high, enlightened, or merry. Given half a chance, elephants get themselves drunk on fermenting fruit. My own favourite tipple is vintage port, fairly rare these days, although production of luxuries is picking up—not everyone has to eat the messes of potage from the factories, nourishing and tasty though the stuff is. The natives of Passion and Melody obviously have a soft spot for their own treats, consequently for Bliss as well.

What do Mockymen get high on? Power, control, understanding the nature of life? Control of information certainly matters to them.

A year and a couple of months after the landing—a year of bliss for umpteen drug users world wide—enough dummies had emerged, as predicted.

Random lottery as to who those were, according to the Mockymen. Very small percentage. Compare and contrast the death rate among heroin users. Loss of taste and smell after the euphoria? You never know what you lost till you lose it—I think Bob Dylan sang that. Balance this inconvenience against the recuperative powers of a Bliss-body.

On Transit Day in timed sequence worldwide well-paid couriers sat upon discs, to be transmitted in a flash of agony to the two star-worlds. After a couple of days spent recuperating they returned, each with a Mockyman as mind-passenger. The alien hitchhikers transferred into waiting dummies.

Some couriers were loath to repeat the experience of transit.

Enough were willing. They would become wealthy. A new aristocracy.

We're told that consciousness—alert self-awareness—plays a vital role in the transit process. A lump of wood cannot transit on its own. Nor a comatose dummy.

Huge distance is a factor, too. Interstellar distance. By all means leap from the space-time matrix of one star system to another—but thou shalt not hop locally. London to New York or London to Mars would require huge energy and could "disrupt catastrophically." Call this the Perverse Square Law. We do not understand it.

We never did catch the nitpicking cybersabber who timed his New Start Bomb to go off at midnight on December 31, 2000, rather than 1999. On that night of the new millennium-according-to-pedants, of the computer records relating to the adoption and the care order for Jamie only the name of his Health Visitor, Dorothea Wilson, survived the trashing. Hard copy files were lost during an arson incident in '03 before anyone got around to re-keyboarding low-priority data.

The news that Dorothea Wilson, now in her late sixties, is living in sheltered housing in Blanchester is more encouraging than if she was in a nursing home. Even if your wits are intact on admission to a nursing home you can soon go gaga in a place where most other residents have Alzheimer's, and the staff dole out pills to keep everyone placid; never mind if you're paying through the nose.

Daddy told me that if *he* suspects he's ever doomed to a nursing home, he'll shoot himself. He has a handgun, trophy of North Africa. A German-made SIG-Sauer 9mm P226. Naughty Daddy, defying military regs and the law. An officer ought to offer a better example. Daddy showed me the pistol after Mummy's death during the superflu of '08. Civil unrest and a lot of crimes against property. I'd been fretting about Daddy living alone at the end of a village lane. Even if he's hale and hearty, the artificial hip cramps his style.

On a Wednesday I fly with Rogers and Peters to Blanchester to meet Dorothea Wilson.

Our landing site is a windswept cricket field close to the T-square of latter-day almshouses. A chainlink fence tipped with razor wire protects the single-storey redbrick mini-community, and I wonder absurdly what happens if a batsman hits a mighty six. Do the old folk hold the ball to ransom? Rather a lot of impacted waste paper and plastic bags festoon the fence. In the spring maybe the Warden will restore the vista. Right now the prospect is bleak and grey.

Rogers escorts me by a wending path to the open gateway of

Daisy Meadows Sheltered Homes. Sounds as though the place is named in honour of a former resident. Couple of hundred yards further along, a big supermarket offers a nice toddle for the elderly if they are mobile enough. They can exchange vouchers for factory-food or if they have funds can pig out on real pork chops.

Through winter-sad shrubbery we make our way to the Warden's quarters, adjacent to a common room: armchairs within, and upright chairs set around whist tables.

The Warden, a Mr Russell, is a retired policeman with first aid qualifications, burly enough to pick up any old person who falls and squeezes their radio squawker. Jack of all trades, no doubt. When I phoned earlier, Russell explained that Dorothea Wilson suffers badly from arthritis, and that is why she is in Daisy Meadows. Most other residents are older than her.

My cover, today, is Home Office. Russell had noted the turbo-chopper. A high-flying arrival on my part. I tell him that we're investigating a passport application by a young man about whose real identity there are doubts—true enough, at least from the young man's point of view! Information about the circumstances of this person's adoption is important. Records have been lost. The young man in question might not be who he seems.

Appeased, or not wishing to know more, Russell accompanies us to introduce me to Mrs Wilson. Zipping up his mac, Rogers parks himself on a bench outside her unit and lights up a slim cigar—I did not know he smoked.

Russell uses a passkey. "Dotty, there's a visitor for you—!"

Let her not live up to *that* name.

Ensconsed in an armchair with a large-print book—my heart lifts at evidence of mental activity—is a stout lady with permed greying hair and pebble glasses. Floral frock and cardigan and furry slippers. Collection of decorative ceramic bells on a sideboard. A feathery pea-green fern in a china jardinière. Were it not for her arthritis she ought to be in a country cottage complete with oak beams and inglenook.

"Bit of a mystery for you to clear up," Russell announces. I'm heartened to see that the book is an Agatha Christie mystery. Mrs Wilson must be able to keep some track of facts.

"The mobile library calls here once a week," Russell tells me.

Don't just smile, *beam*. "And a good hairdresser too, I see, Mrs Wilson!"

She wants the Warden to brew a pot of tea for us before departing, since he knows where everything is. Presently we get down to business.

Soon she's saying, "The poor mite, how could I forget? As I said to Tom—he was my husband, you know, such a lovely man—who could have expected it of a young mum who seemed so creative? If I hadn't paid a surprise visit and heard the baby squeal . . . and if I hadn't popped round the back and looked in through the window . . . She'd been using a lighted candle, Chrissy Clarke had. The baby's foot was all blistered and burnt. There was parcel tape stuck over his tiny mouth. She pulled the tape loose and I could hear her saying to him, *Tell me the number, tell me the number*—as if the baby could even speak, let alone do arithmetic! She was mad. It wasn't only money worries and her husband having a fling with one of those traveller girls with rings in their noses and everywhere. She was insane—"

Mrs Wilson remembers very well. Who can forget witnessing a mother torture her helpless baby with a candle flame?

"I didn't know what to do. I mean, next thing might she stifle the baby? I rapped on the window so hard I broke a pane and cut my knuckle quite badly, then I ran to the car and phoned the police. No one else was about. So back I went to the house and rang the bell and I thumped on the door and shouted. I ran round the side again. Chrissy had taped up her baby's mouth again. The poor thing's face was bright red. She'd pulled a sock on to his foot to cover up what she'd done, even though I'd already seen, and she looked so frantic and demented. She was blowing on him as if that would cool him down—as though *he* was a candle and she was trying to blow him out but she got confused. Well, I was praying Dear God as I went back to the car. I phoned Social Work for them to get an immediate care order signed by a J.P. I was thinking I ought to break into the house . . ."

I scribble notes. "Mrs Wilson, what did Chrissy Clarke mean by 'tell me the number'?"

"Goodness knows! After the police came, and George Douglas —it was him with the care order—she completely broke down. I mean she had a total breakdown, didn't she?"

Scribble again, and I nod, though I do not know. Not yet. One thing at a time.

"Did you clearly hear the word *number*, Mrs Wilson?" This strikes me as very odd. An odd number, hmm.

"I'm sure I did. I remember saying to Tom the same evening, me being quite upset because it isn't every day . . . and he was such a comfort, a shoulder to lean on."

"By number, might she have meant 'do a poo'? Was the baby naked or in a nappy?"

"The nappy was all soaked with pee when we took it off. He peed in pain, is what I think. The candle wasn't the whole of it, you know. When the doctor examined the baby there were some marks —he thought electricity. She might have used electricity as well. That's obscene, Miss—what name did you say?"

"Sharman. Anna Sharman. Don't upset yourself."

"Well isn't it obscene? She should have been prosecuted and sent to a proper prison instead of Ravensdene, that's the psychiatric hospital in Wroxley Wood, Ravensdene Abbey, Ravings the locals call it, someone's in Ravings now, people say, lovely grounds they had there, lakes and woodland, though I suppose the lakes may have dried up."

"Is Chrissy still there?"

"I don't know. I'm sure it was '*tell* me the number.' "

"What did the police or the psychiatrist make of this? What explanation did Chrissy give?"

Mrs Wilson fidgets. "She and—name's on the top of my tongue, Steve Bryant, that's it—they weren't married. They were only living together. So it was easy for him to wash his hands and walk away! The house wasn't theirs, you see. They were only renting it, and finding *that* hard—it turned out there were money problems. Steve was involved with this traveller girl with rings in her nose, and I think, I think he said the baby wasn't his anyway."

"Steve wasn't the father?"

"I think George Douglas told me that after he interviewed Steve. Your tea's going cold." She raises her cup from the little table by the armchair, sips, and makes a face.

"There's more in the pot, Miss, um—"

"Sharman."

"Do you want to pour yours away, Miss Sharman? Have a refill?"

"It's fine." I drink deeply. Disgusting. And it isn't real tea.

"You could have tipped it in the fern, that's what I do."

A bit late to tell me. "So who was the real father, Mrs Wilson?"

"I've no idea. I'm sure George Douglas never said. Maybe Steve told George Douglas he wasn't the father so as to distance himself from what Chrissy Clarke did to the poor mite, and be shot of the responsibility. He must have been scared he might be prosecuted himself. Maybe he was lying."

Curiouser and curiouser. Jamie might not even be the son of one of the parents he was taken from for later adoption. My cover story is becoming quite appropriate.

What on Earth possessed Jamie's birth-mother to torture her

baby with flames and electricity—as if he knew something and could conceivably be forced to tell her? Before he could even speak! Tell me the number, tell me the number: what number could it be, in Chrissy Clarke's demented mind? The phone number of the real father? The winning numbers for the next lottery draw? Mrs Wilson must have misheard. Maybe Chrissy was trying to teach her baby to count and speak before it was capable of either activity. One little toe, two little toes.

When I suggest this, Mrs Wilson dissents. "There were hardly any toys. It wasn't as if they were trying to stimulate their baby. Well, *she* was—she was stimulating it horribly! She was demented."

"She must have been asked what she meant by 'number.' "

"That's the trouble, Miss Sharman. The police were all hustle. They didn't pay much heed when I said what I heard. *Bloody, sick loony*: that's all one of the officers said. And George Douglas was all bustle, then Jamie was out of my hands and off to hospital—and my knuckle was gashed, I needed a stitch in Casualty."

"But you wrote a report?"

Mrs Wilson fidgets.

"My Tom said stick to the facts that make sense. People aren't very good at facts that don't make sense. The business about the number: it was just what I thought I heard, though I'm sure I heard right. So I left that bit out. Did I do wrong?"

Clearly Mrs Wilson may have been perceived as remiss in failing to spot warning signs. She had not wanted to seem given to fancies or inaccuracy.

"Should I have made more fuss about what I overheard?"

At long last she's getting this item off her chest. From my point of view she did just the right thing, because this stuck in her mind.

"No one's blaming you, Mrs Wilson. You've been very helpful."

"How?" She pats the Christie novel as if to identify herself with some old lady sleuth. "I suppose Jamie must have done something wrong."

She wants to detain me, a bit of outside interest having entered her sedentary life. A glance at the teapot. Ah, but an invitation to a second cup might spur my departure rather than woo me to stay.

"George Douglas died of a heart attack," she adds. "He was always overweight."

Stay here, stay with me, the only remaining witness to that past event. Make me part of something interesting.

Eighteen years have elapsed. Chrissy must have been released from Ravensdene Abbey ages ago. Staff changes, records bollix, no one who remembers. If Steve Bryant took up with travellers he might prove elusive. Or dead, from the superflu or from rural vigilantes protecting their poultry and lambs during the difficult years.

"Mrs Wilson, will you tell me everything you can remember about Chrissy Clarke? And yes, I shall have another cup of tea. Seeing as you haven't touched yours yet, should I pour *that* in the fern?"

"Oh please. I feel better now. It nagged, you know."

"I'd like to know *anything* that nags."

Jigsaws.

(And I think of how Jamie cut up clippings before pasting them into his black book, a bit like jigsaw pieces . . .)

Jigsaws: that was the parents' fledgling business. Steve was a skilled woodworker. Workshop and retail outlet in a craft centre beside the canal near Blanchester's train station. And before that, they were . . . where was it now? It's on the tip of Mrs Wilson's tongue—or away in a corner of the room. Her gaze alights on the jardinière.

"Fern, fern . . . Fernhill Farm Craft Centre, that's where they were."

A little bell goes off in my head.

Just a moment, Mrs Wilson, while I unfold my phone, dial my comp, key in my password (*Xcalibur*, deliberately misspelled, the sword which might free England), S for Search: FERNHILL, scan the liquid crystal display.

Yes, yes, of course: God's Legion, Hugh Ellison.

Humpty Hugh, in his seventies, denouncing Bliss. The answer to heroin and Fraz and hop addiction is not some new devil's drug giving a spurious taste of Paradise for a year and robbing dupes of their souls; the answer is Jesus. Mockymen are demons sent by Satan. The Arabs are right in that regard, even if in no other. Turn to Jesus, not to alien demons tempting us with gifts!

Humpty Hugh in a wheelchair, leading his troops in protest at the head of a convoy of lurid vans. God's Legion survived the difficulties of the first decade of the new millennium rather capably, with their Salvation Halls and Glory Farms including, yes, *Fernhill*.

Off to the Kielder Forest with you, Humpty Hugh. Is Ellison still alive?

"Was Chrissy Clarke born again, Mrs Wilson?"

"What do you mean?"

"Did she belong to God's Legion? Was she a follower of Hugh Ellison?"

I have lost my informant, and I need to explain who owned Fernhill.

Racking her brains is hardly the right phrase. Mrs Wilson's lips pout, producing a soft *pop-pop-popping* noise as though she is suckling an invisible teat in search of stimulus.

She stops her popping. "I don't know, but Chrissy Clarke wasn't exactly very Christian in what she did, was she?"

"I was wondering whether she might have been religiously deranged."

"Her baby wasn't christened, you know! And the two of them weren't married."

"So you said."

"That proves she wasn't religious."

Thank you, Miss Marples.

Did Chrissy and Steve leave Fernhill at the same time she discovered she was pregnant? Any connection with Steve's supposed denial of parentage? The real father being someone at Fernhill? A fellow craftsperson . . . Steve says magnanimously, "Let's make a new start, shall we? We'll raise the baby as our own." This does not work out. (And of course Jamie is to blame, seed of another chap.) Steve turns to that girl with rings in her ears and nose and wherever.

A girl of, say, twenty back then? She'll be nearly forty now. If she's still with Steve, what might he have told her?

Ravensdene beckons me. I shall descend unannounced, without any preconceptions.

Chapter 11

The grounds of Ravensdene are sizeable and secluded. A stone perimeter wall encloses acres of woodland and swards and several mud-rimmed lakes, their water level low. Being wintertime, it's hard to say how many of the thousands of leafless trees may be dead rather than dormant. Yet here's a vague approximation of Eden, therapeutic no doubt to the inmates. Masses of rhododendrons, at least, look glossy. From a great dell of scruffy lawn rises an impressive hall of beige-yellow stonework, four storeys high. The mullioned windows of the ground floor are massive. Those of upper floors diminish successively in size. In no way does the building resemble any abbey.

We alight to the rear, near where a tennis net sags limply. Patients in a recreation room break off from their table tennis to stare out at our turbo-chopper. One chap uses his bat to semaphore directions at Rogers and me: follow the terrace of crooked flagstones around to the front.

As we do so, out of hiding comes the sun, adding a rich glow to the masonry. Disconnected from the terrace stands a flight of five stone steps. Rogers hops across and poses on the top, sun-lit.

"Stairway to nowhere. Where do we go from here? What on Earth is this thing?"

"It's a mounting block."

"For knights in armour?"

"No, for an overweight huntsman. This place looks Tudor. By Tudor times bulky armour was going out of fashion." The penny drops. "Dissolution of the monasteries! Henry the Eighth sold the abbey and land to a nobleman—the buyer pulls the abbey down and uses the stones to build himself a stately heap."

"You know such a lot, Miss Sharman."

"I studied history."

"How dissolute were the monasteries?"

Gerry once told me that most men think about sex on average six times an hour. I'm not sure how a social scientist arrived at this statistic. The knowledge that you're a volunteer carrying a counting device must prejudice the outcome. The chip which Jamie wears tells us nothing about his thoughts, unfortunately.

Some male users of Bliss claim that sex on Bliss is the supreme high. Contrariwise, many women say that physical copulation is irrelevant because every bodily sensation is eroticised (though they don't often phrase this in quite such terms).

The bright sunlight haloes fair hairs on Rogers's wrists and the back of his powerful hands, which I had not consciously registered till now. It's been a while since Gerry. Strength in a man is not a trait I need, even though I may desire it. A few years before Gerry there was Julian, with whom I was intoxicated, but Julian wanted to own me. I would have become his possession. I might have basked in this sensation in the way a dog adores its master and finds the meaning of its life in his regard and fondling. So therefore I denied myself Julian.

On the mounting block Rogers is a candidate for my admiration, and he knows it. I may be overrating him because of misdirected adrenalin, the thrill of the chase.

"Come off there, Rogers, you're being silly. You look like a Chippendale statue. They'll think you're a patient I'm bringing in for treatment."

"I'm no historian, Miss Sharman, but I thought Chippendale made chairs, not statues."

He misses the allusion to the New York hunk show of yore. Well, he's a few years younger than me. At Oxford, supposedly for a laugh, Jane and Rachel and I repeatedly watched a video of that musical-with-muscle showcasing the hottest men in the world, in Rachel's college room. Rachel died in the superflu pandemic. Jane became a journalist, then an outspoken Humpty and now she's in Kielder. I would rather not think about either of them.

Rogers hops back to the terrace and nods at the steps.

"Was I getting above myself?" Oh he *is* bright. B-plus for promise. "Don't worry, Miss Sharman, if any of the nutters misbehave I'll protect you."

"Mr Rogers, it may seem low-key visiting an old lady and a rest home for the daft, but this is definitely not a picnic."

He looks suitably chastened.

A noble carved oak staircase ascends from a hallway, supervised by a sturdy male nurse at a desk. Half a dozen patients in day clothes are fussing for a stroll in the grounds, eager to see our helicopter close up. The nurse watcheth their goings out and their comings in, and keepeth check with clipboard and monitor screen, and he controlleth the button which unlocked the door for us.

Since all the patients wear chip-bands on their wrists their whereabouts will show up on his screen in case they try to decamp. Highly unlikely that someone would attempt to liberate one of the inmate of this seemingly benign establishment by air-lift, but who knows? The nurse is stalling the patients till he knows who we are.

We're Home Office. The nurse studies my ID. We're here to see the person in charge.

"That's Dr Akimbola."

African-sounding name. West Africa, Nigeria probably. He may have been in England for a long time, psychiatrist in the Health Service.

"I'll page her."

Oops, Dr Akimbola is a woman. In a regular hospital I would have made no such assumptions.

Several squashy armchairs are vacant. We loiter by these but don't sit down in the presence of mental patients.

An extremely skinny young woman with ratty, flaxen hair buttonholes me. "I shouldn't be here," she whispers. "I'm a *Mockyman.*"

Her fat female companion affirms this with many nods. Dum, and Dee. Obese Dum and anorexic Dee.

"This isn't me," Dee confides. "This is an alien in here."

If only. If only we had a stray Mockyman squirreled away in safekeeping to question—a Mockyman unaccounted for by its kind, a maverick Mockyman. Would a truth drug work on the alien mind inhabiting the dummy brain? Might we regretfully have recourse to Lionel Evans's field of expertise? Extreme interrogation would be disgusting, despicable, and might only produce sheer fiction and lies. No confession would be reliable unless we had independent confirmation.

"I'm another person," schizo Dee repeats. "I'm from the stars, I'm a Mockyman. I have a mission. I'm here by mistake." Yet her avowal has a pat, weary ring to it, as if she is merely reciting without much conviction.

"She really is!" Dum insists in a far more fervent voice. "She told me things only a Mockyman can know."

How do *you* know, my dear? I'm glimpsing the shadowy depths of a strangely tangled relationship. Delusion seems to have transferred from its originator to another person who now bases her sense of purpose upon it. Like religion, really. Dum is a follower of a messiah. The messiah has lost faith in herself, yet she must still mouth her creed for the sake of her disciple. Far from reinforcing Dee's delusion, does Dum's hyperbole subvert the fantasy? Very likely Dr Akimbola sees things quite differently.

A buzz. The nurse talks softly into a phone. The director will be in her office in ten minutes. Another nurse will escort us upstairs.

"Okay folks, you can all go outside now—"

As soon as the front door clicks open, big Dum hauls skeletal Dee with her like some ventriloquist's puppet.

"You stay here when I go upstairs," I tell Rogers. "The doctor and me: woman to woman, mm?"

"Fine by me. Though waiting rooms usually have a few magazines."

"Why not enjoy a cigar outside? Stretch your legs."

He grins.

Dr Akimbola is a buxom assertive soul. Bright green and gold blouse, high-necked and long-sleeved. Voluminous draped purple skirt. Redoubtable matching turban. She's a big splash of Africa in grey England, a morale-booster for her patients. The mullioned windows of her office look out upon a slope of naked chestnut trees and sycamores.

"I love this place, so peaceful in a turbulent world. A paradise. I've been here since before all the troubles."

"You're from Nigeria, aren't you, Doctor?"

"Have you been there?"

"No . . . but I sponsor a girl in Tanzania. I pay for her education. She's fifteen now."

Mary Songa of Morogoro.

Tanzania was always poor. Never a British colony, merely a protectorate confiscated from the Germans, so compared with Kenya there was little investment. On independence the Tanzanians accepted aid from China and followed a mildly socialist line, so the West wouldn't give much assistance. Paradoxically Tanzania weathered the hard years better than many nations because it never had a chance to power up in the first place.

"Sponsorship, Miss Sharman: that's kind of you."

"It doesn't cost much—I think of it as conscience money."

"I'm sure you're being a bit hard on yourself."

"Mary, that's her name, recently she began writing me begging letters on behalf of her extended family. Can't blame her really. But how many people can a person be responsible for? Directly, I mean."

"In my case," comes the reply, "it's a hundred and thirty, including staff. And you might well say this is a privileged haven here—for them and for me too."

"You know, the last time I talked to a psychiatrist . . ." But I can't tell her. The previous interview was part of my assessment as a candidate for security service work.

Dr Akimbola laughs. "Presumably was confidential," she supplies. "So how may I help the Home Office?"

"A Chrissy Clarke: do you remember her?"

"Oh yes, very clearly. On account of the ice house."

"The what?" I'm imagining a refrigerated room, intended to cool hectic inmates. Alternatively, a happy band of patients build a giant igloo out on the tennis court after a rare heavy snowfall. Dr Akimbola swings her chair round and points at the tree-clad ridge.

"Most people can't see it till they're almost upon it, and even so they may walk by. Do you make out a little hump covered in undergrowth?"

Too much sporadic dead undergrowth, too much ivy, too many conflicting shapes of stray branches. And too far away.

"It's an underground domed room covered by earth—once used as a food store. Your forebears took ice from the lakes in deep winter. The ice lasted all summer long. An early refrigerator."

From one of the cabinets Dr Akimbola brings a file to verify the details. Real hand-written notes, thank heavens.

Chrissy Clarke began her stay at Ravensdene by demanding hysterically to have her baby returned to her. They had kidnapped Jamie. She needed tranquillizing. The top floor provided secure quarters for patients who might harm themselves or others. Chrissy was up there for a couple of years, refusing to talk about what had happened between her and the baby, refusing to be helped, flipping between morose silence and mania—the worst case of post-natal depression Dr Akimbola ever saw. Chrissy's former partner, Steve, had not helped matters by ditching her. Chrissy's parents visited, but made no headway.

After those first two years Chrissy seemed to have adjusted and could be trusted to mingle and go on supervised walks. She claimed to have forgotten the circumstances concerning the baby. All of it was a terrible fog, a psychotic episode caused by Steve's adultery. She wanted to look forward now, not back. When her parents visited, she was meek and regretful and lucid.

"Yet a bit like thin ice," adds Dr Akimbola. "And then one day . . . well, we had a new male nurse named Charlie McConnell, not too experienced." She scans the file and nods.

"McConnell took Chrissy on a walk to the top side of the grounds, where she came across the ice house. It's grim and dark inside, a bit like a mausoleum or crypt. Abandoned for decades, and empty apart from dead leaves and beetles. There's a locked iron grille closing off the entrance, but the metal had rusted."

The view through the grille triggered something in Chrissy. She wrenched it open and jumped down into the ice house. Hooting like an owl, she spread-eagled herself against the brickwork, squirming as if she was having sex. McConnell went in after her. *He* said she was calling out things in German.

"In German?" Shades of Jamie's book . . . "What sort of things?"

"McConnell didn't know, apart from *blut*—which means blood."

"I know."

Chrissy pulled down her slacks and knickers as if she was going to do a pee and she beat her palms on the brick wall calling out *blut* and other words. When McConnell tried to restrain her she flipped round, ripped open the zip of his trousers, and slipped her hand inside and gripped his penis. "Fuck me, Carl," she said, "and I'll get out of here . . ."

"But he was called Charlie."

"That's what McConnell *said*, to the then-director, and at the case conference. You see, afterwards Chrissy accused McConnell of assault. She swore he tempted her into the ice house and tried to have sex with her. Her word against his, bit of a dilemma. The head of Ravensdene then, Dr Appleby, decided it was best for McConnell to move on without prejudice to his prospects. McConnell never ought to have tried to manhandle her in those circumstances, not on his own. Chrissy had no way of harming herself other than getting bruised. McConnell ought to have called in for assistance and a witness. When Chrissy came to her senses I believe she tried to exploit the incident. Victim of abuse at our hands; ought to be released. In the ice house, though, she definitely had a psychotic episode, prompted by the surroundings, aggravated by the presence of a man in there with her."

"Whom she called Carl."

"I don't believe McConnell invented this. Still, it was unprovable either way. Chrissy denied saying anything in German because according to her she didn't know any German apart from *Achtung* and *Ja* and that sort of thing."

This Carl might be the real father of Jamie. Craftsman at Fernhill? Am I facing a trip to the Kielder forest to question a defiant, elderly Hugh Ellison about years gone by? Even if Ellison remembers the cast list at Fernhill I can't see him cooperating unless he has mellowed.

In due course Chrissy did talk her way out of Ravensdene. She stuck to her story about the assault, and McConnell had been shifted, so the hospital seemed to have goofed, and Chrissy appeared quite rational.

"Did she go to her parents?"

Not known.

Copy of the file, please, Doctor. You do have a copier on the premises?

"Could I ask why the Home Office is trying to trace her after such a long time?"

I shrug. "While Chrissy was here, did she do jigsaw puzzles to occupy herself?"

"Oh yes. Yes indeed."

"We're trying to fit some pieces together too."

"The big picture, being?"

I shake my head.

The African woman smiles. "You just keep things bottled up, and maybe send a bit more cash to your Mary, for heart's ease."

Before I leave her office, Dr Akimbola mentions that Chrissy's alleged interrogation of her baby would have been in vain even if the baby could have understood her. A baby is born with its larynx very high up so that it can breathe air and drink milk without choking. Only after nine months does the larynx move down, permitting proper vocalisation.

Rogers and I hike up a trampled, earthen path through winter-bare woodland to the ice house. The weed-covered mound looks natural till we head round the back to a short flight of steps and a sloping sunken passageway. Padlock and chain now secure the grille-door. Inside, the murky spherical brick room resembles a dungeon, its floor a metre or so below the level of the entrance. Lock-picking is one of the skills taught by JSSI, but weather has been at work for the past sixteen years or so, and this padlock won't yield. Might as well be superglued. I need to gain entry to experience something of what Chrissy felt.

"Shoot through the chain, will you, Rogers?"

"There's nothing inside but dead leaves."

"Sixteen years ago two people were inside. A man and a woman. The woman assaulted the man. Just shoot, will you? Or shall I?"

Out comes his Glock pistol of light strong polymer. "Watch out for ricochet."

After I distance myself, he aims and fires a single shot—the crack of someone stepping on a rotten branch. The chain rustles loose as Rogers drags the creaky door open. Down he jumps, pistol in hand as if entering a room where a terrorist may be lurking in the shadows. After tucking the gun away, he offers me a hand—the first time we have touched.

Within the ice house it's very chilly and still as though nothing has altered for years. Although the bars of the door have provided ventilation the air is stale and fusty. Patches of mould on the walls are like decayed fresco. As my eyes adjust, I imagine fragments of figures and designs.

If Chrissy associated this place with a sexual act which spawned Jamie, is there a similar ice room at Fernhill Farm? Maybe a cellar? No, farms include barns and milking parlours, not places such as this. Why would she and a lover resort to such a squalid, uncomfortable spot?

I shut my eyes and whisper, "*Blut blut blut.*" Sounds like a dripping tap.

Why blood? No blood was shed. Chrissy did not rake McConnell's cheeks with her nails in a pretence of fighting him off, or in re-enactment of the past.

"*Blut blut.*"

"What are you saying?"

"When I told you that the woman assaulted the man, I meant that she made a violent sexual overture to him in here."

"Sounds the wrong way round to me. But we're talking loonies, aren't we?"

"What's your first name, by the way?"

"Tim."

"So, Tim, how do you rate Peters?"

"Peters. He's a crack shot. He hasn't much imagination."

"Whereas you do."

"Maybe."

"Would you care to use your imagination and pretend that you're a male nurse in here with me? I'm in your charge. A psychiatric nurse is like a bodyguard. I'm a patient called Chrissy who tortured her baby because she wanted it to tell her a number."

"She did *what?*"

"Just what I said. What can it possibly mean?"

"It means she was stark staring bonkers."

"Stark, yes. I want you to imagine that I pull my slacks and nickers down—"

"*You* are wearing a skirt."

"Naturally I shan't do anything of the sort because I would dirty my clothes. Just make believe I sprawl against this wall. With my welfare in mind you come up behind me while I'm chanting blood-blood-blood in Deutsch, and I turn to you and I say, 'Fuck me, Carl, and I'll get out of here.' What do you make of that?"

"Sexual favours. She offers herself to Carl hoping that he'll unlock her chip-band, help her escape."

"Only senior staff can deactivate a band. She's in his care today, so if she absconds he's to blame."

"If he's fool enough to fuck her, then later on she can blackmail him."

"Actually, the nurse isn't called Carl. Carl is somebody else. Carl is the father of her baby whom she tortured, and he wasn't Chrissy's partner. Tell me the number."

"A phone number? As if a baby would know! Safe deposit box? Combination number?"

"Ah—interesting notion." Given Chrissy's money worries, gaining fairy tale access to a cave of treasure might have been in her mind. Open sesame. Back to lottery numbers as explanation?

"Tim, this isn't inspired enough."

When I was eighteen and about to do my A Levels at Cheltenham Ladies College, I was walking through the marketplace in Hereford one bright sunny Saturday afternoon while the traders were packing up. At a fruit and veg stall I spied a ravishing fair-haired youth stripped to the waist in the heat. Such sculpted golden skin. Adonis was trying to get rid of his remaining strawberries. "Last four punnets for a pound!" As I dawdled closer he winked. "Only a pound for four punnets, Miss, juicy and sweet!"—characterizing me as much as the fruit, cheeky chap.

I sauntered onward but not very far. An elastic resistance halted me, and I hurried back. I remember how the belt buckle of his jeans was a Heavy Metal item, a little skull with a rose through its teeth.

"I couldn't possibly eat all these strawberries on my own—"

His tummy, so flat and firm. "They go down a treat with a lager."

I pointed at his belt. "Does that rose come out of those teeth?"

"We can find out."

And we did, later on.

Rogers may be my whetstone on which I may strop myself to sharpen my wits, rather as Chrissy writhed against this brick wall. Up against a brick wall, she was. Nowadays I'm almost twenty years older than I was in that market place and I have authority. Rogers could almost be that de luxe barrowboy, grown up.

"Stimulate my imagination, Tim."

Warily: "Is this a test?"

"Speaking as a man, Tim, does this setting arouse you?"

Dutifully he scans the mottled grubby walls of this . . . *mausoleum* was the word Dr Akimbola used. A place where memories are buried. If a wall is circular, should one speak of a wall or walls in the plural?

"What time of year did this happen, Miss Sharman?"

"Good point. That'll be in the file. I don't suppose sunlight ever reaches in here."

"Entrance faces north, that's why. To keep it cold in here. Maybe Carl came from the north. She thinks he's in here with her."

"So where is the original of this place?"

"Look, I don't know enough about this to guess, and I don't think I *ought* to know enough."

"It's safe to know this much. It's a jigsaw: you don't have the centre. I need some help filling in round the edges."

"Sort of manufactured *cave*, this place," he ventures.

"Would you make love in a cave?"

"If there's sand on the floor and a beach outside and palm trees."

"No, I don't believe it was a holiday fling. I don't think the experience was even enjoyable, if this place is what evokes it."

"Was Chrissy raped by Carl? The assault on the nurse was her revenge by proxy? She never complained about the rape because she didn't want her partner to know. And she couldn't have been on the pill, so back then her partner must have used condoms and rhythm." I nod approvingly at his level of awareness. "But her partner didn't behave very responsibly ditching her—unless her torturing the baby disgusted him so much. He couldn't have joined in too closely on baby care, or he should have sussed what was happening. If the fuck with Carl wasn't rape it still couldn't exactly have been for pleasure."

"But for some other reason?"

"She had a barney with her old man? So she marches off saying, 'Fuck you,' and does it with this Carl? By the time she realizes she's pregnant, she and her partner are lovey-dovey again."

"Are you in a relationship?" I ask him.

He regards me neutrally for a while, lips pursed, before shaking his head.

Chapter 12

A wreath of silver tinsel has joined the trilby and mackintosh which customarily adorn the stag's head on the wall of H-S's office. Christmas is coming, the geese are getting fat. I shall be spending the festive day with Daddy, the two of us on our own. This year Tony can't make it—special reconstituted turkey lunch for three thousand at Kielder as a break from the usual factory food—but my brother will be with Daddy to see the New Year in. Looks like I shall be seeing Tony before then, though. May as well make it a surprise.

Enough rain is sluicing down the window to wash away any spy-bugs which might have climbed up to the thirtieth floor and to blur hopelessly any laser-mike snooping from some distant rooftop, though as a matter of course H-S switches on anti-noise, cocooning us in silence while setting my teeth slightly on edge. We have our own paid ears in quite a few foreign transit stations and ministries, so we must assume that spooks from abroad are keeping an eye on MAL and Hyde Park. The resulting crystal clarity in the room always seems *less* safe to me, even if I know that the opposite is true. I tend to lower my voice. No such qualms bother H-S.

"Sit you down," he booms.

I report about Daisy Meadows and Ravensdene. No joy yet on tracing either Chrissy or Steve.

"And of course Jamie's still with Zandra and Barnabas. Quite a strange scene there."

"In what way?"

"It's so stylized: their butler, their maid."

"Well, we know that."

"Hearing snatches of it brings it home. I think I should fly to Kielder to interview Hugh Ellison. Can we offer him an inducement? Always assuming he knows something useful."

"Aye, well that's tipping him off about our interest, isn't it?"

In view of where Ellison is, a cover story will hardly hold water. Apparently he isn't in the best of health, but his mind is still sharp. If I let him know how vitally interested we are in circumstances of years gone by, now why's that, pray? And in connection with what aspect of MAL's activities? Kielder is bound to be leaky if only because of the permitted supervised visits. How far can I go in confiding in Ellison? If I don't go far enough, I can't expect many answers.

"Do I threaten to let down the tyres of his wheelchair? Do I offer parole?"

"There'll be a Christmas amnesty for some . . ."

All of whom must abide by a sworn undertaking, monitored by chip-band, to remain within ten miles of their homes and to engage in no anti-alien agitation.

" . . .but preaching's in Ellison's blood. I don't think we can safely do that."

The downpour is serving as wobbly supplementary glazing on the window. H-S rises and paces to and fro, those ample hairy hands clasped behind a tweed-clad back as if to correct a very tall man's inclination to stoop and thus be less conspicuous. On a freckled face, under receding fading red hair, his nose is a big complicated cherry-red carbuncle of a snozz, touch of Elephant Man about his proboscis.

"In another few years," he muses, "Mockymen and dummies may be taken for granted. BritGov might decide to downsize Kielder, shut the camp. Unless there are unforeseen side effects to Bliss."

Far too much is unknown. Why are the transit stations on Melody and elsewhere so hermetically cordoned? What is the viewpoint of the natives of Melody and Passion? What if we decide we have received enough gifts to survive and prosper unassisted? I can't see every nation which has a transit station agreeing to shut those. But just suppose. Will the Mockymen merely shrug and say,

"Thanks for the worms, pity you'll be on your own from now!" Do they have a big stick they might wave?

H-S halts. "Telling Ellison about the torture of an infant might shake him and loosen his lips."

"Why are *we* suddenly so interested after all these years?"

"Try this: Chrissy Clarke applies for a position with MAL. Routine check throws up this incident, but bygones are bygones. Looks like she'll get the job. You're horrified, being a sensitive soul. Just between you and Ellison, you're having doubts about the way MAL is run and the people involved, their criteria, the kind of values they have."

"What job is Chrissy supposed to do for MAL? Interest the Mockymen in jigsaws?"

"All right, she's applying for a position at the camp, as a Kielder Kapo."

"Kapo?"

"Female concentration camp guard, Nazi era—I thought Jamie's black book was your bedtime reading." Arched eyebrows, and a chuckle. He's teasing—he knows full well that the text was either torn out or obliterated.

"Now that you mention it, the word does ring a bell."

"So, lassie, *you* don't consider a potential psycho is a suitably humane sort to be in charge of the unmarried women's quarters. Some of the single mums have their wee bairns with them. Confused liberal qualms beset you, Miss Sharman."

French Ambassador at the UN: "If the bodies of Bliss-users will have such powers of self-repair, how long will these people live for?"

Mocky-Lemur Envoy: "Lifetime. Normal human length. Then bodies fail quickly."

French Ambassador: "So there will be no old age for these people?"

Mocky-Lemur Envoy: "Maturity, but not frailty."

French Ambassador: "This will be true of dummies too?"

Mocky-Lemur Envoy: "Dummies being former Bliss users, yes."

French Ambassador: "So what can kill a Bliss body before its allotted span?"

Mocky-Lemur Envoy: "Incineration, evisceration, decapitation, destruction of blood-pump, destruction of brain." At odds with its crisp delivery hitherto, the Envoy utters these words in a stiffly robotic, almost psychotic tone, as if it is reciting without comprehending—or is denying itself comprehension. It continues, more at

ease: "Uncontrollable tumour growth in a percentage of bodies."
French Ambassador: "Will Bliss-users lose sexual sensitivity as
well as taste and smell?"
Hélas, c'est vrai. Ex-users will stay potent or fertile, but as for the
joy of sex, forget it.
French Ambassador: "How do you know this will be so?"
Mocky-Lemur Envoy: "It is so with other humanoid species."

After the twelve-month Peak for Blissheads comes the long shady
valley. Really, we are looking at a mainly non-contributing section
of society being retooled as healthy sober Spartan drones, unless
they fall foul of aftermath-apathy. It's a bargain society can easily live
with. By analogy, if you could receive all the cash you
will earn in a lifetime right now in one lump sum to squander,
many people would think this a wonderful windfall, manna from
heaven.

English was the language of choice for the envoys. Users of
dummies have access to whatever native tongue a dummy spoke
previously, but those first arrivals in the pod-ship must have used a
very sophisticated computer to hack a human language on the basis
of TV output, then some sort of direct brain input to acquire flu-
ency. Into the furnace of the sun went computer and all.

On the flight up the spine of England past the occasional vertebrae
of cities, Peters amuses himself with a mini-comp game while
Rogers scans the grey landscape as if Humpty missiles might rise
towards us unexpectedly. Of course, Humpties have no such toys. I
spy a sun-farm, undulating lake of glassy panels covering dozens of
acres. Thanks, Mockymen.

Before we set out, I had a chat with Rogers. I wish him to be
with me during the interview with Ellison, so that I seem less like
an agent provocateur. Rogers should also seem disenchanted with
MAL, an ally of mine, nodding concernedly. Couple of good
policemen.

After a while he begins studying the game Peters is playing, and
soon he says:

"You should take a look at this, Miss Sharman. I don't think it
ought to be on sale."

The game is called Transit. A tiny figure infiltrates a maze-like
transit station, evading or killing human guards and Mockymen and
dummies that rise from their beds. Very good graphics. Scenes of
the transit station must be based upon inside knowledge, though

with surreal embellishments. I try the game myself, getting killed several times before I have the hang of it. When I finally reach the centre of the maze, in a flash my figure jumps to another level of play: an alien transit station, a new maze, where Mocky-Lemurs try to stop my figure from reaching the outside. Dodging and doubling back, I'm mainly interested in the tantalising fanciful glimpses of the alien station.

"What's outside the alien station, Peters?"

As if a computer game could contain information which eludes everyone else in the world!

"I can't get outside—"

The data-wafer proves to be Japanese.

"Where did you buy this?"

"Shop in Soho."

"Did you keep the packaging? Bring it in tomorrow, and the wafer too. Meanwhile, keep trying to break out."

A game of Breach-the-Mockymen-Cordon isn't something the public ought to be playing. It isn't a concept that should be floating around, maybe for Mockymen to notice. Japanese, eh? I feel mildly paranoid.

Rides and firebreaks cut through the rolling forest of Norway spruce and pines. Down along one firebreak grazes a herd of skewbald goats, brown and dirty white.

We fly over Kielder Water. Murky wet cloud obscures the nearby Cheviot peaks with names like Oh Me Edge and Girdle Fell. Those peaks form a partial cordon around the forests surrounding the camp, size of a small town. Its timber longhouses aren't too geometrical in layout. Gravel roadways wend. Inmates wander freely or are in recreation halls. No forced labour goes on, unlike in Britain's prisons. Local forestry workers live in Otterburn and Bellingham, and bus to their duties. Camp staff live offsite in Kielder Village three miles away. The toothed razor-wire of the perimeter reminds me of H-S's Christmas tinsel. No need for watchtowers in the age of chip-bands and sensors.

Our pilot identifies us for clearance to land on a pad in the administration enclave.

I'm shocked and sorry to see that Ellison has lost a leg. The left tube of his trousers is tucked under his bum in the wheelchair. Evidently the multiple sclerosis is exacerbating. He wears glasses now, and the right-hand lens is dark. Even so, his rough-hewn bulk ensconed in that padded chair with the big wheels, and further chunked out by a white Fairisle sweater, manages to convey a prophetic rather than pathetic impression—except for the single long lock of hair plastered around his dome, which reminds me of one of those airplants growing upon a little boulder.

His attendant has departed. A fan purrs in the ceiling of the white windowless strip-lit room. I set a buzz-box on the table, and my teeth tingle.

"Nothing is being recorded, Mr Ellison, and nothing can be overheard."

"Except," and he pauses before enunciating slowly, "by GodD." The final consonant thuds home like a hammerblow. His right leg tremors.

"Are you getting proper physio, Mr Ellison?"

"Enforced inactivity—is not what a doctor—would orderR." I suppose by inactivity he means not being able to carry on his mission against the Mockymen. Evidently he's experiencing minor speech problems, but the one eye that watches me is very alert and baleful. "Why is nothing being—recorded—except in HeavenN? Are there problems—with the demonsZ now? Is their satanic purpose—becoming apparentT?"

"No, nothing of the sort. The problem is with a person you once knew." And I explain, while Rogers nods conspiratorially.

The news that Chrissy Clarke tortured a baby appalls Ellison. However, he already had an inkling. Ellison had banished Chrissy and her boyfriend and their Majig Mementoes from Fernhill because they perpetrated pornography. They had taken nude photographs of each other and had made jigsaws of these for a client.

The client in question was an elderly Norwegian whom Ellison himself never actually set eye on. The episode stuck vividly in his mind because the Norwegian committed suicide and the police came to Fernhill to interview the two subjects of the jigsaw pictures. From pornography to paedophilia and sadism is a slippery slope, as treacherous as our own compact with the alien demons, unquote.

"This sick old man—blew his brains out—over the completed jigsawsZ—"

"Because of frustration?" Rogers's question earns a glare from Ellison and pursed lips from me. Just as well he asked, though!

Lo, those jigsaws were not primarily nude photos of Chrissy and her chap. They were pictures of the two of them in a sculpture park in Oslo, a park full of nude stone figures. The Norwegian paid them to fly there on a special trip. No, Ellison cannot remember the Norwegian's name.

Here's a whole new insight. In Jamie's black book are quite a few Norwegian words. How and why? Are those words which his mother used while she was burning his foot with a candle flame—burned into his memory. (And how did *she* come by those words?)

"Were there any *grottos* in that sculpture park, Mr Ellison?"

How should he know? All he saw were nude statues by moonlight and the two nude young folk lolling against them.

An elderly Norwegian man pays lavishly for jigsaws featuring a young British couple posing in a park in Oslo. After completing the jigsaws he shoots himself in the head. About nine months later, Chrissy gives birth and proceeds to torture her baby boy, absurdly demanding a number.

"Was the Norwegian's first name Carl by any chance?"

"I never heard—the *Christian* name. Christian, indeed! Pagan, more like."

Did the elderly gent pay to fuck Chrissy at his house, down in his cellar for privacy? Or did he pay to watch while Chrissy and Steve fucked, and this excited him enough join in, resulting in ambiguity regarding the parentage of Jamie? Was the hypothetical cellar well-appointed with thick woolly rugs on the floor and mood lighting, or was it more like the ice house?

"He burned all his—papers, the police saidD. They were at a loss—as to his identity*TEE*."

Was the elderly client "Carl" or not? Something bizarre happened nineteen years ago.

After leaving Humpty Hugh, Rogers and I go to the staff café, where brother Alan may be unless he's at the huge refectory in the main part of the camp. The outlook: forest and low gloomy clouds. Since the lunch rush is over, the café is almost empty. Peters is at a table, concentrating on his game of Transit.

"Any luck, Peters?"

Glance up for a moment and be zapped by Mockymen: "Damn . . ."

"Keep on trying."

Rogers and I fill cups with coffee from a machine and load a couple of bowls with savoury pink factory-stew but I motion him to a different table.

Spoon up a mouthful. "Tastes of rabbit, wouldn't you say?"

"Mmm. Maybe they trap them out there to add them to the gloop."

"We could ask my brother—he's the catering manager here."
"You're kidding." When I shake my head: "Well, talk about
keeping things in the family."
"Not really . . . Just, Alan always wanted to be a chef."
"Does that make you Big Sister?"
"By a year."
"The shaker and doer. Are you and him close?"
To whom am I close? To Mary of Morogoro, proxy daughter five
thousand miles away, unseen except in occasional photographs?
When I don't answer, he says:
"I suppose goat stew must be on the menu other days."
"You noticed the wild goats." Tim Rogers notices a lot. "Those
shouldn't really be there, chewing up the trees. So: what about
Ellison's story? A cellar in the Norwegian's home for a spot of
rumpty-tumpty? And the ice house brings it all back to Chrissy?"
"Why burn his documents and shoot himself? Why not burn the
erotic jigsaws? Do you think the police kept those if they never
traced any relatives? Share them out after a year or so. Sorry Bert,
yours is one of the poofter ones. Frankly I don't think porn was the
point at all."
"Me neither."
Just then, Alan does come in. Hygienic white coat open over a
grey suit, he looks more like some hospital consultant on his
rounds. His black hair is tangled and wind-blown. The Vandyke
beard builds out his chin.
"What are you doing here, Anna?" There's as much shock as
surprise in his voice. I ought to be in London, not here. Rogers
returns his scrutiny evenly.
"Has something happened to Dad?"
"No, Daddy's fine. He's looking forward to New Year with you.
Shame about Christmas. We could all have been together instead
of having separate heart-to-hearts."
"I don't know about heart-to-hearts—the old man and me, well,
you know."
"Surely that's all water under the bridge. A bottle of malt on
New Year's Eve makes mellow. This is Tim Rogers, by the way."
Tony assesses what Rogers must be. "MAL business?" My
brother sounds edgy.
"We came to talk to Hugh Ellison about something."
"Ellison." As if he needs to *remind* himself who Ellison is. "Well,
that's none of my business, Sis. I just feed the body."
"Not as much body as there used to be, in Ellison's case."

"That isn't because of the diet."

A clearing of the throat: "Shall I see how Peters is getting on?" I nod. "Good idea."

Tony takes the chair vacated by Rogers, and we talk inconsequentially. Daddy, the festive season, this and that. Of a sudden my brother bursts out with, "It's so good to see you, Sis!" As if he has caught up with himself at last.

Tony has had a girlfriend or two, but nothing came of it. Undersexed rather than undeclared gay is my diagnosis. He never really confided, a trait I somewhat share. As regards sex, I'm cautious, but now and then the filly must run wild.

It occurs to me: captive audience here at Kielder, bored unattached females. Him, the provider of creature comforts. Maybe there's some ardent militant protestor with rings in her ears and nose, like the traveller girl whom Chrissy's Steve ran off with. Tony isn't bad looking with that nally arty beard of his. He might be ensnared and manipulated.

"You involved with anybody in the camp, Tone?"

"Christ no. Why should you say that?" I've taken him aback again. "Sis, there are *rules*."

"Oh, some glamorous internee, eager for real rabbit pie . . ."

He darts a glance across at Rogers. "You do like to act knife-edge, don't you, Anna?"

"Coming from a caterer, that's quite funny."

"I simply *can't* make Christmas. The leave roster, the Noel turkey feast."

"Aren't you in charge of the roster?"

"In charge, exactly. I need to oversee the feast."

I've no idea why Tony might prefer to miss Christmas with Daddy and me. Unless the answer is simply: me. Too often my chats with Tony turn into badgering when I only intend bonhomie. Something rings false, but I oughtn't to try to put my finger on it.

Chapter 13

"Lassy, it's as though you're asking me to believe in magic—"

Knut Alver was the Norwegian's name. Paperwork and Coroner's report (but no jigsaws) are archived at the police station in Blanchester, and yesterday copies arrived on my desk.

Knut Alver rented a house on the outskirts of the village of Weston Heath thirty-odd miles from where Chrissy lived. He was there for five years. Before killing himself he destroyed all financial and personal records, passport, the lot. The Norwegian embassy was unable to help the police. Alver may not have been the man's real name at all. He's a blank.

Of course the sculpture park is a real place. Pride of Oslo! Monomaniacal creation of a certain Gustav Vigeland. Our embassy sent by diplomatic bag a lavishly illustrated book. There in that park hundreds of nude granite figures express the struggle of life in heavily Teutonic, I suppose I should say Nordic style. The centrepiece is a phallic monolith of bodies questing upward.

According to the book, which is in English, lightning from out of a clear sky struck the top of the monolith, causing some cracking and charring . . . in the very same year and season that "Alver" shot himself here in England. "Thor's Hammer?" enquires the text whimsically.

This morning our cultural attaché in Oslo sent me the exact date of the incident . . . Alver had been dead for several days when found, precise time of suicide uncertain; but it fits.

Almost as if the bullet not only blew out Alver's brains but hit the top of that monolith too. That's the magical aspect which H-S finds hard to swallow, as do I. Shoot yourself upon a jigsaw picturing the park, and cause a repercussion seven hundred miles away.

"Sheer coincidence?" I ask H-S.

"Och, next thing you'll be suggesting that Majig Mementoes was a cover name for some coven of witches up to strange capers."

"Maybe the name appealed to Alver because it suggested something out of this world."

H-S laces his big hairy fingers and cracks his knuckles. "Without yon jigsaws to identify the actual sculptures Steve and Chrissy photographed there doesn't seem much point in going to Norway, unless you fancy yourself as a psychic, Anna." In fact he's a bit ahead of me. "Our born-again dummy: is he doing any jigsaw puzzles at the couriers' home?"

"Not so far as I can tell. He watches a lot of quiz shows in his room. Or at least the screen's often switched on to the quiz channel."

"Random search for information, would you say? As if the missing clue to himself will pop out of the blue?"

Out of the Blue is one of the quiz shows Jamie watches—a random hypertext quiz where the questions (and answers) are as much of a surprise to the ex-centrefold compére as to the contestants. *Beat the Brain* is a more intellectual variation where polymath "Professor Brain" (real name, Alan Short) needs to keyboard answers to the random questions during the contestants' five seconds obligatory pause for thought. Beating the Brain brings a prize. One thing the Mockymen have bestowed by saving the world from ruin is a great revival of trivia. Gobble your factory-food and goggle at the screen.

Jamie also takes long walks. He roams central London. I still have no idea how he came to know Zandra and Barnabas originally. When he first took up residence after his reanimation they mostly left him to his own devices, letting him readjust. Latterly they're starting to play mind-games just as they do with the butler and maid. This may lead to some breakthrough—or breakdown. Robert and Milly don't hobnob with Jamie. I think they resent his presence in the house. Of course I only listen to excerpts on playback. By now my comp is programmed with a whole string of contingency key words: dummy, Bliss, Nazis, SS, identity, baby, candle, Norwegian, jigsaws, and so on. A list almost like one of the haiku in the black book.

Basically I think that Zandra and Barnabas have an inner yearning for normality—and Jamie, having become "normal" (though actually very abnormal), represents a sort of lifeline, which they may nevertheless test to see whether it breaks. Zandra and Barnabas have gone quite far out on a limb, first with their body-scarring, then with courier work and the stylized artifice of their current lifestyle. The strain of their work might snap this limb right underneath them, as happens with other couriers. What do they do then? Hole up in their mansion in Middlesex Square for the rest of their lives, aping decadent aristocrats? Or seek a new way of living? I quite admire their protective carapace, and I think I understand why they are helping Jamie.

Jamie seems fascinated by their extremism—moth circling flame—while at the same time they are power-figures for him, protectors yet also prototypes of how he might, well, discover himself. Individualize himself. Jamie tossed himself away into the drug experience. After a high and carefree time he ought to have ended up insipid, humdrum, purged of cravings and temptations. By freak circumstance he has been recycled back into the world.

Still he has not contacted Ruth and Martin Taylor. It's as if his adoptive parents remain as irrelevant to him as when he ran away for his Bliss-year. Maybe irrelevant isn't quite accurate. More as if they might impede him.

A week has gone by since my flying visit to Kielder. Apart from the "coincidence" involving the sculpture park not much extra light has really been shed. I might even believe that Jamie is a sheer anomaly without significance if not for the cluster of oddities: the suicide of the mysterious Knut Alver and Chrissy's cruelty to her infant child and her frenzy in the ice house.

"No, there'd be no point in going to Norway." I agree with H-S on that score.

"It's the plod of surveillance from now on. At least these days you needna sit in a car for hours on end."

True enough. Shoulder-bug to microcopter to voice-canny comp, comp to mobile multiphone, remote downloading if need be. Comp prioritizing excerpts according to key words, though I dip in at random too. If key words crop up in a cluster I'll be beeped. Default to Jock's multiphone if I fail to respond. Map available of Jamie's movements whenever he goes for a walk, courtesy of the whereabouts of the microcopters trailing the bug. With phone and laptop I can carry on surveillance in bed if I feel so inclined. When I go to Daddy's for Christmas I shall stay in touch. And so H-S and I are able to keep this op to ourselves, for our ears only.

Maybe because adrenalin is no longer flowing, and since there's nowhere special to go to (except perhaps Oslo, to wander round a park in midwinter), my interest in Tim Rogers seems to be on the back burner, an impulse which I shall probably not now indulge, as once I did with that strawberry-selling Adonis of Hereford market.

Still, I did let Tim know part of the picture, because of qualities I sensed in him. Paranoid secrecy can be a bit much at times. Altogether too much! I did tell H-S about Tim's part at the ice house and his participation in the interview with Humpty Hugh, and there was no rebuke from H-S, only shrewd interest. There are times when initiative is called for. I can promote Tim to a player if need be, though right now the game seems stalled.

Of course this occupies only part of H-S's attention while I'm involved full time. No analyst colleagues here on the thirtieth floor would dream of asking what I'm doing and since H-S authorized use of a rota of three microcopters tech support will provide them indefinitely without query. The security service has a long tradition of semi-autonomous fiefdoms and far costlier ops than mine, lasting for ages though sometimes providing little in return. Surveillance of suspected Humpties mounted from Vauxhall Bridge takes up loads of time.

MAL holds an office party four days before Christmas in the largest conference room, specially cleared and decorated for the occasion, overspilling into most of the offices and corridor space on the same level. A hideous hot crush, but deemed worth attending by us spooks of the thirtieth floor in case of any scandalous indiscretions, to which such parties are sometimes prone.

Streamers and balloons and holly; some mistletoe mischievously perched over doorways. Jazz quartet, pineapple punch, firkins of beer, *vin ordinaire* and *vol au vents*. The entertainments committee have been busy. Senior civil servants tend to stay away from the Christmas party but the Minister of Alien Affairs, Ted Morgan, puts in a brief appearance, and a couple of Mockymen are present to observe our customs, each with a security person keeping a protective eye. One of those is Tim.

"Any progress?" he asks me. Progress in my enquiry equating with progress in a possible relationship between us? Babble almost drowns his voice. His discretion is either admirable or a trifle presumptuous. The former, I'm inclined to say.

"Not exactly. Not yet." Nodding towards the Mockymen: "Those aliens any problem?"

"Not yet," he echoes me, grinning. Mockyman and Mockywoman are standing together by the wall sharing a paper plate of snacks. "Give them a few years and they'll look less wet behind the ears."

That's perfectly true. Not even the earliest dummies have aged much yet. This lends a spurious sense of greenness and innocence to our alien visitors, belied by their abilities. The Mockywoman can only be eighteen, in body terms. A tiny hole in her lip and several in her ears mark where piercings were removed quite recently.

The jazz players are funking early rock and roll. Lots of bass guitar. No Mockymusic here in the Ministry. Although it's too crowded to dance, some couples are smooching.

Looking out of place, H-S elbows his way through the throng, nursing a cup of punch.

"This is Tim Rogers," I explain.

"Jock Henderson-Smith."

"I know, Sir."

H-S sips and makes a face. "Tell me Rogers, supposing an *assassin* was to burst in here right now, would you drag yon Mockylass to the floor and cover her with your body?"

"It might be more sensible to slot the assassin, Sir."

"Indeed. Suppose your gun jammed. Would you give your own life to save an alien, laddy?"

"Well, it's the job."

"Judicious answer."

A bubbly buxom young woman breezes up to H-S. "Your eminence from upstairs, we're honoured!"

"Ah, Arabella. Father's well, I trust." Without waiting for a reply to what is not really a question: "I think we're more honoured by the presence of two persons from the stars, taciturn though they be. Don't you feel so, Rogers?"

"I feel," says Tim, "employed."

"Aye, it's a job we're talking about."

"Oh I *see*," hisses this Arabella. "Hush-hush business. Excuse me." And off she flounces.

"Her father's a Tory lord," remarks H-S. "What would your politics be then, Rogers, out of curiosity?"

"Only one choice, isn't there, Sir?"

"There are always Tories—and Humpties."

"I didn't know there was any Humpty in parliament—unless Kielder is a sort of government in exile."

"Vote for them, would you, if you could? If it made any sense. If it stood a cat in hell's chance?"

"What, and be out of work?"

"So where are those two aliens staying?"

Tim purses his lips. All around us are people who expedite alien liaison, and H-S is from the thirtieth floor, and senior. Even so, to reveal arrangements at a crowded party . . .

But he murmurs, "The Dorchester."

"At public expense—as befits visitors from outer space, of course. I sometimes wonder what the *real* expense may turn out to be. Do you ever wonder that, Rogers?"

"I don't know enough to give any sort of answer. Do you, Sir?" Has he overstepped the mark? H-S is frowning.

"In your position," Tim says carefully, "I suppose I'd want to find out—if there's anything iffy."

"Aye, maybe you would. What's your tipple?" Is this another trick question?

"I can't drink on duty."

"I mean in general."

"Lager."

"Of course."

And now H-S must be going, back to his bachelor existence.

"Was that some kind of vetting?" Tim asks after he departs.

I can only shrug.

"Done by the boss himself?" he persists.

"Deputy boss, of this bailiwick."

"What's a bailiwick? A code name?"

A question too many.

On December 23rd I catch the Mag-Lev express bound for Newport, where I'll change for Hereford. Walking along the platform in Paddington Station past carriages already crowded, I spy a little oasis of emptiness and promptly board. Cause of emptiness: a Mockywoman, ensconced. In other countries she might be an object of fascination. Pestered with questions? Asked for its autograph? Serenaded? Maybe I exaggerate. Here, in this particular train, she's the last person anyone cares to sit beside or directly opposite.

She. It. The dummy body is a chubby adolescent's. Creamy coffee complexion, short wiry Afro-look blond curls not unlike lamb's wool except where the skull socket shows, a small steel brooch impacted in the side of her cranium. Outfitted with a big woolly hat, she's using this on her lap as a muff in which her hands are plunged. Her hidden fingers move invisibly as though manipulating some puzzle. Maybe she's counting the time till the train leaves. A tan raincoat is buttoned up to the neck, though it's warm in the carriage. Standard-issue black case rests upright on the floor between stockinged, short-booted legs.

Mockymen seem to regard the gender of a dummy as unimportant. Does this lack of preference tell us something about Mockymen society—for instance that by contrast human males and females are like two peas from a pod?—or does it evade giving us any clue?

British reserve is prevailing amongst my fellow passengers, probably masking mild Humpty sentiments. Who will the Watcher or Watchers be in this carriage, keeping an eye on our interstellar guest? After stowing my bag in the space between the backs of the seats I don't in the least mind plumping myself down opposite this alien in borrowed body.

Her black case is in the way.

"Excuse me—"

Shuffling the case aside with clenched knees, she regards me neutrally out of pale eyes.

"Thanks! And Happy Christmas!"

She nods, then says, "Christmas is happy. This is not yet the Christmas Day." Her accent is nasal Brummy.

Full of bonhomie: "Are you going somewhere special for Christmas?"

"I go where this train goes."

Of course, where else? That'll be Cardiff, I suppose.

"Are you taking that body back to its family for Christmas?" I ask brightly.

What a surprise *that* would be. What a grotesque treat. Aside from the fact that the dummy body must hail from the Midlands, not from South Wales.

"The body does not know about family."

"How forgetful of me! Her mind's in nerve-ana, right?" I make nirvana sound like some disease of the nervous system. "So you'll be spending Christmas in a hotel?"

Other passengers are paying attention while pretending not to. A nondescript man in a raincoat watches me quite attentively, as does his similarly clad wife. With a slight shudder the train elevates itself and we move off smoothly.

I must resist the temptation to regard the mind inside the chubby Brummy as remotely conforming to what her body suggests her personality is. "For soul is form, and doth the body make," some poet once wrote. In outward appearance people usually resemble their personality to a remarkable degree. "Soul" might have sculpted this plump adolescent body (or more likely, vice versa) but the mind inside is now utterly different.

"Other guests in the hotel will be eating turkey and wearing paper hats!" I tell the Mockywoman.

Her fingers burrow inside the woolly muff like a knot of worms.

"The ceremony," she says. "The birth of the child who is later nailed to the tree and becomes a dummy—but the spirit from the sky enters him and he walks."

That's one way of looking at it. The Mockywoman seems strangely riven by the crucifixion story, as if it is at once incomprehensible yet cannot entirely be ignored.

"Goodness, that was two thousand years ago, but it almost *anticipates* your coming here like helpful angels." Innocently: "Do dummies ever revive on their own the way Jesus did?"

"New minds must enter all bodies."

I suppose she means all dummy bodies.

"You must have so much more history than us! A hundred thousand years?"

Already we're passing the big empty common backed by Wormwood Scrubs prison and Hammersmith Hospital and various sports grounds. Someone is flying a kite on the common, and so am I.

"A million years?"

"This is not communicable."

"Is that because a very long history has no meaning? None of it matters in the long run?"

"True." She may merely be agreeing so as to foreclose further discussion.

"What *does* matter most?"

The chubby dummy considers a while. "Continuing signifies. Persisting."

That's true enough. Continue and persist. Sounds stoical to me; but Mockymen have never behaved much like party animals despite their bestowal of Bliss, for a purpose.

"It must be confusing for you having a different body," I suggest. "Different bodies on different worlds. When you get back to your original body that must feel odd too."

She merely stares at me. Me in my body, one and the same, all together. A sudden creepy thought occurs: that maybe this alien has no "own" original body at all, sustained on life-support somewhere amongst the stars. No body to go back to, any more. Maybe the mind in the dummy is ancient. Surely not—who would risk her ancient mind in a host body on a rather barbaric planet where Humpties might take a pot shot? Unless of course for high stakes.

So how are new Mockymen born?

"Do you have children?" I ask her. Pups, wormlings, spawn, whatever.

"This body has no baby in it."

It's now that something bizarre happens. The communicating door sighs open, admitting Santa Claus—in the person of a tall, slim, black dude with a dippy grin on his face, dressed in a Yuletide costume and toting a string bag full of red and green Christmas crackers.

"Black Santa's here from the Coal Pole!" this newcomer sings out. "To make you *coool* at Yule! Why hello, Miss Ectoplasm," he greets a blond lass clad in a white coat, lipstick and nail varnish to match. Thrusting a cracker at her: "Shake with Santa, break it with Santa."

Is Black Santa an entertainer hired by the railway company? Such a gamut of expressions in the carriage: some people studying the scenery as if nothing is happening, others smothering nervous grins, none sure how to react. Parents are trying to curb their off-spring's enthusiasm. That black chap seems amiable, but is also mad or high on ganja or a Blisshead? The target of his attention takes hold of the Christmas cracker uncertainly.

"Do you, um, have a grant for this?" she asks.

"Does he have a permit?" enquires Mr Nondescript.

"Yo, I'm Double-Oh-Seven, permitted to thrill! But ah am in disguise today." The end of the cracker slips out of the lass's hand as Santa tugs. He mimes staggering back, flailing, almost losing his balance. People duck but he bumps nobody.

"Takes two to snap a crack—try again."

Now his gaze lights on the Mockywoman, and he sashays forward.

"Hey, it's a Santa from the Stars! Bringin' all de gifts we could desire. Looks like you had a shock, brown-skin girl. Your hair's gone all white." Peering at her skull socket: "I see someone screwed with your head. So pull a cracker."

One of the Mockywoman's hands wriggles out of the muff.

"What is this?"

"Grip it. Got goodies inside. Hold tight, test your strength. Miss Ectoplasm back there, she's too delicate."

The two Watchers are on the alert as the Mockywoman complies, crushing the end of the cardboard. Santa jerks. Cracker rips with a *bang*, startling the Mockywoman.

"Illegal assault! Raise alarm!" Sounds like the recorded voice of a car security gadget. The Watchers do not overreact. They know what a cracker is.

Santa looms over me now.

"You see any assault?"

On the seat by the Mockywoman lie a rolled-up orange paper hat and a tiny plastic elephant. The Mockywoman still clutches her section of cracker like a broken gun.

"Complaint, disorder, riot, ailment—"

"It is all right," I assure the alien, loudly for the benefit of the Watchers. "No harm is happening." My own words seem stilted and alien.

"To hear dummies talk," Santa addresses the carriage at large. "It's a symptom of a syndrome. Name of the syndome is schizophrenia. Government says they come out of a hole in Jekyll and Hyde Park, but it is not so! There is an epi-demic of schizos." His finger stabs at the Mockywoman. "Primo, you lie zonked out— then up you bob hyped to go." Two fingers now. "Duo, thinking you're under alien control. Trio, voices in your heads. Four-o, wonky grammar. All signs, my friends, all signs. There's no aliens inside you, there's just your own minds all broken up from usin' Bliss."

This is quite ingenious avoidance-thinking on Santa's part. He may have undergone therapy, or maybe he worked in an asylum, picking up jargon, becoming an amateur authority on disorders. Mockymen aren't aliens at all—oh there *were* those original Mocky-Lemurs from the pod-ship, you could see on TV that those were real aliens; but thereafter, it's all in the mind. If only.

"So why," I feel bound to ask Black Santa, "does the government let these supposed schizos roam around where they please? That's not only our own government. It's governments all over the world."

I never get an answer to my question. Abruptly the train is slowing. Santa is off-balance for real, dropping his bag of crackers, clutching for the back of the seat on which lie party hat and plastic toy. We're coming to a halt in West Drayton station. On the platform a couple of policemen in radio-linked hard hats and fleecy blue-grey blousons are staring into the carriages passing them by.

Santa Claus in a red gown isn't hard to spot. Soon the officers are with us.

It seems unfair to be arresting Santa, even if he is loopy and bothering people. Imagine instead employing him to rack his brains about the motives of the aliens.

But anyway. Fare Avoidance, Public Disorder, Breach of the Peace, et cetera. I assume Santa was spotted boarding at the last moment. Maybe he vaulted a ticket barrier in Paddington.

"Illegal assault!" whines the chubby Mockygirl with the white afro.

Et cetera now includes Menacing a Mockymen.

"No, that isn't true, Officer. I have been sitting right here all the time."

"Are you acquainted with the offender, Madam?"

I could pull out a warrant card, outranking any regular police procedures; but the alien might wonder about my motives.

Santa cackles. "Madam don't know me from *Adam!* I'm Black Santa from the Pole of Coal."

The other officer scans the carriage as if hopeful that a voice will denounce me. Most people avoid meeting his eye-shielded gaze.

"She friendly." Mockymen speech sometimes does seem like that of schizophrenics, infantile and faulty in grammar. Not always, but now and then.

"Too much friendly," adds the faux-girl. "I need to think."

What about, what about?

"You had better shift your seat, Madam."

"Where to? There's nowhere else."

"That isn't my problem, Madam. Leave this Mockymen alone."

"So I'll stand." I haul my bag to the end of the carriage and lean against the partition.

After the officers have led Santa away and the Mag-Lev moves off again I return to my previous seat, occasioning a mild smattering of applause, though not from Mr and Mrs Nondescript.

The pale eyes of the Mockywoman regard me. "You do not obey. You do not fear penalties."

"I need a seat, that's all."

She shuts her eyes and hums to herself. Mute Mockymusic.

Because of the thrumming of the train and the buzz of conversations in this almost full carriage I seem to be in a hive hurtling west —a hive containing an intruder, sure enough, but the alien in her mimicry is humming along with the other bees.

This crowded hive, this social engine, is heading towards the future. I know no one in it personally, yet I am a part of it, part of society; and society is immense, comprising billions of mortals, even after the deaths of the dire decade—which in percentage terms did not really cut too much of a swathe—and irrespective of a downturn in fertility; still huge, still hurtling futurewards. If I should die, a multitude of lives will continue braiding onward, a great rope of continuing history. Individual strands start and cease but the rope as a whole endures, the cable of continuity. Before the Mockymen came it seemed the rope might tear asunder, but surely not now.

Mummy died in the superflu, Daddy will die presently, Tony shows no signs of perpetuating the family name, and in another few years I shall be slipping past the age for kids even if I feel the need. Our strand will end, yet the great braid will persist so that in a sense my signature will remain writ upon time, however faintly and minor, a vicarious participation in future events.

Persist, says the Mockywoman. Persist. A million other species on this planet persisted longer than we have, to date. What might the persistence of aliens cost us?

This sense of myself as part of society is something I have not experienced before so immediately and viscerally, so interwoven with my identity. The insight comes as a surprise, an astonishment. Maybe here's the first touch of death, the first intimation. Yes, in-Tim-ation! Tim could become a parent, perhaps, not merely a prospective lover.

Even a child of mine would not matter much compared with the greater continuity, the engine of the human world enduring energetically, me for the time being a small cog in it, a little parcel of fuel and substance consuming herself as part of this progress.

Chapter 14

Daddy is waiting in the station car park, in his adapted Volvo.

Since I last saw him three months ago he has let his silvering hair grow a bit longer than the military crop I'm used to. Same twinkle in his eyes, of pleasure at seeing me, though he's reticent as ever when away from the sanctuary of home. Good journey? Fine. You look well, Anna. You too, Daddy. Customary small talk.

As usual he detours through the centre of town right past the Cathedral. The famous Mappa Mundi is in the museum at the west front: the confined 13th century view of a flat Earth centered on Jerusalem, long before we dreamed of worlds called Melody and Passion, about which we know far less than the old monks knew about Africa or China. The sky's clearing nicely in time for a splendid sunset. Ruddy golden light shafts from the direction of the Black Mountains and Wales upon the pinnacled ecclesiastical masonry. Soon after we cross the narrow old river bridge, we turn east on to a B road leading down the Wye Valley. D road, more like, bumpy and rough with tarmac psoriasis. Already wintry dark is creeping upon us.

Cattle in the fields are white-faced shadows. Elderly cider-apple orchards loom like big reefs of dried grimy coral, but I know that I'm in golden territory, and home, where the lazily looping Wye wends through meadows. In the headlights: a huge knot of mistletoe in a skeleton-tree, the parasite we have chosen to symbolize love and affection.

Withyhope village is night-shrouded by the time we arrive. Fairylights twinkle in windows, holly wreaths hang on doors. Down the lane we lurch to Cwmbach Cottage, which in fact is a substantial timber-framed and plastered house, black and white, with tall redbrick chimneys. "Come back, come back," whispers its name, though actually the Welsh word means little valley. Back I have come yet again.

There's a glass of port for me and an Isle of Jura single malt for Daddy.

"Tony mentioned he'd seen you. Surprise trip to Kielder to visit Hugh Ellison, eh?"

I nod. "You know, a funny thing happened on the Mag-Lev." I tell him about the Mockywoman and Black Santa, including that stoical alien philosophy regarding persistence.

"I suppose," Daddy says, "being able to swap your body when you please is a neat way of persisting. I wouldn't mind swapping this body for a younger one. Maybe the Mockymen are immortal and there aren't so very many of them. Just a few million in the universe." This thought seems to uplift him.

A log fire burns in the lounge, for cheer as much as for warmth. Bit of a haul for Daddy to carry in logs when the electric heating is perfectly adequate, but he has done so for me—just as he has brought out the artificial fir tree and hung baubles all over it. The mantleshelf is packed with Christmas cards, many of them treasured old ones. The card I sent by special YulePost has pride of place: a 3-D scene of skaters in perpetual motion on a frozen lake. Lean years and electromail mostly killed off greetings cards but they're making a comeback. Triumph of trivia, or of the human heart.

I *want* to tell him about my enigma, Jamie. I need keep nothing from Daddy. He must feel at such a loose end, retired, out of action, going to dine with the Regiment occasionally, occupying himself with history books and memories. On the sideboard in a black frame stands Mummy's photo amid her collection of china miniatures of poultry, a hundred bright-plumed birds. We kept a few beady-eyed hens when I was young. I do want Daddy to feel in touch.

"Just between you and me and the fireplace, the reason why I went to see Humpty Hugh is quite strange—"

*   *   *

Naturally I omit details such as the chip in Jamie's shoulder. Afterwards, Daddy says softly, "So your Jock Whatnot believes in the
agent provocateur approach . . ."

"How do you mean?"

"Telling Hugh Ellison you have misgivings about MAL. You and
Jock Whatnot don't have misgivings, do you?"

"H-S regrets internment, but we can't have amateur activitists
indulging in agitprop and causing incidents."

"As opposed to *professional* activists? This Jamie business . . .
you're devoting a lot of energy ferreting around, to find what? A
chink in the Mockymen facade?"

"If dummies recover spontaneously, MAL doesn't understand
everything."

He sighs. "Anna, we know as much about the Mockymen as
natives gleefully clutching smallpox-doped blankets. That's in my
humble opinion, which counts for nothing at all. I wouldn't mind
another splash of Jura before dinner."

Which I shall be fixing. There's half a salmon in the fridge.
Poached, the fish'll be. Oh not by some naughty villager from out
of the reviving Wye. That is how I shall cook it.

I dream well, and I usually remember what I dream. By dreaming
"well" I mean that I am comfortable with myself in my dreams.

I suffer no haunting if—for instance—Jane from Oxford days
features in a dream, Jane whom I sent to Kielder (in itself no
great injury compared with murdering the anti-alien lobby as in a
certain South American country). One recurrent dream affords me
exuberant intricate adventures followed by an escape into sweet and
rewarding privacy.

Typically the architecture of my dreams is that of a huge city
designed by, say, De Chirico: a maze of sun-drenched arcades and
piazzas, rotundas, cafés, boulevards lined with enigmatic statuary,
and college cloisters and quadrangles. Accessible from cloisters
and quadrangles are elaborate libraries based on memories of my
college library and the Bodleian, with many ups and downs and
galleries and rooms leading into rooms, on and on.

Thrilling intrigues are afoot in this city. People whisper to me
and whisper about me. Bizarre events need investigating. Guns are
fired during pursuits and escapes. Quite often I'm being chased,
though I always elude capture. The complexity of the dream events
is something I relish rather than these being a cause of frustration.

In any of the libraries there is always a secret room known only to myself, resembling a priest's hole but a bit bigger. I can reach it from a gallery overlooking a reading room, by swivelling a bookcase or by sliding a panel aside, revealing a narrow, twisting, dwarf-scale staircase. This leads up into the sanctuary room, where a small window overlooks a courtyard. I am very secure in my room, very comfortable and contented.

Last night, unusually, Daddy was part of a four-man patrol dressed in camouflage clothing who were hunting me. Daddy had a wooden leg. One trouser leg was cut away, revealing a contraption of wood and straps helping him gimp along. He was carrying a rolled blanket.

"I only want to give you this blanket," he called out, "so you shan't be cold in your room." How did he know about my room?

Wrapped in the blanket was a huge salmon, head protruding. Behind a pillar lurked Black Santa.

"Watch out for the fishy, Miss Dishy!" he called out cheekily. "It got a mind of its own."

"What sort of mind's that then, Santa?"

"A Mocky-mind! That fish is a dummy."

The salmon writhed and gasped. Being slippery, it might escape, hence the blanket.

"Where did you get that fish?" I shouted to Daddy.

"We caught it. I'm going to grill it in the library. You need the blanket for your room."

Black Santa had become Rogers. We were inside a library now. Hastily we climbed an oak staircase to a wrought-iron gallery. Below, the three able-bodied members of the team began building a barbecue out of books. The big salmon flopped about on the floor, protesting in a gurgly voice, "Complaint complaint!" Daddy started mounting the staircase with difficulty, empty blanket in hand.

"Anna, you need this to cover you while we grill the fish—"

I showed Rogers the way into my hidey-hole. Up we squirmed into the private room.

"Nobody can find us here," I promised.

"But Miss Sharman, there's no *blanket*. Nothing to lie on. How can we make love?"

I began to laugh at our dilemma.

Daddy and I enjoyed a quiet, affectionate cosy Christmas. My presents to him were a first edition of Jonathan Swift's *History of the Four Last Years of the Queen*, plus a box of liqueur chocolates which we polished off between us.

Before I came across the volume in an antiquarian shop in

Charing Cross Road, I had never realized that the author of *Gulliver's Travels* wrote a genuine history book. I couldn't help fancying that here was a Mocky-title concealing a different text within, in the way that a respectable Victorian daddy might have a volume of French pornography rebound for his library with an innocuous title tooled upon the spine. That's why I bought it. In fact the queen in question proved to be Anne of two and a half centuries ago. Here was a double bluff: a book which appeared to be a hoax but was actually authentic. Really, it belonged in my dream library.

Daddy's present to me was a gorgeous kimono, sprays of cherry blossom on the front and on the rear an incredible Samurai.

Stepping towards someone, I would be bouquets of soft pink petals. Turn my back, and I would be an armoured warrior, though only a silken one. In the boutique in Hereford's olde worlde Church Street where he bought this, said Daddy, the manageress told him of a Japanese proverb: As the cherry blossom is to flowers, so is a Samurai among people. In Japan maybe transvestites wear such kimonos, because its sexuality seems ambiguous. I wore it most of Christmas morning over my day clothes till it was time to start the turkey, a modest-sized bird which would only take three hours.

On Boxing Day Daddy drove me into Hereford to catch the train.

Back here in my flat in Hampstead, while a Sibelius symphony plays, I sit in the kimono and I think about Daddy in my dream "grilling" a captive Mocky-creature and Tony's shock at my turning up at Kielder, and him reporting my visit to Daddy (though this was perfectly natural), and Tony being unable to be with us on Christmas Day but due to keep Daddy company on New Year's Eve. My subconscious says that something is fishy. Telling Daddy about Jamie may have been a grave error.

If I drive to Herefordshire on the last day of the year—or rather, if I *have myself* driven to Withyhope village because I may be going into an uncertain situation—it will be to peep at Come-Back Cottage to reassure myself that only Daddy and Tony are present, then we can slip away again, Tim Rogers and I.

I may of course be fantasizing to infuse new zest, in which case Daddy deserves better from his daughter than shitty suspicions! (Two-sided, eh Anna? A bit like the splendid kimono I gave you?)

No, I do have genuine misgivings, compounded by my having foolishly told Daddy about Jamie. I missed the signals but my subconscious did not.

Mulling this over, I let a few days pass before I contact Rogers. A problem connected with the investigation. A rather private problem, best discussed at my home.

Meanwhile Mary of Morogoro sent a home-made Christmas card, which arrived late although sent early enough: a drawing of an elephant pulling a sleigh loaded with presents. It would take a jumbo jet to heave enough gifts to satisfy local needs.

I try to imagine Morogoro from Mary's descriptions and drawings. Hills, heat and dust, corrugated roofs, rutted red road, baobab trees dangling pods, some wild animals still surviving. Another world. The nearest transit station is in Kenya, in Nairobi. Tanzania will not allow Bliss within its borders, nor any of its citizens to be dummies. Proud, anticolonial, and poor.

In the evening, I shower, then don my new kimono, belting it tight. The carpet pleasantly tickles my toes.

When Rogers arrives—brown leather jacket, thick tartan shirt, stone-washed jeans—I exclaim, "Are you early? I just got out of the shower."

"Early for what?" He eyes my kimono. "I see I didn't need to bring a bunch of flowers."

Nor has he.

"My father gave me this for Christmas." I spin around. "He's Major Donald Sharman."

Rogers's blue eyes narrow. "And your other side puts up a fight, hmm?"

"No, I wouldn't say so." Rough sex isn't to my taste.

He nods, understanding me.

"What did you get for Christmas, Tim?"

"Nothing much. Not yet."

I know from records that he is separated from a partner, and has no kids. Name of ex-partner: Maria-Constanza Nicolazzini, an Italian girl, probably glamorous, perhaps inconstant.

"Let's sit and talk about my problem." Here on this sofa covered with a pastel green throw reminding me of misty fields. "I got in some lager. Or I have wheat beer."

"Lager's fine."

"You can smoke a cigar if you like."

"Only when I'm in the open, thanks."

We are not in the open quite yet.

*   *   *

I draw my right leg up under my left leg, curling my toes against the back of the knee, the other knee pointed at him, obstacle or invitation.

"I was at my father's for Christmas, Tim. I think Daddy and my brother may be involved with Humpties. I think they plan to kidnap a Mockyman and grill it to make it talk."

"If they're found out, they face the high jump."

"Exactly."

"Which would compromise you. *Not* the major consideration, of course, when family's at risk."

"Quite. I need to reassure myself that these suspicions are empty —that I'm just being paranoid."

"If you aren't, would the deputy boss be able to intervene?"

"The trouble is, stupidly I told my father about Jamie, so this is a touchy matter."

He glances at my exposed knee, with a desire which he is bridling.

"I thought I was giving Daddy a sense of connection. Now the *reason* why Jamie matters—"

"Oh dear. Is this it?"

Take a deep breath. "This is it. Are you game? Or you could leave. It's up to you."

"Tell me, what turned you on to the service? Was it glamour— the thrill of being a manipulator? A thrill that's frustrated by routines and," chuckling, even though he's in earnest, "endless legwork?"

"I do think there was some idealism involved. And some despair as well, at the way the world was going. I think that remains true. I feel something may be deeply wrong."

"You can be the pivot, putting it right. Not a cog but a pivot— even if it's way out of bounds. I can't decide if you're basically a romantic or an utter cynic."

And neither can I!

"How do you define romantic?"

"A person whose quest can cause trouble."

"Would you step out of bounds?"

After a moment, he nods. "In for a penny."

So I tell him about the dummy spontaneously reviving.

Presently he says, "So there's a black project going on. Within the service, lurking inside of MAL. Operation Alien."

"Any chink in the armour. Any hole in their security screen. Any anomaly. This could vitally concern the human race itself, not just national interests. And we don't want Humpties screwing it up."

"That's you and the deputy boss and how many others in high places? I suppose that's a silly question to ask."

I don't want him to harbour illusions. "It may not be many people at all."

I don't know who else H-S recruited except for one person, that being Jonathan Lascelles, currently one of our UN delegation in New York. To the best of my knowledge Max Adams at Hyde Park isn't one of us, nor anyone who was involved in testing Jamie; they were just doing a job for H-S, results for his eyes only (and for mine). I don't know whether H-S was the initiator or whether any government minister is involved because I never had a need to know.

The twinkle in Tim's eyes is quite disarming. "That makes this all the more romantic, doesn't it?" He finishes his lager and sets the empty glass down. Me, I have hardly touched my own glass of port. "Supposing Humpties do kidnap a Mockyman for grilling, can you—can we—um, muscle in on the act?"

"It may not be so simple . . ."

The alien may be able to send a distress signal more clamorous than the woman on the Mag-Lev's verbal protests. Telepathy between Mockyminds is an outside possibility. Another far-out possibility is that a distressed Mockyman might be able, by an act of will, to reconfigure the residue of nanomimetic Bliss in the body it wears into some sort of beacon. We have to consider all possibilities, when the downside might be the withdrawal of alien patronage from our country; or other sanctions unknown.

"Right," says Tim, "I'll check a car out of the pool on New Year's Eve morning—just an ordinary car. And we'll spy on Major Sharman, and prove you wrong."

"We should get into position earlier than that. Spend the previous night in Cheltenham."

"In a spare room at GCHQ?" He's joking, of course. The Government Communications Headquarters gathers and analyses data on alien activities in foreign countries, friendly or not so friendly, but ours is a private eavesdropping operation.

"I was thinking more of a hotel." I shift my position. "Do you speak Italian, by the way, Tim?"

"You ought to know, since you've been reading my file."

"I thought you might have picked some Italian up, from . . ."

"Maria-Constanza. *Grazie, avanti, ravioli*. Not what you'd call speaking."

"Just as well we don't need Italian in Cheltenham or Hereford. What was she like?"

"What went wrong, you mean?"

"Something of the sort."

For a moment I think there'll be reticence; but no.

"I called her Stanza—she was a bit of poetry to me. The wrong lips came to utter her. She conned me."

"I was at school in Cheltenham."

"School, as in schoolgirls?"

"That's right."

"Posh school?"

"Posh enough. My father keeps no dog to bark or bother you. He has a false hip—couldn't walk a dog as much as a dog needs."

"So we don't need to take a drugged beefsteak with us."

"Oh, and he has an illicit pistol. A SIG-Sauer 9-millimetre P226."

"How do I recognize your brother if there are more people than him and your father there? Does he look like you?"

Curtains are bound to be closed at Daddy's, though in the event of a chink Tim will have a mini-camera with him, as well as a limpet-mike to sucker itself to the wall.

"What do *I* look like?" I ask him.

And now he proceeds to discover.

By New Year's Eve the weather has taken a sudden cold turn. Freak wind gusts in from the Arctic. By tomorrow very likely the temperature will be mild again. Which is worse: warmth and storms, or an honest, old-fashioned, skin-cutting chill? Daddy sometimes speaks as if the cold winters of the past equated with moral fibre and discipline. Well, here's a taste of bygone days.

Tim and I are snug in this car with tinted windows, as we enter Withyhope. We're both wearing dark police outfits: the fleecy blousons rated for mountaineering, the warm waterproof trousers with breathable membrane; and a couple of military-issue, woolly hats, the rims of which we can pull down. Last night and this morning Tim and I were snug as bugs in rugs in Cheltenham, lying in late because we would be staying up late. In bed, we listened in on Middlesex Square. Barnabas was away on a courier trip to Passion. Zandra came back home from Melody, all tensed up, and snapped at Jamie, then, oddly, apologized.

The Cider Press pub is all up lit and alive, visibly packed.

Despite the keen wind the door stands wide open. There must be such human heat and fug in there.

Come back, come back: down the lane we are coming almost silently, lights doused, towards Cwmbach Cottage. If Daddy and Tony are fooling with Humpties, what's to be done to protect them? "At the end, Tim: look."

In a way it's worse than I feared. Or is it, perhaps, better? Two unfamiliar cars stand in the driveway but in front of the house itself are a couple of Land Rangers—as used by the Regiment. Unmarked of course. This might still be an innocent New Year's Eve party, though neither Daddy nor Tony mentioned any such thing. SAS officers, giving aid and comfort to Humpties? Hardly bears thinking about. Or does it? Two hundred yards short of the house, we stop.

"Do I turn around for a quick getaway?"

"No, I'll take the wheel. This lane goes down across a shallow ford then out through fields, and joins a road. If there's any trouble I'll blaze down and pick you up. Remember to get the registration numbers."

He tucks us in flush with the hedgerow. Once he's out I shuffle across.

I do catch one glimpse of Tim, a brief movement of darkness, no more, which is as it should be. The mike comes alive and I hear the natter within the lounge. It's all recording. Tim will have hidden the little scrambler-booster radio unit in thick hedge or wherever. Into the cellular phone network goes the signal. After he gets back we'll park a couple of miles away in a lay-by and eavesdrop for a while.

Someone's talking about Dehib, the drug that releases a person from inhibitions.

"Trouble is, the person might just start masturbating like a monkey—"

No doubt about it: conspiracy to kidnap. Or maybe dope a Mockyman by trickery and pretend to be paramedics assisting it. Its dummy might be malfunctioning. How disorienting for it.

If they are still undecided on means of interrogation they cannot be too far advanced in planning an abduction. Maybe all they ever do is chin-wag, although the presence of those two Land Rangers suggests serious attitude. It's just after nine when I see Tim ducking back towards our car and shift myself over into the passenger seat again.

Tony is talking. Tony, here from Kielder where Humpty Hugh

roosts in his wheelchair, and other harder cases than Mr Ellison. The car bomb which exploded near Marble Arch shortly after the opening of the transit station was denounced by Humpty Hugh, not long before his internment. In fact that bomb was the trigger for internment, and we almost certainly did not put it there to excuse stern measures.

It's ten o'clock. The car engine purrs to keep us warm.

I hear Daddy say, "My daughter tells me, about a month ago at Hyde Park a dummy revived of its own accord—"

Shit, shit.

"Shit," murmurs Tim aloud.

Of a sudden my phone burbles. At this time on *New Year's Eve?*

"Anna Sharman here."

"Anna, it's Jock—" Such urgency in his voice. Has he ever used his first name with me before? "Where are you?"

"I'm near Hereford."

"But you went there for Christmas!"

"I needed to come back again." Cwmbach, Cwmbach. "What's wrong?"

"Has your comp not paged you?"

"Not a peep."

"It paged me all right! I'm at MAL, Anna—get here as fast as you can. On the way, replay Jamie from about eight o'clock. *Have you your own transport?*"

"Yes—"

It's an alert, our first ever. Key-word density in the vicinity of Jamie's chip has triggered this. The software decided I'm too far away to bother with, damn programming flaw only shows up now. Of course H-S won't go into details on a phone.

"Be careful, the streets are hectic tonight."

"Jock . . . I'm with Tim Rogers. He's involved."

"Damn glad to hear it. Another pair of hands."

Chapter 15

And as I was to discover later:

On Barnabas Mason's journey home from the Hyde Park Transit Station, a crowd of partying Blissheads were blocking Oxford Street. The driver of the bright new hovercab—a middle-aged Sikh, wearing the traditional turban—halted his vehicle where sprawling young bodies gaped up at the sky. A rocket exploded. Its bang, followed by a cascade of lights, seemed like some awful migrainous discharge in Barnabas's brain. People rarely used to shoot off fireworks on New Year's Eve when he was a kid.

The gust from the cab's skirt blew rubbish about. To let in some fresh air he thumbed down the window, but only briefly—the breeze was so raw. The Blissheads couldn't care less.

Mr Singh (what doubt could there be about a Sikh's name?) hit the horn a few times, and the cab mooed loudly like some cow impatient to reach its parlour and be milked.

A policewoman waved the cab onward over the lolling bodies. Unless anyone sat up suddenly, they wouldn't be injured. The battering from the downdraught might seem a splendid massage.

They passed Centre Point, lighthouse in the heart of the city. New Oxford Street was fairly clear of revellers. When the cab finally floated into Middlesex Square, however, the small oval park in the centre was full of flesh.

Mockymusic wailed. A bonfire burned low. Flames licked from

hot embers, remains of the woody old briar roses—many were conspicuously absent from the flower beds. Up from an empty wine bottle whooshed a rocket, to burst above the rooftops. Like fallout from a steel-smelting furnace silver stars showered.

Eyeing the fun were a couple of private security men who could not have made much effort to stop the square being invaded. Summon riot police? The whole centre of London was one big anarchic street party. In fact those security boys seemed to enjoy seeing this little paradise being trashed. *Nothing we could do about it, Squire!* The sight of so much bare flesh must appeal, too.

Barnabas had come back to London in the midst of something resembling a Roman Saturnalia. Ring in the year of 2016. Salute it with pyrotechnics and orgy.

Outside the mansion which he shared with Zandra Wilde half a dozen youths dressed only in luminous Day-Glo loincloths capered in a circle, lashing out at one another with thin whips as though such exertion might banish the chill of the night. Actually they were shivering with delight, not on account of the cold. No pain, no pain. Delirium. Rapture. Bliss.

As Mr Singh deflated the cab's skirts he lamented: "The world's going to the dogs." People probably made the same comment century after century.

"It already went to the dogs and come back again."

Singh was incensed. "Mockymen have taken over, mark my words! Just look at these young fools squandering themselves—only to become dummies!"

"Very few of them."

"My son, sir, my own son—!"

"So your son's become a host body? I'm sorry. He still exists, Mr Singh. He's in a nirvana state. Perfect peace, perfect bliss." Perfect nothing.

"That's what the Mockymen tell us! But no, Jogindar hasn't become a dummy *yet*."

"In that case very likely he won't. Within a year he'll be immune to Bliss."

And immune to most bodily sensations, having burnt up a lifetime's capacity for pleasure in one prolonged spasm, rather as the roses were torched for a quick thrill.

"You're a courier, aren't you? This house . . . You're rich. You condone our boys and girls using Bliss."

Barnabas ached to be inside, in calm and quiet. The accusation angered him.

"If only *I* could use Bliss, man! All I know is pain."

"Not a father's pain."

By the bonfire two adolescents, boy and girl, stripped naked. Stepping on to hot embers, they began fondling. Mind over body. Joy banishing harm to skin and flesh and lungs. The little flames caressed so pleasantly.

Just so long as they didn't stay in the fire *too* long.

"It's disgusting," snarled Singh. "Obscene. Filthy!"

Irritated, Barnabas payed Singh without tipping him and stepped out of the cab. Already the skirts were inflating as though intent on knocking the departing passenger aside. Squeezing the remote in his pocket, Barnabas hurried past the flagellants to his front door.

Zandra was dining by candlelight. Robert the Man was in attendance, in black frockcoat, grey trousers, starched linen shirt with bow tie, white gloves. Milly the Maid wore her frilly costume, bobbly blond curls spiralling down from a lace cap. Although nearly forty, she carried this image off to perfection. In the holo-arena on its podium black American dancers as etherially tall as basketball players performed *Swan Lake*. Such *jetés* worthy of Nijinsky from the Harlem Ballet. Robert ducked his head in a quick bow. Milly curtsied to Barnabas.

Zandra exclaimed, "Barabbas!" She was wearing her low-cut cream satin gown. A diamond necklace glittered against her lovely, scarified, milk-chocolate skin, jewels upon a patterned brocade of flesh. She had only toyed with her dessert, a slice of rich white pashka cake studded with candied peel. An open bottle of Champagne stood in the chiller. Gorgonzola sweated on a board like a sizeable biopsy sample of diseased lung tissue.

Ritual elegance mattered deeply to Zandra, so Barnabas kissed her raised hand before his lips brushed against her cheek, notched with its tribal-style scars.

"How was it?" she asked.

"Excruciating as usual."

"Ex-cruc-iating." She lingered over the word. "That means being tortured on a cross. Or being racked." A smile in Robert's direction seemed predatory and glacial.

The butler hastily asked, "Will you be dining, Master Barnabas?"

Only Zandra used the nickname Barabbas. Their little joke. The bandit who escaped crucifixion—whereas Barnabas was crucified anew on every trip. As was Zandra. As were all couriers. Unless they quit.

"So what has your mother cooked?" Barnabas was hardly hungry after his ordeal.

"Poached salmon, sir, with steamed asparagus. Followed by spatchcock guinea fowl, and then . . ." Yes, the pashka.

Robert's mother performed her feats of cooking down in the basement servants' flat. No need for her to mingle with the masters, unlike Robert and Milly who were such *treasures* in their willingness to enact a charade of old-fashioned butler and maid. These roles must afford them a sense of comfort and security, whatever playful menace they were obliged to tolerate.

"Bring me just a little, Robert."

Keep the rest as perk for yourselves. Luxury food was part of the extravagant chic, compensation for the pains of couriers. If Robert and family weren't in the employ of Zandra and Barnabas, they might be eating factory food.

"Will you be dressing first, sir?"

"Of course." How could he sit at table in a black jump-suit?

Two places were set. One was Zandra's. Fish knife and fork were absent from the other, though this would be remedied.

"Jamie only had some salmon," observed Barnabas.

"I suppose I upset him earlier on."

"Zandra dear, there are flagellants outside."

She toyed with a knife. Simply a hooked pronged cheese knife, true.

"Shall we invite them inside to perform for us and Jamie?" she asked archly. "Greet the new year, in style?"

Milly was trying not to notice how Zandra played with the knife.

Barnabas's jump-suit hid his own scars: the plumed angel wings arching down his back as if about to unfurl from his skin, an effect which had been difficult to achieve relying on mirrors.

"Shall we invite them, Barabbas?" Zandra was amusing herself at Milly's expense. She despised immature amateur flagellants, because Blissheads experienced no insightful pain. At times such as this, after trips, the two of them might behave like a pair of vampires who employ vulnerable human servants. Mostly they were impeccable polite, and they did pay very generously.

It was Zandra who invited Jamie into the house fourteen months earlier, on a whim.

At the far side of the park in Middlesex Square stood a semi-abstract sculpture. A man was running, bowed forward, a boy perched upon the saddle of his rump. Depending on angle and light it might seem that someone was riding a two-legged dinosaur through the park. Alternatively, man and boy appeared mixed together anatomically, legs and arms confused.

On three successive mornings Zandra saw Jamie staring at the sculpture, either standing or sitting huddled in a donkey jacket for an hour or more.

Tousled fair hair, fresh open countenance: the youth looked seventeen, eighteen. What could be so special for him about that piece of sculpture? On the fourth day of the vigil, despite drizzle curiosity carried Zandra outdoors, clad in long purple velvet robe and spike-heeled boots. The youth gawked at her facial scars and her great frizz of hair cut like the sarcophagus headpiece of an Egyptian queen—into which a mouse had munched a little tunnel at the bottom of which was her skull socket. She was an apparition.

"Would you like some coffee when you've finished here?"

Hauntedly, he nodded.

"I mean indoors, out of the weather, not on the doorstep."

"Indoors. . . ?" He seemed nervous of her invitation, a wild animal which must be coaxed and lured. Scamper off, puppy dog, before it's too late!

"I shan't *eat* you, boy."

He stared at her scars.

"My butler will serve us coffee." See: there is more than merely me in the house. "So have you finished yet?"

Her poise and bearing subdued him.

"I suppose so."

In the pink room Jamie perched on the Victorian spoon-back chair fastidiously as if wary of creating a mess. The drum table, on which Robert had placed a tray bearing cafetière and plate of amoretto biscuits, separated Jamie from Zandra as though she was a clairvoyant and he her customer—for a sign of the zodiac decorated each of the round table's twelve drawers, implying a fortune-telling game.

On the wall, an ornately framed sepia photograph showed an Indian holy man hanging prone from a scaffold, fleshhooks in his shoulders, back, and calves. Hands steepled prayerfully, the Sadhu appeared about to be launched by this apparatus into the unknown, even though he could move nowhere without ripping his flesh. Jamie would not look that way more than once.

"I don't know who I am," he confessed. "There's no way to find out."

"You have lost your memory?"

"No. Or maybe."

"That sculpture in the park reminds you of something?"

"Yes! It's so out of focus."

"It *is* a bit abstract."

He had run away from home, so it transpired, because he could not discover himself at home. He sought out Blissheads because amongst Blissheads he could find free shelter and he wondered whether a sort of joyful oblivion would be preferable to the torment of identity-crisis. Find yourself with us, a girl had invited. She and Blisshead friends were living in a squat near Euston Station.

As yet, he had not taken Bliss. Instead he roamed and he had come across this square with its garden and granite sculpture. He might have dreamed of this garden and the granite man and boy. Or rather, the place itself seemed a dream, a distorted aspect of some grander original, which he ought to know.

"That boy emerges from the man as if he's bursting out of a chrysalis. The man has hold of him, though he can't see the boy's face. I think the man is going to throw the boy over his head like a wrestler, then he'll have the boy in front of him—"

"To do what with him?"

"I don't know! To be him. To become him. That's his son, the next generation. No, it isn't. I don't know. I *am* going to take Bliss so I won't care. Maybe I'll see the truth of the man and boy."

"You'll take Bliss and come back here to look?"

"I don't know what I want. Maybe wanting will stop and I can just *be*."

"Jamie, you can come back here any time. *I'd* like to know what the sculpture means."

"Really?"

"It'll be amusing to know what you make of it, and of yourself."

"Amusing?"

Jamie did not return until a year later when he rang the door bell.

After donning his dinner jacket, Barnabas fluffed out his afro and checked that his skull socket wasn't showing, in the shaven area up above his right ear. Spruce as a lord, he descended.

Zandra remained at table, watching the Harlem Ballet perform *Swan Lake* for the second time, while Barnabas forked up some salmon, and then some pashka. Transit-nausea had passed away by the time Robert served coffee and brandy. Zandra dismissed Milly and Robert. If the servants wished they could go to Trafalgar Square to frolic and sing *Auld Lang Syne,* though probably they would dislike the bedlam.

After a while Zandra said softly, "Barabbas, something happened."

"Between you and Jamie?"

"No."

"Something *they* would like to know about?" Meaning the Ministry. At this hour on a New Year's Eve Barnabas wasn't sure whether to expect a routine post-transit phone call from a ministry lackey. "Is there something you haven't reported?"

She whispered, "I have a fugitive inside me."

His first thought was that the agony of so many transits had finally deranged Zandra, an anguish so different from the measured, meaningful pain they had once imposed on themselves to sculpt their bodies. She had become deluded that her alien passenger was not downloaded into a dummy after transit, but still lurked inside her.

"Do you mean you didn't download? That isn't possible."

"Oh I did download. But you see, I had two passengers, not one. The fugitive was concealed behind the official one. Only the official one was sucked out."

Schizophrenia. Split personality. Her mind was fragmenting under the strain of the pain.

She laid a tiny black leathery pouch upon the table, loosened the drawstring. On to the white linen tablecloth rolled a jewel the size of a quail's egg. Such iridescent facets of light—the diamonds of Zandra's necklace seemed trivial by comparison.

"On Melody one of the Ivory-dummies approached me. The Mockyman showed me this. He said he could plant himself inside me, using it."

Not a neural socket, but a jewel.

"Via my eyes, Barnabas. By both of us staring into this."

Were it not for the splendid unearthly jewel surely Zandra was inventing all this as a game. Or else she was deluded.

"How can the optic nerve carry so much data?"

"The dummy called this a quantum crystal. As soon as I looked in the jewel, even before I knew what he wanted, I was seduced."

The experience of accepting the fugitive had been quite without sensation, so said Zandra. Just prior to transferring itself to Zandra, the rogue Mockyman had injected his dummy with a delayed-action toxin. No trace of poison would remain. The toxin would mimic a massive fatal stroke, or the Ivoryman equivalent. A corpse would be found. Used up.

"How awkward for this fugitive if you changed your mind at the last moment."

"I couldn't! After I looked in the jewel I was enthralled. Barabbas, the Mockyman said that his mind would surface in me within a week or so if I don't transfer him to a dummy."

Not by using her skull socket, not in a supervised transit station, but by means of the crystal.

"What is he a fugitive from?"

This, the Mockyman had not confided. There was no way to ask the creature within her. Not yet. He was submerged.

Compared with Melody and other worlds, Earth must be a wild frontier where a fugitive could lose himself.

"Your runaway must have been a worker in the Melody station, or he wouldn't have understood English—"

What assets does the fugitive have? Knowledge, of course. Knowledge of unguessable value.

"I need an unregistered dummy, Barabbas. Look into the jewel first, though. It's fascinating."

Barnabas sipped some brandy.

"Will I be seduced and captivated?"

"Look through the jewel at one of the candles."

He trusted Zandra. Aside from their love, they were allied by the knife, by their proud scars, by the pains of transit which mocked what they had formerly endured to make an art of themselves.

"Just look. Hold it steady as a knife. Think about me."

Was the theft of the crystal the fugitive's crime or merely a means of escape? Did it intend to hide itself anonymously on Earth throughout a dummy's lifetime or would it try to carve out some niche for itself? Suppose they told the Ministry what happened. Sorry we took our time, Gents, we needed to think this through. The Ministry could upload Zandra's fugitive into a spare dummy, then they would have themselves a captive Mockyman unrecorded by its own kind. Zandra and Barnabas might be locked up for the rest of their lives to protect this secret. They were already guilty of abetting a crime against aliens.

The jewel was heavier than expected. Denser. Barnabas held it to his eye.

No Short Cuts was the name of the private club in Kensington.

Some similar clubs were sleazy—back street, back room—but not this one. No Short Cuts was sumptuous, subsidized by the pop

star who called herself Suzie Cicatrix, for even during the awful
years cult entertainers thrived.

Bar, sauna, little swimming pool, around which members would
show themselves off to kindred spirits . . . And now Barnabas was
there again, he was there, beholding Zandra for the very first time,
splendid sublime Zandra wearing only a bikini brief and her scars.
Total memory, perfect recall: that's what this was!

He could see each scar upon her breasts. He could smell the
mild chlorine of the pool. A Brandenburg Concerto played softly
through the speakers, for Suzie Cee's own hectic brand of music did
not suit this lux sanctum where she could unwind.

Soon, Zandra would in turn be captivated by the angel graven
on his flesh. Soon, he would be learning that she was a freelance
escort.

Zandra was as upmarket as escorts can be, exotic, almost too
intimidating to lay a finger upon because of the decoration of her
flesh. What a shiver of excitement for Asian businessmen. In this
dilapidated land, gateway to troubled Europe, business still struggled on. The whole world was disfigured by famines and droughts
and endless minor wars triggered by climate change and scarcities.
Yet Zandra scarred herself willingly, wondrously, as did he. Their
scars were the emblems of self-control, enhancement of themselves,
ownership of themselves.

And soon she would be learning that Barnabas was a bodyguard
to the Minister of the Environment, Julia Hennessey, except that
bodyguard is a dorky word. He was a Close Protector, a CP-er. His
angel stayed hidden from vulgar eyes though he always felt himself
protected by her wings. Who could ever shoot him (and her) in the
back?

It was not superstition which made him carve his own flesh, but
artistic courage. Soon, they would rhapsodize together, Zandra and
he. The tilt of her chin, her fabulous Egyptian hair, her liquid eyes,
her scars, the whiff of chlorine, the music of Bach . . .

"I'm there," he gasped. "No Short Cuts."

He forced himself to lay the jewel upon the table. She was right:
looking into the jewel was ravishing. To be exactly as one had once
been seemed so *innocent*—never mind what shit the world was in
six years ago just before the pod-ship arrived, to change his life, and
hers.

"It brings memory back so perfectly! So totally!"

"*Let me see—!*" Pushing the door wide, Jamie was in the room,
agog at the lustrous crystal.

"How long were you listening?" Barnabas cried.

"I came down . . . to tell you I'm going to leave. I can't stand being near . . . that sculpture—it torments me."

"You're going nowhere, boy."

"I feel so *compelled*," Zandra interrupted tensely, "to give the jewel back to its owner."

"Oh God, is that him surfacing inside you already? Pushing up a periscope?"

"No, Barabbas, no. I can imagine what *that* would feel like."

Jamie came sidling forward, begging, "Let *me* look in the jewel." At this moment chimes interrupted the music of Tchaikowsky. A logo invaded *Swan Lake*: a green star enclosing the initials MAL. Very expensive smart house-system, detecting one's whereabouts and routing calls accordingly.

"I'll be an accomplice. I won't betray you—"

Fluidly Zandra rose and slipped behind Jamie, one hand over his mouth, the other touching the prongs of the cheese knife to his windpipe.

"Hush, Jamie, hush—"

Although he had use of his arms, Jamie put up no resistance, limply accepting her control, sinking into her. Barnabas nodded queryingly toward the doorway, but Zandra shook her head.

"Just hush, Jamie."

By choice their holo equipment would receive images but lacked a mini-camera to transmit a picture of the dining room—no need to frogmarch the boy nor hide the jewel.

Debriefings rarely yielded anything interesting. Allow the courier time to get home and have a stiff drink rather than bother him with routine questions while he was disoriented and nauseated.

"Accept Call!"

The logo duly swelled, to be replaced by . . . Danvers. Glisteny oval face, retro horn-rimmed spectacles, oily receding hair, a fellow going on for fifty. He peered in vain. "Mr Mason?"

"Here I am, Mr Danvers. All ears."

"Anything special to mention?"

The usual question. The usual answer:

"Nothing different." No glimpse of the world of Passion. No encounters with Lemurs who were not dummies, every last one of them.

"Except," Barnabas added, "I feel a bit ragged after this trip. I can't face another for at least a month. Miz Wilde, neither. We might go to the Cotswolds for a break."

Danvers grew wistful. "Ah, the Cotswolds. I remember the snow there when I was a boy. Tonight it's chilly enough for snow. Or frost, if the sky stays clear."

"We shan't be taking fur coats with us."

"What made you so ragged this trip, Mr Mason? Can you put a finger on it?"

"It's cumulative," Barnabas told him brusquely.

"Does Miz Wilde feel this cumulative effect too? She mentioned nothing about it earlier."

"Have *you* ever been tortured at regular intervals? Felt yourself being torn apart?" What could Danvers say to that? "It's no big deal, but we do need a rest."

What Danvers did say was: "I want you both to have a full medical before your next trip. Will you call me to fix a time after you get back from the Cotswolds?"

"Yes, yes. Though it isn't necessary."

"Nevertheless."

"Happy New Year to you, Mr Danvers. End Call."

Danvers disintegrated amongst tall black dancers. Releasing her grip on Jamie, Zandra tossed the cheese knife upon the table.

"Zandra, do you suppose your fugitive was telling the truth about being able to surface spontaneously?"

She pursed her lips, so fully fleshed. Barnabas often thought of some magenta orchid.

"In case I try to cheat and keep the jewel for myself? I told you, I feel a compulsion."

"Please let me look at the jewel." No one was restraining Jamie, but he must know that he needed their consent.

"This compulsion—do you remember everything that happened between you and the fugitive?"

"If I've forgotten something, I wouldn't know what it is, would I?"

"*I've* forgotten something vital," Jamie fussed. "Please let me use that jewel."

"Zandra, have you tried looking into it and concentrating on when you met the Mockyman?"

A quick shake of the head.

Barnabas rolled the crystal across the tablecloth. "Sit down and look in it. Just you be patient, Jamie."

CHAPTER 16

"I'm in a pearly room. The Ivoryman's showing me . . . Oh it dazzles me so—!"

Of a sudden Zandra uttered a shriek and the jewel flew from her hand. She clawed at the cloth, toppling both candelabra. Great flimsy shadows capered as if ghosts of the Harlem Ballet had escaped into the room. Several candles stayed alight, charring the linen where they fell. Screaming, Zandra flailed at the air.

"Lights On!" At Barnabas's cry the electric chandelier blossomed brilliantly. He squashed each candle flame with the palm of his right hand, a very minor pain.

Zandra had stuck the edge of her hand into her mouth, gagging herself. She rocked to and fro in intense concentration before finally she relaxed, panting.

"I felt him stirring. He was rising up in me. What a stupid stupid thing to do—"

If the servants did hear something, they might imagine that Barnabas and Zandra were playing with razor-sharp knives. But screaming was no part of body art. Nor had Zandra and he scarred themselves physically for quite a few years now. When she and Barnabas first met at No Short Cuts they were already perfect and complete. Subsequent scars had been mental, due to transit, the torment of disintegration and reintegration.

"He was stirring. It was like childbirth starting. The first contractions . . . If I go to sleep tonight with him in me—"

"Like *childbirth*. . . ? But you never—"

Zandra looked daggers.

"I never knew—"

She must have given birth to a child while a gawky young teenager growing up in poverty, before her beauty became exceptional. He knew so little about that part of her life. They scarcely ever discussed the years when each had been growing up. Those were irrelevant.

His own years in the army were also of no real meaning. He had had two main choices in life: the perpetration of disorder or its suppression. He had improved himself much since then. They both had, together.

A child . . . Where was her child now? Growing up in an orphanage? Adopted by strangers?

Zandra whispered, "It died. The cord strangled it. They cut me open, but it was born blue."

It, it, it. Girl or boy, she wouldn't say. He wouldn't ask. The fruit of her own womb was neuter; it had been neutralized. Maybe Jamie, despite being a blond white boy, was a proxy son, a photographic negative, black skin rendered as white.

"It would have had brain damage. They let it die after they cut me."

The first cut of the knife . . . Later cuts had been by choice. Not imposed, but freely sought.

And Jamie was hearing all this, shocked and unnerved yet still avid for the jewel.

"They tied my tubes. Don't want no penniless black bitches breeding. Just as well, in my case."

Just as well, when she had been freed by the knife to become the beautiful escort he had met at No Short Cuts rather than a single mother bringing up a brat in a slum; and freed to be here now, a rich courier.

"Did you remember anything important?" Jamie blurted.

"*Important*. . . ?" Zandra shook.

"Oh rip yourself, boy!"

"I mean what happened in the pearly room between you and the Mockyman."

"Mustn't lose control," muttered Zandra. "Mustn't." She gazed past Jamie, hardly heeding him. "I felt the alien in me, fluttering, stirring . . . Barabbas, it has to be tonight! So it has to be Robert's nephew. There's no time to find a different dummy now."

"We *can't.*"

"It would be so unfair? It would spoil everything? What else can we do?"

"Was this possibility in the back of your mind when you—?"

"I *know* what's in the back of my mind, Barabbas! A Mockyman, about to take me over as its dummy, early."

Ever so slowly Jamie was straying closer to where the alien mind-crystal lay, like a cat stalking prey. A glance in his direction, and he wasn't moving at all. What, me? Stealing nearer? Pure imagination.

Robert and Milly and Mrs Johnson were such treasures. Barnabas had never confronted them with his knowledge of their family secret. When he and Zandra bought the mansion and needed staff, a security consultant probed Robert's background thoroughly.

Robert's sister Joan was married to a certain Alex Corby. Alex was one of the long-term unemployed, living on meagre welfare in South London on a grim estate between Kennington and Brixton, beyond the range of gentrification which saw the south side of the river become fashionable for a while before the Hardship Years set in.

Alex and Joan had an only son, Billy. Billy became one of the early Blissheads. Bliss was circulating freely on such estates as his, so much less troublesome a drug than Crack or Fraz or Hop.

After a year's use, Billy became a dummy.

The Corbys did not register him. They could not bear for him to be carted off by BritGov to Hyde Park to be fitted with a neural socket and be a body for Mockymen to use. Not to see him again—unless by chance, on a street, a puppet used by an alien.

How expensive to hide Billy at home. Bootleg medical equipment to keep him ticking over in his nirvana state. Bribes to the local estate boss. Robert and Milly paid the bills for this from the generous salaries they earned.

"It'll be a weight off their backs," argued Zandra. "They must be so sick of it all by now! Billy's mother will be the one who's obsessed. We'll tell her that the jewel will awaken her boy."

"And when something else awakens?"

Zandra sounded on the verge of hysteria. "You have a gun, Barabbas."

When he gave up his CP work he had surrendered his licensed weapon. But after they acquired the mansion he bought a gun in a pub for a thousand in used banknotes—not a Glock with inbuilt silencer such as he used before, but a vintage Browning. Their privileged sanctuary might attract malice or mischief.

"If the Corbys don't agree it only takes a tip-off to the Ministry to have Billy picked up. Then they've lost him anyway."

She and Barnabas had talked and acted callously on other occasions because of the trauma of transit, but this was real.

"Better, we'll say that the Ministry told us to do this."

"To a dummy hidden on a lawless estate?"

"Aren't Robert and Milly loyal to us?"

"I'm loyal to you," Jamie butted in. "I can't leave you now. Not knowing such things. Please can I look in the jewel?"

"You want to be the focus of attention at *this* moment? Now, of all times?"

"It only took Zandra a moment to look. Maybe the Mockyman will leap into my mind, then you won't need to involve Robert."

"And you won't need to whine about your shit-forsaken identity any longer. The Mockyman isn't in the *jewel*."

"If Zandra and I both look in it at the same time—"

"Look in it for God's sake," cried Zandra, "look in it now. Get this over and done with. We haven't time."

"Oh thank you, Zandra!" Occupying a chair at the disordered table, Jamie snatched up the jewel, jammed it to one eye, stared through it at the electric chandelier.

His arms and head and whole body were quivering as if he was clinging tight on some juddering ride. He panted, hyperventilating as though some orgasm was upon him. Then he slumped forward upon the table. Sobs racked him, sobs of release, of deliverance.

He raised his head.

When he spoke, only his voice was the same.

". . . almost twenty years—I know those from Jamie. How the world has shifted! I don't think I would have told you—but I'm affected by being him. He's so excited, finding his heritage. The writing in the book is revealed."

"Man, you're talking like a loony!"

"I'm not mad, Barnabas. I'm adjusting. But you're right that I'm a man not a boy—though the boy is me."

"You're fucking *pretending*!"

The fair-haired lad spoke rapidly in a Scandinavian language.

"Does that satisfy you? My name's Olav. The floodgates opened. I know who I am all at once. I'm reincarnated at last. Jamie was a dreamer seeking to wake. I'm the one who awakes. He becomes my dream."

Zandra moaned. "I can't take this in."

"This crystal from the stars restored me to myself. I'm Olav, the same name as the Saint of Norway. I am the One, I am the Two, in the poet's words."

"How can you—how can you be *reincarnated?*"

A smile. "With difficulty, so it seems! Yet I succeeded." Rising, the lad examined his reflection in a gilt-framed mirror. "Yes, I see who Jamie is seed of. Very apt." He stroked his cheek. "How fresh: such vitality, such vigour. Jamie took this for granted. Why did I not rejoice at every single moment? Because I knew I was incomplete. But to business, my friends! We are allies. Your need is urgent, Zandra. I'm no raw youth. Long ago I was an officer of Norwegian SS volunteers. I have been in some fierce actions, believe me."

"Did you say SS? You were a Norwegian and you belonged to the SS?"

"Many true Norwegian patriots did. British men also, though not very many, and only a handful were much use."

"Do correct me, but weren't the SS the fuckers who ethnically cleansed millions of Jews and gypsies and anyone who wasn't quite *white* enough, eh Olav?"

"I was not involved in any atrocities, Barnabas. Your skin colour is of no importance to me."

"Spoken like a true racist. You're talking as if you set out to be reincarnated. *How*, in hell's name?"

"Barabbas," pleaded Zandra, "we cannot cope with this as well!"

"She's right," said whoever Jamie was. "You must summon Robert and apply pressure."

"With you here?"

"You need to keep an eye on me till you can trust me. I'll be quiet as a mouse, unless I see a way to help."

"Now, *now.*" Zandra rose and tugged a brass knob on the wall. Down in the basement a bell would jangle. How much more gracious than summoning Robert electronically.

Olav rested his head in his hands.

Robert's eyes were always a bit bulgy.

Slim moustache. Chestnut kiss-curl across his brow. Watery blue eyes. Amenable open face.

He had already changed into pyjamas, over which he had donned a purple paisley dressing gown. Early to bed, eh? No time to resume frockcoat or gloves. A green cravat did duty for a bow tie. The stained, scorched linen seemed the obvious reason for his summons, but disregarding the mess Barnabas invited him to sit and share a brandy.

"Cheers, Robert. Now I want you to listen carefully. We know about Billy Corby . . ."

Their butler's eyes had always bulged a bit.

"For the past three years," Robert said at last, "we put up with your elegant menace, and you knew all along."

"If you had to endure torment each time you do your job—"

"Maybe Milly and I do! You're paid a small fortune every time you turn a trick." Robert was verging on vulgarity. Valued agents of BritGov by no means sold their bodies like whores. Understandably he was upset. "You don't mind the lad listening while you strip me bare!"

Lips pursed, Olav gazed steadfastly at Robert.

"Jamie is in our confidence," said Zandra.

"Oh really? Has he cut his flesh, then? Initiation ceremony, is that it? And you offer us fifty grand to sell Billy . . ."

Too exorbitant a sum might trigger fantasies of extracting more

"Ministry money," mused Robert. He sniffed the air—brandy fumes, spent candle smoke—as if testing for truth. "For an illicit experiment, *sir*? And I go to gaol if I snitch. You must think I'm simple."

"Not at all. To have carried out your charade of butler and maid so believably—"

"Charade!" Robert drained his goblet and set it down with such a thump. "After this, there won't be any need to carry on pretending." Still, he seemed to be weighing pros and cons. He leaned forward. "You see, sir, my brother-in-law's the real problem, not Joan. Alex was all washed up long ago. He's still clinging to one hope for the future—his son, even though that's stupid. If Billy gets a bed sore, Alex is vile to Joan. She's so scared. She can't tell the authorities because Alex would kill her. He's a bastard. Alex is the problem, do you understand what I'm saying, Master Barnabas?"

Robert was at the wheel of the Mercedes, alongside Barnabas. Zandra fretted in the back beside Jamie who was really Olav, unbeknownst to Robert.

Before bringing the Merc out of its garage in the mews—the stables of an earlier era—Robert had put on cord trousers, a pullover, and an anorak. His chauffeur's uniform with peaked cap would look seriously out of place on an estate. Barnabas had donned a long cream raincoat with big lapels over his dinner jacket. Zandra had draped herself in a black velvet cloak with scarlet lining, making herself seem vampiric. Jamie was wearing that black leather jacket over shirt and jeans.

Robert told Milly that they were going to an all-night casino, a story which hardly squared with his attire. How out-of-place would the Merc look on that estate? They might seem like a visiting crime boss and gorgeous moll and bodyguard and young protégé.

They avoided obvious bottlenecks such as Trafalgar Square or Piccadilly, yet wherever a pub was, a mass of drinkers spilled from it like human algae in bloom. Threading their way down to the Thames took a while. At this rate they would be transacting their business with Alex Corby around midnight, when a big official fireworks display would explode over London. Bang, bang, bang.

Barnabas was so tired and Zandra so stressed that it was hard to think clearly.

Robert might indeed be intimidated, but Barnabas was being pressured to kill a man, something he had never done before. Seriously wounded, yes, but not killed—despite his stint in the army, despite security work. An active service unit of the Scotch Bonnets tried to assassinate Julia Hennessey, and he fired to kill but the buggers had been wearing vests made of vectran.

If push came to shove, how could he kill a person in cold blood, however worthless and sad and bad the man is?

His utter reluctance wasn't on account of risk. Probably the police would scarcely bother to investigate a killing on such an estate. Quite likely they would never even find out about it. Joan Corby would need sanctuary in Middlesex Square for a while till she recovered her spirits and a flat could be found for her—and the local boss would investigate the abandoned house before too long and disappear Alex's body.

What would the estate boss do then? Try to work out what happened and exploit the situation? Try a spot of blackmail? Barnabas wasn't feeling sick at heart because of this *risk*, either. Killing someone, however trashy they may be, was a wicked thing if avoidable. It was wrong, it was evil.

"Look Robert, we can tie Alex up at gunpoint, do what needs doing with Billy, then simply bring Joan away with us for her safety."

"My brother-in-law won't leave things be. Don't you see he'll have nothing to lose peaching on me and you for revenge?"

"Maybe he'll go mad with despair and hang himself."

"Are you suggesting, sir, that we hang him? So that there's no bullet left behind? We can't exactly rely on *Alex* to hang himself."

Stand Mr Corby on a chair? Fix a rope to a light fitting? Kick the chair away? See him choke? God no.

Failure tonight might mean that the alien took Zandra as its dummy. In the back of the car she uttered a noise somewhere between a moan and a low growl. Almost, they might be driving her to some hospital to give birth.

As they crossed over Lambeth Bridge, the Houses of Parliament were a radiant sight. In another half an hour the clock tower would be on screen nationwide.

Most of the buildings in the sprawl of housing were double maisonettes: two-storey flats stacked upon one another, of yellow brick with small balconies. Quite a number were boarded up, massive metal shutters giving the look of mothballed little battleships. Tiles had been stripped from some roofs as if a maniacal giant was determined to break in, to lift out the inhabitants and devour them. A few dwellings, revealed by those streetlamps which were still functioning, sported flouncy lace curtains at their windows, defiantly and bizarrely houseproud amidst the squalor.

How far Barnabas and Zandra had transcended similar circumstances. Thanks to courier work they were aristocrats, though their scars had made them secret aristocrats even before the aliens came.

Clapped-out vans and derelict cars shared kerb space with the occasional smart BMW or Audi, prizes of crime presumably, and as such immune to theft or vandalism.

As Robert turned left then right through the estate, wary of potholes, a bunch of young kids scampered down lanes between buildings, reappearing further along their route. Despite the lateness of the hour maybe there were several wolfpacks of children. No older teenagers were roaming. Raving it up in Trafalgar Square? Or out burgling some other borough?

Robert stopped the car outside one of the piggyback maisonettes. Sheets of steel hid the lower windows and concrete blocks walled up a forsaken doorway, but curtained light showed in the upper habitation.

"Upstairs—" Robert was either informing Barnabas or ordering him.

Joan Corby was a drab plump pasty woman, wrapped in a quilted dressing gown. Fear seemed a permanent resident in her eyes, though not fear of opening a door so late at night—they paid for protection, didn't they? Or rather, Robert did. In bewilderment she gaped at splendid Zandra and Barnabas, paying less heed to the fair-haired lad accompanying them.

"Robert. . . ! Who—?"

"*Who's there?*" Through in the lounge a screen was churning out sounds of festive Scottish dancing, merry overture to the death of the old year and the birth of the new.

"*Who is it, Joany?*" The man sounded drunk. He did not bother to come to the door. Even if the Corbys did not feel vulnerable to late-night callers, Joan's husband must be a shit.

Robert whispered, "We've come to sort things out, Joan. Sort them out, do you know what I mean? Wipe the slate clean."

The lounge was so cramped after the mansion in Middlesex Square. Tatty three-piece suite. Trio of china mallard ducks on the wall over the fireplace, which must have been there since the middle of last century. On screen lads and lasses in kilts were dancing a reel. In old jeans and checked shirt Alex Corby nursed a can of lager, a bloated, lolling man.

"Bit early for first-footing, in'it? You're s'posed to come after midnight. With a bit of coal in your pocket." He chortled. "You know that, eh? Coal for luck? You two don't need coal. Shake your hand'll do fine." He struggled up but did not offer his hand.

"We came to see Billy—"

Alex paled. "You've *told!* You aren't going up there, not bloody tonight. Next bloody year Billy's going to wake up."

The scene on screen shifted to a picture of Big Ben, the minute hand of the clock creeping towards midnight.

"We can wake your Billy up," pledged Zandra. "Midnight is magic time." She must be half out of her mind with worry.

"Billy belongs to Master Barnabas and Madam Zandra. They paid for him. Now they've come to collect." Robert was deliberately provoking Alex, winding him up.

"Bloody Master and Madam!" Alex might be drunkenly quoting Robert's own words from some previous occasion. "You want him for a dummy, that's why you're here!"

Barnabas slid the pistol, shiny and black, from his raincoat pocket. 9-mm Browning self-loader. Magazine capacity twenty, but few people loaded the entire complement of bullets against the increasing pressure of the spring.

Brandishing the lager can, Alex blundered at Barnabas. Instead of firing, Barnabas parried the can which was thrust at his face. Grappling, boozy-breathed, Alex butted his brow into Barnabas's jaw. As Barnabas's grip loosened, urgent fingers plucked the pistol away. The loud bang, the bright yellow flash of a shot, the swift stink of cordite: Alex tumbled against an armchair as Joan shrieked.

Gun in hand, Jamie bent over the body, then straightened.

"He is dead. Heart shot." A little blood had sprayed his shirt, and Barnabas's raincoat too.

Outside, down below, the Merc also shrieked piercingly—and a child squealed in the night. The car had electrified itself because fingers tried to tamper. Non-lethal, but painful. Robert darted to the window and parted the curtains, but quickly abandoned his inspection—kids must have fled. Massed voices began singing *Auld Lang Syne*. With wonder and wariness Robert eyed Jamie.

"I suppose thanks are in order."

The Browning was returned to Barnabas, and to his pocket.

Joan sobbed, in shock.

Robert hugged her. "I'll phone the boss tomorrow, let him know about the body. He'll arrange for disposal."

"Hang on now, we never—!"

"It's best, to pay him off. Yes Joany, Master Barnabas can pay. You'll stay with us till we can all move out together. Somewhere better than this."

"And Billy'll be with us?"

"We'll see . . ."

Zandra was breathing deeply, forcibly, like a woman in labour. "*Upstairs*," she urged.

A thin cotton sheet veiled naked Billy's lower half, almost hiding the big nappy he wore. A heater put out enough warmth to take the edge off the chill. The lad's eyes were open, as with all unused dummies. Lachrymal lubricant seeped from pipettes. His cheeks gleamed from leakage. Occasionally, automatically, he blinked. Over him towered the intravenous feeding equipment, its tube in his arm. He swallowed, another reflex.

Jars of ointments and creams and bottles of aromatherapy oils crowded a shelf. Joan must have given her son's body amateur physio every day, for he looked in reasonable shape, not like a corpse pulled out of the Thames. Even had a bit of a tan. An infrared lamp accounted for that. What servitude Joan had endured for years. Despite all her ministrations, Billy must have lost a lot of muscle tone.

Robert held his sister's shoulders, to comfort her but also to stop her from interfering as Zandra took the pouch from an inside pocket of her cloak, removed the jewel, and leaned over Billy to view him eye to eye.

Billy stirred. He blinked rapidly. His hand rose feebly to sweep the pipettes aside. Barnabas pulled the feeding tube away.

"Billy?" Joan's voice was the squeak of some trembling baby animal.

With difficulty the youth propped himself up, the effort seeming to exhaust him.

"My . . . mother. Mother mine—"

The Mockyman was making a fair guess, unless it had been able to trawl memories out of the host brain. In this bedroom it saw: Zandra, whom it already knew—she was standing back, looking so relieved. On account of skin colour Barnabas must be her mate or a relative. Robert and Jamie-Olav, unknown. The fraught shabby white woman was surely bloodkin.

Distant bangs: the noise of big rockets exploding . . .

Joan wept again.

"Mother," said the dummy. It must be surprised at how frail it felt, contrary to expectation. Fixing its gaze on Zandra: "Give. Crystal. Into hand." As if to draw strength from the jewel.

Robert murmured, "Master Barnabas, maybe you—or Jamie—should shoot it now?"

Dispose of the Mockyman—and keep the jewel? Risk the death penalty if BritGov ever found out?

"Give crystal."

Two strides took Zandra to the bedside, where she thrust the jewel into the open palm, which closed up tightly. Such willpower. Couriers knew about willpower.

Barnabas failed to produce his pistol. "Christ, we don't need to kill it, just leave it here." Enfeebled in the middle of this predatory estate. With the local boss due to be tipped off now, apparently. The boss would arrange, and would keep his lip buttoned supposing one of his men acted as executioner. Easiest of all would be for him to torch the house. Billy seemed too weak to go anywhere of his own accord without several weeks of recuperation and exercise.

"Billy's body isn't Billy any more," Robert assured his sister. "You're free now." You would think he had planned this all along.

"But he's my Billy!"

"No he isn't, Joany. Not any longer." Patting her: "You've come through. You don't have any more duties. You're out of this prison."

"What shall I do now?"

"It's a new year, so it's a new life." Eyeing Zandra: "By the way, Madam, happy new year."

"Robert, I'm sorry about our—what was it?—elegant menace."

"If it made me and Milly hate you? That's a very special admission on your part."

"You're both so talented. So versatile!"

"That relied on me and Milly being opaque to you, so to speak. We oughtn't to have personal problems—like a dummy hidden in the cupboard. You knew all along. That's unforgivable."

"It turned out well. For all of us!"

More sharp bangs sounded, far off, as if a gun battle was in progress.

"Is there war?" asked the naked Mockyman, sheet still over his loins and legs. "Who fights?"

How much did it understand about its circumstances? Did the alien who ensnared Zandra deserve sympathy?

"We can't possibly leave the crystal here," stated Jamie. "Suppose that boss takes it and looks into it. He may try to sell it. Suppose a rumour reaches the authorities."

"He'll probably burn the house down to destroy the body."

"Without first looking round for what he can loot? Abandoning the equipment in here? Talk sense."

"*You*," said Robert, "certainly talk differently. And as for you using that gun . . ."

"Don't bother about me—bother about the crystal. Zandra, you fulfilled your compulsion by giving the jewel back. Now we can take it away again."

"Hey, who's the master here?"

But Barnabas merely shrugged, nor did Zandra hinder Jamie as he approached Mocky-Billy, although she was trembling and beads of sweat studded her scarified skin. Mocky-Billy tried to clench his fist but the enfeebled fingers were no match as Jamie prised.

"Give me the little bag, Zandra."

Restoring the jewel to its pouch, Jamie handed it to Barnabas. "Keep it safe."

"I really don't know about you two, Master and Mistress. Maybe you've been humbled after all."

All Barnabas said was, "I am so sodding tired. We must go."

As the Mercedes returned over Lambeth Bridge, from midstream outside the Houses of Parliament one of the fire-fighting boats sprayed celebratory plumes of water high into the air. In the back of the car Zandra held Joan to comfort her—Joan could scarcely notice scars in the darkness. On Joan's other side, Jamie-Olav was deep in himself. Barnabas had almost fallen asleep but jerked back to awareness.

"Stop here, Robert, right now." They were halfway across the river. A car sped past, full of young men. Stepping out, Barnabas headed for the parapet followed a moment later by Jamie-Olav.

"Wait, what's your idea—?"

Streetlamps burned along Millbank and the Albert Embankment beyond the wide oily darkness of the Thames.

"I'm going to get rid of the damn thing, throw it in the water."

"No. You must not!"

"What do you care? You've already been reincarnated, supposedly! Think you might need a refresher course?"

"It is stupid to get rid of something so unique."

"It's trouble. I can't take any more tonight."

"Make no decision when you are tired and confused. That is never wise. You need to sleep on this."

"I need to *sleep* full stop."

"Come along then. We all need to sleep. Come along." Gently Jamie-Olav guided Barnabas back across the pavement, as if assisting a reveller who had vomited into the river.

Chapter 17

It's a hundred and fifty miles from Hereford to London. Once we join the M4, Tim speeds down the outside lane of the motorway where the surface is smoother. Can't be doing the suspension much good, even so. My phone is turned up so that Tim can hear the Jamie news. We're cruising at ninety when, just beyond Swindon, a police hover-chaser whooshes out of hiding from behind a bridge abutment. Sirens and lights. This wastes precious minutes while I show my credentials. A stop for petrol and toilets at a service area steals a few more minutes. A bit after midnight we pass Reading.

It's been one astonishment after another: the maverick Mockyman, the alien crystal, the reincarnation in Jamie of a Norwegian SS officer named Olav . . . The old Norwegian gent who commissioned the jigsaws of that park, then shot himself: it links, it links. Reincarnation seems incredible—*planned* reincarnation by some means that remains a mystery—but I'm crediting it, I am.

That gem without price may offer a way to penetrate Mockymen security, a means for a human being to stow away in a courier unknown to the Mockyman passenger. And then somehow to transfer to a vacant Ivoryman dummy left unattended? It may take a number of routine trips before our courier has a window of opportunity—and who will the volunteer courier be? Imagine: looking just like any other native, our agent slips out of the Melody Hilton, through into Ivory-land. Damn, but we're going to find out the truth.

Three moons are in the sky, perhaps. Perhaps two suns. How long have the Mockymen been operating on Melody? Is there some kind of opposition, hopefully more clued up than our homespun Humpties? Can our agent make contact? With help, will she be able to return, filled with intelligence? She, or he. Assuming she can understand Ivoryspeech, courtesy of her dummy, where does she go, what does she do, how does she pay for anything?

Of course this will need to be a deeply black operation, unsanctioned, undisclosed, at least till results are known. My mind hums with possibilities—and problems.

There has always been a big mystery as to how consciousness can possibly be transferred from one body to another. How a mind can be disembodied. Memories are experienced by a body. They should be unique to that body, indivisible from it.

Manifestly the Mockymen know otherwise. Them—and also our Norwegian, seemingly.

Maybe the crystal can be copied here on Earth? Thank heaven that Jamie-Olav talked Barnabas out of throwing it into the Thames. What a diving and dredging operation that would have been to retrieve the "little bag" from the mud, always supposing that the current didn't carry the bag away downstream. Thanks very much, Jamie-Olav. I hear you loud and clear.

"Anna, where are you?" H-S's voice booms in the confines of the car, overriding the link with my comp. Adjust the volume hastily.

"Maidenhead turnoff coming up." Slough next, then the London Orbital.

"Divert to South London, the Corby house. Are you on real-time yet?"

"Yes, yes."

"I've trawled the address from Corby's benefit records. Got a pen?"

"Just a moment."

Roof light, notebook, pen.

"Go ahead."

Difficult even to print legibly, with the poxy much-patched tarmac vibrating and juddering us.

"Got it."

"I'm sending a team from the Sleeping Beauty Squad. I fear they may be a wee bit drunk, and they'll have to collect a van that's been squirreled away, so you may arrive first at the scene."

"Did you say drunk?"

"A bit tiddly. I bleeped them both at parties. Tonight's regular duty crews aren't of our persuasion."

We're to rely on two chaps who are *tiddly?* A special van may have been squirreled away and two Sleeping Beauty chaps recruited to the covert network—but the network can't be as extensive as I hoped. No wonder H-S was happy to have Tim on board. Can H-S merely have been playing boys' games all along, never really believing we could have such a breakthrough, still less a double coup, rogue Mockyman on the loose *and* an item of alien tech-magic? The network has been a sort of hobby to him. Starting tonight, it's for real, and now we have to improvise.

"Sir—"

"Jock: call me Jock."

Yes, we're on first name terms now all right.

"Jock, one of the crew isn't Gerry Walsh by any chance?"

How insufferable if Gerry and I were on the same side all along but never disclosed this to each other! We might still be together, not that I wish for this now.

"Their names are Colin Munro and Bob Maclaren. Those two whisked Jamie away from Hyde Park." A transfer that Jock himself arranged. "Reliable chaps. Knew their families. Been in London a year now. Why?"

"Curiosity."

We're passing the turnoff to Slough. I switch on the routemaster. Little screen glows. Key in the name of the Corbys' street. Yes, follow the M4 all the way in through Hammersmith, jink down to the Embankment, cross the river at Vauxhall Bridge.

"Where do we take the Mockyman to, sir?" Some formality still seems in order.

"I'm working on a safe house right now."

He's *working* on one?

"Wee spot of difficulty with the place I set aside. Tree came down in the last storm, wrecked the roof, repairs in progress right at the moment—well, not *right* now, second of January the builders get back to it."

Contingency plan? There isn't one. H-S must own that house. Country cottage somewhere. If he tries to use a regular safe house, rival intel officers will wonder why. Too many ambitious individualists. Would I have had a backup house in case of the totally unexpected?

Maybe I do have one—and maybe I can solve the dilemma about Daddy.

"Jock, are there any of us in Hereford with 22 SAS?"

A pause, then, "No."

"I found out that some officers are Humpty sympathisers. They're even plotting to kidnap a Mockyman."

"*What—?*"

"My father's involved."

"He *told* you?"

"No, they use his house as a meeting place. I was worried. I was snooping. My brother is involved too."

"The Kielder chef."

"Yes. Look, I'm afraid my father knows a bit about Jamie because I confided in him before I realized."

"Shite, lassie."

"That doesn't matter now, because we can enlist them. They don't need to snatch a Mockyman—we have an untraceable one. My father's house is fairly isolated, down at the end of a village lane. There's a cellar."

"We *do* have several balls in the air! Preferable to a balls-up, I suppose. Do you know who these conspirators are?"

"Not yet. I have tape. Tim has vehicle registration numbers. Pair of Land Rangers will be from the regimental pool."

"You're sterling sure about this conspiracy?" Oh, witty, if that's his intention. The SAS base at Hereford is called Stirling Lines. Lines, as around a camp. Stirling, as in Sir David, founder of the SAS.

"Jock, I'm positive."

"How much puff do you have left in you, Anna?"

"We slept in late this morning—yesterday morning, I mean." It's gone midnight already.

Dryly: "Did you just. I'm trying to juggle London and Hereford. We'll need to box clever as regards Middlesex Square. Seven people in that house by now. Yon Olav is a loose cannon and no mistake—unless it simply isn't true about him."

"It seems true."

"*How did he do it?* Well, we'll find out! I suppose you need to smooth the way with your father. Prisoner escort." God, back again to Hereford? And miss descending on Middlesex Square? "Trouble is, I want you in London tomorrow. Help question Olav. Jamie. Whoever. The rogue Mockyman sounds too feeble for interrogation yet."

"If the Sleeping Beauty team have a routemaster in that van they'll be using—"

"They certainly do."

"I can give exact directions for when they reach the village itself."

"Bloody long drive if they're sozzled," Tim chips in. "Don't risk a crash with the alien on board." We're coming up to the M4-Orbital interchange. "How about if I drive the van to your dad's, since I know the place? I think I can do all the necessary talking to your father. I can stay there till there's backup."

Backup from the pro-Humpties of the Regiment . . .

"Excellent suggestion, Rogers," comes H-S's voice. "Much appreciated. Bottle of thirty-year-old malt for you."

"Are you up to it, Tim?"

"What, a bottle of malt?"

"No, the *drive*."

"I'll have to be. Because you need your beauty sleep. Big day tomorrow meeting Olav, hmm?"

"I did meet him at Hyde Park."

"Different him. So that's settled, okay? Assuming our Mocky-man hasn't wandered off."

Don't let that be so!

In a way it's better that Daddy hears from Tim about my snooping. I'm in a bit of a spin emotionally about it. Plainly my prying was justifiable because my suspicion proved to be correct and Daddy could have burned his fingers badly; Tony too. But was it also sneaky and underhand of me? Scarcely the deed of a daughter? On the other hand, Daddy was deceiving *me*—as I suppose he was bound to, considering my job, even though ironically both of us were pursuing a similar goal. That's the whole trouble with secrets. Everything will be out in the open now—between Daddy and me— though I hate to think how fraught the situation could be were it not for this bolt from the blue, the rogue Mockyman. Without the alien, I could scarcely disclose my true motives to Daddy. I did go some way, I suppose, if unintentionally, by telling him about Jamie.

Self-justification is such a dubious device.

"Thanks, Tim," I say.

A jewel which can evoke memories perfectly, as if the past has returned. . . ! Will I myself peek into it after we have it in safe-keeping?

As we drive deeper into London I can't help but hark back to the Gaudy I went to at Oxford four years ago. Student reunion. Make that five years. For almost an hour now it has been 2016.

Gaudy from *gaudere*, to rejoice, as in the drinking song

Gaudeamus igitur, once beloved of students in Heidelberg and such places. Strictly, a college Gaudy ought to happen every ten years but the dreadful decade intervened. Civil unrest, superflu, world not unlike Edgar Allan Poe's doomed fishing boat heading into a maelstrom. Then of course the pod-ship arrived.

Graduates of my college are supposed to be champions in the race of life, but the first decade of the new millennium was hard to cope with. I was curious to see who would turn up at the delayed Gaudy, and what had become of them during the past fifteen years. I was also curious to see my former tutor who was Professor of Modern History by now. Flamboyant Richard Cornwallis would hardly miss an opportunity to dress up.

Although arguably the oldest in Oxford, architecturally the college is 19th century Gothic. I had requested my old room, which overlooked a graveyard and steps descending to a public toilet beneath the pavement. Crane your neck and you could admire the tall spiky memorial to the martyrs Latimer and Ridley who in reality were burned at the stake around the corner in Broad Street. Opposite Thornton's bookshop (lots of excellent second-hand history upstairs) a metal cross set in the tarmac marked the exact site of the agony.

I arrived in time for an "At Home" hosted by the Master in the old senior common room under the library: loads of chilled Hock (it was June), and a throng of people rediscovering one another, or failing to. And there I met Jane again, fiery journalist Jane. Jane Morris. She had cropped her red hair and plumped out a bit instead of being all knees and elbows. Seemed more like a sister of hers, than herself. Of course, we embraced.

"It's so *good* to see you, Anna. You look just the same! What are you doing these days?"

"Oh, I'm with MAL," I said brightly.

Her look narrowed. "Doing what?"

"Records, archive work, keeping the files in order."

She began to pump me for anything I might know which was not public knowledge. Especially about that *concentration camp* in the wilds of Northumberland.

To change the subject I said, "I wonder if Rachel will come?" The lodge porter, old Charley who was now white-haired, ought to have handed out a guest list and seating plan for dinner along with our room key, but there had been a cock-up. Instead we would be collecting the details from the buttery just before dinner.

"Rachel's dead. The flu. Didn't you know?"

"God, that's awful."

"*Awful* is what's happening to this country. We're a banana republic, with aliens as the men from Del Monte."

"Don't you mean a pineapple republic?"

"Very funny. Third world from the sun equals third-world planet."

"Oh get off your high horse, Jane. The benefits are obvious already."

"Spoken like one of Himmler's pen-pushers. These aliens are buying us."

"They're offering a lot more than bags of beads."

"Because it's all peanuts to them. Lesson of history: beware Greeks bearing gifts."

I looked around. "Talking of history, Richard doesn't seem to be here."

Jane looked shifty. "Richard?"

"Cornwallis."

"He'll be at high table tonight."

"Do you know for sure?"

"Actually, I phoned him."

"Have you two been keeping in touch?"

A shrug: "Hardly that."

Conversations were in progress around us about pandemics, new technologies, ozone repair, the continuing demise of parliament, all very cutting edge. So what did Jane want with the Professor of Modern History?

To the best of my knowledge, Richard scrupulously (or sensibly) never slept with any female undergraduate or postgraduate of his own college, although otherwise his affairs were legendary; meaning perhaps that legend exaggerated. You might spy him in a wine bar or on the street with some catwalk-calibre darling, invited up from London where he had a flat. He was independently wealthy.

His Oxford pied-à-terre was about a mile from the college. During our second year Richard stubbed his toe. Walking to college was a pain, so a note invited me and Jane to his flat to read our essay of the week and partake of coffee and scones with clotted cream, as I recall, and strawberry jam. (The essays were about Bismark and the rise of Germany. Germany was a speciality of Richard's.)

Scrumptious, was Jane's girly word for him. I preferred hunky. We could confide this to each other since Richard was so clearly out of bounds.

"*Scrumptious*," Jane declared to him as we sat in his book-lined

study—apropos her scone laden with Devon's best which she had
sculpted into a tit of cream tipped with a strawberry nipple. He was
sporting a white brocade shirt with chunky gold cufflinks, maroon
velvet waistcoat, and polka-dot cravat. No need for an alien jewel to
remind me of this.

Fifteen years after that occasion, was Jane hoping to sleep with
Richard at last? We headed for our respective rooms to glam ourselves for dinner. Same graveyard outside, same public lavatory,
same memorial. How poky the room seemed. Paintwork was tatty,
probably always had been.

Suitably dolled up, I sauntered past trees, rose beds, and lawn
towards the hall. Scores of chaps and a lesser number of women
were converging on the buttery below, for pre-dinner drinks. In their
dinner jackets and cummerbunds and bow ties chaps are the real
peacocks of such occasions, and none was displaying plumage more
so than Richard, whom I quickly spotted dallying with Jane at the
base of the stone steps leading up to the hall. His dinner jacket was
a brocade creation more like tapestry than tailoring, and his tie
veritably blossomed: a bouquet of black satin camellias spilling
down a rich white silk shirt. His coaly hair was almost as luxuriant
as I remembered, swept back like wings about to unfurl, godlike,
from his head. His jet-black eyebrows were arch, and arching. And
he wore a long black academic gown, which on him seemed posi-
tively Transylvanian. I noticed that other fellows of the college were
wearing gowns too.

On closer approach I wondered if he had taken to tinting his
hair, though maybe this was a bitchy thought.

"Hullo, Richard."

"Anna, what a pleasure. When I learned that you were coming
—yourself and Jane—that's really what decided me to be here."

Oh such charm.

"Why are you all wearing gowns?"

"A note came round from the Master. He must want us to
appear dignified. First Gaudy for ages."

Dignified, oh yes. And perhaps a bit self-important and paro-
chial. Aliens were on Earth in human bodies, and the dons of
Oxford looked like bygone pedagogues as if some time-slip had
occurred. Minds as keen as mustard, though.

"I wonder if there's any Mockymen in our midst?" I joked.
"Here to experience a bizarre human ceremony."

"Oh I hardly think so." Surely not among us, not among this
élite. No man of our college would stoop to Bliss. "What Jane was
saying to me just now . . ." She flashed a look of caution at him, but

he paid scant heed. ". . . about history coming to an end with the arrival of aliens is, hmm, *provocative.*"

He expounded. In the millennium year of 1000 A.D. many people had expected that the world would come to an end. The year 2000 had ushered in a decade when it seemed that the same was truly starting to happen, at least as regards human civilization. Then: bingo, a turnaround in our fortunes thanks to the Mockymen.

"We're in an aftermath situation right now. There's a physical phenomenon called hysteresis—not to be confused," and he winked, "with hysteria. When a body is stressed, there's strain. Remove the stress, and strain lags behind. This lagging is hysteresis. I would suggest that the arrival of the aliens released the strain human society was increasingly subject to, but the stress—in a psychological sense—attached itself to the aliens in the form of anxiety and paranoia." Oh, he might write a scintillating paper on this subject. "Especially in the case of Britain," he added, "since we are an island. Islands are supposed to be defensible, but the aliens can intrude as if from nowhere, into people's heads. Shall we discuss this in more depth later on, Jane?"

She was frowning, but she brightened. "I'd like to."

The invitation did not exactly extend to me.

"And you, Anna, how do you rate history nowadays?"

"Oh, I intend to *make* history—though whether it's ever written down . . ."

He laughed.

Jane was trying to seduce the celebrated and vivid Professor of Modern History to her Humpty views. Her hectic journalism was already a cause for concern.

We were being summoned up to hall, so I hastened to collect my seating plan before I ascended.

Four long tables, sixteen a side, plus high table; about a hundred and sixty of us were gathered. The organ in the gallery over the door was playing stirringly. Same old high hammer-beam roof; same portraits of past Masters. Milling around, nodding and smiling, people were fitting themselves on to the wooden benches polished by generations of bums. I wasn't close enough to Jane for easy conversation.

Of my immediate neighbours I recognized only one, a red-faced fast-talking Welshman who turned out to have become a lecturer in geography at Aberystwyth. Directly opposite, a beaming Indian had little to say but seemed in seventh heaven.

Yum, roast guinea fowl on the menu, after the avocado with

crab, and before the summer pudding. White wine glass, red wine glass, port glass. College doing us proud. Eighty guinea fowls died to please us. Fall silent, organ. Grace from the Dean. Servants brought our starters and poured white wine.

The chap on my right, an Australian microbiologist, really appreciated being next to a Sheila such as me, though I did not appreciate him quite so much. I pointed my fork up at a high clerestory window engulfed by a vast cobweb, completely beyond the reach of a feather duster even on a thirty-foot stick.

"Way out of reach," I told him.

"She served us guinea fowl," someone was saying loudly, "and she carefully explained to everybody, 'This is *not* chicken that has gone off—' "

The port accompanying the summer pudding wasn't bad at all. Then there were toasts, the final one prefaced by a ten-minute, rapid-fire spiel of wit from a young Fellow, designed to reprogramme us with that sense of effortless superiority which is the supposed hallmark and unofficial motto of the college.

"A few aliens may have come to Earth recently and caused a spot of hubbub, but college traditions endure," et cetera. General laughter and table-banging.

The hospitality was really generous, not least in the Senior Common Room afterwards—meaning the new SCR, of concrete and glass, adjacent to the hall, new in the sense of thirty-odd years old. Set out on a huge oak table were three choices in abundance: chilled bottles of lager, Newcastle Brown Ale, and brandy, sufficient to last a lot of people until one in the morning.

Brandy glasses in hand, Richard and Jane were ensconced in a corner, almost rubbing against one another. Richard disappointed me. He was so self-satisfied. Within half an hour the two of them had slipped away. Heading up St Giles towards his flat, no doubt. The sofa in Richard's college room, where we had once sat primly for tutorials, was inadequate; and Jane's overnight room would be as stark as mine.

The following week I set wheels in motion to detain Jane, to dampen her anti-alien fervour. The suppression of Humpty activities was necessary for the health and wealth of the nation. Rabble-rousing was not the way to achieve anything useful.

I had told Richard that I wanted to make history. For years I had felt that I was preparing myself for something exceptional, and when Jock revealed the conspiracy within the heart of authority this struck a deep chord.

As I say, Jane never reproached me in my dreams for her internment, which actually kept her out of trouble. Just last week I dreamed of her. She and others had broken out of Kielder and were escaping over open moorland. I was with them.

A vivid shooting star streaked across the night sky, then another. Those were not military flares but celestial phenomena. When a third bolt of light came, I knew beyond doubt that portions of a comet were crashing into the atmosphere. Scarcely had I realized this than a tremendous white flash arose beyond the horizon — hundreds of megatons of impact. In a few minutes a blast wave would reach us here on this bare moorland. This was not a nightmare. I wasn't terrified. Since I understood what was happening I was apprehensive but also fascinated. I called out to Jane to follow me because I knew that nearby a shaft with hundreds of circling steps descended deep into the ground. She scorned my advice. She couldn't understand the consequences.

Reaching the place, I plunged down and down — until I came to my hidey-hole, as the earth shook above me. By now Jane would have been swept away.

Chapter 18

What a scary shit-heap this estate is. Abandoned homes shuttered with metal, derelict vehicles, great pools of darkness—it's like a huge version of an urban warfare training village. Thank heaven it's so late, or so early in the morning. May our car with its darkened windows seem as sinister as the neighbourhood.

Back in Middlesex Square there's silence. Jamie-Olav is either asleep or lying awake ruminating. He mentioned *adjusting*. Incorporating the Jamie life into the far longer span of Olav. Jamie was a confused lost soul, sense of purpose alternating with perplexity. What of Olav? Willpower, *persistence*, to quote that Mockywoman on the Mag-Lev, self-assertion carried to the extreme. Had he been chums with all those ghastly mass-murdering Nazis in South America? He must be thinking his way through what Jamie knows of the world nowadays, assessing it all with a different inner eye.

"Tomorrow morning," I muse to Tim, "Zandra and Barnabas are bound to want to hear Olav's story. He may open up to them more readily than to strangers. So we won't swoop too soon. Though we daren't delay long."

Ah, here's the Corby home. There's even a number on the building. Ugly square twin decks on top of an armoured hull. No sign of lights. No sign of any van, either. No one is about.

"We'll wait. They'll have paramedic equipment." Hopefully zonk-juice too, to make transport easier.

"Extreme stuff, reincarnation," says Tim.

"Absolutely. One of the big mysteries about dummies and transit is how you can possibly separate a mind from a body. All goes back to Descartes."

"I think therefore I am."

"Oh, you know?"

Chuckling, "Einstein is E equals MC squared, there's my whole repertoire for Einstein. Descartes is I think, et cetera; and that's about it."

This isn't quite the time to talk about dualism, the idea that the mind is a sort of presiding entity inhabiting the brain, so that a mind could take up residence elsewhere, in a new body or in a machine —an idea fast falling out of favour until the Mockymen came along. Not the time at all. I'm too nervous.

"You're quite an extreme item for me, too, Anna. But after Stanza I'm not naive. Enough said. I'll only stick my foot in my mouth."

"A cigar would fit better."

"Right. Let's keep it light. Enough heavy things are coming down."

"I'm glad of you, Tim." Truly I am.

"Olav will have to collaborate, won't he? Realistically no one is going to prosecute him for war crimes or send him back to Norway —"

"—but the threat exists?"

The jewel is far more important than Jamie, but if Olav genuinely reincarnated himself he is like a Mockyman minus the hi-tech.

"*Anna, any sign of that van?*" It's Jock.

"Not yet. All's quiet, though."

Tim looks in the mirror. "Van's coming."

Unmarked. White.

Munro and Maclaren are both hefty Scots, and indeed are still sporting kilts—one mainly red, the other blue and yellow—with matching tartan socks. No time to change into something less conspicuous. The element of fancy dress adds a bizarre touch to this operation, as if a pair of psycho bank robbers are disguised in Walt Disney masks. Any baffled witnesses might be discouraged from sticking an oar in. The two Ms have a military bearing—Jock's own tiny Tartan Army—nor has their drinking been Glasgow-on-a-Saturday-night but something more robustly lairdly.

There's scant time to become acquainted.

"And you'll be?" one of them asks, to be certain.

"Anna Sharman. With Tim Rogers."

"I'm Colin Munro. This is Bob Maclaren. We're to do as you tell us."

"Jock has briefed you?"

"Indeed."

"Any sedatives with you?"

"Aye. And sluicing around in our bloodstream too."

"That doesn't matter. Tim will drive you and the van and your patient to where it's going. Are you armed?"

"Pistols. And shotgun in the van."

"Bob, will you guard the vehicles? Colin, bring a stretcher—"

The door proves to be locked but Tim kicks it open easily enough.

Mocky-Billy is in the lounge, collapsed upon the sofa near Alex Corby's corpse, starkers except for a nappy. He got this far —sliding or bumping downstairs I suppose, then crawling and hauling. Willpower, willpower. On the TV lots of wurzels are having a knees-up down in the West Country. Turn it off so as to be able to hear any street noises.

Munro promptly unrolls the stretcher then slides a needle into Mocky-Billy who flails weakly but soon subsides. His nappy is wet and smells of piss.

I dash upstairs to the marital bedroom for a blanket and to the bathroom for a towel to replace the nappy. Can't waste time searching Billy's room for where his mum kept spares. Back to the lounge.

"Hoist his bum, Tim."

Off with soggy nappy, and toss aside. Tie the towel round the pasty loins. Then it's heave-ho by Tim and Colin on to the canvas, wrap the parcel, pull the straps tight.

Under five minutes, and they're bearing the parcel between them down the external flight of stairs.

Maclaren is pointing a pistol towards the neighbouring building, so out comes mine too. Only now does it occur to me that with Tim assigned to the van I shall need to drive out of here one-up, on my own.

An engine revs in an adjacent street. Soon a car noses into view —an old Audi, I think. It halts at the junction, idling. Our van and our car are both facing in that direction.

"You mustn't be followed, Tim—"

Nor must I be, nor must I.

Van doors are open now. Medical equipment, monitor screen, a short-barrelled black shotgun on a rack. In goes our guest, out comes the shotgun. It's a Franchi Special Purpose Automatic. Munro dangles it by his hairy leg, not showing it off.

"Well?" he asks me.

The Audi moves again, entering the street we're on, then stopping again. Two men inside are trying to make out what on Earth two kilted clansmen are up to. Shouldn't have left that junction. Can't they see we're armed?

Headlights glare from the opposite direction. A truck is on the move. Now the Audi swings out across the street—it's going to block us.

No, it isn't. Mounting the pavement briefly, it retraces its route to the junction, plugging the side street instead, pointing the same way as us now. The truck's loitering. They're like kids challenging us.

Being in the lead, I shall need to drive off first.

Munro loses his balance for a moment, and I smell the whisky on his breath. Tipsy in charge of a shotgun. As passenger, he'll be on the wrong side of Tim to aim at the Audi to immobilize it.

"Give Tim the shotgun," I tell Munro. "He has to ride with me in the back to begin with, then we stop as soon as we're clear, and transfer. Have you used a Franchi before, Tim?"

He hasn't.

"On full auto it fires four shots a second. Effective range is fifty metres. 12-bore slugs, can reduce a rock to powder. You only need aim low at the engine. There's no need to slaughter the occupants."

How likely are the men in the Audi to have an illegal shooter with them? What would their purpose be in using it? Sheer bloody-mindedness? Or to try for my tyres?

Pulling away fast, van following close behind, I duck my head as I accelerate past the junction. From behind me: boomboomboom. In the mirror: one nackered Audi. Windscreen shot to shit. The truck had picked up speed but it comes to a halt by the damaged car—to give help or to avoid a similar fate. We're away, we're clear.

At the edge of the estate I squeal to a halt and Tim leaps out.

"Anna, take care."

"You too."

And I speed away.

Those fellows who tried to interfere will surely check the Corby home next and find a corpse, but no wife or dummy son in the building. Gunmen in tartan, moll getaway driver, shotgun: what does it add up to? At this late hour their boss may be sozzled or fast asleep. Ah, but tomorrow Robert is planning to phone the boss, and the boss may alert Robert about us unexpected visitors. We can't delay our trip to Middlesex Square too long.

Jock will be on tenterhooks. I must call him.

The alarm clock shrills. 0700, January 1, 2016. A holiday for people who have been up revelling half the night, though not for me. Tim must be asleep at Daddy's right now. Absolutely he *has* to be. I could call his mobile but he'll be exhausted. By now Daddy has a different perspective on his daughter, along with a renewed sense of purpose. I'll call Daddy around seven-thirty, no make it eight. He'll be up by then even if his sleep was disturbed last night. Of course it was disturbed. In the cellar of Cwmbach reposes a Mockyman. If not, why not?

Linking to Olav, real time, yields silence. He's asleep. When will he rise? And Zandra and Barnabas? I'll have time to replay their return to Middlesex Square.

At Oxford Jane and I once took acid together. I wasn't interested in raves and Ecstasy and Yaba, but acid was supposed to be a key to reality, so to speak. We took our microtabs of LSD in the Botanic Gardens on the lawn by the bank of the river Cherwell just after lunch. Half an hour later I was seeing Jane's face as a flexible mask designed to portray a gamut of feelings in almost theatrical fashion. The faces of other visitors to the gardens were likewise all masks displaying traits. In everyday life such exaggerations must enable us to recognize personality and mood, which otherwise we would miss. Throughout that afternoon Jane seemed like an artificial, if organic, caricature of herself. A semblance of Jane.

And nowadays masks are walking about in the world: aliens, wearing our bodies, though that may not be the worst duplicity . . .

There by the Cherwell I was vividly aware of the cunning artifice of existence: faces that exhibit people to us, but which are contrivances of evolution akin to the patterns on butterflies' wings. Yet I was a mask as well, as I noticed in the mirror in my room after we returned to college.

Another thing I saw that afternoon was the gears of the world, the structure of relationships. A bird flying by *kaleidoscoped* across the sky like that painting by Duchamps of a nude descending a staircase—stages of a process all seen simultaneously. The bird's wings webbed their way from one place to another within a prismatic mesh of light, propagating through the array like a pattern of ripples moving over water rather than the bird physically shifting from one place to another. I remember thinking that an alien being might see his world in this way—not as a collection of objects, but as *process*. Applied to human relationships, you could as it were "pause" a person's mask, alter it by means of an astute word, and let the process resume, having changed the other person's mind without them realizing.

This is sheer Descartes: a miniature person or pattern, the Self, roosts within the skull, strings connecting her to nerves and muscles. Ergo, this Self can relocate into another body or into a machine. Much research work into mental processes has insisted that this is nonsense and that the conscious Self is no such animal. Taking rides inside couriers, downloading into dummies, or being reincarnated ought to be impossible. Except, here are the Mockymen. And here's Olav as well.

In that lovely botanic garden, as in the world at large, life was a system of competitive consumption, plants striving for space and light, beckoning bees to fertilise them, *using* other beings, as other beings use one another, flies thirsty for our sweat, spiders trapping flies; and thereby beauty and vigour and richness. Use-of-others was not selfish but something lustrous and radiant, it seemed to me— which perhaps was a seductive illusion. Do the organs of a body use one another in this way? Does the liver lead an independent life?

Oh, Jane is alive and well, and Daddy is saved from an illegal escapade for the sake of something far more valid, all be it still highly illegal. When Jock first *kenned* me (his word) as someone suitable to recruit I became one of an esoteric few—perhaps too few!—the aim being to acquire hidden knowledge, now within our grasp. In my warm bed I stretch like a cat, and flex myself.

Memo to self: a cat lacks a conscience. A person who lacks a conscience is as impaired as those rare persons who cannot feel any physical pain. Not courier material, such persons as those. The pain of transit reaches parts that other pains cannot reach.

"Daddy, it's Anna. Oh this is an open line. I just wondered, did you get my present?"

A pause while Daddy digests the need to watch his words.

"It certainly came as a surprise." The reply is so neutral. "So you knew I was wanting to look after a pet? Kind of you to choose one for me." Maybe he's being sardonic.

"The opportunity came out of the blue. Has Tim said how?"

"He has."

"And has he said anything about . . . an exchange student from Norway?"

"He needed to mention your protégé so I'd fully appreciate your, um, justifiable concern at my knowing about him. But he didn't go into great detail."

"Fascinating, isn't it?"

"Deeply."

"Did the two Scots fellows hear about Norway, too?"

"Oh no. They were both taking a gander at my wine cellar—spent quite a while down there sorting things out. They're upstairs in the guest room sleeping it off. What bothers me a bit, Anna, is, if you *hadn't* found a pet for me, what would have happened instead?"

"Nothing dire. I would have sorted it. But I was full of curiosity."

"As it turns out, I'm inclined to say that the world needs curious people."

"Forgive and forget?"

"Of course. We see eye to eye."

"I would have hated it any other way, Daddy. Where's Tim, by the way—in my old room?" Occupying my largish single bed . . .

"No, he's on the sofa here, stirring. Wanted to keep an eye on the wine cellar."

"Can I speak to him?"

"When I say stirring I don't mean he's ready to run a mile. He'll be out cold till lunchtime." Yes, Major Sharman (Retired) is in command of his house and unexpected guests.

"Look, I'll be in touch. Love you, Daddy."

"Right. Yes; love. Goodbye."

Chapter 19

Mrs Johnson produced a belated breakfast of scrambled eggs, crispy bacon, deviled kidneys, and croissants. Having abandoned butling togs in favours of cords and an open-necked shirt, Robert served the dishes, then proceeded to sit at table and pour himself a coffee.

Zandra ignored the breach of propriety. "Have you phoned that boss?"

"Half-ten on a New Year's Day? You're joking. I'll phone around one. His head might be back in gear."

"How did Joan settle in?"

"She bunked with Milly, and I slept on the sofa. Milly's staying downstairs all today to look after her."

"That's no problem."

"I dunno about *no* problem. That sofa ain't any feather bed. I ought to move upstairs, temporary. Use the other spare room."

Zandra flexed her manicured fingers. "I really don't think so, Robert."

"We'll see. Milly and Mrs J need a story as holds a bit of water. You don't want me spouting off about alien jewels and fugitives and whatnot, do you?"

Jamie-Olav pointed a fork at Robert. "*You* are an accessory to murder."

"You pulled the sodding trigger. Something's not right about you at all. Something to do with that jewel, is it? You come in here off the street, all mixed up and in a fog, then last night suddenly you're capable of doing what Barney here couldn't bring himself to do."

Jamie-Olav speared a kidney. "Don't overreach yourself."

"There you go again! What are you, Jekyll and Hyde? Jamie Taylor and Herr High and Mighty?"

"The point is that your employees are important to the State. *You* are not important. Their indiscretion might lead to them becoming long-term guests of the system. Yours is more likely to lead to elimination. Of youself and family. As unwanted witnesses. I know this. I'm not trying to sound sinister."

"What makes *you* so important to anybody?"

"I have *remembered* a little secret which ought to guarantee my welfare. You have no such saving grace, Robert. Now let's agree on your story before your mother's splendid cooking goes cold. Then you can go downstairs and caution your kinsfolk."

"You aren't Jamie. You're a dummy with a Mockyman inside!"

"If it helps, think of me as schizophrenic and unpredictable — just so long as you pay attention to what I say."

Barnabas spooned scrambled egg on to his plate. "Be wise, man, be wise."

"So," said Zandra to Olav, "that's put Robert back in his place for a while. I think I'm a bit scared of you myself."

"Shall I tell you what scared is? Shall I tell you about the escape from Cherkassy?"

"Where's that when it's at home?" Barnabas asked.

"It's in the Ukraine, one hundred fifty kilometres southeast of Kiev. The Reds encircled sixty thousand of us there at the beginning of 1944."

"Sixty thousand *Norwegians?*"

"No of course not. Along with regular German forces was the Wiking division of the Waffen-SS. Wiking was made up of Reichsgerman and Scandinavian regiments as well as Dutch and Flemings and the Belgian Walloon *Sturmbrigade*. This international division earned high esteem."

"Not among Russians, I don't suppose."

"On the contrary! Red commanders sweated if they knew they faced Wiking men. Well, nobody *sweated* — it was too bloody cold. Though in February an unexpected thaw turned the ground into a bog."

"What year did you say this was?"

"1944—and I was there, believe me. The Luftwaffe couldn't resupply us by air because of the thaw. Mist and smoke reducing visibility to a hundred metres even by day, and by night. *Nacht und Nebel,* literally. Night and fog! The constant pounding as the pocket shrank to something like ten kilometres by ten. Air bombardment and shells and rockets raining inward. Sheer hell. Us destroying equipment as we shortened our lines since we could only keep what we could carry. Our few remaining Wiking panzers tanks turn back heroically to buy a little time, sacrificing themselves. Ach, such blood and sacrifice! On February 10th we make the final breakout. Swarms of Reds pour after us as we lumber through mud in our fur-lined winter anoraks. At midday blizzards begin to rage, which gives some cover. As Red tanks close in, thousands of us drown trying to cross a little river which has become a raging flood—I mean *thousands.* And the survivors, their soaked clothes are freezing solid. In rearguard action the Walloons lose seven out of ten men. Hauptsturmführhrer Degrelle, he survived and became brigade commander—he received the Knights Cross later, as did I. And thirty-two thousand men escaped from hell. *That* is being scared."

"So you won a cross."

"Knights Cross of the Iron Cross."

"And the Russians won the fight, thank God, or like as not there'd be no black folk in Britain today."

"I told you, Barnabas, I was never involved in racial exterminations."

"Just sort of in general killing?"

"You don't understand the perspective back then—the need to stop Communism from swallowing the Nordic lands. This was a matter of national salvation. Also, early on in the war Hitler was the only game in town, and he seemed a strategic genius. How could we imagine Britain could continue to resist? And without the stepping stone of the British Isles America could not have intervened."

Zandra broke in. "Last night you told us that you set out to be reborn. Deliberately! *How did you do it?*"

"It is not something you can do."

"It has to do with the statue in the park, right?"

"Yes, yes." Jamie-Olav pursed his lips. "This isn't something you or I can duplicate ever again. It's futile to tell you."

"Sod that," Barnabas exclaimed. "You wouldn't remember a fucking thing if not for Zandra and the crystal—not to mention us giving you house-room when you needed it. So bloody well tell us.

Did you boil down a few Jewish babies and drink the juice? Is that why you don't want to say?"

"Someone did die. But voluntarily! Not so that I could live again —the sacrifice was for a national purpose."

"You sort of muscled in on the act?"

"You make it sound so vulgar. That's why I'm reluctant."

"We might sully the memory, you mean? Who died, man, who died?"

Jamie-Olav whispered, "It was my sister."

"Fucking hell, your own sister . . ."

Zandra peered intently. "*How* was this done?"

Jamie-Olav shifted uncomfortably. "She was . . . assisted. But she chose this."

Harsh laughter broke from Barnabas. "I bet she had second thoughts when it came to—what *did* it come to, exactly?"

"Her throat . . ." The words came out slowly and strangulated. "It was cut. In a ceremony."

"Nazi voodoo, with a human chick instead of a chicken! Your own sister, man . . . So who exactly cut her throat?"

Jamie-Olav remained silent.

"What was the ceremony?" persisted Zandra. "What's the connection with the park out there?"

It's half-eleven in the morning when Jock and I arrive in the MAL car outside the mansion in Middlesex Square. Just the two of us, softly, softly. Is that one of our smart microcopters alighting on the guttering and slipping out of sight? Or just a dead leaf or scrap of rubbish whirled up high by the wind? Not something you would normally give a second glance.

"Bear in mind, lass, that our Olav may look wet behind the ears but he has all the guile of a lifelong survivor. If there's a whiff of a rat, he'll smell it. So far as he's concerned—same goes for Zandra and Barnabas—we're big cheeses, real ripe gorgonzolas oozing authority."

Quite! Whether or not gorgonzolas smell more persuasive than rats, our target trio mustn't suspect that we are only a tiny cabal within the security services. Jock won't remain for the full interview —gallingly for him—because sequestering the alien crystal takes precedence.

We don't know if Robert has phoned the estate boss yet or not. Most likely not.

When Robert opens the front door, suspicions cloud his face.

Oh but Jock Henderson-Smith and his niece here, Anna, simply happen to be in the area. May as well kill two birds. Need a word with Mr Mason and Miz Wilde. Wee official matter. Do convey apologies for our being a bother during a holiday. Take my trilby, will you?

Soon we're shown into a drawing room overlooking the small park. On a wall there's a framed photo of a fakir hanging by hooks from a contraption resembling a medieval catapult. My fingers itch to open the drawers in the drum table tarted up with astrological signs. We sit in the spoon-back chairs and wait for several minutes.

Under any circumstances tribal-scarred Zandra and Barnabas would make a stunning entrance.

"I told Mr Danvers we wanted time off—"

In the presence of a lady Jock has arisen courteously. "Och, this isn't to do with Danvers. Let me show you some ID." Settling down, he lays heap big ID on the table, as do I. So of course the two couriers sit and scrutinize. The four of us around the decorated table.

"Coffee?" offers Zandra, feigning normality.

"No, let's leave your man Robert out of this for the moment. He has enough on his mind. I'll come straight to the point. The point is yon alien crystal that you have in this house—"

Zandra and Barnabas both tighten up like a couple of snails given a tap upon their shells.

"—the jewel yon Mockyman made you bring back, Miz Wilde, along with his mind inside your head. We have Billy Corby safe and sound for a spot of cross-examination, but I want the crystal now for safekeeping, if you please."

"How. . . ?" breathes Barnabas.

"And after we've had a little chat my colleague here wishes to speak to Jamie, better known as Olav."

"You bugged our home!" Zandra's indignation goes into high gear. "MAL bugs *all* couriers' homes!"

Jock inclines his head, seeming to confirm this reasonable deduction.

"Before we even moved in! You buggers, buggers."

"Let's not overheat ourselves. We'll sort this out calmly and use-fully for all concerned."

"I'm not living in a house without any privacy."

"Miz Wilde, the alternative might be you living in a far more controlled environment. We didn't come here to be unpleasant, though. You've done your country a service: that's my attitude.

You've offended, but productively. So will one of you kindly produce the crystal?"

Barnabas mumbles, "If I do give it to you . . ."

Jock wags a finger. "Laddy, we aren't talking deals. Go and get the damn thing. And don't tip Olav off while you're about it—"

While Barnabas is away, Zandra stares fixedly at the photo of that fakir immovably held by hooks. Then Barnabas is back, depositing a little leathery black pouch on the table before resuming his seat. Jock empties out a lustrous gem as big as a fair-sized marble, picks it up between thumb and forefinger of his big hairy hand.

"Don't look in it—"

"I shan't, Miz Wilde. I wouldn't wish to be confused by discovering that I'm actually my great-grandfather. Just checking this isn't a marble." Back into its pouch goes the crystal. Casually he drops the pouch into a capacious mackintosh pocket, since he hardly came equipped with a case chained to his wrist.

"This bauble will need some scientific investigation by the best brains in the land, and we'll be finding out what Mocky-Billy has to say for himself. Meanwhile, you're to carry on with your ordinary lives. Though excluding courier trips—you'll stay off the rota since you wanted a rest. Remain in London. I cannot emphasize too strongly the need to be discreet."

"What about Robert?" Zandra asks.

"Ah, what the butler mustn't see . . . Robert intends to organise a house clearance, I believe." Jock cocks his head at me. "You know, lassie, we ought to have burnt the place down last night. Loose end, that. Robert's a big loose end."

"Olav scared Robert quite a lot," Zandra hastens to say—trying to protect him? Guilty conscience? "He warned Robert about . . . dire consequences, if the authorities ever find out."

"And now we have. I suppose Robert'll want to know our business here, if he's become uppity."

"We shan't tell him."

"Could be fraught and inconvenient, him and family staying on here with you. Tell you what. Let's say that under new regulations MAL is going to vet everyone who lives with a courier. That's what this visit of ours is about. So if Robert and his tribe scarper now, suitably paid off, vetting won't apply. I presume you can run this place yourselves for a month or so, since you won't be doing courier work. That's better than having minders installed by us."

Minders? We certainly couldn't install minders without giving the game away.

Zandra is already nodding when a doubt hits her.

"Robert isn't going to have some sort of accident, is he? Olav said—"

And *I'm* wondering exactly the same.

"Olav, yes." Jock stands up, towering, patting his pocket. "I must be on my way. Miss Sharman will be your contact. After I'm gone she will continue this fruitful discussion with your house guest present. I'll bid you good day and a harmonious 2016. Get rid of your servants but make sure you have their forwarding address."

I, of course, will call for a taxi when I'm done.

Can we safely let Robert run loose?

I would love to put a recorder on the table but Zandra and Barnabas believe that hidden microphones are already listening.

What Olav reveals may be only—*only!*—of intrinsic interest, irrelevant to the mystery of the aliens. Or maybe not. Those popular books and vids about people recovering memories of past lives through hypnotic regression always struck me as tosh, to the extent that I paid much attention. Historical details supporting people's claims that they lived before could easily come from the ocean of background info to which we're all privy about life in past times—books, movies, whatever—which claimants have been exposed to, even if the conscious mind forgets. Olav may be the first genuine claimant.

Claimant, claimant . . . *Tell me the number, tell me the number . . .*

Of course the number must be that of a Swiss bank account! Chrissy Clarke knew what Olav had been and she wanted the Nazi money. Alas, Jamie only had speechless baby responses and no memory of a previous life, so her tortures by candle and electric shock were in vain. Those were forgotten by Jamie, blotted out. Here's something to shock Olav with.

While Barnabas is away fetching Olav, Zandra leans towards me. "Will you promise that nothing bad happens to Robert? Oh is there any use asking!"

Actually, her asking focuses me. I'm very unclear what Jock has in mind regarding Robert. We simply haven't had time to go into it. Get rid of him. . . ? Hoping he'll keep his head down and his nose clean, when he knows about a rogue Mockyman? A disgruntled ex-butler can't be allowed to endanger what might be the security of the human species. But to have him slotted, as Tim might phrase it: that has a very foul taste to it, very foul indeed.

"Tell me, Zandra: who does Robert care about more, Milly or his mother?"

Zandra shakes her ebony-Egyptian head in refusal as if I'm a sniper asking her to select a victim.

"I'm trying to help, Zandra. Whom will Robert worry about more?"

"If *what* happens?"

"If one of them disappears—if she's held somewhere for a while. Him unsure, and scared for her life if he does or says anything he shouldn't do."

The German Gestapo used to intimidate and control people by this method. A loved one would disappear into—what was it? —night and fog. That was the motto for their policy, *Nacht* and something or other. Right at this moment, taking this particular leaf out of the Gestapo book seems almost humane.

"A hostage for good behaviour, Zandra. I think I'll be able to persuade Jock."

"Why not *detain Robert*? Take him somewhere secure. I don't understand."

Of course not. She doesn't realize how we're operating on a shoestring and have no state machinery to call upon. And I must not alert her to this. If Robert himself is seized, how do I guarantee his survival? Under Jock's bluff bonhomie how ruthless may he—or some other fellow conspirator—be? *I don't know.*

Carefully I say, "Millie may cause a fuss, get in touch with Humpties, seek publicity, to try to find out what and why. The other way round, Robert keeps the lid tight on."

"I see," she says. Maybe she'll puzzle away at this. Why doesn't mighty MAL detain the whole household? Can't be for lack of personnel, surely?

No, her main concern right now is protecting Robert.

"Anyway, Zandra, if we took Robert how would you know that we were genuinely detaining him and that he's still alive?"

"Jesus."

"Zandra, I'm trying to be decent about this, compatible with the need to act firmly. This isn't easy for me—though of course your job involves a lot more anguish than mine."

Maybe Daddy's contacts in Hereford will be a better bet than Jock's damaged house, when repaired. As for the kidnap itself . . . two burly Scots and a white van, I suppose. Jock was thinking on the hoof, improvising. But then, so am I.

"Which one, Zandra?"

Reluctantly she says, "Milly. Though why not Joan? Joan's Milly's sister—"

"I know she is."

"Do you also know what colour my nickers are?"

"Some things," I reply, "are sacred."

Such as the lives of bystanders, if they can be safeguarded.

And what are we trying to safeguard but the future of billions of people, supposing our paranoia about the aliens has some basis?

Joan is no use. She's a burden. Despite all the aid and comfort Robert has given her, he might just decide to wash his hands. Has to be Milly. What shitty decisions to be forced to make. Surely it's better that I make them myself wherever possible.

No, I am not forced. I choose. And hope for the best.

Through the doorway comes Barnabas, followed by. . . .

Jamie has the look of my blond, blue-eyed Adonis of Hereford market, though he lacks the gorgeous tan. His is a fresh-faced, appealing look, of young farming blood with a touch of rural noblesse. When I was at Hyde Park questioning him, I recall how I imagined him marching off to the trenches of Flanders a century ago, flower of England about to be reaped. Son of soil, and land, and all that. In the light of what I know now, of course he looks distinctly Norwegian.

I smile graciously. "We've met before—"

His expression acknowledges this but he keeps mum.

"I don't know if you paid much attention to my badge last time, but the name is Anna Sharman, Ministry of Alien Liaison. You're a bit of an alien in England yourself, Olav. I'd like to know the number of the bank account in Zurich that your mother tried to torture out of you when you were a baby."

He braces his hands on the drum table between us.

Zandra nudges the empty chair beside her, and he subsides. He breathes in deeply then squares himself, gazing at me levelly.

"Did you say torture. . . ?"

"With a candle flame and electric current. That's why you were sensitive about your feet—Ruth Taylor told me you were."

"This is . . . sudden."

"We've been investigating you for a while."

Barnabas bursts out with, "Is that why you bugged the house—just ours? But when?"

Olav's eyes have widened.

"Come on: the Swiss bank account."

His eyelid twitches, and he rubs it as if to erase the tic.

"I'm not sure what to say."

"Never mind about the Nazi money for now, Olav. And let's leave the jigsaws and the Vigeland Park on the back burner. Tell me how you accomplished reincarnation in such a suitably Nordic body."

His mind must be working overtime.

"What is my *family* name?" he asks abruptly.

This is a question I cannot answer. "You used the name Alver."

"So you do not know everything."

"We know enough."

"My mother actually . . . tortured me?" This has got to him. The thought of him so vulnerable, pain being inflicted, something he never took into his calculations.

"You forgot because you were just a baby then. If you look in the alien jewel I suppose you might relive those episodes, though I don't imagine you wish to. Anyway, my associate has taken the jewel with him. Yes, Chrissy Clarke tortured you dementedly. Evidently she was plumpish and dark-haired. But as for the lover who sired you . . ."

"*Lover?* He was my nephew. Great-nephew."

Norwegian. Of course. How clever. Reincarnation down the family tree. Affinities.

"So you hired your great-nephew and Chrissy to fuck . . ." In something like the ice house. " . . .in a crypt." Crypt is a general enough term.

Puzzlement, definite puzzlement.

"I did not hire them, though I realize it must have happened somehow. Where was this crypt?"

This does surprise me. Maybe I was wrong about the ice house.

"You didn't hire them to have sex?"

"No, but obviously they did so because I resemble Carl Olsson. There's no other explanation. He was at their home. A crypt. . . ? Tell me about this crypt."

Now he is making demands of me, but I shall let this pass.

"To be honest, I can't. I thought you would know."

Zandra slides a long slim finger into that hole in her hair and twists it about, as if the skull socket within is some control device by which she can crank up her attention and intelligence, using her fingernail as screwdriver. Barnabas is frowning intently. The two couriers are so enthralled that they seem to have forgotten their own predicament.

Olav says, "Olsson came over from Norway with her because of nightmares they were having. I think they must originally have met in the Vigeland Park . . . The sex must have been part of their attempt to . . ." He snaps finger and thumb together. "The crypt— of course I know where it is. It's in Slemdal. *Emanuel* Vigeland's mausoleum. The brother of Gustav the sculptor. Yes, that would be a perfect place. I didn't give Olsson enough credit. Instincts guided him."

"Unlike you, who plan everything. Though not the womb you would be born from."

"I expected there to be a racial affinity, but it is a direct blood affinity."

"Comes from spilling family blood, eh?"

This irks him. "I am not a monster. I eventually made use of existing circumstances. And thus my sister did not die in vain! Listen: I already told Zandra and Barnabas that my rebirth is not repeatable—"

"But uniquely interesting, I'm sure you'll agree. So what was the precise method?"

Obviously he must cooperate—just as, in his former life, he cooperated enthusiastically with Nazism because of ardent Nordic and nationalist ideals.

I do realize, from Robert's point of view downstairs, that my visit must seem to be protracting itself unduly . . .

Nutty as fruitcakes, a lot of the Nazis and their fellow travellers were! Except, Olav is here as witness to success in one of their crazier magical undertakings—although the outcome was not as originally envisaged.

According to Olav, initiates of the Vril Society (no connection with Bovril, the meat extract drink) would stare at an apple cut in half so as to begin to awaken the superman in them. Proto-super-men would play an occult Tibetan card game of destiny. When not vivisecting prisoners in concentration camps to determine racial characteristics, the Ancestral Heritage Department of the SS (with a bigger overall budget than the American Manhattan Project to build the atom bomb) organized expeditions to Tibet, bringing back elixirs and "Aryan" bees which produced special honey. A colony of Lamas settled in Berlin, and another in Munich. In the quest for superhumanity many weird avenues were explored, as Nazi bigwigs sought a kind of transcendent consciousness.

Olav evidently views many of these shenanigans as absurd, at least from his perspective of maturity, though he may have been hooked at the time. Being classified as a top-notch Aryan, and an SS officer into the bargain, he was privy to certain rites.

Mingling of male and female secretions (and blood and soil) played a part in some ceremonies. In a literal sense such mingling was the modus operandi of the Lebensborn movement set up to breed superior Aryans by bringing together SS heroes and suitable maidens. Apparently Chrissy's capers with Carl Olsson in the crypt had been along the right lines.

Blood sacrifices took place. Arguably, the millions of victims who were gassed, then burned in ovens were sacrifices as well as being victims of racial purging—not that Olav knew at the time about that non-military aspect of the SS, oh no.

So far as his reincarnation is concerned, the crucial magical rite was an Odinic variation on a Tibetan ritual, the name of which means "Cutting Off." In his Himalayan homeland a Tibetan initiate who undertook this rite would perform a special dance, the steps of which formed geometrical patterns. (Geometry was available aplenty in the Vigeland Park, which seen from the air resembles a huge mandala.) The initiate would brandish a magic dagger, and offer for destruction a body held dear, namely his own. He would imagine himself being torn apart and devoured, amputating himself from the world and his spirit from his sacrificed body, wiping thought from consciousness so as to free the will.

"*The will, the will,*" enthuses Olav. All a matter of will, of supreme will. "How did I survive Cherkassy? Cherkassy is in the Ukraine—we were surrounded, bombarded, besieged . . ."

"You told us you were scared as shit," Barnabas chips in.

"*I did not say I shitted myself.*"

"Okay, keep your hair on."

"I survived by will! As we fled I willed that I would not be killed by a shell or a rocket. Others might be killed because they expected to die—like beasts, brave enough beasts, but in a slaughterhouse. My fear went away like fog dispersing. My consciousness became clear as crystal. I *knew* I would escape. I knew I would escape from Norway too. A properly focused will can achieve anything. I was perfectly clear about this when I shot myself."

"The ceremony in the park," I remind him.

Yes, the cutting off from the world, to make a psychic cordon which would safeguard German forces in Norway. His sister's death was the pinnacle, the anointing, the consecration. This rite stirred up potent forces which focused themselves in that park. And there the power remained after the German will to fight collapsed. What about those Tibetan lamas? Those experts in Cutting Off and similar mysteries?

So far as Olav knows, the Tibetan adepts who did not die in the Battle of Berlin were massacred by Mao's soldiers in the late 1950s.

The sheer irrationality of many Nazi activities in the eyes of the enlightened democracies made the Allies unable to credit such occult capers. Historians deny that any such aberrations played a significant role, but Olav knows otherwise.

"Small fry, us," sighs Barnabas. "Small cuts, after all!" He's referring to the scarification club in Kensington.

"The Mockymen also have a will to persist," I tell Olav.

"Do you know, Anna Sharman, it was believed in occult circles that in the distant past superior inheritors of the Earth descended from the sky, from the Macrocosm, to occupy the bodies and brains which had evolved on this world! Old Ones without bodies of their own. But we forget this, whelmed in flesh. I think this did not happen in the past at all. I think it is a vision of the future, an intuition of the coming of the Mockymen, superior to us—occupying our human bodies, preparing to supplant us. They masquerade as men. Nazism was misguided, yet the Nazis spoke of the Jews in our midst as members of a different species masquerading as human beings."

Barnabas jeers, "So was that actually an insight into the future? Your Nazi buddies just got the timing wrong?"

"I am making an analogy. Obviously these aliens do not value the human race except as vehicles for their own purposes, whatever gifts they give. How could it be otherwise in the struggle of life?"

I have been listening to him for over half an hour. Ever since Olav entered the room everything uttered has been recording. Now I need to go away and do some very clear analysis—and downstairs Robert will be chewing his nails because I have been up here so long.

"By the way, Miss Sharman, my family name is Frisvold."

"Frisvold. Well, Herr Frisvold—"

A shake of his blond head. "I am not a German."

"Mr Frisvold, you will keep yourself available here."

"Where else should I go to? Stratford?"

"I was thinking in terms of Switzerland, to collect your inheritance. You can go out for walks and drinks; visit parks with statues in them." Don't even glance at his shoulder. Let him imagine surveillance by smart mini-cameras on rooftops, all networked. "Don't

go too far. We can find-you quite easily. You're ours, Mr Frisvold."
"Yet you allow me liberty. As was obvious, when you came here
with only one companion."
"No one has banned reincarnation. We're a democracy."
"And my good hosts remain at liberty, despite jewel and dummy.
So we appear to have some sort of understanding." He actually
winks at me in rather a lecherous way. I may be the first woman he
has fancied since his resurrection. Dirty old man in a personable
youth's body. Or maybe Jamie's hormones are affecting him.
Zandra's too daunting for him, and Zandra's black—if that bothers
him after screwing Indian women in Paraguay, no doubt.

A leer, definitely a leer in Olav's look; and him once the heel-
clicking SS officer, as I imagine him to have been, a black-
uniformed blond beast. Now he's studying me, trying to determine
whether his wink intimidated me at all, what buttons he might press
to manipulate me. Oh I will not be manipulated at all. It is I
who must manipulate. And a lot of manipulation needs doing, by
too few hands.

"Mr Mason: if Robert hasn't phoned that boss yet, tell him not
to. If the boss phones here, Robert's to say that MAL found out
about an illicit dummy and came down very heavy. He can't say
more."

The estate boss ought to drop his stolen clone-phone like a hot
potato in case smart software can somehow pinpoint him. As to why
Billy's life-support gear remains in situ, let the boss puzzle about
that but stay well clear. Alex's corpse, rotting or mummifying?
Unpaid rent and uneasy neighbours? An untidy business, best left
alone for the regular police to find out about some time or other,
and be baffled, and maybe notify the Sleeping Beauty Squad on
account of the bootleg equipment.

"Robert is going to stay here," I say. "Miss Wilde and I agree it's
best. There'll be a control on his behaviour—she'll explain later.
You'll tell him that MAL already knows what happened because of
the bugs in this house and that we're assessing the situation carefully. No one here is in danger, but the house is under surveillance,
and anyone leaving will be tracked."

Olav rises and looks from the window.

"By two old ladies?" he enquires.

"Technology has moved on apace, Mr Frisvold. We use microcopters and mini-cameras. We prefer not to be conspicuous. Rapid
reaction personnel are on standby."

"They did not react rapidly last night. Barnabas very nearly
threw the alien crystal into the Thames."

I sigh, as if vexed. "We retrieved Mocky-Billy soon enough, once monitoring flagged what was happening. And I really do not need to explain any more to you, except that we regard cooperation as preferable to coercion just at present."

On the subject of coercion, there's an illegal gun in the house. Barnabas must keep it in a safe and secret place, and he bottled out of pulling a trigger last night. Not such a good idea to tell him to bring a gun to hand it over. Gun in the hand is dodgier than one locked in the drum table or wherever—no, the drawers of the drum table have no locks; gun'll be upstairs somewhere. There, let it stay.

CHAPTER 20

On January the second Jock turns up at my flat so that we can go to Hereford together. He has borrowed a car from "a friend." We can scarcely use a chopper any more; far too prominent, and the pilot would know our destination. Even using a vehicle from the official pool poses a risk. The journey itself should provide ample opportunity for him to hear all about my interview with Olav but he wants the broad outlines right away, even at the cost of delaying our departure, because lass we have a passenger with us who doesn't necessarily need to know yet about a resurrected Norwegian Nazi. Who's that, then? Wait and see.

I'm to drive. The car proves to be a newish Volvo Landsman, and the passenger waiting in it is chunky dark-haired Lionel Evans, the Welsh courier. I thought I knew Evans moderately well, and I never realized that he is one of us.

Courier—and connoisseur of the history of torture. I feel very iffy about his inclusion in our trip to question the Mockyman. Daddy's Regiment already includes interrogation specialists, though in what you might call a preventive role. Men are subjected to sensory deprivation, loudspeakers blaring white noise, drugs, and a certain amount of physical abuse to train them to withstand what the Gestapo used to call "intensified" questioning, should they be captured by ruthless enemies. All this, thank goodness, falls quite a way short of actual torture. Rules of the Geneva Convention are only bent somewhat. Rite of passage, really.

Evans's presence sours the trip for me and make me feel ambivalent about Jock, but I still need to sweet-talk Jock regarding Robert, so I hold my horses (if not my horsepower) as we hum westward along the M4, the suspension coping well enough with most of the irregularities.

Traffic is fairly light. Not too many metal mammoths charging along. Dull day of grey sky and sad misty fields—the temperature has risen again after the sudden cold snap. With luck there won't be drizzle and spray later on in the journey.

"You aren't reacting," Jock says, which causes me to jerk as I check my mirrors and the vehicles ahead of us.

"To Lionel being with us," he prompts me.

Measure my words. "I think the Mockyman will have little choice but to answer all our questions. What other option does it have? Why shouldn't it cooperate?"

"And if not?"

"Maybe it has a way of isolating itself from the sensations of the host."

"Only if it's a passenger. Not if it's the pilot. Not so far as we know."

"I don't think extreme measures are appropriate." Especially not under Daddy's roof—not in my own old home, full of memories. Nor anywhere else, either!

"Speculatively, lassy, suppose there's a nuclear device hidden somewhere in London, and the clock's ticking, and you have your hands on the terrorist who hid it. Would saving millions of lives justify extreme measures?"

"This isn't the same."

"We don't *know*, not for sure."

"Anyway, the Billy body is weak."

"De-billy-tated, is that it?"

"Pressuring the Mockyman might cause, I don't know, a heart attack. A stroke."

"You think we can simply propose a deal. Be honest with us and we'll be nice to you. How could we have confidence, lassy? Shouldn't we tickle him a wee bit?"

"This is loathsome. Why should we have to?"

"It isn't a human being, it's a dummy."

"Occupied by a mind."

"Aye, my sentiments exactly—deeply distasteful. I wondered

what your reaction would be. You're playing your cards too close. I think you want something, Anna. Not a promise that we won't use physical pain—something different. What is it?"

I almost miss a van signalling, at the last moment, to pull out ahead.

Jock says, "My idea in having Lionel with us is to scare the living daylights out of our guest, should the need arise. Mockymen seem to take great care to avoid pain."

"*We* feel the pain of transit instead of them," Evans growls behind me, in a getting-one's-own-back tone. He's wearing an aftershave that is at once cloying and acrid. Personally I never wear perfume. Rather than enhancing a person I think that perfume represents phony assertiveness.

"If need be, Lionel will describe to it in exquisite detail—"

"Oh, exquisite."

"—the nauseating history of torture."

"Devices such as the Spanish Boot—"

Crushing feet for the use of, as Evans proceeds to regale me. And the Copper Boot, boiling feet for the use of. And the Dice (with screws); and still we're only in the foot department. And the Eye-Cups, and the Scavenger's Daughter; and the Wooden Horse plus water torture . . .

"That's enough! I can't steer straight if I'm squirming and feeling sick. This is histrionic. It's melodrama."

"Aye, it's all very primitive and barbaric, and that's the whole *point*. Bygone torments seem more terrifying and disgusting than modern techniques, even if modern methods are often worse. Our Mockyman's an advanced alien on a comparatively uncivilized world."

"The tormented body is a liar." I've heard Evans say this in the past. "The mind best torments itself."

I protest, "But you don't have any of those devices. You might need to show it things, the way the Inquisition showed Galileo, not just talk about them."

"Actually," Evans confides, "I'm a collector. Mostly of replicas, I confess. Some, made specially for me."

What must *his* home be like? Like a German dungeon? Do he and like-minded cronies play-act putting his toys to use, not too extremely? Consenting adults in private. Or is it all solo, like masturbation?

"We have several choice items in the back of this car. Thumbscrews, a Copper Boot, the Eye-Cups." Just a few feet behind me.

"Contingencies, lass. We might need a bit of melodrama if sweet reason and Dehib fail."

Full marks for imagination—or is Jock out of his head? The Mockyman certainly isn't in *its* right head.

"So, Anna, what are you wanting to ask me about that requires a spot of subtlety?"

Right. The Robert problem. I explain my preference. Kidnap Milly, and salt her away with dire threats. Today this seems as lurid as Eye-Cups, whatever those are.

Jock chuckles. "I was planning to sequester Johnson rather than his wife, even though we'll be stretching resources." Ah, not to slot him, after all. Thank God for that. "The objection *I'd* raise to your proposal is that we'd be leaving a very pissed-off man in the couriers' mansion, a man with criminal connections."

"His acquaintance with the estate boss is hardly that."

"Left at liberty, he's more likely to cause trouble than his wife would."

"What, and risk his wife?"

"There'll be a fraught mood in the house, upsetting our couriers."

"I think our foreign friend can handle things. This way, we'll be reassuring Zandra."

"Och here you are worrying about everyone's feelings all of a sudden, even a Mockyman's."

It's true, it's true. How to live with oneself. Scruples at the very time when a crisis is upon us! Maybe this is the best time for scruples.

What if the Mockymen have no secret agenda? Will we be able to believe this? Soon we'll be passing Reading and the turnoff to Pangbourne. Pangs are the watchword of today.

"Jock, if we take Robert instead of Milly it'll lower my rating with Zandra and Barnabas."

"Because you won't have twisted me round your little finger?"

"We may need their good will."

"Aye, when we use the jewel. If Lionel here doesn't feel up to smuggling a stowaway spy." So that is the other reason for Evans being with us . . .

"I'm certainly game," Evans says, "if it's possible."

"Or if the spy doesn't fancy Lionel. We might need more than one reliable courier—though we aren't carrying out any experiments with the jewel till we hear what the Mockyman has to say about it, and till we believe him. Right, Anna. We shouldn't alienate Miss Wilde and Mr Mason more than necessary. Munro and Maclaren will take Milly. She'll be easier for them to handle. And now I'm feeling peckish—always did when I was a lad, off to the seaside and such. That urge to gobble the packed lunch right away. Which services shall we stop at?"

One that sells a lovely corned beef sandwich, I hope.

In Come-Back Cottage curtains shut out the fading afternoon. Illumination in the lounge comes only from the standard lamp with its big, silky, green tasselled shade, casting a glow over Mummy's multicoloured china hens and roosters, as if we do not wish to shed too bright a light on our activities, or our identities. Gone are Christmas tree and cards; and not Twelfth Night as yet.

I become mother and hostess, setting out ginger-and-orange cake while Tim helps with crockery and cups. He's so pleased to see me. In the kitchen, he already confided that Daddy nursed mixed feelings at first but now in his view I'm ace, a trump card. (Still, Daddy did put my skaters card away.) Naturally Tim's agog to know what happened between me and Olav, and I promised him, *later*.

Munro and Maclaren are still here and still in their kilts—they'll be returning to London before the interrogation. Along with Major Mike Denbigh from the Regiment, we're seven for tea—I keep thinking we're eight but the eighth is in the cellar; Tim might take him some fruitcake.

Denbigh is about Tim's age, with a lightly sandblasted moon of a face, deep-set watery eyes, corn-stubble hair. I would say that his is rather a psychotic face except this cannot be true. It may seem so to those he interrogates, his other speciality being paramedic. Obviously Daddy holds him in high regard, and vice versa. Denbigh is wearing one of those survival jackets with umpteen pockets and pouches, and a cravat knotted round his throat.

He and Daddy and Jock need to suss each other out, since in other circumstances a senior "Military Intelligence" spook attached to MAL would have been witch-hunting this Humpty faction within Britain's elite special forces rather than plotting along with them. Something of a fantasy with Major Mike, until now, the conspiracy? Has its roots in the SAS maxim, "Think evil." Think of the worst conceivable thing that might happen and work out how to cope. What if the Mockymen are not benefactors but cunning invaders?

The idea that an advanced alien civilization might be predatory received a thumping knock on the head with the coming of the

Mockymen to help us in exchange for what seemed precious little, even though that little is important to the Mockymen. All those popular paranoid novels and movies of the 20th century about alien invasions really reflected our own long history of invading one another. Rome invades most of the known world. Mongols invade. Britain invades India and Africa. Germans invade most of Europe. Italians invade Abyssinia (*Duce*, it is the only place left to invade!). And invasions were often conducted by chaps who seemed pretty alien to the invaded: Aborginals boggling at Captain Cook, Cortes in armour on horseback amazing the locals. This happened so often that obviously anyone odd-looking turning up with strange equipment is in the business of invading. Map this on to imaginary aliens. Then real ones turn up offering new lamps for old, fusion and food synthesis in exchange for worms and weeds.

Denbigh and others were dutifully *thinking evil.*

And now an irruption of reality has precipitated the need for action.

What a surreal tea party this is. Daddy, revitalized though hampered by his hip, treating me with a mixture of crisp professionalism and qualified parental approval. Denbigh, some fuse sizzling in his mind underneath his own disciplined though mutinous esprit. Evans with his Copper Boot and Eye-Cups in reserve. Two kilted clansmen. If we were drinking toasts in Isle of Jura and swearing do-or-die oaths we might seem like fruitcakes ourselves, but we are merely sipping tea.

And coming, now, to the matter of Robert and Milly, soon sorted.

Denbigh will send an unmarked van and three men well trained in hostage situations to London tomorrow. Difference being, they shan't be freeing hostages; they'll be snatching one. I will phone Zandra, patching through my comp to erase source-of-call, to alert her to a goods collection concerning her maid. I'm keeping my word, I shall say.

In the Brecon Beacons west of Hereford the Regiment carries out its endurance tests, yomping over the mountainous terrain in the foulest weather. On the southerly fringe of the Beacons the whale of Mynydd Llangattock mountain sprawls across many miles, bearing Ebbw Vale on its windswept back. To the east is pretty Abergavenny amidst wooded hills. Nearby is Llangattock village which lends its name to the flat-topped massif. From girlhood I remember picturesque stone bridges over streams and canal; rows of former weavers' cottages along lanes, stocks and whipping post inside the church to discourage drunkenness in days gone by; but the village was wiped out ten years ago by superflu and forsaken. Use one of those empty cottages?

No, no, that would be too visible.

Beyond the abandoned quarries pocking the limestone crags, the looming mass of Mynydd Llangattock is honeycombed by a maze of tunnels and caves extending for miles. Entry has been banned for years, but the military are pretty much a law to themselves in these parts, and Denbigh and chums are expert cavers. Inside Mynydd Llangattock they have kitted out a den. Boys' games, boys' games. I can hardly visualize a liberated Hugh Ellison in his wheelchair being concealed in such a place! Now the den comes into its own.

"Are you *sure* an abandoned cottage wouldn't be easier?"

Denbigh eyes me from deep in that big golden bun of a face as if I'm a guileless girl.

"How would you heat the cottage, Miss Sharman?" Possibly by using the portable generator which is squirreled away inside the mountain. "At least underground that woman will be able to get some exercise."

"Be sure to keep her blindfolded all the way to the caves," Jock tells Denbigh.

Of course. Come the time for her release, Milly will have no idea whatever she has been inside a *Welsh* mountain.

"Are there books to read in your den?" I ask Denbigh.

"Quite a few thrillers and, um, magazines."

I can imagine what sort.

"Better clear those out and stock up with big fantasies and historicals." Actually I've no idea of Milly's reading tastes, if any. "Maybe some romance."

"We'll load a bergen full of books."

With the departure of the Scots we are five (plus one out of sight). Jock will need to use the spare room tonight; he can hardly share Daddy's bedroom. Assigning Evans to the sofa puts Tim and me in my old room in the ample single bed. I'm not sure if love-making will enter into it, here under Daddy's roof, whether to celebrate a breakthrough or to exorcize demons, depending on what happens in the cellar.

Which is lit by a single bare bulb. Plugged in to the only power point, a fan heater purrs. Wearing a pair of Daddy's pajamas and a dressing gown of green towelling, Mocky-Billy is resting on a camp bed, eyes shut. Jumble has been shifted to make space for the camp bed and a portable chemical toilet. Our guest's bowels have been on holiday for years. There's no odour as yet. We never did get round to sending down a slice of ginger-and-orange cake. A tray on a small, low table holds a bowl smeared with porridge, a glass stained with milk.

It's my first real chance to study the borrowed body. Face and neck a bit chubby, though with a mellow tan. Rather a surly, wilful face. Mulish, self-indulgent. His hands are podgy in a baby way, but the nails are beautifully manicured.

Jock shifts the tray so as to use the table as a stool. The rest of us will have to stand.

"Wake up, Mockyman."

Mocky-Billy is already awake.

"You stole me," he whines.

"You're a bit of a thief yourself, eh? I mean that mind-transfer crystal—we'll come to that in a moment. Actually we saved you from an unpleasant fate, left helpless in that house. You ought to be grateful. Are you grateful? And prepared to show it?"

Mocky-Billy's gaze drifts from person to person in this cluttered little cellar, fixing finally upon Tim who is at least familiar. He licks his lips.

"This body is feeble."

Is this a lament? Or a disclaimer that we can't expect too much from him?

"Aye, well your dummy was lying around unused for four years. After a spot of exercise and feeding up you'll be right as rain."

"Exercise . . . may be difficult . . . in here."

"You can do sit-ups and push-ups. You aren't going anywhere else unless you answer a bunch of questions truthfully."

How can he ever be allowed to go anywhere else?

"I am tired."

"Snap out of it, laddy. Do you have a name?"

The Mockyman considers.

"Billy," he suggests. Is he trying to convey an impression of feeble-mindedness?

"I mean an alien name."

"Is Billy not a good name?"

"Not for you. We might think of you as human. Appearances are deceptive. We don't intend to be deceived."

"Ah . . . *Loosh-shi-cartoo*, then?"

In alien lingo for all we know this means box-of-cornflakes.

"Car-too," echoes Jock. "That'll do fine. Sounds like cartoon. A mockery, not a real person. Well, Mr or Miss or Neuter Cartoo—do you have a sex, by the way?"

"This body is boy."

"That's the body you're wearing, aye. What's the real you? Do you have an original body stashed away among the stars? What's your alien method of reproduction?"

"Bodies reproduce."

"That's usually more effective than merely thinking about it. Tell me, if you are to fuck a human Mockywoman is the outcome a human baby with a Mockyman mind of its own? Do you produce a Mockybaby between you?"

"This can happen."

"So. Let's say there's some sort of mind-fuck going on at the same time as the copulation. Yet to date none of you have done this on Earth, not so far as I know. Now why's that? What are you waiting for, laddy?"

The interrogation was a qualified triumph—the main caveat being whether the genocidal masterplan of the Mockymen as revealed by Cartoo bears any relation to the truth.

"Do you think it's for real?" Tim asks me in our room afterwards.

It's always possible that Cartoon-man was slandering his fellows out of self-interest, feeding our paranoia in exchange for protection as our source of intelligence.

In the bathroom I changed into my kimono of soft flowers and armoured warrior, and carried my day clothes back to the room, which the heater warms comfortably. During my absence Tim donned a black kimono which looks brand-new, bought specially with an evening such as this in mind.

Actually, I believe that the correct name for both our garments is *yukatas*. Kimonos are full-blown affairs for wearing outdoors, not in bathroom or bedroom. In his yukata Tim looks like a Ninja assassin minus the head covering. There's a print by Hokusai of a Ninja. Only the man's eyes and brows and a bit of his cock-shaft are visible amid his black garments—he's raping a woman whose husband he tied up. She's supine, oh so white against his coaly robe, her arms roped beneath the small of her back, her legs heaved vertically up into the air by the intruder.

A tube of toothpaste has appeared on the bedroom washbasin. I already cleaned my teeth in the bathroom. It's important to remember to clean one's teeth. Dinner tonight consisted of pork pies hastily devoured in the basement, washed down with lemonade, maybe a dubious omen when pork pies rhymes with lies.

"He did genuinely crack, didn't he, Anna?"

I have little wish to remember the function of Eye-Cups as lovingly detailed and demonstrated to Cartoo by Evans, but nor can I exactly forget.

Jock and Denbigh were in a hurry, competing with one another. Cartoo was prevaricating.

An old Persian torture, explained Evans. Speciality of this planet, torture is! Ways of inflicting hideous pain. Did you know that, Mockyman? On this leather head-strap are two eye-sized cups like the wide-open beaks of hungry nestlings. These are for holding the eyelids open, which hurts quite a bit, believe me—but the cups also include ingenious channels which will slowly leak corrosive acids into the bottoms of the eyes. The resulting agony can derange a victim to death.

This was stomach-turning enough for an onlooker, never mind what Cartoo must have felt, having the cups attached very lightly to test the fit while Denbigh held him firmly by the arms. Don't really need those eyes, do you?

We all acted out the nauseating charade very seriously until I wondered whether Evans was actually going to produce a bottle of acid—or possibly fizzy water with which to fill the channels in the bottoms of the cups. Cartoo obviously had no means of retreating inside, away from nerve impulses. He began shrieking.

Denbigh injected a weak dose of Dehib, and the story came out amidst pleas for the preservation of Cartoo. It is not a reassuring story, as the rabbi might have said after reading *Mein Kampf.*

For several millennia the Mockymen have had no bodies of their own. The original Mockymen exploited and poisoned their home environment to a point where it became essential for survival to transfer their minds into machine-bodies, into mobile robots or static computers. Their technology was swanky enough for this. And their understanding of the mind too, evidently!

They let the environment rot. As machine-immortals they would persist, contemplating the mysteries of the universe and of consciousness and contemplating an evolutionary leap to discarnate intelligence, hoping to become free-ranging energy-beings, while lesser native species of their world went extinct en masse amid fumes and viruses and mutating toxic moulds.

They could not make the hoped-for jump. As time passed, the

artificial immortals became prey to maladies of mind. Memory overload. Identity dissolution. Obviously they must begin to reproduce naturally again.

How? By recreating bodies in sealed habitats and downloading into those bodies? This would be a cul-de-sac when their world was scarcely habitable. How about regeneration of the ecology? They learned much, but the scale was too daunting. And it would be a backward step.

How about recreating bodies *plus* emigrating to habitable planets of other star systems?

It appears that there exist an affinity between all life which evolves in a certain setting. Not only as regards gravity, chemical balance, quality of sunlight, such things, oh yes, but there's also this subtle harmony between all life which has arisen from a common source, like a secret signature. Set alien life down upon an impeccably habitable world and in the long run it simply will not thrive.

So then: modify the intruding alien life for compatibility? That would be complex—so many variables—and besides it's unnecessary . . . if you can download mind into readily available fully evolved meat.

Meat which can mate with other marionette-meat, and produce true mind-offspring.

The great evacuation necessarily took hundreds of years. Send numerous robot probes to check out likely solar systems for suitable natives. Blank blank blank blank, then bingo. Follow up with a starship carrying hibernating original Mockymen. Make one's presence felt as superior beings. Upgrade some of the natives, make with some technology, build a transit station, kit out a priesthood and devotees with skull sockets, let there be Bliss, produce dummies, establish sufficient bridgehead . . .

All takes time at first. Then after a while, whoomph, the dummification plague. Dummified by nano-viruses—super-Bliss at high speed—most of the natives of the victim-world, those not needed as additional host bodies, simply die of neglect; potential hostile threat thus eradicated. Survivors provide a pool of breeders of bodies destined for future dummification so that Mockymen can transfer when their current bodies wear out—and of couriers to link with what will in time, after the process repeats with variations, be a dozen Mockymen worlds.

There are only enough authentic Lemurs of Passion or Ivorymen of Melody to service requirements. The populations mainly consist of Mockymen in Lemur and Ivory bodies, though obviously these populations cannot indulge in any over-breeding.

And Earth is next in line for treatment, once with guidance we have repaired our environment, brought things back into harmony, a far simpler task than cleaning the cesspool of the Mockymen home-world would have been. In twenty years time the food-factories will rejig themselves to manufacture and emit the dummy-plague and the Mockymen of Melody and Passion will send cadre-minds to Earth stacked four-deep in Lemur-couriers and Ivoryman-couriers by means of those crystals.

The crystals are a relatively recent innovation. Hard to manufacture. Many units defective. Held in reserve for the in-flooding of stacked minds after global dummification. Assorted side effects.

Oh brave new world of Mockymen, human in body, alien in mind. People have romanced about us humans going out to the stars and altering our biology until we became, in effect, the aliens of our fantasies. However, it is otherwise. The aliens will become us.

Leaving aside our own conduct towards aboriginals and natives in the recent past, *how can the Mockymen contemplate doing this?*

Persistence requires that a species should occupy as many star systems as possible. Eggs must not all be in one basket. A sun might flare up. A nearby star could explode. A comet or big stray rock could collide with a world at any time, blasting it back into the era of bacteria and little else. A species confined to one world is really risking it.

Nor can one risk being in a minority on a world.

A residue of us will remain purely human, supervised and used as breeders and couriers. All is not lost.

Besides, our world is grossly overpopulated. And besides again, being dummied doesn't hurt.

Will the Mocky-Humans continue to live in the manner of human beings, imitating what they have stolen? Playing football and going to pubs?

No, the grand scheme is still to become energy-beings and somehow survive the collapse of the universe umpteen billion years from now and live on in a brave new universe. Mockymen Forever, that's their motto! With each new world they acquire, apparently they gain a few new outlooks—this being reason number three for planetary piracy. Put enough outlooks together, maybe in the long run you can become something like a God.

So why did Looshy Cartoo steal the crystal and flee from Melody? Why come to such a barbaric place as Earth where Eye-Cups and Copper Boots are still knocking around?

That's because Cartoo is an alienated alien, a deviant among

Mockymen. He and some chums of his were not such regular guys. Basically Mockymen society is a drag. Wary of mind-maladies, determined to think alike despite a dozen different kinds of stolen anatomies, full of creed and screed about persisting until they disembody themselves one fine day, effectively Mockymen culture smothers diversity.

When the Mockymen turned up on Melody, just as on Earth hundreds of different languages were in use. Now for simplicity only one native language is used by Mocky-Ivorymen and by the residue of natives alike. A minimum of one Ivory language needed to stay in place for vocal convenience, Ivorymen mouths being ill adapted to the original Mockylingo. The same applies to Passion and the other star-worlds. They're like monolingual countries— France, Italy, et cetera—adjacent to each other thanks to transit, all linked by a shared polity, and constantly in contact so as not to diverge from the glorious common goal.

Keeping in contact means using couriers. Couriers endure the pain of being torn apart and put together again, consequently courier selection involves ordeals and initiation rites to weed out the unfit—who can serve as future dummies. The rump population of genuine natives evolves quite a masochistic/machismo culture with a strong accent on sacrifice.

Like young lords slumming it, Cartoo and cronies took to visiting the local indigenous cantonment for kicks. Not kicks in the behind—Cartoo is as squeamish about pain affecting his own person as any Mockymen. But to gawk at the exotic rituals of the aboriginals for frisson, chills, and thrills. There but for the grace of our destiny go we. We, of course, will never suffer—a highly ambivalent attitude, it seemed to me. A scapegoat, denial-attitude: load the sins—no, the fear of retribution and of suffering, an otherwise universal condition—on to other beings, the goats they keep and use. There was something deeply sick about the serene Mockymen.

Once you acquire exotic tastes you tend to want madder music and stronger wine. Cartoo is only "in his first body" and thus debarred from transit. In any case he would not have passed scrutiny as a stable candidate to transit to Earth, though his role-in-life took him to the transit station where he could gawk at human couriers.

As yet, Mockymen are only a few needles in the haystack of all the persons on Earth. Us locals might recognize Cartoo as an alien in human guise but Mockymen were *not* to be hassled. In the unlikely event of being accosted on Earth by a fellow Mockyman he could bluff his way in the language of Melody, to the extent that a human voice can cope with its sounds.

As for twenty years on, that's quite a long time away for a lad in his first life even if trivial compared with the long term. He would cope.

After spilling these beans Cartoo finally passed out, exhausted. When Denbigh returns tomorrow we're to reconvene, after having slept on this very disturbing story, supposing it bears any relation to the truth.

Presumably the aboriginal Ivoryman population contains no resistance movement. Any such group would need to be a very persistent one, passing down a hidden flame from generation to generation in the hope of some opportunity arising eventually. When Mockymen are masters of nanotech and viruses and molecules and whatnot, I can hardly imagine what sort of opportunity. A spontaneous unstoppable plague affecting only the Mockymen? Their population is hardly vast—breeding new citizens such as Cartoo carries with it the need for replacement dummy bodies, so they can't multiply willy-nilly. But they're, well, persistent.

No, there won't be an Ivoryman refusenik coterie; their culture has been thoroughly warped.

"But if we could contact Cartoo's *cronies*," I'm telling Tim. "I mean, to confirm all this about us having a couple of decades left, then being harvested—"

"Why not snatch another Mockyman and see if it tells the same story?"

"When it sees the cups and the Copper Boot? It might be able to let off some alarm signal—we'd be dealing with a motivated Mockyman, not a black sheep. With Cartoo's assistance we can work out how to infiltrate."

"You hope." And him in his Ninja gear.

"I do hope."

"Cartoo might be setting the passenger up for a nasty surprise."

"Not if thinks he'll be eye-cupped if I don't come back."

"If *you* don't come back? *You, Anna?*"

"Me, Anna. We need sneakiness. The sort that spies on your own father. And we *are* a bit short-staffed."

"But what about your body?"

This sounds like a timely question in the circumstances, both of us being bare-fleshed under our yukatas.

"You'd be leaving your body, Anna—what happens to it?"

Supposing I can use the crystal the way Cartoo used it, to squirrel away undetected behind a kosher Mockyman passenger, will I be able to reoccupy my vacated body on my return from Melody? Without previous use of Bliss and subsequent dummydom will my body continue to tick over on standby like a dummy? Does Cartoo know the answer? This business of the mind being able to separate from the body is a major riddle.

Suppose I *can't* reoccupy my own body, plenty of dummies are available at Hyde Park, supposing we can use a dummy without loyal MAL staff or a Mockymen adviser smelling a rat. Afterwards I could be a different woman, twenty years younger. I could even be a bloke. Is this an enticing prospect or not?

"I wonder if I need some tips from Uncle Olav."

"Jesus, you were going to tell me about him!"

So I was, so I was. Cartoo's disclosures have completely distracted us from the SS resurrectee. . . .

I'm no scientist nor philosopher, and religiously I'm a blank, though I hope I do have some ethics. But really there are two giant puzzles.

One is why anything exists at all. Why there is a universe. Since there must be a universe before I can ask this question—me being a part of the universe—I'm caught in a conundrum. The opposite to a universe cannot be "eternal nothingness" because even this is an idea and therefore something, not nothing.

The other puzzle is how any creature can have awareness of itself so as to be able to ask such questions. The universe being necessary, what is the most important feature in it? It's me. Myself. My awareness (and yours and yours and yours). In other words, consciousness.

Maybe consciousness isn't necessary. The universe existed before any life or mind evolved. Self-awareness emerges in a baby some time between conception and . . . when, roughly speaking? Half-time in the womb? Birth? The start of talking?

Talking has to be important. In the absence of language mind cannot express itself, so Self cannot yet exist. Awareness of your surroundings, yes, but not awareness of yourself which must be uttered in words to yourself and to other minds.

How strange that a passenger in a dummy can use its language in the absence of the personality which that language generated. How strange that a presiding personality can be piped from one head into another when the head ought not to contain any such thing as "Captain Self" or "Pilot Self" who can switch from one vessel to another. According to some of Earth's best minds (at least until the Mockymen came) the Self should be a parliament, an assembly of deputies in ever-shifting coalitions, not a kingdom with a throne which can be vacated and re-occupied.

Surely the inter-connections in all human brains vary rather like computers with subtly different architecture—how much more so the difference between human mind and alien mind! So how can the software of one run on the hardware of another? And how can that software extract itself—not copying itself, which would give rise to two Selves, but shifting elsewhere?

If it can shift, does it need any receptacle at all?

Many people believe in ghosts: software, perhaps impaired in its understanding of itself, yet cut loose from any body. Many people believe in a soul which can pass into some hyperdomain called Heaven, or which transmigrates into a new body. How many fables ancient and modern are rooted in the conceit of a mind which can leave the body, to take up alternative residence—in the body of another person or beast or in an alien anatomy elsewhere in the universe or in a machine or as a pattern of energy.

Thus, the Mockymen. Thus, Olav Frisvold. The Mockymen know nothing about Olav, who perhaps fulfills some of their criteria for disembodying. . . .

Chapter 21

It's dark and early when we awake, each of us still chastely wrapped in a yukata. Last night was altogether too much to contemplate love-making as finale.

Thank our lucky stars for Jamie-Olav. If we hadn't been tracking him we would have remained totally in the dark about a fugitive Mockyman unless Zandra or Barnabas decided to come clean. Cartoo would likely be dead, the crystal would be in the Thames. We would know nothing about any genocide plan.

I snuggle. Tim is hard against me, but he has to excuse himself to tippy-toe to the toilet to piss.

"Open the curtains, will you?" Even if there's no hint of daylight as yet, things always look better of a morning. Lo, we have survived another night.

When he returns, he holds me.

"Are you serious about giving up your body? Supposing H-S lets you try."

"Olav gave up *his*."

"There wasn't a lot of mileage left in that one. I know I don't have any rights over your body—it's yours, damn it all. How can you contemplate. . . ?"

"I might learn to think like a Mockyman. No fixed abode, no fixed a-body." Spoken like an Italian mafioso. "Know thy enemy."

"If you have to use a dummy afterwards you'll hardly be able to carry on in the same job."

"Isn't that rather a minor consideration?"

"Surely you like being you."

"Not always—believe me, not always."

"I like you being you."

"Celebrate, then," I tell Tim. "We have quite a lot to celebrate." And oh he affirms this body of mine. And I rejoice in him.

"What Olav told you about Tibetans being in Berlin during the Second World War, Tibetan *magicians* for heaven's sake. Here we are, worrying about whether Cartoo is telling the truth—but is Olav? Granted that the Nazis were screwballs—"

Quite. Olav's presence in Middlesex Square nowadays, January 2016, seems to authenticate his explanation, but does it actually? What's the old saying about swallowing a fly and straining at a gnat, or is it the other way round? At Oxford Richard always taught us to be sceptical.

"True enough, Tim. Right now it's time to freshen up for Cartoo's confessions part two. I'm for a shower." Nudging him: "Gonna wash the man right out of my hair."

"Which sort of hair?" he asks cheekily.

"*You* had better check on Cartoo. Help him empty himself."

"Okay, and I'll start sorting breakfast. Full English, hmm? I'm starving. I might even make you some corned beef fritters."

For breakfast, God, such a love-gift.

"If you bump into Jock don't tell him what I'm thinking."

"You're the boss."

"No, Jock is." Only in a limited way, as regards our small conspiracy against MAL and BritGov and the UN and the whole sodding Mockymen Reich.

What if our actions could receive some unofficial sanction? I don't think that's possible, considering the deadweight inertia of the permanent government, nearly nineteen years in power, hauled us through the Hardship Years into the blue water of Mockymen goodies they did, same captain at the helm, lock up the Humpties, don't rock the boat, benign ossified centrist dictatorship. Jock may or may not be on good terms with some cabinet minister, but we only have the unsupported word of one maverick alien.

Once Denbigh is back in attendance, while Daddy minds the fort upstairs, the interrogation proceeds though without any more recourse to Eye-Cups or Dehib. Cartoo has become a thorough snitch, and just as well for him, though we must take his revelations with liberal pinches of salt. Same as last night, we need to waste time on what words mean since Billy Corby was not exactly college calibre, though Cartoo is quick on the uptake.

Anyway, *Su-loo-la* is adherence to the Mockymen credo of perpetuity in host bodies unto the Great Liberation from time-bound flesh (or circuits), the hypothetical transfiguration into pure energy. There but for the grace of Su-loo-la go we. Cartoo fulfilled a junior role in the testing of mind-crystals and mind-transfer apparatus. New refinements, new tweaks, always ensuring absolute safety, gilding the lily. Being in his first body, a junior is all he could be.

Despite re-embodiment, the breeding population of Mockymen stays in check partly due to euthanasia. Mind-maladies often accumulate from body to body, and mercy-killing is the remedy— policed largely by "Monitors," specialists in handling regrettable situations such as accidents and emergencies, lunacy or major deviancy, or natives misbehaving. Monitors carry pacifying "pistols" which disrupt the nervous system, although use of these is very rare.

Some Elders in their umpteenth bodies survive from the time of the original Mockymen diaspora and constitute a "Council of Wisdom." Those Elders don't exactly go in for public appearances. By now I'm sure they must be fanatically bonkers or very complacent due to habit and repetition.

Mockymen security may seem nifty at keeping human couriers sealed away from the real Melody or Passion, but of course a human being is highly visible.

"We bloody well need to confirm your story, laddy—!"

Supposing a human courier knows the relevant door code and avoids being spotted, he or she might enter the section of the station close to the arrival rooms where Ivorymen dummies are stored—not in one huge ward, thankfully, but in many smaller chambers. Downloaded into an Ivoryman dummy, and in possession of another door code, a human stowaway might with luck stroll out into the alien city, so long as behaviour and apparel appear normal . . .

Wouldn't the corpse-of-himself which Cartoo left behind in an important sensitive area have prompted the Monitors to launch an investigation exploring all possible implications? Especially when a crystal went missing?

Not necessarily so! Cartoo had filched the crystal a year earlier during the course of his duties, swapping it for a rejected defective specimen which supposedly had been destroyed. The substitution would not come to light just yet. And in that room he had suffered a seemingly natural if premature death.

"So how did you lay hands on the toxin, laddy?"

Why, from his crony To-mees-troo who is in his second body and who works in a biology laboratory . . .

"Suppose someone like us uses yon crystal to hide in a courier, when they came back will their mind be able to pop back into their own body again, just like going into an empty dummy?"

This, Cartoo does not know for sure.

Midway through the afternoon, during a recess while we are up in the lounge, Jock roars at me, "Are you out of your head?"

"No, but I *will* be! What's wrong with me volunteering? Someone has to."

"One of *our* boys," says Denbigh. He must feel that baby-sitting a bewildered woman in a cave is not quite employing the full resources of the Humpty faction within the Regiment.

"No," begs Daddy, "for God's sake, no. You're wanting to be too special, Anna."

"Sending in a soldier's no use," I tell him, "no matter how used he is to blacking his face and hiding under a bush for a week. That isn't what I'll be doing."

"Our men are trained to pass themselves off and melt into the background."

"Major Denbigh, would *you* volunteer? Maybe lose your body permanently?"

Denbigh hesitates rather too long before producing a defiant "Yes."

"Any reservations in the volunteer's mind would endanger the mission."

"You caught me on the hop, that's all."

The prospect of being in Evans's head for a time scarcely appeals, though presumably I shall not be aware of him.

"Och lass, heed your Dad." Yet Jock no longer sounds nearly so opposed. He's had a moment to think how much better it is to keep all the strings in his own paws.

Daddy mounts an appeal and Tim is also looking very sad, but personal considerations are minor when the fate of the human race may be at stake, and Jock is hardly pitching in. I hope Daddy will be proud of me.

A call comes on Denbigh's mobile. Parcel collected and en route. Milly will be snug under Mynydd Llangattock by tonight.

*   *   *

Questioning resumes.

Ribbons are what distinguish Mockymen from one another in public. Inside the transit station, as we know, anonymous plain tunics are worn. That's so as not give our couriers unnecessary insights into Mockymen society. Out in the city—which is called Faluinu—tunics are adorned with "life-ribbons," serving as costume adornment as well as ID. Workers at the Melody Hilton and those in the transit station who will encounter humans shed their glad rags prior to a spell of duty.

Money: there's none at all. Everyone is a mutual partner in the great Su-loo-la enterprise.

Public transport: it's free, in the form of vehicles sliding along magnetic monorails. Wheeled vehicles are for official use. Walking is normal. Mockymen cities aren't huge, nor many in number, though obviously Faluinu is expanding because of specializing in contact with Earth.

Intrinsically rewarding though Earth's bugs and weeds may be, what the Mockymen primarily needed was transit stations in as many human nations as possible and a nice varied supply of dummies to practise with to get the hang of being human in readiness for takeover.

Transit stations linking with other Mockymen worlds including Passion are all located in different cities, reached by air. Buildings and streets are smart, able to clean and repair themselves. What a ghastly utopia it sounds, built on regulated genocide.

Foodstuffs are synthesized as per the dietary requirements of Ivoryman bodies and come in the form of little pyramids and cubes and cones, a whole gamut of different geometrical shapes variously flavoured and coloured like all sorts of candy at a fun-fair. Eating with companions becomes a game with quirky rules, involving capturing choice items of food from your fellows or losing items. I should avoid such social occasions. It's enough to give one indigestion—aside from me not knowing any of the rules.

Social occasions, ha. Sporting stolen ribbons I shall need to find my way to where the nearest of Cartoo's cronies lives, a female who is named Pha-po-lidoi. . . .

Another night at Cwmbach, and what of Tim and me? Already I feel the need to detach myself, though without offending him. It's as if for me loneliness needs to begin here and now in preparation for the much greater loneliness of being in alien flesh on a distant world.

I think I can cope with the loneliness. In a sense, I have always done so. Or did I become lonely along the way, losing myself—which I shall now aggravate by abandoning even my own flesh? Might my grand gesture amount to a kind of suicide? And a sort of rebirth, too?

We're still in our day clothes, Tim and I.

"I lost Stanza. Now I'll be losing you."

"Not necessarily."

"You're *hoping* to lose your body, aren't you, Anna? To become somebody else afterwards."

"Am I only my body?"

"Of course not."

It's the right answer emotionally—the answer that has appealed to generations of people. The body is only a seat for the mind. The mind is the true person rather than the bones and brawn and brain. This ought not to be so, but the Mockymen show otherwise.

"If you come back and climb into some dolly-dummy I'll feel like I'm being fucking unfaithful going to bed with you."

How sentimental men can be. He idealized his Stanza—she was living poetry to him. Her cheating wounded him not in his ego but in his private den where he made a shrine to her. And now my image replaces her. Are the image and me the same thing?

"If there's the opportunity, Tim, would you like to help me choose a backup body?"

"Now you're playing with me."

Oh no, he must harbour no such idea.

"I'm not, Tim, I'm nervous."

"You hide it well."

"On Melody I'll be needing to hide the real me rather well. What I mean about helping me choose a dummy is, if you approve the choice, that'll be an anchor for me. Something to come back to."

Is he becoming angry, or sad?

"How could I point at a body and say I'd rather have this than you? Maybe you ought to have a shot at being a man—we could go out and swig lager together like buddies. You'd need to give up port as a tipple. Pint of port doesn't sound right, and a chap downing port in a pub is a bit nancy. He'd be a young chap, wouldn't he? Bound to be. I'd seem like a queer with a boyfriend. We'd end up going to gay bars. What am I talking about? I'd be aching inside."

"I don't want you to ache. One more time, tonight? Kimonos at midnight?"

There's a lump in his throat. "I don't think so. It would seem greedy. I'd just like to hold you. Pyjamas and shut-eye."

"You're a good man, Tim."
And it's true.

Jock must return to London. The crystal needs scientific attention —X-ray crystallography, et cetera, nothing damagingly invasive— and the man for the job will be back from holiday. Ned Rawlings, reliable chap, he'll work nights in the MAL laboratory where he's regularly involved in trying to suss out Mockymen technology, and keep shtum. Info for Jock's eyes only. The two Scots will sit in on these tests (though not in kilts) as guardians of the crystal—they'll need more briefing. Tim will stay on in Cwmbach Cottage with Denbigh, deepening the dossier on Melody and Faluinu City.

Tim has a good mind and the motivation not to let me blunder into any unavoidable shit. Me, I need to choose a spare body, just in case.

Jock and Evans and I will drive by way of Cheltenham and Oxford, the route a crow would fly, though driving will be slower and rougher for the first half of the way. We'll call on Professor Richard Cornwallis to pick his historian's brains about those Tibetans in Berlin. Richard's at his flat; I just phoned. His voice was guarded and cool. I suppose he bears a grudge because of Jane's detention following the Gaudy, but he can hardly refuse a seemingly official visit.

During the drive through the Cotswolds we listen in on excerpts of life at Middlesex Square, as overheard by the chip in Jamie-Olav's shoulder.

Robert was shaken to learn that MAL knew all about Billy and the jewel due to the couriers' home being bugged. Whatever he said was in whispers but Barnabas's reply came over loud and clear.

"I can't give you any fucking money because our accounts are frozen as of now, said Little Miss MAL. That's so as we can't try to do a bunk, and neither can you, capiche?" Inspired, inspired.

In deep shit they must stay put and do nothing.

Apparently no phone call came from the estate boss, so that particular big fish must have decided to behave like a sensible small fry and hide in the weeds. Leaving one dead body unattended to. Be damned if our two Scots should venture another visit to tidy up.

Zandra and Barnabas were generally keeping fairly mum, as was Olav. Simmering small talk was all. Until—fast forward—the arrival of the regimental specialists in kidnap situations, and Milly's removal.

Robert accused his employers of setting this up with MAL.

"Where the shit are they taking her? Where's *somewhere safe?* Kielder, is that it? She isn't a Humpty! Is that where? For how long?" "Robert," said Zandra, "we have no idea. You must calm down." "You knew this would happen. You knew!" "Did not." "Liar." Sounded a bit like children squabbling. "I didn't know *this* would happen exactly—but I'm glad it has. Do you hear me, I'm glad!" We could hear Zandra very clearly.

Olav chipped in: "I told you the alternative would be *you* disappearing permanently because of what you know. Disappearing into a hole in the ground with a hole in your head. Thank your lucky stars."

"What *are* you? Who are you?"

"We already went into that, Robert. The less you know about anything, the better."

"*Joan* is doing her nut about her sister—she thinks those geezers were from the estate."

"Rather than from the State itself."

"Bloody estate, that's all she's known for years."

"Let us restore some sense of discipline and position around here, Robert," said Olav crisply. "That will be good for morale. We should behave as we did before any of this happened."

"You cheeky sod, you can't be serious. Milly, taken off in a van —she'll be frantic. Kielder, you have got to be kidding. She could gab off unless they keep her all on her own—"

Olav, again: "Think straight, Robert. Only you mentioned Kielder."

"You *do* know where they took her!"

"We do not. She is a hostage, to guarantee that you do nothing out of line."

"While what? For how long?"

"Robert, we simply do not know." Zandra's tone was soft and sympathetic. "Jamie's suggestion is not such a bad one. We need to be actors, feigning normality so that we can all live together in the same house until this is over."

"Me, still play at being your servant? That's convenient for you!"

"I appreciate how worried you must be—"

"All because of you! Because *you* brought that fucking Mockyman and its jewel here. It's you who ought to be punished, not me."

"I had no choice. We have no choice. There's no point in recriminations. MAL is too powerful. We're being let off lightly for now because the crystal is valuable to them; and so are we, as couriers."

"But not me, not your bloody butler."

"Robert, I interceded for you with the woman from MAL."

"What do you mean, interceded?"

"I begged her not to let harm come to you." Oh do be careful, Zandra. "So this is what she decided."

"They want you to do something for them. Some courier thing."

"*Robert,*" snapped Olav, "are you stupid? The walls have ears. You must control yourself."

Which he did.

Misty-murky in Oxford. Water meadows breathing out. Now that the Thames flows more fully again, the water table is recovering.

We pull in to a little slip-road by an arcade of shops fronting the buildings where Richard roosts. Mock-classical arcade; Gothic revival brickwork above and behind. First time I'll have been inside since scones and jam in the early Summer of 2000. Evans will stroll around to stretch his legs—Eye-Cups aren't in order here, historical though they may be. Make sure you keep the car in sight, boyo.

Richard's flat seems smaller than I remembered, maybe because even more books are competing for space, though it's as plush as ever. Here's the little lounge where I read out my essay. Richard's once-sumptuous mane has receded and thinned. It's still jet-black, as are his impressive eyebrows, but I can easily see through his hair now. Should he knock off embellishing himself and suddenly become grey and old? He's still trim, in white silk shirt, natty brocade waistcoat, fawn twill trousers.

The flat's cool. He's frosty. No coffee is on offer.

Jock presents his impressive ID.

"I shall let Anna handle this, since you know one another—"

"I wouldn't say we *know* each other exactly. A single encounter in the past fifteen years hardly amounts to *knowing*."

In a funny way, the implicit accusation is exactly what I want to hear, alienating me yet further.

"We're interested in the activities of Tibetans in Nazi Germany, Professor," say I.

Richard steeples his fingers, as he used to do during tutorials. "So what has Nazi Germany to do with Alien Liaison, aside from any passing resemblance you yourselves may bear to the Gestapo?"

"Watch your words," Jock growls. Then he grins charmingly. "Equally, it's your words we want to hear." The grin vanishes. "Your words, not ours. Do be of assistance to his young Majesty's Government. We're thinking of releasing a few more internees."

"I see. Such as Jane? How gracious of you. How can I help expedite this?"

*   *   *

Having heard me out, or at least my version of what interests us, Richard chuckles sourly.

"Tibetans in Hitler's Berlin, *possibly* . . . But you should think of them as more like student activists. Young, politically motivated, fanatical about the liberation of Asia from Anglo-American-Jewish influence. A lot of Nazis thought Churchill was Jewish, you know. His American family connections, and his looks. Your Tibetans would be rather like that Indian chap who raised an army to help the Japanese boot the British out of India in the cause of independence. If you're looking for occultists, personally I would suggest Himmler's masseur, Felix Kersten, rather than lamas from Tibet. You're sounding quite like Nazis yourself, setting up departments to investigate crackpot ideas. Is this what mingling with aliens brings? Do the aliens want to know such things?"

"Maybe they do."

"And you want to keep them happy. Sell them some snake-oil as well as worms."

No comment.

We talk a bit about Norway.

Did we know that the Norwegians never let the opera singer Kirsten Flagstad back into her native land after the war? Her husband had been a minister in the Quisling government—too much singing of Wagner went to her head. But as for some occult barrier around Vikingsville. . . !

We cannot reveal that a supposedly reincarnated ex-SS officer is currently resident in Middlesex Square, useful though it might be for a historian to interview such a man.

"Himmler was convinced he was the reincarnation of some old German hero," I mention.

"Heinrich the Fowler, that's right. What of it?"

"You might say that the Mockymen reincarnate themselves from one body to another. Could there be any credence in Himmler's notion?"

"Where *have* you been keeping your brain, Anna Sharman? Oh, are you people trying to tell the Mockymen that we can swap bodies by occult Nazi methods? Borrowed, I suppose, from Tibet. Is that it? Restore a spot of planetary pride in the face of superior technology! You got starship, massah, but we flap our arms, shout abracadabdra, and fly."

"The point is it oughtn't to be possible to separate mind from brain. Mind should be a circumstance of the brain."

"So yours is still working, after all." Richard's fingers steeple once more. "I recall talking to Cartwright of St John's when those transit stations first started up. He refused to believe the stations were what the aliens claimed, for that very reason."

"What did he think they were?"

"He thought maybe aliens were landing secretly; that they were actually very small and were being surgically inserted into the bodies of dummies in the stations, and that nanotechnology was customizing the dummies' nervous systems or whatnot."

"This is Julian Cartwright the philosopher? Believing in a UFO soap drama? Secret landings, alien crayfish or scorpions in the skull?"

"He merely said maybe. At least it's a materialist explanation. Cartwright's a thorough reductionist."

"I assure you the stations do exactly what they're billed as doing."

"No need to assure me. I have no hot line to the Humpties." He stands up. "If that's all. . . ?"

"Aye, maybe it is," says Jock. "For the moment."

"Of course if you would come to the actual point, whatever it is, I might save you a wild goose chase."

For a moment Jock hesitates. Yet Richard can't possibly be trusted.

"It has not been a pleasure meeting you," is the parting shot when we leave. Fine by me.

No, not fine really. Quite sad. Depending on what transpires, Richard may re-evaluate me.

Chapter 22

I'm at Hyde Park with sturdy Colin Munro of the Sleeping Beauty Squad. In the big cool fluorescent-lit storage hall a warmly wrapped-up nurse—of Asian parentage, and more inquisitive than her white colleagues—watches us from her desk as we stroll the aisles between waterbeds. Why we are sightseeing all these naked bodies? The nurses on duty are new to me. Very boring job; rota them in and out regularly. No chance for Tim to be here. Events are moving too fast.

Which shall it be? This red-ringletted girl? Her boobs are too big; they would unbalance me. This fey skinny blonde with rings in her nose and navel?

Presently the nurse comes over. "Can I help you?"

Her badge names her *Fatma Ladak*. Lovely light brown skin, rather officious bovine face. Wedding ring on her finger.

"Not at the moment, thank you, Mrs Ladak. We're simply looking for someone."

"I can consult my records." Over which I fancy she may labour, at screen, as painstakingly as a child sucking a pencil . . .

"We need to look at faces," Munro says.

"Is it a male or a female you're seeking?"

"A female," I tell her. Of course it should be a female. I'd be silly to settle on a young man. That would be a crazy whim.

"If you come to my work station I can show you all the faces on screen. All the patients are colour-photographed."

"We're aware of that, nurse. We need to see them in the flesh. Will you let us carry on with our job?"

Huffed at Munro's disinterest in records, Mrs Ladak returns to her desk.

How about this long (or rather, tall) black beauty? She bears a fleeting resemblance to Mary of Morogoro as Mary might become in another few years given good food and grooming. Such fine sculptural slopes to her face, jaw jutting pertly, slim flaring nose, high tight cheek bones: she looks more in command of herself and of life in general than she could possibly have been to become a Blisshead. I could become an elegant black girl.

Admittedly, this is all only a contingency plan!

Here's a girl who looks fairly like me. She could be a younger sister of mine. Oval face. Black hair, though longer than mine and ratty—it could easily be trimmed. Little chin, not weak but just neat. Browner eyes. A good number of little milk-chocolate moles all over her arms and legs and trunk, one larger one poised above her belly-button. Those are charming; they make her skin interesting. Shall I be black beauty or shall I be my ever-so-slightly piebald sister?

"*She* looks like you," Munro murmurs.

"I know."

Would I seem to be a caricature of myself?

"Quite lucky, finding a match."

"Yes, but I think I'll be the young black woman over there." Not a girl any more, when and if I inhabit her.

"The long-legged one?" Oh he noticed her.

In solidarity with Mary, my proxy daughter far away. In homage to Zandra Wilde, bringer of the crystal and of Cartoo. In order to be different from what I have been.

"She's a head and a half higher than you—you'd be stilt-walking. Are you sure?"

"I can always use a new perspective."

"I should have thought you'll be having your fill of new perspectives."

"Exactly. That's it exactly."

So now we can go over to Nurse Ladak's terminal, since the chosen one is in her sector.

Quite a number of dummies have no known identity. Goes with the habits of Bliss users. Naturally any photo in the register of missing persons can be matched to a face, but MAL does not officiously contact relatives for identification—that would be crass.

Persons Unknown are not assigned banal names equivalent to the American John and Jane Does. Someone had the whimsical notion of giving names suggested by the original bed number here at Hyde Park, and the idea stuck. Number 43, we discover, is Fuchsia Tree. Miss Tree, identity a bit of a mystery. Unused, as yet, by any Mockyman. Her brain is virgin in that respect.

Munro is forthright, not furtive.

"Mrs Ladak, I cannot say more than that MAL needs to carry out a few tests on a certain physical type. Do remember that you signed the Official Secrets Act to work here. We're withdrawing Miss Tree from circulation forthwith, and I'll need to deny access to her file—"

Jock's flat is in Clifton Place, a few stones' throws from the northern side of Hyde Park where the Long Water bounds Kensington Gardens with its statue of Peter Pan. The terrace is Georgian. Jock occupies the top two floors of a house near the Sussex Square end. In the flat below him is a divorced airline pilot who is often away on long hauls. Occupying the ground floor are a pair of gay men who co-own a restaurant; they sleep in late, and are out till one in the morning except on Mondays, their personal sabbath. In the basement is the infirm old lady who once owned the entire house till she had to sell off the flats one by one at a loss during the difficult years. None of these are likely to be at all intrusive.

The lower of Jock's two floors boasts high ceilings, nice plasterwork, impressive old fireplaces, thick blue-grey Wilton carpeting. Quite a collection of old snuff boxes in a glass case: enamelled, solid gold, silver and wood, tortoiseshell. Upstairs—the servants' quarters of a bygone era—is more compact; and in a spare bedroom up there my mindless body will lie hooked up just as Billy Corby's was. Tim will move in to the house during my mental absence. He'll be the one to change my nappy.

So here we are in Jock's lounge by night: myself and Tim and Lionel Evans, poring over Cartoo's shaky cartography of the Melody Station and Faluinu city, and drinking Highland spring water with a dash of whisky, a sort of homeopathic dose of alcohol. In Jock's opinion total abstinence might make us twitchy and inattentive.

During the past few days at Come-Back Cottage Tim and Denbigh have amassed many more details—routes and ribbons—so that I shall be able to do precisely that: come back. I shall of course need to go in-depth with Cartoo again.

As for alien tipple and substance abuse, the original Ivorymen got high on fermented sap and other plant derivatives. Mocky-Ivory-men eschew intoxication, which is for inferior beings who can be manipulated through their addictions. The pusher-man does not partake, except for the "guild" of biochemists—if they screw up their bodies while experimenting, they can swap to a new one.

"It's a shame," I remark to Tim, "that this can't all be programmed into a game like the one Peters was playing—preferably using virtual reality." Next thing, I'm telling Jock about that Japanese game of transit.

"Aye," Jock says after hearing me, "I suppose this info could all be made into a VR experience given time enough and a contract with some cyber company which signs the Official Secrets Act, and programmers who breathe not a word, and beta-testing it on yon Mockyman to cross the eyes and dot the tees." He crosses his own eyes drolly as if staring at a display a few inches in front of his head. "Then you'd be like a spaceman in a simulator rehearsing for total safety. I'm thinking that the longer we hold off, the more can go wrong. Suspicions in MAL or Security, or in Hereford. Changes of arrangements on Melody. It's all very dicey as it is."

"I don't want delay, Jock."

"Good lass."

By the end of the session my head is humming with Melody. We'll go through all this again tomorrow and the next night, probing for flaws and pitfalls. After I've learned my party piece, it'll be back to Herefordshire for a long *tête-à-tête*.

Early of a blowy rain-spitty afternoon Tim is driving Jock and myself along the Wye Valley to Withyhope.

By now we have the technical report on the crystal: diffraction patterns, vibration directions, fast rays and slow rays, axes, hyperbolic isogyres, et cetera. We're much the better informed, but none the wiser. And we can't risk a test transfer of my mind into Evans and back again into my own body in case of failure.

What if I am sussed on Melody, and Mockymen interrogate me? What means might they use? By our unofficial espionage do we risk provoking the premature release of dummifying and genocidal nanoviruses?

"Jock, *after* I come back what exactly are we going to do?"

Or after I fail to come back but nonetheless have managed to brief a courier in the Melody station . . .

For a while he does not answer, then he says slowly: "If Cartoo's story is corroborated I believe we need to destroy the stations on

Melody and Passion. Break the link with Earth in no uncertain terms."

"By persuading BritGov?"

"I wouldn't pin my money on that—it's other people we need to persuade. Suppose members of the Regiment seize the despatch area of Hyde Park. Suppose volunteer couriers carry portable nukes through and detonate those the moment they arrive in the alien stations."

"Jesus *Christ.*" Tim almost fails to slow behind a lumbering tractor, hay bale impaled on a yard-long spike like some mechanical dinosaur's horn, winter fodder for the cattle. Blind bend; he waits for a clear view ahead. Talk about speaking the unspeakable.

"Jock, are you forgetting about all those foreign nationals who'll be in the two stations? There could be a couple of hundred people —American couriers, Japanese couriers, Brazilians, everyone."

"Aye, we'd be unpopular internationally. Have a bit of explaining to do."

As we surge past the tractor, our acceleration is wilder than need be.

"You'd be more than unpopular," Tim says. "Crucified is more like it. Blowing up hundreds of people, Christ, that's bloody terrorism."

"On the plus side, laddy, it's an instant death, at least for the couriers."

"Jesus fucking Christ, it's mass murder."

"No, it isn't *mass* murder. Mass murder is millions of people, the sort of thing the Nazis did. Mass murder is what will happen to the human race if we don't act. What else do you suggest, eh?"

"But *nuclear* stuff . . ."

"Would you rather hump a hundred kilos of Semtex and maybe not do the job entirely? Is that nicer? Leaving some couriers injured and stranded? Does that salve the conscience? Seems worse to me. Do you agree we need to break the link?"

Tim does his best to steer efficiently and safely.

"Maybe the Mockymen can adjust their other transit stations. Recalibrate."

"No, the equipment that sends our couriers to either Melody or Passion is dedicated. It's specialized. The Melody and Passion stations are dedicated to receiving Earthfolk, not couriers from other worlds. The redundancy is in having Melody and Passion both linked to us. They won't be able to use their non-Earth stations to relink. They'd need to send another pod-ship."

"You hope."

"I *bloody* hope, laddy. All the stations in other countries will come to a stop. Out comes our evidence; plus Cartoo. After that, everyone will be blowing up their precious transit stations."

"Is it so easy to lay hands on a couple of nuclear weapons?"

"I'm thinking about it."

"Who are these volunteers who'll vapourize themselves?"

"There's that too."

We ride in silence until Tim says, "Why not do it without Anna going there, risking alerting the Mockymen?"

"There has to be corroboration. This could all be slander spun by a malcontent. An agent has to go in, otherwise—"

"—BritGov will revive beheading especially for you?"

"Otherwise we don't stand a chance of laying our hands on any decent kit."

Decent, indeed. Interplanetary nuclear terrorism.

"And if Anna isn't able to report back? If she's rumbled there can't be a second chance."

"We'll cross that bridge—I *think*," Jock interrupts himself, "*Winterbourne Gunner . . .*"

"Who's he?" Tim asks.

"It's not a he, it's a place. Just beside Porton Down."

"Porton, the bug lab?"

"Aye, four or five miles outside of Salisbury, stone's throw from Sarum Castle. My first thought was naval ordnance at Portsmouth, nuclear depth charges, but they're a bit heavy. And there's Kineton in Warwickshire for shells. No, Winterbourne Gunner's the place. Chem-bio warfare, and nuclear kit too, hundred kiloton yield. Portable and adaptable; that's the ticket. Closer to Hereford. Officer in charge is . . . a Colonel Macdonald, Hamish Macdonald . . . I think Hamish will understand the need if we have a spot of corroboration . . ."

God, the cogs are turning.

"Our Major Denbigh very likely did some training in chem-bio at Winterbourne Gunner . . ."

And all on my say-so, finally. Horror wells at the thought of so many people incinerated in a fireball. The agony and blast and flash-injuries of those not in the immediate vicinity—the aliens in Faluinu city: burn them and blind them, do they not scream? Survivors can shift into new bodies. It's the human victims who will haunt me. Could be several hundred of them, an entire plane-load.

A plane disaster kills hundreds of people who are so terrified during their last minutes—by contrast with instant oblivion, alive one moment, atomized the next. If you're next door to a nuclear weapon when it explodes do you know anything at all about it even for a fraction of a second? Surely you simply cease. Security services have caused plane disasters in the past.

Let's suppose I'm a Buddhist saint. Let's suppose I'm teetering on the edge of a cliff with a child, the whole future, in my arms, and I can only stop myself from falling by slamming my foot down exactly where a beetle sits minding its own business. Do I slam my foot down?

Sergeant Matthew Woods, Denbigh's reliable regimental Mocky-sitter, has run an extension cable down into the cellar so that our captive can watch TV. This access to information implies that Cartoo will become part of our world rather than face oblivion. As reading matter he has a big English dictionary. He must have been mulling over his fate. He rattles his chain and asks Jock, plainly the cock of the roost, "What will happen to me?"

The chain is new, as are some folding chairs for us to sit on. Already the Billy-body is recovering rather well from years of immobility. Sergeant Woods is helping Daddy upstairs by doing a spot of cleaning. We can't have Mrs Jones coming in to vacuum while a prisoner is locked in the cellar.

"If all you've said's true, we'll be generous, laddy. Big-hearted. We reward cooperation."

Can I count on aid and shelter from Cartoo's cronies? He was obviously the most deviant among them. How wayward are they—or are they simply dilettantes?

"They admired my enterprise. They helped."

"Using yon crystal's full capacity, if we offer your friends a chance to come here, will they do so?"

Talk about springing a surprise, almost equivalent to setting off a bomb. Myself and three aliens inside Evans's head—talk about too many ladies locked in a lavatory! How to hide four vacated dummy bodies somewhere in the Melody transit station? Maybe *in* a lavatory or similar . . .

"Isn't this rather ambitious, Jock?"

"My flat'll be a wee bit full, and our boys in the Sleeping Beauty Squad'll be busy. But that'll be extra confirmation, and it'll encourage experienced assistance for you over on the other side."

I can see the sense of this. It's just that adding this little extra twist—does this allow more to go wrong, or less? Such as chaos;

such as an alien ending up occupying my own body or Fuchsia Tree's.

"This stacking. . . ," I begin.

First in equals last out, so it transpires. Last in equals first out. A brain can hold a lot of mind. Biggest computer in the universe. Three Faces of Eve, so to speak.

Jock demands, "Will they do it, Cartoo?"

"Pha-po-lidoi and Shi-sill-aidoi, most likely. To-mees-troo, possibly. If I write a message. The message must truly say I am in good life."

If the courier we meet on my return to the Melody station needs to give a ride to two or three of the Mockyteers as well as me, who'll be piggy at the bottom of the pile?

"Aye well, your transfer back to your own body may be more problematic, Anna, than Mockymen into dummies. Heaven forfend, I'm not saying that it will be, and we shall have the black girl on hand as backup. Any blockage in the outflow could be unfortunate, wouldn't you say?"

Quite true, quite true.

Out come the maps of the Melody Hilton and of Faluinu. . . .

Daddy need not know about these extra kinks in the scenario. Everything's hunkey-dorey, Daddy-o. As a military man he realizes this can hardly be so. Best laid plans, et cetera. He's not the one to sap my nerve. Tony, of course, must be kept entirely in the dark, being too close to Humpties. Be good to have Tony here—on compassionate leave, to comfort Daddy in case I don't return—but it's too dodgy.

While we were down below, Sergeant Woods, useful chap, fixed us a supper of cold cuts and pasta salad into which we all tuck. Nice nutty-tasting pasta spirals, scrumptious ham, good mustard. A plate goes down to the cellar for our guest.

Matt Woods is a stocky Liverpudlian whose nose might have been reconstructed in a boxing ring. Ruddy countenance, gingery crewcut. His looks belie the intelligence evident in his keen twinkly eyes and his occasional judicious observations. He knows the general mission outline. Denbigh made a good choice.

Woods eyes me. "You'll be first person really to visit an alien world. That's quite something. Still, I can't say I envy you."

Do I envy me?

The first person really to visit—only to close the door for a very long time.

Once again Tim and I will share my bedroom. Last time he simply held me. Now I crave him.

Before we leave in the morning, Cartoo inscribes his affidavit message on a sheet of paper which Evans will carry to Melody in his clothing, crammed in some small plastic tube, a baton to hand on to Ivory-me. The script resembles some zany musical notation. Cartoon claims that the text is as we wish, though of course we cannot be certain. Might as well be in Tibetan. The real name of Melody is Vroa, an Ivoryman word for world. Never knew that before. By now we know more than anyone else on Earth knows. Hope it's enough.

It's big hugs for Daddy and me as we part, perhaps forever.

Chapter 23

Olav has been telling Zandra and Barnabas some more of his exploits. Presumably he hopes we'll be overhearing how capable he is—especially with regard to his getaway in 1945 via Spain to South America, an episode superficially less contaminated with shit than sister-sacrifice or Waffen-SS activities (though personally he never was involved in atrocities). His escape might almost amount to a deed of derring-do if it weren't for the Nazi associations. Even the Nazism has a sort of sick fascination, a perversely glamorous frisson. A previously civilized nation mesmerized by primeval passions and mass rituals, bewitched by banners and anthems and uniforms and torchlight, almost as if a collective magical rite was being enacted.

This focus upon the art of escape stirs and troubles me. It's almost as though Olav is intuiting the action I'm intending, or some variation upon it. Don't I need all the tips I can get? We need to involve Zandra and Barnabas more deeply too.

Between missions couriers generally rest over on Earth for two to three weeks. On Melody or Passion the turnaround time is rarely more than a couple of nights, to recover from excruciation and transit nausea. Despatch back to Earth is flexible; couriers' wishes are heeded. True, there's an ever-changing international crowd in the alien Hilton, but it's tedious being stuck there. Although sizable, the place is clinical, more like a large hospital, each private room equipped with its own dispenser of utilitarian rations. No communal dining room, no bar, no health club—and no TV in the rooms. Couriers roam the corridors and hallways for exercise. To relieve the monotony: card games in those halls—and sometimes, given the nature of many couriers, pageants of piercings, tattoos, and scars, not unlike activities in the native cantonment, I suppose. Camararderie obviously exists between couriers, though also tensions between Chinese and Russian or American couriers, say.

I can't stay too long in Faluinu city. My return to the transit station *must* be with the assistance of Cartoo's cronies.

We sit around the dining table of Middlesex Square, me and Tim and Jock opposite Olav and Zandra and Barnabas. For a warm-up we want to hear more about Olav's escape route, a topic on which he is happy to enlarge.

From Oslo he flew by night down to Spain in the company of Leon Degrelle, the Belgian fascist leader who had washed up in Oslo after the fall of Berlin—a dangerous flight when the considerable swathe of territory to be crossed was either war-torn or already under Allied occupation, though not daunting to the swaggery Belgian, who was a consummate survivor, much decorated by Hitler.

The aircraft descended on the beach of elegant San Sebastian, out of fuel and with quite a bump, which put Degrelle in hospital under guard. Just along the coast the port of Bilbao was the entry point by ship for art works and other treasures looted by the Nazis. Ever since the outcome of the war became obvious to all but total fanatics or the deluded, plunder had been flooding into Spain. There were networks for booty and for escapees too. Spanish companies which previously were covers for Nazi espionage activities against the Allies in neutral Spain now retooled for the Scattering. Soon Olav was in Madrid, hub of fugitives. In the October of 1945 Olav left from Malaga on a merchant boat bound for Rio along with a Gestapo man, both of them dressed as Franciscan monks.

Likewise I shall dress as an Ivoryman, wearing not only a false tunic but a false body . . .

"The secret of escape from harm," Olav tells me, "is to focus the will to create a blank space where you are, an emptiness which nothing shall enter. Not to be a target for shell or bullet or hostile gaze. You must cut yourself off from the web of the world. You must *will* this, and walk serenely . . ."

Once again he favours me with a wink, less of adventurist lechery this time than of complicity.

And he says: "You're planning to infiltrate the aliens, aren't you, Miss Sharman? You yourself, none other. You'll use the jewel to hide yourself in a courier the way the alien did. That's why you're really here."

Jock is on full alert—as are Zandra and Barnabas. But really, it had to come to this.

"It isn't an authorized security operation," Olav presses us. "It's your own initiative, isn't it?"

"Your imagination's running away with you, laddy—"

"Why are we not in detention? That would draw attention. Detention, attention, hmm? Milly isn't in protective custody, she was simply kidnapped."

H-S says severely, "You people here are guilty of smuggling a criminal alien, withholding an important artefact, complicity in concealing a dummy, murder, crimes against humanity in your case, Frisvold, in your previous incarnation, the list's bloody endless. We've been too soft with you. Gives you the wrong idea."

Olav explodes with laughter. "But I am on your side absolutely, Mr Henderson-Smith! I count myself privileged to assist if I possibly can. Did I not tell you—no, it was you I told, Miss Sharman—of the perception that bodiless beings from the sky would steal the bodies of the human race and supplant us? What may happen is so terrible that our racial mind sensed this across time."

"Racial mind, laddy? Up to our old antics, are we?"

"Certain . . . visionaries . . . sensed this."

"Hocus-pocus merchants, more like."

"They were wrong to think this happened in the past. It was a warning of what *will* happen. You have evidence, don't you? The captive alien has told you."

"Och."

"You can't trust your government to believe this because of all the gifts and because the alien is a criminal. The policy—the one you yourselves police—is to suppress all anti-alien agitation. Just as the bomb-plotters conspired against Hitler, so you plot against your own Gestapo, from within."

"I hardly think that's a fair analogy."

"You practically admit it. A few of you are involved, but not many. Though you are the wise ones."

"Endorsement from such as yourself is scarcely a bouquet of roses, Mr Frisvold. But actually. . . ," and Jock reaches his decision, "you're absolutely right."

Jock's gaze takes in Zandra and Barnabas. "According to our one and only source, who might just be a pathological liar, the human race has less than twenty years left on the clock unless we scupper the Mockymen's schemes. MAL as a whole, and the intelligence service as a whole, and BritGov know bugger-all. We dare not let them in on any of this until we've confirmed it or most likely we'll never be allowed to do so. Good work Jock, have a gong and bugger off to Bonnie Scotland. Nearly twenty years till doomsday, did you say? Home Secretary has a dicky ticker. We need medic-nanotech before we rock any boats. Do I sound bitter? Patriotic, I hope. *Truly* patriotic—to my species. You know about patriotism, Frisvold, and how it forces some choices upon us that seem criminal unless they happen to succeed . . ."

Jock proceeds to regale him and wide-eyed Zandra and Barnabas with the whole caboodle, excluding only the proposed theft and modification of portable nukes.

"And you'll be happy to hear this house isn't bugged at all—"

Zandra gapes. "*But how—?*"

"It's Frisvold here who's bugged. Mini-mike chip in Jamie-Olav's shoulder. We inserted it when we were testing him at Hyde Park."

"The cuts! The anaesthetic!" To his credit Olav does not promptly slap a hand to his shoulder.

"Oh man," mutters Barnabas.

"One small cut for mankind. We use microcopters as relays. There'll be one sitting on the roof right now, but Anna will be calling them off and erasing all the surveillance records and compressing them into a black hole."

"In case anyone bugs the buggers?"

"Aye, Miss Wilde. You'll have your privacy back. You can keep the chip, Frisvold."

Olav purses his lips. "People like yourself are necessary. Not everyone would agree, but I do."

Barnabas needs to assert himself. "One small cut, did you say? Just don't you take the piss out of us!"

"I wasn't, Mr Mason, believe me. It's simply the way my mind works, and my tongue."

"That's an interesting statement, Mr Henderson-Smith."

"In what way, Mr Frisvold?" How polite we are being.

"Over the last few days I have been webbing, as Jamie would put it—to understand better how I passed into his body."

"In case there's a chance of pulling off the trick again when you grow old?"

Olav shrugs. "I thought my achievement could not be repeatable, but the way that the aliens switch minds from one body to another—just as you soon hope to, Miss Sharman—makes me wonder."

I'm paying full attention.

While trawling the web Olav has come up against the Descartes Conundrum, much batted around in connection with the Mockymen. "I think, therefore I am." Memorably put; stands to reason—seems plain common sense. Yet what is this Self which presides in a person, supposedly experiencing life and responding appropriately? When we're asleep there's no Self; Self does not exist. Later, Self starts up again; self-awareness resumes. Yet there seems no place for a central Pilot to perch, as Captain-of-your-soul, as spectator in the mental theatre. A brain is an assemblage of parallel hardware produced by evolution, all sorts of processing proceeding in shifting coalitions of multiple superimposed functions, reinforcing or damping one another. On this assembly of semi-intelligent agencies acting in concert, a serial model of conscious awareness runs—telling a story to itself, the story which *is* your Self. Stories have gaps. Consciousness has gaps, of which we are oblivious so long as the story proceeds. Driving from London to Hereford I fail to register miles and miles of the journey but my story seems continuous.

And what tells the story which gives us awareness? Why, words. Language. A narrative engine, which gives rise to our Self. We tell the story of who we are, and so we are aware.

Words compete for utterance, whether uttered aloud or internally. The winning words of themselves give rise to meaning. We do not fit our thoughts to words—words shape the thoughts we think, appropriate to our situations. So how can our Self quit our hardware and word-swarm, and exist elsewhere, as ghost or soul or as passenger in another's brain or as operator of a dummy?

"Your words say so-and-so, Mr Henderson-Smith, and thus you concoct your plan. Hitler's words burst from him in his speeches, changing him extraordinarily and imposing themselves on the world, and becoming true to the amazement of his generals—until his words became mad ranting about imaginary armies. You must believe your words as I believed in my will to survive."

Olav seems intent on establishing himself not only as a Houdini but as a soap-box philosopher.

"And you will either win, Mr Henderson-Smith, or—"

Of a sudden Tim rises, darts to the door, yanks it open.

I don't think Robert was leaning any weight against the wood. Its sudden removal merely makes it seem as though he was, as into the room he stumbles.

Quick recovery, though. Too quick for Tim who stepped aside like a matador, the door his cape, and now faces a Browning pistol in Robert's hand. Unlikely that Robert ever used a gun before but the hammer's cocked, so there's a round in the chamber. Barnabas's damned gun it must be.

"Don't anyone move—I'll shoot anyone who moves."

Tim is assessing. He's just a bit too far away from Robert. He stays utterly motionless—as does Jock. Zandra and Olav are twisted around awkwardly. Non-plussed, Barnabas is staring at his own gun.

"How did you get that?"

"Stuck it in the drum table, didn't you, when we came back here on New Year's morning."

"But I can't have done. I wouldn't have done."

"You were far gone, Master Barnabas. I shifted it. Wasn't much use till now. Waving it wouldn't bring Milly back. *Back off, you!*" to Tim. "Back off one step at a time, and slowly."

Being closest to Robert, Tim occupies most of his attention; and I'm edging a hand gradually inside my jacket.

"This is *stupid* of you, aside from being impertinent." I might admire the hauteur Zandra summons up if it didn't make Robert shift focus momentarily.

You," scowling at me, pop-eyed, "stop moving. You're all bloody traitors, not government at all."

Tim has halted.

"So," says Jock slowly, "that's what the Butler heard, is it?"

"I know what I heard. Get further back, you. *Abracadabra.*" The holo-space lights up obediently, default depth-picture of a coral reef, schools of brightly coloured little fish, huge sea anemones. Exorbitant, state of the art. "*Phone.*"

An icon of a phone appears amongst the unheeding fish, an art nouveau contraption of black and chrome, very elegant, not unlike a little antique sewing machine.

"Wait a minute," says Jock. "If you heard us properly you'll know the human race is going to expire in twenty years time if we don't do something about it."

"Twenty years is a long time."

"Oh is it, Mr Johnson? If you think you can peach on us and rehabilitate yourself scot-free, think twice."

"Scot-free? I'll be free of *you*, Jock Scotty."

"Och, a scot is a payment people had to make in olden days, and I don't believe you've been paid yet, have you, Robert?"

"Stuff that."

"Aren't you forgetting we're looking after Milly for you? We're taking care of her."

"The police will get Milly back—it's the police I'll be calling, not your mob. I'm not stupid."

"The rozzers won't know where to start looking, laddy."

"It's all your fault, opening the door. I would have gone away—I might have agreed with you. Not now I can't. We can't kiss and make up after this. I've no bloody choice."

Soothingly, "Of *course* you have a choice. You're needing a wee time to think. Let's not be premature. There's no hurry. You're in charge. The whole point about taking Milly was to safeguard you. The same still applies."

"Not after what I overheard. You're bloody criminals. And *he's* a frigging freak." Superstitious horror grips Robert as he gapes at Olav. "You oughtn't to be alive! You aren't natural, you're a monster. *Em*," says Robert, and coughs. Sounds as if he's clearing his throat. He isn't, he'll say the whole word next. Emergency, em-bloody-urgency, and the phone will obey.

As I thrust my chair back, momentarily the pistol snags on my jacket and Robert—

Bang bang, missed me missed me, holes in the wall there'll be, BANG-hammer blow in my chest—

Bloody bad luck for me, fire enough shots one of them hits a target.

Bang-bang-HAMMER-bang, final bang would be Robert going down to Tim or Jock.

Lying on the carpet now, hunched on my side. Breathe without bloody coughing. Half a brick in my left lung. Bladder of blood, it'll be.

Hold out for half an hour, even an hour? Em-bloody-urgency but there'll be no ambulance siren. Jock took off almost straight away to fetch the crystal.

Tim kneeling, crooning to me as if praying, though I'm hardly heeding him. Bye-bye to this body and no mistake. Olav inspecting my injury, knows all about war wounds, saw thousands, blew his own brains out, empower yourself Anna Sharman. I'm not ready but I'd better be! Stakes are so high. Fucking lance of pain.

Barnabas seems more upset than Zandra. Resents the stain on her carpet? It's shock that she's in—so must I be, I'm shivering, those nauseating fishes, at least the telephone's gone away. Fucking half-brick's bigger, one of Evans's tortures. He's on the other side of London, a courier too far. Has to be Barnabas or Zandra.

Sleeping Beauty Squad to dispose of bodies, Robert's and mine. Joan and Mrs Johnson down in the basement, how to cope with them?

Where's Jock, where's Jock, where's Jock?

Losing control. Drowning choking. Pain pain. Sickening shimmering fish, power of the will, control, keep control.

Argument above my head: who has the nerve for the mission? Barnabas bottled out of shooting Alex Corby. Killing's a different kettle of fish. Nerve isn't something Barnabas lacks—agony of transit.

She did her best to protect Robert. If she hadn't kept her word to me she wouldn't be lying on the floor. All because Robert freaked. I can accept her, I can do it. One of us has to.

Do we?

Damn right you do, she's dying—

Duty to the human species—

That's fine talk, coming from you!

Did what I believed what was my duty to my country—

Yeah, genocide!

Genocide's what coming to us all if you don't . . . if I could be a courier—

Why don't you try it?

Don't be stupid. I have no experience—

After the famous escape from Jerky-ass and all that willpower?

No experience of transit stations—

Besides, I already had a stowaway in me—

And at long last here's Jock, panting like a grampus, gleaming jewel in his big welcome paw. *Well done lass, well done, you'll be fine now.*

And it's the lovely scarred face of Zandra I'm looking into, her eyes wide deep pools, the crystal between us. And I'm being sucked out of myself, peeled away from the bloody brick—

Anna-anna-anna-anna-anna-anna, baby-babble, nonsense noise. Yet Anna means *I am.*

Words vie to be voiced. I am, in my secret room, the room of me.

Other times in this room I had a dream-body. Dream-limbs. Not now.

The room is so empty. No door. And the window: it's blank.

Nothing beyond the window: not merely darkest night but sheer absence. This room is space inside nothingness. I am this room, this space with only an inside, not an outside. Other times I had a dream-body. A dream-body could go through a door but no-body cannot, so there cannot be a door.

And yet I am Anna. *Anna* means *I am.*

Who is Anna, where is she? In limbo, in limb-zero. Words vie, words arise.

Olav: the name occurs. Oh laugh? No: Olav, Olav. *Olav* means *he is.* I am, you are, he is: verb of being. Olav is.

You are, you are, you are:

"*Anna—Anna—?*" Beautiful scarified face, splendid black hair, jewel between her fingers, softly glowing ceiling, slender equipment looming, tubes disconnected from me.

"You're Zandra!"

So melodious, my voice. She has given birth to me.

"Do you know where you are, Anna?"

Oh yes. "I'm on Melody—I hope. Robert shot me." Music to my ears.

"Then we did it. Get up, get up." She returns the crystal to its pouch and hides it away.

What is this body that sits up and swings its bare legs from the low squashy couch, plants its feet upon the rubbery floor? My naked flesh is like flexible porcelain. My fingers explore. Between my legs, a flap of supple petals are white artichoke leaves. Two hollows in my smooth chest, hard nubs inside, engorging like peeled lychees, filling the hollows up. My hard hairless skull. The skull socket is more obtrusive than with hirsute humans. I am alien: Ivorywoman, Mockywoman.

In the room three other dummies just like me lie on couches, tubed to such elegant machines. Draped over one: my tunic waiting, adorned with bright ribbons. Zandra succeeded in pilfering as per Cartoo's instructions. On the floor, soft shoes resembling suede moccasins.

"Here's Cartoo's message." Into a pocket of the tunic I shall wear Zandra tucks what must be Jock's tiniest sold gold snuffbox. Nice touch, being a gold one. Makes me feel valued. How trusting of Jock.

"Your boss said bring his snuffbox back—unless you need to barter with it. Do you remember where to go?"

Agglutinating coalescing syllables arise and I answer her in trills, in words no human being ever knew before. And then in such tuneful lilting English: "I remember everything."

Zandra hesitates. "How is it with you, girl?"

"I feel I have hidden aspects—this body might surprise me."

Tentatively she strokes my cheek, then one of the lumps of my chest. The petals of my groin are stirring, stiffening, opening. Deliciously a pinkish stub emerges just a little way, something that could fit into a tiny egg-cup or big thimble. I imagine Ivoryman sex as mutual suction rather than penetration. I feel robust, flexible, sinewy.

"I think I'm not a girl at all."

"I must go. Evans is here too. We'll stay as long as we can. He made as if he freaked-out and started a fracas. Quite a few people boiled over. Others were heading for the disturbance, Mockymen too."

"Monitors with pacifiers?"

"Dunno. Get dressed now! Hurry, Anna."

How can I hurry a body quite new to me?

Though I must. No time to tell me how much time passed between my death and my resurrection. No time to tell me about Mrs Johnson and Joan.

On goes my tunic. Missing tunic, missing dummy: how much attention will these cause? It's utterly *impossible* that any human being can be responsible because no human being can possibly know any door code.

"Give me a minute to get back station-side without being spotted. Good luck, you bugger—"

She cues the door, peeps out. Short corridor then a final door to station-side. Off she goes, door clicking behind her.

No outcry yet, not yet not yet . . .

No outcry at all.

What's the code to get out of here, city-side? I've forgotten. No I haven't.

I'm terrified. I mustn't be.

What Cartoo neglected to inform us about is the sheer brightness of Melody's sun, and the heat. Plainly an Ivory body evolved to tolerate these conditions but I'm wary of the arclight in the shot-silk sapphire sky. Melody's sun illuminates the city so powerfully that shadows, rather than yielding dark strong contrasts, are saturated by reflected and refracted multi-coloured light. Already my skin bears an iridescent sheen, not of sweat but of some oil which films me, without feeling slimy, however. Other beribboned Ivorymen waiting nearby glisten about the head and hands. The air smells of musky pollen and vinegar.

The city, oh the city of Faluinu . . .

Geometrical, crystalline, hence all the prismatic effects. Buildings are clusters of polygons and rhombs and pyramids, a bit like a Mockymen banquet I suppose. Everywhere the ground is yellow like stiff polenta, buildings rooted in this as if they grew rather than were built. It's alien, it's alien. I'm walking in a dream. No I'm not. This is reality.

Behind me, the transit station looms huge yet low, a dome bristling with spiky pyramids and prisms and horns webbed with silvery . . . *nests*, where ribbon-tailed birds roost under silky awnings. A bird takes flight, claws dangling, clutching what might be the skeleton of a snake for disposal elsewhere, gossamer trailing faintly behind it. Melody's birds spin nests like spiders and they snack on snakes. Apparently no one minds them colonising the convenient roof of the transit station, or maybe the symbolism appeals.

Imagine a baby nuke going off in there: instant searing obliteration, hot hurricane ripping into the crystalline buildings in the neighbourhood. Very nasty indeed.

A curving line of low T-shapes—fence posts without any fence—stretches away in both directions; and a noiseless pink sausage with a row of large diamond-shaped portholes slides into sight, riding smoothly along the punctuated track—the gaps are wide enough to steer a balloon-tyred bubble-vehicle through, though few of those are in sight. The mock-Ivorymen over there were waiting for public transport. A door-ramp descends. Some passengers walk off; the others board. The sausage whispers on its way.

And I set off. There are no crowds, but a number of pedestrians are heading here and there.

In the omnipresent yellow surface, patterns of corduroy ribbing form rippling paths and roads—not carrying pedestrians along, no not mobile travel-ways in that sense, but vibrating underfoot, distinguishing themselves from the rest of the surface veneer. When I stray off the route I know at once I have done so from the feeling of deadness. Scared and exhilarated, I seem to be conducting myself appropriately, not lurching or jerking.

Slim transparent arteries carrying what must be water are embedded in the static areas, the effect resembling earthquake cracks filled in with glass. When rain falls these must serve as drains—though there's no sign of any gratings—otherwise a city-wide shallow lake could form. I feel that the whole surface is reactive and responsive, self-cleaning, self-repairing. Here and there frondy trees arise not from soil but directly from the yellow crust.

It comes to me that the season is Simmer, not Summer, and that Spring is known as Swell. Writing on buildings means nothing to me, and because the written language eludes me it would be pointless to take out Jock's snuff box to read Cartoo's message and reassure myself. Mockymen on Earth can read, but I am not as them. Side effect of using the crystal while on the point of death, maybe, like losing a skill after a major trauma.

Here is a café-cum-meeting place: behind a whale-size, curving window clientele partake of coloured drinks and wield food-tongs at tables resembling complicated chess boards. Oops, from within a monitor is eyeing me, sporting the scarlet-and-green amidst the Maypole of costume accessories. I must not gawp. My skull socket itches as I pass by purposefully but I don't scratch at it.

Behind another window delves a deep chambers of wares and whatnots attended by several large floating frisbees which presumably require no fingers in this cashless society. Maybe the machines manipulate items by some kind of magnetism and keep afloat likewise.

This must be the ultimate high, to walk in an alien city, in perfect disguise. A peak moment worth swapping twenty years' of life for, here's genuine quality time, rich with new perceptions.

Turn left here, according to Cartoo, along a ripply lane hemmed by towering amber honeycombs . . .

I'm getting there, I'm getting there.

Pha-po-lidoi lives in a habitation resembling two pyramids, one inverted upon the other, a giant angular egg-timer, golden-hued below, violet above, unmistakable. What strength there must be in the structure.

There's no concierge, either alive or automated. Crime isn't a feature of Mockymen society. A hallway stretches into the heart of the building, walls and floor and ceiling crusted with tiny glass blobs—an empty hallway; thanks be for Mockymen population control. In the distance, softly lit from within, arise two free-standing spiralling flights of steps. The right-hand one will carry me upward to Pha-po-lidoi's level, so Cartoo said. Right for up, left for down.

So I head for those—*I'm in a great tube adrift in outer space, stars and nebulae ablaze amidst utter darkness.*

No, the stairs are still exactly where they were, glowing softly. All the blobs of glass are part of a display like so many pixels in a wrap-around VDU. This corridor puts on a show for its users—great décor, real morale-booster for would-be masters of the universe. Truth is, it's hauntingly beautiful. Quite stunning. Probably the corridor can display any number of scenes. Not even worth a mention by Cartoo, this surprise in the vestibule. Will the shockwave from Jock's baby nuke reach as far as here? I've no idea.

The steps corkscrew upward into a shaft in the ceiling. Climb and they will carry you upward, according to Cartoo. How, pray? They seem quite unlike an escalator.

As soon as I set foot, I'm rising slowly. The step I stand on moves upward smoothly and quite inexplicably. Stand still, stand still and trust.

Progress is slow. So that passengers don't fall off? Climb, Cartoo said—he didn't say stand still.

Here goes; and the speed of ascent picks up. Heigh-ho, vertigo. The system has to be safe; Mockymen do not risk themselves. This must be ordinary, normal, not a fun-fair crazy house stairway. Now I'm inside that vertical shaft—I've gone through the roof of the inner lobby. Here's an opening on to a pearly corridor, intermittent doors coloured like heraldic shields. On the wall a single cross glows green: first floor. Ascend to the level marked with three crosses, quoth he. What happens with these weird escalators if there's a rush of users? Maybe there never is a rush.

Three green crosses: here's Pha-po-lidoi's level. Take one step back and I'm stationary.

In the empty corridor I pause for breath, two exits behind me, up and down. Hers will be an orange door with blue chevrons half way along the corridor.

As promised, here it is. Touch the plate with Mockyscript upon it.

Warble: "Pha-po-lidoi, this is Loosh-shi-cartoo."

The door replies, "Pha-po-lidoi is absent. What message?"

Now it's time to say, "Ho-thlee, Ho-thlee, Ho-thlee," changing the pitch of my voice each time for this password which Cartoo tried to teach me perfectly in Come-Back Cottage despite pronunciation difficulties.

Open sesame. The door slides apart, admitting me to a little welcoming-room which is sealed off from the rest of the apartment during its owner's absence. Light comes from silvery panels in the ceiling.

"Ho-thlee" closes the outer door behind me. Furnishings are a creamy couch, a soft chair, a pedestal bearing a scarlet cube with no features, and what looks like a refreshments machine though I've no idea how to use it. My legs are shaking—at last I can sit down.

Pha-po-lidoi's tunic is adorned with mainly green and yellow ribbons. She has worked up a sheen, outside, and smells faintly of sandalwood. She's startled, since obviously I am neither Shi-sill-aidoi nor To-mees-troo nor anyone else of her acquaintance who knows her password.

"I bring you a message from Loosh-shi-cartoo," I warble, and open the golden snuff box. . . .

.

Chapter 24

Amazed by these tidings from Earth, Pha-po-lidoi calls her two chums from her main room simply by addressing another scarlet box which puts her in touch without her needing to touch it.

Long upright window and slanting outer window, the space between filled with clear liquid or gel as if the whole is a giant prism. The floor is a firm foam, primrose yellow. Two saggy couches and soft chairs of golden fabric. A great glassy pixel-picture of water in swirling motion—a kind of screen-saver? A long low table inset with lines and dots like a Go board.

Pha-po-lidoi attends to hospitality in the form of a trayful of tasty little cubes and pyramids plus cup-o'-juice brought from a kitchen cubicle. Scarcely have she and I snacked than To-mees-troo arrives hot-foot, or rather sheen-skinned, followed soon by Shi-sill-aidoi. How alike all Ivorymen look. No wonder they need ribbons, though ribbons are used on all the Mockymen worlds, quoth Cartoo.

Except for Cartoo, present only on paper, the gang's all here and agoggle as dusk thickens outside and crystalline buildings glow inwardly. Across the fading zenith a bright little dart descends, from space perhaps. The liquid or gel in the double window distorts vision somewhat.

I'm with aliens, in their home.

*   *   *

I'm a wow with Pha and Shi, to trim their names as they themselves do. And To-mees is highly attentive. Do I detect an edge of reserve, a mild corrective to the enthusiasm of the two females? He has lived more than one lifetime. Maybe he's more formal by nature. Maybe I misread him. Maybe I misread many things.

How varied and vivid the Earth is: that's my first theme—and how welcome they will be as asylum seekers.

"You will have refuge. We need you as witnesses. We want variety to continue. You will be rewarded."

"Say more about places and creatures," Pha flutes.

I tell about flooded Venice and the Alps, about horse riding and skiing and elephants, describing these as best I can. God knows what will tickle their fancy. I feel like Julie Andrews piping about her favourite things, raindrops on rosebuds and whiskers on kittens. A lot of elucidating is needed due to alien vocabulary. Maybe because of Olav I find myself mentioning the Second World War, huge tank battles. Bad idea? Earth might seem a dangerous place to visit, and ourselves deserving to be supplanted. Let me reassure my audience that such havoc is a thing of the past. (Pantomime chorus: *Oh no it isn't.*)

Mention of mayhem seems to interest To-mees considerably, or to appal him—I can't tell which, but he has to hear. More, more: the trenches of Flanders, Hiroshima, North Africa. Let's hear it for human diversity.

"This behaviour must be innate," To-mees surmises, "for purpose of population control. But your war machines kill the capable as well as the incapable. I would very much wish to view images of these encounters."

Sweety, your dream can come true on Planet Earth. Millions of hours of footage, factual and fictional. I do wish this topic had not arisen.

"Tell me," says Shi, "about sliding down mountains on sticks of wood—"

Indeed. Skiing is a much more salubrious form of competitive risk-taking.

"Tell us more about racing on wheels—" Frisson, or fearfulness?

They're hosting a sort of devil. They're tasting forbidden fruit. Cue sushi, spaghetti, strawberries.

I must not seem merely an exotic novelty. Or maybe I ought, to entice them to Earth.

"We must save our world's rich variety by shutting your transit stations—"

"Why have you not done so already?" To-mees asks me.

"Loosh-shi might speak falsely. We need more than one witness."

Witness to planet-theft, body-larceny, controlled genocide . . .
Surely these rebels against Su-loo-la perceive that such behaviour is
bad.

They pass Cartoo's message from hand to hand once again.
Finally To-mees folds it and pockets it in his tunic.

"You offer us vivid experiences. If you shut all stations, other
travellers from our world will be marooned on your world along
with us." (Oh, so then you will not be so fucking special — or do you
fear recriminations?) "What will happen to those other travellers?"

"Each separate nation will decide on this — unless our forum of
nations agrees. But *you* will be honoured guests, our saviours."
Can't say fairer than that.

"Will your varied separate nations willingly shut all stations?"

Ah . . . Perceptive of him. Take a deep breath.

"Couriers from my part of the world will carry small destruction
devices here, and to the other link-world. Small devices, but with
enough power." There, I've said it. Bridges burned. Rubicon
crossed. "And you will be treasured on my world."

"In your part of your world. In a part of that part, perhaps. Treasure is sometimes shut safely away."

Did Cartoo write anything about the cellar he's stuck in just
now?

"You'll certainly need some protection," I admit. "At least, to
begin with."

"Loosh-shi thought he would be anonymous. Did he approach
you in free will?"

"Not exactly. He had a problem with his dummy. The dummy
was weak and in a dangerous place, so he cooperated and we
reached agreement."

"How did he contact you?"

"To tell the truth we found him. And saved him."

"But how did you find him?"

"By good luck."

"You honour us with candour. But—"

"But," interrupts Pha, "will your destruction devices not take life
from many persons in the station?"

"To save millions and millions more! Our people will lose lives
too."

"Because you will not tell them, so that all seems normal?"

"For the greater good." I can hardly believe I'm saying this.

"How far will damage extend?" Pha seems deeply nervous—I *think*—yet at the same time she is entertaining the idea, forcing herself to confront it.

"The station shell," To-mees informs her, "is made of—" I don't know the words he uses. "If a stone-from-space hits, it would bounce. The strongest explosion will be contained although doors will blow open."

Even in the event of a baby thermonuclear explosion? Maybe so . . .

"How much you know, To-mees," says Pha admiringly.

"By living two lives, that is how. No harm will happen to our city except that it will lack the purpose of transit."

"If the dome contains the explosion," I say brightly, "then no one will feel any pain or even know what happens."

Due to being vaporized instantly—is this a justification?

"It may even be best for our race," To-mees declares, to my surprise, "if the stations are destroyed. The people of Earth may infect us with serious mind-maladies. But," he presses on, "how did you find Loosh-shi?" He seems to accept that the station can be destroyed in what one might call a surgical fashion, but he's persistent about what happened to Cartoo. Hardly surprising since this reflects on the treatment they themselves may expect as defectors.

Take another deep breath. Be candid.

Tell them about the Jamie-dummy who awoke because he had already had the mind of Olav inside him. Give them a quick outline of my search, to the extent that setting and circumstances can be conveyed. Olav who fought in the world war; Olav reincarnated, but only emerging thanks to Cartoo's mind-crystal.

Maybe it's an unedifying guide to the bit of the world I'm inviting them to, or to myself; but my audience, particularly in the person of To-mees, is riveted.

"This person achieved a newborn body by power of will?"

"There's no doubt of it."

"Why did Loosh-shi not write this in his message?"

"Because he doesn't know. Not yet."

"You keep it secret."

"It is your secret too now."

"Yes . . . our secret, ours. How many of your people achieve this?"

Don't lie, don't tell any porky-pie. So far as I know Olav is unique. Maybe other people do achieve reincarnation but never really awaken, so there are only stray memories of an earlier life, bits and pieces. In Olav's case there were exceptional circumstances.

"What circumstances?"

The ceremony, the sacrifice of his sister.

The three aliens warble at each other too quickly and quietly for me to follow, then Pha addresses the scarlet box. Mockymusic fills the room softly, cosmic chords interwoven with a couple of mischievous fluting melodies. Quite like a couple of people tiptoeing through a forest of vast trees, trying to take one another by surprise. Quite unlike the wailing and skirling of the Dum-Dums or the Zomb-Eyes. And now comes a savage thumping beat, an alien *Rite of Spring*.

"This is an ordeal ceremony of couriers," Pha informs me.

Blut stein macht schild shutz, I think to myself.

"You will meet the reborn fighting man, I promise you." Not just raindrops on rosebuds and skiing down snow-slopes, but Olav as added inducement, and war movies. If only Olav was a hero rather than a war criminal.

"Will you come to Earth and join Loosh-shi-cartoo?"

"Maybe," says To-mees.

"If you take too long we might not be able to reach the right courier."

The music has faded.

To-mees says, "Your proposal needs thinking about twice then three times." (And how long will that take?) "Pha can take liberty from duties. You will want to see more of Faluinu while we decide." There's a kind of flatness, a lack of emotion, to his tone—again, I *think*—as if what I have said has been taken in but cannot entirely be incorporated, even though it is fascinating to these misfits. Well, it's a lot to take in.

Who wouldn't want the opportunity to be guided round an alien city? Yet shouldn't I remain in this safe house? I have come this far without mishap. Strolling around sightseeing seems reckless. On the other hand, I'm inviting greater boldness from them. A commitment. Yes, I must see the city, not hide here.

"I would love to see your city, but what if I attract attention?"

"Pha will be careful. You need different ribbons. I will see to this. And you need a name."

A name, a name. We settle on Yaan-ah-sha. I'm no longer Anna Sharman but Yaan-ah-sha.

We have spent a long time together. It's night, and the window has become black as a wall of coal. To-mees needs to go, taking Shi with him.

"Loosh-shi's message," I say, "shouldn't you destroy it?"

"Why?"

"For safety."

"It is a message from a friend. I will not drop it in the street." A message to all three of them, but To-mees is senior.

After Shi and he have gone, Pha demonstrates the use of the cleansing cubicle, then lends me an unadorned night tunic. Don't crumple your ribbons is a popular proverb. Pha fetches more cup-o'-juice and sits by me on the couch where presently I'll doss down.

She is utterly attentive. Or maybe scared that I may misbehave. Would I want to be left alone in my apartment with an unpredictable alien? Perhaps the long success of the Mockymen has led them to view other races as rather manageable.

I ask her, "To-mees said something about human dummies maybe infecting long-term users with mind-maladies. What did he mean?"

"There are different kinds of mind-maladies, Yaan-ah. To-mees understands these things."

According to her, undesirable traits can well up from the original architecture of the brain, quirks at variance with the Mockymen way. If us humans are markedly hard-wired for violence and aggression, after a while our brains may begin to bollix up the sober new residents. Drugs and nanotech might not batten down the hatch; the root-brain beast might still rattle its chain.

By collaborating in blowing up the stations, my deviant friends might be saving the Mockymen from a load of future problems. She stares at me constantly as if not quite able to believe.

Then there is the problem of storage capacity for memories, supposing that you live on and on in body after body. To-mees (our expert) says that a brain can store about a thousand years of subjective experience. Lots of surplus capacity there, you'd suppose; nature went in for a spot of over-designing.

Not so as regards the Originals, members of the Council of Wisdom, and subsequent persistent Mockymen. They have been around significantly longer, and become full up. Full up means cerebral crisis—the brain over-writing earlier memories and even crucial abilities. Since persons never evolved to live for a thousand years and more, there's no orderly programme for info-dumping. The brain dumps at random. Pour a huge wad of mind into a dummy brain and *fizz-pop*, uh whadja say my name is? Not enough memory for system commands, as my very first computer used to protest long ago. Long-life persons can go blank to the on-going world, gaping vacantly.

No wonder the fans of Su-loo-la wish to become disembodied minds, presumably with no constraint on capacity.

To avert the fizz-pop factor, you use deleter-drugs for memory editing. But you wish to retain as much of yourself as you can. So the longest-living Mockymen are a bit too full for mental agility, flexibility, new approaches and insights. (Tekkin' over other species always served us reet, lad; that's the Mockymen way.)

"Excuse me, Pha, but can't long-living persons add on *extra* memory? Fit something to the skull sockets?"

Something nanotech, or a neural net plug-in unit, needn't be very big. Mockymen are the nanotech mavens. Gizmo could even be inside the skull, super-miniaturized. Probably it would be better on the outside, readily detachable. When you swap to a new young body you simply unplug your extra memory from the old noddle and plug in to the new one.

"This is not Su-loo-la, Yaan-ah. Apparatus binds us to bodies."

"But you use apparatus."

"Therefore Su-loo-la is in vain! Our worlds are in vain, our purified worlds." Purified, I presume, of most of the former inhabitants, Mockymen for the use of . . .

To-mees is the authority on such matters, so it seems.

Pha is glistening. "How can a being kill itself with only the *hope* of being reborn? Without the certainty? How can a being *kill itself?*"

"Well," I say lamely, "we're accustomed to death." Of course we are not personally accustomed to dying, since we only ever die once. Until Jamie-Olav came on the scene to prove otherwise! "Human beings quite often give their lives to save other human beings."

"I am in my first life," she says. "How is it to know you will not continue living?"

"I suppose we try to pack a lot into one life, and be satisfied."

"I think I can grasp this idea. Would I gain a second life on your world, or would I live one like you?"

I shrug—if she understands a shrug. Maybe she thinks I am uncomfortable. "Ultimately everything dies."

"Su-loo-la will save us forever . . . But Su-loo-la is a dream."

*   *   *

I can't get to sleep. Undreaming sleep is the little bit of death that constantly abides with us, yet we know nothing about our nightly non-existence. Images and impressions of Faluinu and the aliens whirl in my mind: now a gaudy fairground roundabout, now a maelstrom. I pretend sleep.

Pha stands in the doorway, watching me. I think of a stoat and a rabbit. Really, the Mockymen are the stoats but right now perhaps Pha is the mesmerised rabbit.

Stoats, weasels. How do you tell the difference between a stoat and a weasel? Weasels are weasily identifiable, but stoats are stotally different.

Pha has gone. On the verge, I hope, of sleep—because I must sleep, I *must*—I remember another joke.

"Lazarus, come forth!"

But Lazarus came fifth, so he didn't get the job.

Chapter 25

Postcards from Faluinu:

Dear Jock, Dear Tim,

To-mees popped round early on with my new regalia, obtained, I gather, from a ribbon-printing machine at the Public Library of Ribbons. Yaan-ah-sha is supposed to be a nurse of dummies, so I wear striped green and yellow ribbons prominently among assorted others.

Although To-mees could not stay long he did ask me more about Olav. Olav is of great importance. That he should have deliberately embraced death so as to defeat death seems like throwing a stone into the sea in the hope that the next wave might wash up a nourishing food-cake, not the kind of gamble any sane being would undertake.

"It's part of our heritage," I said. "Sacrifices and self-sacrifices." It is not the Mockymen way.

In a sense I too made this leap in the dark, or into the dark, assisted by Robert's bullet, even though I did not actually die at any stage.

I briefly raised the subject of plug-on memory. Apparently this would give rise to independent sub-minds which would tend to compete with one another. Not a case of "After you, sir!" or "Be my guest, feel free," but rather, "Who do you think you are, buster?"

On his way out, To-mees closeted himself quite a while with Pha in the welcoming-room, to discuss me in private. Upshot: this evening there will be a special dinner for the four of us in her apartment, featuring gourmet items.

Duly kitted out in my new attire, I ride a sausage-train with Pha through the crystalline metrop which, incidentally, doubles as a city-size sun-farm.

Our destination is the residential school for juveniles, where Pha's single offspring lives. Visualise a cylindrical honeycomb with a slim spire on top. From the peak of the spire a translucent white skirt descends to prop its fluted hem upon on a perimeter of pillars twenty feet tall.

Circling the honeycomb under the shelter of the skirt are concentric rings of pedestals ranging from knee-high to chest-high interspersed with free-standing flights of steps to nowhere—like the mounting block at Ravensdene, remember, Tim?

Pupils, of assorted heights themselves, wear lightweight virtual reality crash helmets along with baggy white pants and silky yellow vests. Either they sit on pedestals, receiving tuition through their helmets, or they're on the move, quitting their previous perch to sprint to a vacant one elsewhere—as well as running up those steps to perform solo callisthenics. It's a busy scene, combining mind and body workouts. The number of pupils is by no means large.

We wend our way through the pedestals and the capering or concentrating students to a vestibule of the honeycomb habitat. Pha announces to a scrutinizing eyeball set in one wall, "Pha-po-lidoi comes to see Rho-pha-ploo."

We wait till a miniature Ivoryperson comes trotting from the playground-workplace, helmet in hand. By way of greeting Pha places her palm on his head—in common with his schoolfellows he lacks a skull socket as yet—and Rho places his free hand on her elbow.

"My womb-parent," he trills. "Thank you for life."

"My issue, persist." Persistent people, the Mockymen. Removing her hand: "Have you learned to stand alone, Rho?"

The child glances at the nearest vacant paediatric pedestal as if about to dart to it to demonstrate.

"I belong with my fellows," he says.

"What if they turn their backs?"

"Why would they?" The Ivorykid eyes me. "Is this a Monitor, even though the ribbon is missing?" Maybe he suspects his womb-parent of deviant attitudes.

"No, this is my accessory, Yaan-ah-sha." I'm not sure what function an accessory performs. An appendage, an accomplice? Something casual, or the very opposite?

"Continue!" the kid says to me. A courtesy-cliché or an invitation?

"What are you learning?" I ask.

"Thinking and facting, Yaan-ah-sha."

Learning to think the right thoughts, I guess, as opposed to irregular ones; then suiting the facts to the thoughts, maybe.

"And respect for long-living," little Rho adds. "I will live on the new world when I am older. I will continue till I am like an Original."

What a prat. Perhaps Pha came here to remind herself of his prattishness.

"Suppose," says Pha, "your fellows turn their backs, is there a special person to stand beside?"

"Yes! There is Mai-too-eedoi."

An Ivorygirl.

We leave quite soon, and as we walk out from under the great canopy I ask her, "If you come to Earth will Rho suffer anything because of you?"

"Rho may be investigated for possible inherited mind-malady. I think he will survive." I wonder if Pha is being ironic.

What is the quality of her care for Rho? I can't tell. One of her ribbons (cerise with blue stripes) commemorates the production of a male offspring. A battle honour; but does one wish to perpetuate the battle for the rest of one's life? And why, in the first place, did she undertake a planned pregnancy assisted by mind-fuck (thanks for that, Jock)?

The sun beats down. Faluinu is so bright yet there is a deep darkness here, of denial.

Dear Tim, Dear Jock,

Here's Faluinu Hospital and Body Bank, a pile of coloured blocks kicked over and arrested in mid-fall upon slim columns. Fanciful architecture is a Mockymen infatuation, taught half a world away in the metrop of Laafeelu. Most human architecture, aside from such as Sydney Opera House or the Guggenheim in Bilbao, must seem prosaic by comparison.

Another imaginary camera click: here's the local Su-loo-la Study Centre where Mockymen muse on how to become disembodied minds. Silver zigzags slither up the facade of slim pyramidal skyscraper like snakes or like sperms trying to eject themselves from the tapering tip. So far they aren't succeeding. Close by is the Residence of Originals, a mammoth bunch of grapes composed of opaque blue globes.

Click: here's a double-helix mini-skyscraper in blue and gold where Earth's worms and weeds are screened for pharmaceuticals. That place is due for redundancy, if we have our way. Likewise, the adjacent New World Evaluation Centre . . .

The Evaluation Centre is a vertical stack of five planets, perched one upon another, not to scale. Ringed Saturn is topmost, balancing upon bandy red-spotted Jupiter. Jupiter sits on an outsize Mars which rests upon a white Moon bigger than Mars, cratered by portholes. The biggest and bottom-most globe is blue and white Earth, its continents picked out in a sort of metallic decoupage. Behold your new solar system, Mockymen.

Finally Pha escorts me to the cantonment of genuine Ivorymen, those courier-grade pain-buffs whose many surplus offspring are destined to become host-bodies (after injection with personality-mind-purge, Bliss without the rapture).

By contrast with the bizarre geometries of the rest of the city almost all the buildings here are identical oblong blocks, rows and rows of them all roofed with shiny solar collectors. Indeed this is a type of farm, for free-range Ivorymen. Can Mockymen ever empathise with their subject populations to any greater degree than we empathise with our own herds of sheep and cattle? True, they need to exist in the bodies of natives. But if we have a pig's heart transplanted into us, do we grunt, do we bother about the sacrificed porker?

Pierced by several gateways, a head-high wall circuits the camp. A spur of the monorail enters but Pha and I approach on foot. Pedestrian access is scarcely supervised. A few bureaucrat Monitors sit in mobile offices, little opaque-roofed vehicles on fat wheels, doing screen work. If something out of the ordinary occurs I suppose they would react.

To our right a VTOL plane rises skyward from compact Faluinu airport. Beyond the cantonment is thick green forest.

The monorail terminates inside a windowless building, where Pha says that skull sockets are inserted and bodies are dummified.

Inside the cantonment Ivorymen roam freely and Ivorykids play healthy games. We pass among them without attracting any hostility, indeed quite the opposite. Our ribbons give us admirable status. Minor deities paying a visit. Members of the master race. After a whole lot of centuries this is the way things are. What alternative can there possibly be?

Reminds me of Kielder, in a way. Except, here's an ordeal plaza, equipped with devices resembling a cross between gymnastics equipment and the contents of a torture chamber. Dear Mr Evans, you ought to be here, even though no fest of endurance is under way at the moment. In a few hundred years time will the rump of the human race live in places such as this? In that hot sunshine I sheen, and shiver within.

We stroll around this utopian version of Auschwitz-Birkenau for a while. A sausage-bus carrying a dozen senior kids is touring on an educational outing; no VR helmets this time. No native throws a grenade, there being none, nor the inclination neither. Young masters are visiting. One day, little Ivorylad, your body will belong to a Mockyman and you'll be fulfilled, your destiny accomplished. I feel no inclination to address a native, which in any case would probably be inadvisable.

"You will come to my world, won't you, Pha? Novelty, variety, a new start."

"We may decide tonight."

Dear Tim,

This evening, rather than Pha using the food machine, Shi and To-mees both arrive with boxes full of scores of variously coloured little pyramids and cones and cubes.

"We shall play a child's version of the food game," announces To-mees.

The food is set out at the four corners of the Go-board table. Rules are: advance two items at a time. Pyramids capture cones, cones capture cubes, cubes capture pyramids. After playing, pass a third piece to the neighbour on your right. You can either eat or bring into play an item received from your left-hand neighbour, but if you have passed on a cone and received a same-colour cube or pyramid you must eat it. Et cetera. Object of game: to acquire blue pyramids.

To-mees also produces a flask of violet liquid which Pha pours into four little cups.

"This," he explains, "is a drug used in promoting mind-mix, but it has other uses in conjunction with," and he taps a blue pyramid.

Eating a blue pyramid requires a sip of the violet drink, not something which features in the children's version, I fancy, though in order to play as children do we must now remove our beribboned clothes . . .

When in Rome! I'm in their hands. We sit around nude. How smooth we are.

Blue pyramids are utterly delicious. The chaser drink has an insipid, slightly oily taste. Rah for blue pyramids! I seem to be winning a lot of them. Beginner's luck, eh. Pha does well. Shi captures one or two, To-mees none at all.

Food's disappearing, drink's disappearing, most of the room's disappearing. The floor's softening remarkably, more like a sprung mattress now, and Pha is passing me nothing at all this time but instead is taking hold of my hand, my chest growing lumpy and the stub stirring amidst the artichoke petals of my groin, oh these are devious deviants beguiling me drugged into an alien orgy, and why not indeed, why not lie on the soft floor pressed alongside Pha, our unfolded groins softly and exquisitely sucking at one another, thrill of my life . . .

Her Pha-ness, her farness coming closer and closer, inwardly, like a baby whale rising up from within the sea which is me, to break surface and behold all there is to see. Talk about a whirlwind affair, more like a whirlpool one.

Briefly we blend, I'm her, she's me, I'm alien, she's human, I've always been alien, you and I are making love, Tim, Pha is experiencing what it is to be human, and now I know why she had her child, in an attempt to make herself feel connected, continuous with Mockymen past and future, not an isolated person but part of race and society, and presently we're separate again, and I'm human, me, myself. We have worked up such a slippery sheen. We lie side by side while I emerge from intoxication and aphrodisia.

"Why did we do this, Yaan-ah?" she asks.

Isn't it obvious? "So that I form an attachment to you."

So that Pha—and therefore Shi and To-mees—become vital persons for me, whom I will go out of my way to cherish and safeguard once they are in our clutches. Come home with me, *home*, true home, Cwmbach, come back with me. Free spirits, who must have freedom. And this must apply to Cartoo also. Whatever crimes the Mockymen commit against Ivorymen and the Lemurs of Passion and other alien beings, these four must bear no blame.

"Attachment, yes."

What of all the infiltrators who will be marooned on Earth when transit evaporates? Granted, they planned us great harm. So far they only brought benefits, give or take Bliss and dummies. Even Bliss is a benign alternative to drugs which were causing great social chaos and misery to the profit of rogues and criminals. With the castaways can there be any reconciliation, spearheaded by Pha and her friends? To the ongoing benefit of the human race, because of alien knowledge? How about new bodies for old! But for *whom* precisely? And decided how? For the best and most prized people, or for the richest and most powerful? And how would dummies be obtained?

Won't work, can't work. Not in any sense fairly. There are altogether too many of us human beings.

Mockymen persist because they never behaved fairly to other beings. Other beings were only raw material. Does fair equal fool? I hate to think so.

I am filled with foolishness for Pha and her friends.

"I will come with you to your world," Pha tells me, which is what I have been wanting to hear all along. How could I leave her behind?

"Pha, I think that was the peak experience of my life." Like a peak it was not wide in span, but vistas linger. Phew. "Do you often drink that drug with the blue food?"

To-mees is the expert on such matters. "We do not, because the experience is too fast and intense and not widely known about. Mating to breed offspring with suitable minds takes longer and guidance."

"If Pha goes with you gladly," says Shi, "then so shall I."

"What about you, To-mees?"

"There may be problems unless I stay behind to tell untruths. Let us resume our clothing."

Shame, shame. Ivorymen bodies are so lovely. But we need to talk undistracted.

Amazingly, my mission is succeeding.

One vacant body, Cartoo's, being found on the floor of a dummy-room: unusual natural causes, right? Plausible, when he had duties at the transit station.

But then, not so many days later, three bodies to be found in similar circumstances? Oh pull the other leg!

Might a dodgy deal with some human courier be suspected? Might Monitors become exceptionally wary from then on of *incoming* couriers? When the volunteer with the heavy suitcase arrives, while he's still in shock from the torment of transit might they paralyse him?

In the opinion of To-mees it is best that the deaths are seen as a suicide pact. Suicide is a sign of insanity. Human beings are creatures of death—causing death, and dying in turn. Confronting one is like encountering an abomination, in the face of which it is better to extinguish oneself. Hence the venue for the suicide, a demented attempt to achieve Su-loo-la *right now* by quitting the body. Hence the desire to confront a human courier prior to suicide, for a human being is the Death-That-Walks. The Angel of Death, as it were. As To-mees, the witness to the suicide, will affirm in due course. This seems like demented logic, but To-mees is the authority on mind-maladies.

"You will be taken for assessment," Shi warns him.

Ah, but as soon as To-mees has affirmed he will swallow a memory-purge concealed in his mouth.

"I will think about the destruction devices—those will vanish first from mind. Then I will think about you—"

"And you will forget us."

"Thus I shall not miss you."

"Your memory, To-mees! You will continue losing it randomly."

"Only until the Monitors supply an antidote, which they will surely do as soon as they realize."

"This will not happen soon enough. You will not be yourself any more. How can you rejoice in our exploit?"

"By rejoicing beforehand."

Is he unstable, with a self-destructive streak? Willing to throw away chunks of his memories and personality? Willing to be evaporated if the nukes arrive while he is held at the Faluinu transit station?

"And the Monitors will assess me in the Hoo-hoo House which is far from the transit station."

Not quite so self-destructive, perhaps. Self-sacrificial—grand gesture? Memo to self: Monitor HQ is called the Hoo-hoo House.

"You will really do this for us?"

Sounds flaky to me as a plan. Apparently not so to Shi and Pha. Seems downright splendid to them. Alien attitudes are not mine to question.

Despite my afterglow of euphoria some questions do occur.

"To-mees, how will we manage to be alone with the courier?"

"We will claim that we are a research unit from the Su-loo-la Study Centre in Lafeelu, and we shall all wear the proper ribbons."

Sounds crafty.

"Will our courier have time to transit before the Monitors get involved and question her?"

"The courier is merely a circumstance in the suicides, not an agency."

Okay, I'll believe this since Pha and Shi both seem to regard it as self-evident.

"And who am I supposed to be, To-mees? Pha and Shi are both identifiable—"

"Not physically with any immediate ease."

Ivorymen all looking so alike, quite so; though I can tell Pha and Shi apart, especially after what I shared with Pha.

"Human beings are much more grotesque in their physical differences than most other races."

Supposedly many Asians look alike to non-Asians, but not to Asians themselves. Do the Mockymen not easily recognize differences between the dummy bodies they inhabit—hence the ribbons! —otherwise they might need to acknowledge the individualities of natives too?

"Surely they're identifiable by virtue of going missing—and presumably by being known acquaintances of yours. Didn't officials contact Cartoo's associates after his supposed death?"

Not so, apparently. Natural causes.

"So who am I supposed to be?" Especially when a dummy went missing recently.

"I will have totally forgotten," To-mees says triumphantly.

Can't argue with that.

Chapter 26

Dear Tim/Jock,

I woke this morning with rather deep feelings about Pha. Our love-making, even though rapid and drug-induced and in company, continues to bond and haunt me. The sensations last night were literally overwhelming—me being her briefly, and she being me. This is quite different from falling in love.

Though how should I know? I coasted into relationships rather than *falling* for someone. I find it hard to imagine anyone glancing across a crowded room, as in the song, and falling in love right there and then willy-nilly. My Adonis of Hereford market was an almost instant choice but that was only a physical attraction, lust.

Was I manipulated last night? Of course I was; yet at the same time this seems irrelevant. Am I crazy to be nursing such feelings for an alien? She and I resemble two bald smooth mannequins in a painting by Chirico. Extreme circumstances! I'm alone on an alien world, consequently I imprint on my hostess. And this afternoon we hope to leave this world, so long as To-mees has time to lay his hands on amnesia-juice as well as more spoof ribbons . . .

Do you understand that I have vouched to Pha with my very being, Jock? My promises must be kept, my assurances honoured.

This morning Pha will have time to show me the Heritage Centre, bidding adieu to her life in the Mockymen realms. I wouldn't mind sneaking a look at the Hoo-hoo House—the competition, eh Jock?—but that might be inadvisable. For breakfast we share nutty and fruity-tasting biscuits plus cup-o'-juice, but these don't have us rolling on the floor together. What human body will Pha assume in England? Tim, the prospect confuses me. I'll need your strength in sorting this out.

"Pha, couldn't a collective suicide note be left in the dummy-room? A big eye-catching note—so that To-mees can come with us too, and keep his memory?"

"He needs to stay to cause confusion and misunderstanding."

What do you feel for me, Pha—what do you feel?

"Surely you and Shi will miss him? Have either of you . . . have you drunk that drug with him, the way we did last night?"

Apparently not. The circumstances never arose.

"How long have you known To-mees?"

"Two years."

I would have imagined far longer.

"At first, Yaan-ah, there were only me and Shi and Loosh-shi. Because To-mees joined us, Looshi-shi was free to undertake his adventure."

So three is company even in Mockymen circles. Though of course To-mees expedited the adventure.

"Was it To-mees's idea for you and me to bond?"

"Oh yes. He could obtain the drug."

To-mees is a useful friend to have.

"You'll miss him."

"I will be with you on your world, Yaan-ah. You will arrange things there, the way To-mees does here."

Be with me, be with me—might this become a bit stifling for me? Probably my feelings will moderate themselves once the nervous anxiety of being in Faluinu has gone.

Meanwhile we walk a ripply route to the Heritage Centre. I would love to hold Pha's hand but actually I must be her captain, even though she pilots me this morning.

In the linked crystal chambers of the centre are displays of the Mockymen worlds. The holo-dioramas alter every half minute.

A party of bald smooth Mockykids troop through ahead of us accompanied by a tutor or, for all I know, a science-priest of Su-loo-la.

Here's Passion, identifiable by the Mocky-Lemurs in the scene. So this is what Passion really looks like! A frigid though ruddy world lit by a tiny bright sun and by a much larger dull red one. Snow-flakes like clots of dried blood blow through a forest of growths resembling barrels perched upon barrels, withered fronds at the top. On roller-wheels, great igloos with sails scoot across a frozen plain. In a lake of steaming slurry, held back by a dam, a spacecraft is taking shape. An enormous cavern with phosphorescent walls houses a small city in the form of an inverted maze cut into the floor . . .

And here is a world I must call Blue.

And one I must call Tree.

And another deserving the name of Swamp. Amphibians those Mockymen are, upright frogs with what look like corks in their skull sockets. The ribbons on the kilts and webbing they wear must be waterproof. Do those Mocky-frogs spawn? Do they lay eggs? Remarkable, really, that Mockymen have continued breeding at all when they have an alternative means of survival. Might I myself feel an element of, well, racial pollution, if I was to breed as a giant bullfrog, with another giant bullfrog? Undoubtedly Olav would! But of course they have the mind-fuck drug to promote a stable Mockymen psyche in offspring.

"Is your home world here too? The way it originally was? The way *you* once were?"

No. That is abandoned. To show the original Mockymen bodies would be to suggest that those represent some sort of ideal, now tragically lost. The Mockymen harbour no racial prejudices. All races are equal, and equally are commandeered. Could lead to the unity of all intelligent beings in the galaxy. All of one mind, mostly.

"Tell me, Pha, do you feel love?"

She cocks her bald head. "We say there is love, there is lust, there is liking. Love is obsession, love is addiction, a sort of pain."

"And you avoid pain." As a breed you make aliens experience it instead of you. "So why do you visit the native ordeals?"

"Fascination, at their obsessions. Those who are obsessed may achieve. Yet obsession captures the obsessing person in a tight circle of behaviour, the way the once-wild natives are captured and need no cordon, for they have made their own cordon in their minds. After lusting with you I am obsessed with your world, Yaan-ah. Going there will expand my circle of capture into apparent freedom, so big will my available circle become."

Let's hope so, Jock, let's really hope so!

The four of us turn up at the transit station kitted out in our false ribbons. No hand luggage—that would be pointless—but slung from To-mees's shoulder is a small machine to record the supposed findings of our study group.

We are the four wise Mockymen from the Su-loo-la Study Centre in the main metrop, To-mees explains to a Monitor. We need to examine a female human being courier of black skin who is a minority citizen of the Earth country known as Britanoo. Americoo will do, but Britanoo is better for our purposes because one of our group has learned Britanish in liaison with the New World Evaluation Centre.

"We suspect that being female and black and of a minority may predispose to mind-maladies. We suspect this potentially affects their brain-passengers."

To-mees sounds like some crackpot Nazi doctor with a bee in his bonnet. If this were Earth, at this point sheafs of authorizations should be produced, but we're wearing the right ribbons, and why tell such a story otherwise?

"Human beings in general may be specially prone to mind-maladies," continues To-mees. "So we need to examine a case more prone than most, and while not in her native environment. We have thirty-three questions to ask her, designed by our committee."

Another Monitor joins the first, an Ober-Monitor apparently, and To-mees trots out his rigmarole anew. I hope I'm not showing a sheen of anxiety. Believe us, you sods, believe us.

The Ober-Monitor eyes To-mees's ribbons.

"An oddity occurred here recently, Senior Expert. An unused dummy went astray."

Oh dear me.

"So did a tunic."

Oh double dear.

"I know a case," To-mees asserts, "of a dummy functioning in automaton fashion without conscious control—this happened in Lafeelu about ten years ago. I surmise that your missing dummy may have walked automatically to the local cantonment." Oh ingenious.

"This merits attention, Senior Expert. But days previously a body was found defunct here."

"By natural or unnatural cause?"

"Natural."

"Then how can that be linked with the later event?"

"Is it possible," Shi chips in, "that the defunct body and the absent dummy are the same? Could the body have been comatose, not defunct, and mistakenly have been placed with dummies?"

"Not as reported."

"If a person misreported, hoping to avoid responsibility for error—"

To-mees hushes her. "Such errors are not our concern, Assistant Expert."

"It is the easiest explanation."

"No doubt," says To-mees, "an enquiry is under way. We would be glad to receive a copy at our Su-loo-la Study Centre for information. Seeing connections where none exist is natural yet often fallacious. This cannot concern our need to ask a black female human being thirty-three questions. We must fly to Lafeelu with our results—we shall ride couriers to the other link-world to consult, and repeat the test. This is an important study. Will you facilitate the interview, Senior Monitor?"

"One of you understands Britanish?"

That's me.

"To learn Britanish in Lafeelu is zealous of you."

Gosh, we're nothing if not thorough in the Lafeelu Su-loo-la Centre.

"I assigned my Assistant to that task," says To-mees. "We liaise with the New World Evaluation Centre."

Please do not contact a scarlet box in the stack-o'-worlds building here in town!

"I myself do not understand Britanish, Senior Expert," says the Ober-Monitor. "I shall seek assistance from a Speaker on the other side to locate a subject for interview."

"Excellent. Though we must not inhibit our subject. Already four of us will face her."

"You understand the need to change tunics for plain ones in a robing room before this interview?"

Of course, of course.

Zandra looks like a panicked panther, being escorted in by the Ober-Monitor and by a Speaker-Monitor from the Hilton side to find herself facing four seated Mockymen. After even my short time spent among smooth Ivorymen, and especially after my wonderful bonding with Pha, a human being seems like a kind of caricature, a grotesque. A lovely, familiar one, though.

Plain room, plain table, plain chairs, one seat left vacant opposite us. To-mees's comp upon the table. This could be a board of enquiry into a captured infiltrator who has identified her. Me, of course, she cannot tell from Eve or Adam.

"Please sit," I warble melodiously, and Zandra complies. Do I risk a big wink? She might, just might, betray herself and us.

Although the Speaker-Monitor departs, the Ober-Monitor remains like a guardsman at ease.

"We must not inhibit our subject," To-mees repeats. "Five persons is too many. We will need to concentrate on the answers afterwards at great length while the nuances are fresh. May we ourselves send her though the door when we are done?"

"That is not prudent, Senior Expert."

"It would assist us greatly."

Come on, make with the bloody door-code—even though Zandra already knows it, as do we. And then piss off.

"My duty is here, Senior Expert."

"With respect, I outribbon you, Senior Monitor. I take responsibility."

"I shall say nothing more."

"I shall find fault in my report."

True to his word, the Ober-Monitor says and does nothing whatever.

This is just not going to work. We are not going to be left on our own.

We'll have to rush the Ober-Monitor, collar him tight, stop him from shouting out, pour some of that drug into him to scramble his memory, stun him with his stunner—the pacifier's in a holster under his tunic, reachable through a slit, he didn't leave it in the changing room.

We can manage this so long as we don't trip each other up. How do we sort out who does what?

Blandly To-mees tells me, "Proceed with your preliminary explanation in Britanish to the subject."

Oh yes, to clue Zandra up; to cue her—Zandra is nearest to the Ober-Monitor.

"Only us two speak English," I warble. "Don't show any surprise. The Monitor refuses to leave. I'm Anna and these others are Cartoo's friends."

Relief mingles with misgivings.

"Did you remember to bring you-know-what?" Zandra asks. Only *I* would know what that is.

I place Jock's little snuffbox on the table. Could be a miniature recording device.

"Zandra, before we can transfer we need to take the Monitor by surprise. Immobilize him. Three of us will transfer. To-mees will stay to cause confusion."

"Yes. I see. Anna, you're supposed to brief to me in case any-

thing goes wrong." She's right, of course. "How much can we talk?"
Thirty-three questions' worth of talk. Time is passing.

"Pha here, and Shi," with nods at my supposed fellow re-
searchers, "they'll confirm all that Cartoo said. I've seen what
the natives are reduced to. The Mockymen will steal our world. It's
all true. Zandra, if I don't make it, Jock must treat Pha like royalty.
And Shi and Cartoo as well. I've promised faithfully."

Her scarred face peers at me quizzically. Pha's face is so smooth.

"Girl, you've had an affecting visit."

"Tell Jock a baby nuclear blast won't breach this building, so
casualties will be kept low. I suppose that goes for Passion too."

"To contain passion is quite a trick." I think she's trying to calm
her nerves. "Is it daylight outside?"

"Burning bright."

Never to be seen again by a human soul. But I have trod the soil
of Melody. No I haven't, I have trod the stiff ripply polenta.

"If the Mockymen cotton on and cut London off, Operation
Bye-Bye can be routed through Dublin." Fraught matter, the Regiment commandeering a friendly nation's transit station. Operational decisions aren't down to me, thank God.

"You'll be telling him yourself, girl, before the day's out."

In a lovely young black body, of course I shall be.

"Is there anything else that's vital?"

Vital, vital, what else could be vital? The stack-o'-worlds building, the Heritage Centre, the Hoo-hoo House? Pha can explain
about those. I don't really need to brief Zandra. I'm only putting off
the moment—when we tackle the Monitor; when the crystal is on
the table; when I lose all knowledge of what happens.

"Zandra, when I say 'go' I want you to moan and hold your
head as if you're in distress. I'll come round the table to investigate.
The Monitor will be concentrating on you, and I'll get him in a
choke-hold. You go for his hands and hold them tight. I'll be telling
To-mees what to do."

How strong will the Monitor be? How sinewy? I've no idea.
Surprise will be on my side. Zandra's strong. Three of us should be
able to restrain the Monitor.

"Are you ready?"

From inside his tunic the Monitor pulls out his pacifier, fat purple tube with black grip. "Stay still," he flutes in English. Zandra
jerks around. Seeing the stunner, she utters a moan for real.

"Stay still," the Monitor repeats in Ivoryspeak, then using English again: "You are in custody."

Already his free hand is in his pocket, pressing something.

Already the door is opening and two more Monitors are in the room, stunners at the ready.

"Phaaaa!" wails Shi.

"Shiiii!" wails Pha.

To-mees rises nimbly and I'm tensing myself to follow through, in vain though this may be—but no stun-gun veers to cover To-mees—those Monitors aren't in the least alarmed—all To-mees is doing is getting out of the way and the Monitors bloody well know it!

To-mees the Mocky-friend, To-mees the two-time twister.

"Betrayer!" I shout at him.

"He cannot be," Shi says, voice aquaver.

"Unbelievable," Pha says.

All the rigmarole of phony ribbons and memory-drug and Su-loo-la study group sweet-talking and chiding the Ober-Monitor who understands English perfectly well: it was all a sham, a charade. Lead us along then pull the rug right from under us.

"*What's happening, Anna?*"

"To-mees-troo is a fucking cheating informer, that's what. He sold out."

My attempt to get back to Earth might have failed in any case, but this is sodding wicked.

For a moment I imagine the door flying open and Denbigh and boys from Hereford bursting in, all kitted out, all singing, all dancing, all shrieking still from transit, but on the ball absolutely, hostage rescue in full swing.

Dream on.

"My regrets," To-mees flutes in Ivoryspeak. "Pha, Shi: you and Loosh-shi are subjects of my research in mind-malady on behalf of an Original of Faluinu . . ."

To-mees didn't snitch on us just yesterday nor the day before. To-mees the wised-up one has been studying Pha and Shi and Cartoo for the past two years by playing along with them.

Then I walk into their lives from another world and the situation alters radically. The folks from the Hoo-hoo House must know about Jock's baby nuke plan by now.

Why assist Cartoo's escape in the first place? Oh why?

The chances of Zandra and me ever returning to Earth to report anything? Pretty low, I'd say. Zandra is eyeing me in bleak despair.

This must be shattering for Pha too. She's breathing deep and low, almost moaning. Hooo, hooo, is the noise of her breath. Shi has quite a sheen on her. Assessed and euthanased, that's the prospect.

"We almost made it," I tell Zandra by way of consolation. So near yet so far. Yet this isn't true. We made it this far because we were allowed to. Game of cat and mouse? To flush out Zandra beyond a shadow of doubt?

"Why did you let us hope for so long?" I rage at To-mees.

"To study the event," is his reply. "And to bring it back to its starting place."

For the sake of tidiness and symmetry? But that means . . .

"When did you first know about me, To-mees?"

"You were known about before you left this transit station."

So much for strolling blithely through an alien city. I was under some sort of surveillance all along like Jamie with the chip in his shoulder.

"Why did you let Loosh-shi escape in the first place?" Endangering so very much . . .

"The Original decided. Yaan-ah, you do not have thirty-three questions to ask. The Original has one to ask of you."

Four sets of plastic cuffs appear. Kindly place hands close together on the table in front of you. Can't ask Zandra where Lionel Evans is. I don't know if Zandra can take the heat and brightness of this world. Probably we won't be marched to the Hoo-hoo House or taken by sausage-train. Bound to be in a balloon-wheeled vehicle.

CHAPTER 27

Indeed. The vehicle proves to be a bulbous side-loading ten-seater, opaque apart from at the front. Don't want the citizenry catching a glimpse of a tall, scarred, black alien with a sumptuous hairstyle, do we now? Zandra is squinting past two Monitors pointing pacifiers and the Ober who is steering, catching what she can see of bright Faluinu. Temperature is okay in here, moderate. We're still in ribbonless anonymous tunics.

Presently I spy the Bunch-o'-Grapes building ahead of us. Those big blue globes each the size of an early warning radar dome swell up above us as we roll closer, our speed slowing.

We're heading down a ramp into darkness uttermost. Vehicle lights come on.

"Zandra, this is the Residence of Originals—it can't be the Hoo-hoo House too."

"What's a Hoo-hoo house?"

"That's their security place. I haven't seen it but this can't be it—this is where Originals live. We're being taken to see the one To-mees reports to."

"Is that bad, or is it worse?"

Which indeed?

Glimpse of a grotto inset with a myriad glassy beads, our lights splashing back at us momentarily, then suddenly glittering constellations of stars and dust clouds glowing violet and rose as if our mini-bus is transformed into a space vehicle hurled far from Melody, and Zandra gasps, but this is a show I'm used to by now, simply on a rather larger scale than in Pha's building.

"It's a display, that's all—"

At least one other vehicle is parked in this cosmic grotto. A few vacant nooks in the wall of stars: our mini-bus is pulling in alongside one. We stop. Side slides open—upon a cubicle. Out into this we must climb, cuffed. Once we're inside with our Monitors, the cubicle closes itself and I feel it ascend.

Two more Monitors meet us in a short vestibule of arched golden glass opening into a sizeable circular atrium. Glassy beads coat the floor and ceiling of the atrium. Some silvery doors, all shut, presumably give access to adjacent chambers as well as to whatever is above and below—this inner space accounts for less than a third of the interior of the globe.

Free-standing slim columns, shoulder-high, support contraptions slowly spinning around like complicated weathervanes. Other slender pillars are topped with cups cradling what look like huge eyeballs. And several crystalline thrones are arranged in a semi-circle . . .

While To-mees looks on, us prisoners are enthroned. In place of the cuffs, white bands tether our wrists to each arm of the thrones. Our feet remain free though the wrist-tethers feel quite unshiftable. This is altogether too much like a preliminary to intensified interrogation. Fear increases sensitivity to pain. I must be calm. How can I be calm? By telling myself that the Original dare not meet us unless we're completely immobilised. He must take absolute care of himself.

The Monitors withdraw beyond the thrones. The eyeballs on pillars gaze at us.

And before our eyes appears. . . .

Suspended upright in mid-air: the naked amputated trunk plus head of an Ivorybody. Tubes lead from the groin and from the behind, ending where the field of view ends, for of course this is an image not reality.

The two arms and two legs are present, wide-spread, encased in some protective or preservative sheath—arms raised above the trunk, legs forking out below—but *separated* from the trunk, detached from it.

What we are seeing is a total amputee fitted with tubes for draining waste, but with the severed limbs still present, pickled perhaps, embalmed by some means, tantalising near to the trunk yet divided from it.

I suspect the image is rotated so that what is floating supine in some chamber above our heads is here viewed as vertical. Maybe what holds that trunk and those limbs in position is edited out, unlike the tubes.

This is an Original? Lopped of its limbs . . . No short cuts, anyone?

Pha and Shi are both sheening, as if here is an image of a punishment for them or an experiment which might be performed upon them: dismemberment and enforced persisting.

A helmet hides most of the Original's head apart from the mouth. I suppose he or she is viewing us through those artificial eyeballs on pillar-stalks.

Its lips move. Emenating from all over the atrium, the voice flutes as sweetly as an angel's.

"You from the New World: tell me all about the human being who was reborn."

Of course: that is the holy grail of Su-loo-la, a mind on the loose. A mind detached from any body. Olav disembodied himself and persisted before he became Jamie.

Several thousand years old, this Original? Remembering only edited highlights of its long succession of lives. And now quite literally unhinged, though in a Su-loo-la-friendly orthodox fashion?

"Tell me every detail."

I don't suppose an Original is accustomed to being denied a wish. Do I have any bargaining power? Only my knowledge of Jamie-Olav and whatever spin I can put on this. Surely the baby nuke idea is shot to shit. Complete failure of mission, unless this Original is in two minds about the merits of the New World—what did To-mees say about it maybe being best if the stations are destroyed because of the mind-maladies of human beings? Alas, the holy grail is on Earth, so it seems. Goose and golden egg.

"Begin."

"With respect"—no, I shan't address him as Great One or any such—"what exactly do I gain by telling you?"

"Gain? If you do not begin to tell me, then a Monitor will use a pacifier upon Pha-po-lidoi. He will use it repeatedly. Until euthanasia."

Disrupting her nervous system, then disintegrating her mind
. . . Not Pha, *no*, not my Pha—she's sheening, hearing this. Is this
why To-mees wanted us to use the drug, to bond us so closely?

"Next he will use the pacifier similarly upon the black courier."

That's why the Original wanted Zandra fished out of the transit
station. Small mercies, Zandra can't understand what's being said.

"So tell me."

"If I do, what happens to us?"

"You remain a source of information."

"And Pha and Shi and Zandra?"

"Those are your accessories."

Quite; but what does that imply for them? Us all being kept here
like Cartoo's in Daddy's cellar, either interminably or for as long as
I remain a useful source?

"What guarantee do you give?"

"I guarantee that otherwise a pacifier will be used."

As threats go, undoubtedly this is nowhere as vicious as Eye-
Cups . . . Only human beings could dream that one up. I'm beginning to think that an actual atrocity, the infliction of severe pain,
may be impossible for the Original to contemplate or perpetrate
. . . because, because . . . if he could do such to another, it could
be done to him. Always distrust everything. I'm beginning to wonder whether what I am seeing is genuine—a true image—or a
macabre simulation, a pathological symbol of a desire to be rid of
the body, to become a free mind . . . For Pha or Zandra to be
pacified to death is still . . . terminal.

Not a whole lot of choice, really. Olav seems to be the only card
I have.

"I shall tell you freely—if you will tell me a few things first."

"A few things in exchange for one?" enquires the amputated
angel poised before me.

"In exchange for many things, actually. The point is, what you
are asking is complicated. Answering me may help me answer you."

"Give an example."

"How is it that a mind can transfer from a brain into another
brain the way it does by using your transfer equipment? If I don't
understand this I'm handicapped explaining about the man who
was reborn."

Not perhaps handicapped so much as desperately wishing to
know.

Religions and popular beliefs have made an item of the self
being independent of the body and brain, but how in heck could

this be so? In a sense it's the biggest, the watershed question; and till a few years ago it was beginning to seem to be a non-question, a nonsense question, one which would surely evaporate within another century unless the world crashed back into barbarism, and superstitions held sway instead of rational lucidity.

If enlightenment could advance, rather than collapse, I suppose the theme of much great art and writing and fantasies—the sovereign mind, the autonomous soul—would become mere picturesque childish psychology, infantile pre-civilized patterns of thought, magical thinking. What would we have lost? Cultural infancy. A few thousand years of it. What would we have gained? A mature realistic future in which we could edit out our assorted mind-maladies instead of trying hamfistedly to police them. Maybe intelligent life is a sickness of the universe, not the icing on the cake. I can't bear to believe this.

The mind-maladies so deeply ingrained in us! What price the wood without the grain? Grain is the memory of growth.

"And?" enquires the Original.

Here goes. "And why did you let Loosh-shi-cartoo escape to my world?"

"Because he would stay the longest of any of us, having no choice. We would be able to study him later and discover the long-term effect of being a human."

Oh. All part of the research. Yet the Original has deigned to answer me! He has answered a question.

"Were you not worried that Cartoo might betray you?"

"It would be senseless to disclose himself—the very opposite of his aim. Who would believe in him, compared with all the benefits your world enjoys?"

One lone, untrustworthy voice. Quite true.

"Some of us believed him."

"Not enough, I judge. Here you are, bringer of information, not collector."

"By the time you study Loosh-shi-cartoo it'll be too late to realize how unsuitable human beings are—all our wars and violence and frenzies."

"Your atomic weapons, which you would have the madness to carry to our worlds! Our thinkers were aware of the possibility of such devices." Maybe that's the ticket for me: nuclear madness, latest instalment in the career of Homo Sap.

"Knowledge about nuclear weapons is suppressed—is that it? What if your colonists go mad on Earth?" Yes, what if they go ape!

"What if they make use of our nuclear weapons? What if they can attack your other worlds?"

"This exchange is interesting, akin to debating with my equals in the Council of Wisdom."

The whole Council cannot meet very often, if ever. All the logistics of couriers and dummies and a dozen worlds. So: how autonomous are the various Originals? The residents of the Bunch-o'-Grapes: a sub-council managing Melody—united in Su-loo-la, yet with a lot of individual scope, and their own Monitors loyal to each? Seems highly irresponsible of this Original letting Cartoo decamp to Earth—not something a committee would approve.

Grown sceptical about the takeover of Earth now that investigation is in full swing? Is that it? Inject a tiny chance of failure in the person of Cartoo, if fate so ordains? Maybe Cartoo's liberty resulted from the Original having too much on his mind and editing himself. Missing things out.

I am sure that the amputated image is false. It's the closest that the Original can come, vertiginously, to what Olav talked about as the rite of "Cutting Off"—the sort of transcendent caper that shamans (but not this one, me!) went in for.

Does the Council meet personally, or as holographic images?

"Have you really had your arms and legs removed or is this merely the way you like to show yourself to visitors?"

Pha and Shi are twittering softly, aghast I think.

The Original is silent for some time

"What's going on?" hisses Zandra.

"I'm trying to deal with him up there." What sort of *deal?* Treat with him? Cope with him?

I wish I was locked up in Kielder. I wish I was Humpty Hugh confined to his wheelchair. I wish I was Milly squirreled away under that Welsh mountain.

Hesitantly, I venture: "Other members of the Council must see you as very powerful—being cut apart like that."

"Explain what you mean."

"Seeming to be cut apart is a potent image of something unattainable—the leaving of the body, the freeing of the mind, the defeat of death—not by going conveniently into another body, but by accepting destruction. I honour you for conceiving this." Appealing to vanity is always a bright idea, though I'm treading on eggshells. "It's a pretense, isn't it? Upstairs, you are all together."

"Be silent!"

Are those eggshells cracking. . . ?

Upstairs, in his head, he is certainly not altogether. But is he mad . . . or alternatively *sad*, even pitiable?

"I'm sure only persons loyal to you are listening, and they already know your secret. I admire you so much for conceiving of this way to present yourself. It is very brave—and visionary."

"Continue."

"I think it is unreal. You cannot really cut yourself apart."

"It can be done."

"You are focusing your mind upon the possibility. That is a great insight, Original. It is very original. In your next life would you enter into a limbless Ivorybaby?"

"You come here in your only life . . . For centuries we of Su-loo-la have contemplated . . ."

"But you shy away. Because you already are cut off—from what I know. From suffering and death."

"I am thinking." Time passes. Maybe the Original is taking the Mocky-equivalent of a tranquilliser.

"I must know," the Original resumes. "I must know about the reborn person."

"To tell you clearly, I need to know what you know about *minds*."

There. I am presenting this not as a bargain but as a definition of terms.

"Anna—"

"Zandra, I have to concentrate."

I wish I was anywhere else. I wish I was in my private room. But I cannot be. Anna Sharman has gone to the stars and the only way back is by coping with riddles and with an alien who has complete power over me.

I wish I was Houdini in a straitjacket.

And so, I am instructed.

Why is red "red"? Unless you happen to suffer from colour blindness, each shade of red is experienced identically by everyone normal. Blood is not perceived as scarlet by some and as pink by others. A rose is a rose is a rose. So why is red "red"?

A particular wavelength of light enters the eye, sure enough. Yet inside the brain there is only darkness. No miniature observer watches the show with an inner eye, nor is there a show to watch.

So how does almost everyone experience the selfsame redness?

Tastes, too. And smells. Well, not all stimuli, since sensitivities vary. But if a stimulus registers it is experienced identically by members of a species.

Individual mind is *coherence*, quoth the amputated angel. Awareness is coherence, quantum coherence, so he calls it. I understand well enough once I mentally adjust the Ivoryspeak terms to human popular science parlance. Yet there is a higher coherence too, a harmonizing coordination between separate awarenesses, so that my experience of red is also your experience of red. The idea of redness reverberates in the fabric of reality. And fundamental reality is not things; it is energy. Nor is space vacuous—vacuum seethes with potential energy vastly outgunning all the blazing of all the stars. Nor are separate places really separate—if two particles have ever been in contact they retain a "memory" of the encounter; and once upon a time, in the beginning, when everything bloomed out of infinitely potent nothingness, absolutely everything was in contact. Hence, the coherence of physical laws which in themselves are like abstract ideas; for the universe registers itself—and Self registers in the fabric which is not material fabric, quoth the Original. Here is the root of Self. Since the universe consists of possibility-states, Self can be uprooted-rerouted from one locus to another.

Why is red red? Because all is registered.

At body-death the Self remains recorded but it is no longer manifest to itself until perhaps the end of time and space when the vacuum swallows its cosmos back into itself, at which point the manifest and the unmanifest become one and the same. Ha: life after death as permanent amnesia—or as an unnoticed pause lasting for billions of years yet also no time at all. And then what? Awareness resuming once more? Awareness of what? Of the totality of all life and lives? The aim of Su-loo-la: disembodied awareness *now*, within the material universe, able to interact with the material universe through energy.

Olav remanifested himself in the world, ostensibly by power of will, though he only emerged when Jamie looked into the quantum crystal, a crystal that, according to the Original, infolds-unfolds inner dimensions.

Do I understand? Maybe.

"You will tell me now."

Right. Very well. The tale of Olav Frisvold and Jamie and Zandra, her too, so that she will seem central to the matter, precious rather than peripheral. . . .

Questions, questions. The sacrifice in the park, mind-maladies of Nazis, the Odin cordon and blood-shield, the Tibetan ritual of

Cutting Off and rite of rebirth, Tibetans dying in Berlin or being snuffed later on by the Chinese People's Liberation Army, the discharge of energy when Olav shot himself, the sacrifice in the park . . .

How much does the Original understand of what I explain about the ways of another world, as delivered in Ivoryspeak? Enough, so it seems, enough—though at the same time this all takes a long time.

When my voice becomes reedy I need pitcher-o'-juice by my side and my right hand free, then I need to be led away to pee in a cleansing cubicle, and next Zandra must have her turn, and Pha too, and Shi, and afterwards on the Original's instructions a much-needed snack is served, the food machine providing human diet-bars for Zandra just as in the Melody Hilton—she must be going crazy having to sit listening without comprehending anything.

All the while the Original floats before us, dissected, neither wetting his whistle nor sucking on any food-tube, so the image *must* be an edited, idealised version, even though the lips move whenever he speaks.

Hours have passed. Till at last he says, "It is necessary to encounter this human Ola-foo in the body. You must bring him to me for study."

Bring Olav *here?* By me going back, inside Zandra? By Jock and Tim and company hustling Olav from Middlesex Square to Hyde Park and *transiting* him without anyone else intervening and blowing whistles and raising Cain at what we're doing without authority? Blowing our cover, and all for nothing! Aborting any chance we have of dealing decisively with the threat. Oh we'll set up a top-secret study group. Report in four year's time, after we get more goodies in the larder. Meanwhile, you people are right out of it. Max-security prison. Throw away the key. Years of interrogation. A purge of the Combined Security Service and of the SAS.

Admit it: "We who have the reborn person are only a small group, Original. Just a few persons. We are acting without permission. What you ask is too difficult to carry out."

And even if Olav *was* a Nazi, it's vile to trade Jamie-Olav to aliens as an experimental specimen.

Olav is a holy grail for the Original, something desirable in the utmost. Something to be exchanged not for a handful of lives but for something far more significant. Mockymen, leave us alone. Let us bomb the transit stations.

"You already came here without permission," that sweet voice says. "Therefore you will succeed a second time. Otherwise Pha-po-lidoi and the black courier will both be dissected and sustained. Hands then feet then individual joints."

To-mees seems perturbed—fingers flexing. Pha is hooing to herself and Shi has gone very blank and drained.

Zandra hisses, "Why's she whimpering, if that's what she's doing? What's the big cheese saying? What the shit's going to happen?"

"Nothing to worry about for the moment." Don't let Zandra know. Never let her know. This has to be a ghoulish threat, as was ours to Cartoo.

Using anaesthetics, so that no pain results? Might this be the Original's way around a dilemma? Can't contemplate pain, but can casually talk about cutting off limbs. This Original must realize, at least intellectually, that this is a horrid threat to someone who only has one body. That's because he has contemplated his own severed simulation. Many Mockymen might scarcely understand. Lose a limb or so in an accident, swap to another fully functioning body as soon as one is available. This Original has to be something of a superstar. No wonder members of the Council hold him in esteem, assuming that they do so, and I think they must—here he is, allowed free rein as regards the New World Project. But he's a very flawed prodigy.

If I go back to Earth, and swear affidavits about my discoveries and then kill myself, making sure the reason is known, I shan't need to think about what is happening on a world far away to the woman who saved my life and the alien woman who bonded with me.

In what body would I go back to my world if not in Zandra's? Transiting directly in this Ivorybody? Enduring all the pain that Zandra knows so well? *Get back to Earth by whatever means, get out of here no matter how.* No, not by abandoning Zandra and Pha. Mustn't even think of it.

"I can only go back within the black courier." And would I abandon Pha?

"There remains a courier who is your accomplice."

The Original knows about Lionel Evans—who, at this very moment, must be searching the Melody Hilton for Zandra—where the hell has she vanished to?

"If I can bring Ola-foo, will the four of us transit back to my world?" Zandra, Pha, Shi, me.

Or will he keep Pha and Shi for assessment? Might he keep all of us?

How practical is it to bring Olav? Him to Hyde Park, false ID, no great problem. Might need to drug him to handle him; might be kinder to drug him. The Mockymen supervisors can already have been wised up. Me and him on the transit disc together, him cuffed hand and foot, half-zonked, me holding him tight. Some variation on this.

Olav vowed to do anything he could to assist against the Mockymen. Such a betrayal.

Why on Earth should Jock hand Olav over in order to rescue one human courier and two aliens he never met? The baby nuke scheme can never surely happen now—that's a blessing in a way— but how do we save the human race?

How can I enforce any supposed bargain? The Original has no reason to comply with any promise—not that he has made one. He has not answered me. Maybe he is communing with elsewhere through the helmet.

I have to get back to Earth, on my own if it's the only way. That's my mission.

I must not behave like a shit.

What else can I do?

I thought that I was becoming a better person. I wish I was Milly hidden under a mountain. What do I choose, what do I choose? To save. To abandon. Get out of here, Anna. At all costs. No. . . . But I don't have any choice, do I?

"Zandra, I shall have to transit to Earth in Lionel. We're going to give Olav to the Original in exchange for your freedom." Jock willing. Jock won't be willing. "I'll be back in a few days, Zandra."

"Exchange Olav for me? Girl, you got to think of a better lie than that!"

"Olav's a criminal. You're important to BritGov."

"Oh, pull the other leg right off me." Such withering contempt. Little do you realize. Little do you. Oh shit and shit.

"You white worm, Anna Sharman. Worming out."

"I am *not.* There's no other option." I can't bear to look at her. I'm ripped, inside. I will commit suicide if I fail. When I fail. I cannot live with this. I cannot go on living. Maybe Nazi Olav could, sister-killer. I have to seem confident and plausible for Zandra's sake even though she sees me as scum. I must lie to myself as much as I lie to her. If only I could die right now, instant oblivion.

"Original, after I bring Ola-foo I want Pha and Shi to come with me too." As corroborators of Cartoo's story—how very unlikely that scenario is now! "Ola-foo is worth a huge amount to you, Original. I know he is. You'll make a great breakthrough in Su-loo-la. You'll be honoured above all other Originals."

"That is true." He admits it, yes.

"Also in exchange, you must let us destroy the stations here and on the other planet."

Mockymen investment in Earth amounts to one starship launched from Passion, which can't have come cheaply, a transit station there and its twin here on Melody, the economy of Faluinu and a corresponding city on Passion, buildings, analysts, scouts, quite a bundle though perhaps only comparable to what us human beings routinely squander in an average war.

Plus the potential of a whole planet ripe for the plucking.

"If the stations are destroyed you will save yourselves from contamination by our aggressions and madnesses."

What a plea to make, that we are too sick to steal from.

If I fail there's no point in him carrying out his threats against Zandra and Pha. No point at all, except in my own haunted mind. The only function of such a threat is to manipulate me. I must put it out of my mind. It will not be carried out. It lacks any substance. When I fail to bring Olav, the Original will decide that amputation was not such a threat as he theorised. Or might he pull the legs off the spider anyway, to study the mental consequences?

Zandra will be terribly lonely . . . Oh but Jamie-Olav will be here too. At least let me imagine he will be here.

The ache of leaving Pha; the misery of leaving Zandra. A sickle moon half the size of Earth's moon hangs beyond the dome of the transit station like some mad surgeon's scalpel blade. The snake-snacker birds are spiralling down to roost.

Accompanying me in the vehicle which the Ober drives are two other Monitors and To-mees, tool of the Original. As we pull up by the station To-mees warbles rather flatly, "You will come back. You will not abandon Pha or Shi."

Is he trying to reassure himself? Exonerate himself? He must believe the Original's threat, but I cannot cannot cannot. Silence is best.

Silence, until Lionel Evans is brought into the selfsame room as before.

"I'm Anna," I tell him quickly. "Things went wrong. They knew I was spying. They took Zandra hostage—"

"Hang on, what are you talking about? I don't know any Anna. What are you?"

"Lionel, you're blown but it doesn't matter! You're going back to London with a passenger piped in, and me in you too underneath. You're going back tonight."

He eyes the Monitors. For a moment I think he will persist in his bluff.

"Straight-up?" he asks instead.

"Straight-up. I have a message for H-S."

"What message?"

"For his ears only."

"Shouldn't you tell me in case. . . ?"

In case I can't transfer into Ms Fuchsia Tree, quite.

The English-speaking Ober intervenes. "No failure will occur. Now is best."

Maybe there's reason to put our skates on. Shifts may be due to change in the station. Mockymen loyal to the Original may go off duty. Maybe the various Originals in Faluinu are rivals, like Renaissance Cardinals kissing each other but all craving to become Pope. The Ober places the confiscated jewel on the table.

"Sit opposite yourselves." Opposite each other, he means.

We do so.

"Pick up the crystal, courier."

"Let me get my head in gear first." Evans sits breathing deeply.

It isn't only the business of taking me on board, it's the sudden imminence of transit-agony. Torture-time.

Put myself in his place? Oh I am going to do just that.

After a couple of minutes spent composing himself, Evans lifts the crystal.

Crystal, crystal in your hand. Now I must lose all knowledge of what happens.

Chapter 28

"Anna—"

Lionel withdrawing, Tim looming—and Jock alongside. My hands, arms, all my skin is black, I'm Zandra no I'm not. A sheet goes over my lower half. But I'm not not not in Jock's upstairs room. I'm in a strip-lit room in Hyde Park, and alert by the door is moon-faced Major Denbigh in camouflage gear and boots and badged cap, holster at his waist.

Members of the Regiment have seized Hyde Park without waiting for further evidence? How can this have happened? We've been sussed, found out! Jock and Denbigh and Co jumped the gun.

BritGov must know. We must be surrounded. Can any por-tanukes be here?

"Don't send the nukes, Jock," is the first thing to say, in a lovely, soft, rich, throbby voice unfamiliar to me. "The Mockymen know about those. They can stun anyone carrying queer kit—"

"Hwisht!" he hushes me. "Why, you're a fine black Scots lassie —Edinburgh, by the sound. Don't fash yourself. We have no nukes here, not as yet. Welcome back to Britain, with its new military government."

Tim clasps my shoulder. "Welcome back, Anna—there's been a coup."

"What—?"

* * *

Coup, coup? No time to tell *me*. The urgent priority is for Jock and Denbigh to hear all that I know—gushing out of me in this unexpected Scots voice of mine.

The status of the original natives of Melody, fate planned for the human race, betrayal by To-mees, the amputated Original, Olav as holy grail of Su-loo-la, Zandra held captive under vile threat which at least she doesn't know about and which just has to be sham, can't expect Jock or Denbigh to care much about Pha . . .

All this while I'm sitting wrapped in a sheet, black legs not dangling but firm on the floor as I sit tall, and I'll be walking tall too, as tall as Zandra.

Zandra. Pha. And Shi. What if the threat isn't sham? How shall I know? Dreadful vision of a courier arriving with a package addressed to me, and in the package a dark human hand or foot!

"I tried," I say, "to link handing over Olav with letting us blow the stations—the Original seemed to think us having nuclear weapons is a really sick symptom—maybe the Mockymen are better off without our bodies. If we do give Olav to the Original—" Oh what am I saying.

"Lassy, if he's such a grail, have you not thought that him staying here protects us against them starting those plagues of theirs ahead of schedule? Start a plague and Olav most likely goes dummy along with almost everyone else. Have you not thought that he's our shield? *Schild, Shutz,* eh?"

Schild. Shutz. Schild. Schutz. The beastly litany in the park.

"We'll shift him to somewhere really secure." Denbigh's in his element.

The house on Middlesex Square is already under military guard, by no means the only place to be so. Same goes for Downing Street and for most government buildings including Centre Point and the headquarters of Combined Intelligence; the firm wasn't too sharp at spotting the actual subversives at work in the country.

"Not too canny at all!" Jock tells me gleefully. "And us farting around with our spot of mischief while a proper conspiracy was brewing. *Mind you,* lassy, if it *hadn't* been for what we were up to—"

Cartoo's confessions triggered the coup, finally tipping the balance for some senior officers who although sympathetic—the armed forces had been nursing grievances for years—hitherto were reluctant to behave "like a bunch of South American generals." That, and the fact that Jock and I stumbled upon dissent at Hereford—tip of an iceberg, so to speak—and that my jaunt to Melody might easily bollix up with unpredictable repercussions.

Mr Bee and his cabinet and supporters are in custody, en route to Kielder camp. Mockymen are being arrested. Most amazing of all, as though to make space for new internees, the old hard-case internees have been released.

"You ought to have seen TV this morning," Tim tells me. "Humpty Hugh rolling out of Kielder in his wheelchair. 'Course, that was staged for the look of it, and he can hardly be part of the Government of Salvation—though that's what it's being called."

Absolutely not: Hugh Ellison's too ill, he's a religious raver, he's totally unsuitable. Still, a touch of figurehead symbolism shows that our General Abercrombie has his sights on hearts and minds. It's a full coup, not a half-baked one. I could dance (once I get used to my longer legs!), I could weep, I could cry out with joy.

Lionel is in no state to dance. He's hanging in but he's pallid and shaky with transit nausea.

"That was my worst bloody transit yet—" All the extra anxiety in addition to agony as usual. It can only be half an hour since he was torn apart and put together again. No idea whether the passenger he decanted is an agent for the Original, but in its dummy that passenger isn't going jaunting anywhere, not any more. Jock and Tim have been staying here at Hyde Park with Denbigh since shortly after the coup, since if I did return it was urgent to debrief me.

Evans groans. "I'll have to catch up on all this later. Are taxis still running?"

"You hang about," Jock tells him. "Kip in the medical wing."

"Among dummies?" But off he lurches to do as he's told.

"This business about your Olav being the bees' knees," Denbigh says to me, "it's just what we need. Ace card. Blocks the Mockymen from playing their joker. You're a heroine, Miss Sharman. Only problem: might that Original character decide you were doing disinformation about Frisvold?"

"I don't think so. I really don't."

"I'll go with her assessment," Jock says briskly. "Of course Britain's only one wee country taking action—and actually what action do we take next, if the baby nuke idea's unsound?"

Denbigh broods.

Daddy. I'm forgetting about Daddy. Sly fox, he must have been in on this for years. It'll be his turn for a surprise when next I see him in the person of Fuchsia Tree.

"Does Daddy know I was shot, Tim?"

"We didn't wish to worry him, Cartoo being there and all."

"Don't tell him. Just say that I've come back, and that I'll visit as soon as I can."

"You shan't be phoning?"

I mimic Jock. "Och, laddy, how would he tell that it's me?"

Zandra and Pha and Shi: oh God, what can be done? What ever can be done?

Denbigh contemplates Tim and me, then finally addresses Jock.

"Big problem with your portable bomb is the volunteer chap. Not quite in our own tradition to vaporize oneself, hmm? *Almost* certain risk of death, that's one thing—chaps volunteer. Absolute guarantee of death, bit different. It's quite Islamic, though. Direct beeline to Allah's bosom for the lucky fellas. Blow themselves up and they're in paradise."

"What are you getting at, Major?"

What has been happening, to Jock's astonishment and mine, is covert military contacts with the religious leaders in a certain Moslem country which would have no truck with the Mockymen —contact first broached through British Moslem fundamentalists who kept their noses clean when the likes of Hugh Ellison were kicking up a fuss. Which country, Denbigh refuses to say.

Contacts in which Daddy has been involved . . . Daddy, with his Arabic. There's been an understanding for a couple of years now. Combined Intelligence knew sod all about it.

"Army's been screwed by Intelligence for years," is how Denbigh puts it. "Bosnia, Ireland, Hardship Years, Scotch Bonnets, whatever. Intel not supplied fast enough or fully enough. Never giving us the whole picture. Spend ages setting up an op then cancel at the last minute for supposed political reasons or ramifications. And all the time, cutbacks going on. Parachute Regiment without planes of their own, bloody hell. And never mind the rigged endorsement referendum couple of years ago."

"No evidence it was rigged," says Jock. "That's Humpty nonsense."

"Electronic polling secured by encryption. Encryption controlled by GCHQ. Well, *we* control Cheltenham now. The truth will out."

Nukes in London are not on. Nor in Dublin neither. Stands to reason. Government of Salvation couldn't countenance it. Lose popular support right away. Terrible international stink. If it's done far away by Moslem fanatics, carried out in a third world country which you wouldn't expect, using kit supplied from Britain, well-shielded automated bombs that go off two ticks after they lose an inhibiting signal, accompanied by a religious fanatic who's merely along for the ride, no need to push a button—different matter entirely.

It so happens that Moslem bigwigs in a certain country had been angling for a nuclear solution to the aliens along lines such as this, but they lacked the necessary kit. General Abercrombie could hardly slip them nuclear kit while the status quo prevailed. Discussions remained provisional: an understanding that if and when the situation altered. . . .

"It's bloody well changed now and no mistake." Denbigh is excited, face shining. Maybe he's being indiscreet but Jock and Tim and I are such a central part of what's happening. Oh no he's judging this correctly, is Denbigh. We do need to know. He's trusted to make judgements. No accident that Denbigh was the officer who came to Come-Back Cottage.

"How long to set this up?" Jock wants to know.

"Week or so, then a week or so more to completion. Fly the kit out with technical support so our mad Mullah pals know what they're doing. They smuggle the kit to sympathisers in a neighbouring secular country to cover traces. In the other country armed fanatics seize the transit station. Big bangs on Melody and Passion. Mockymen stop coming. Religious extremists take the blame. We're clean. Nothing to link us. Piece of cake." And Denbigh adds wryly, with a wink of a watery eye, "Allah willing."

And of course the Mullahs can be apprised of the secret of the food factories, programmed to release the dummifying plague years hence. It can be the Mullahs who wise up the world. Independent confirmation can come from New BritGov . . .

"Cartoo may need to be trotted out as Mockymen defector."

Jock is sceptical. "Won't that seem to be a direct link with us?"

"We're such unlikely bedfellows, us and the Islamics. There's the beauty of it. We're running ahead of ourselves. I must see the General toot sweet, tell him in person. Better come with me, Miss Sharman. All three of you. Are you up to it, Miss Sharman?"

"I think so. Where is General Abercrombie?"

"Dulwich."

Ah, at the Regiment's London home, south of the Thames. A more salubrious neighbourhood than where Alex Corby lived and died. Abercrombie himself is regular army but, sensibly, special forces are acting as his Pretorian Guard during the upheaval.

What about Zandra, what about Pha? Pha seems so far away,

Zandra too. No way of extricating them. The Original's threat is a fake. Never carry it out. No severed foot or hand incoming in a few days' time. What do I tell Barnabas?

It's time to visit the wardrobe department to choose gear for Fuchsia Tree. How soon do I kill myself? After I have saved my country, my world.

How will I kill myself? Gun barrel in my gaping mouth, pointing upward. Pull the trigger.

After the vivid daytime brightness of Faluinu, London seems monochrome, an antiquated black and white movie following upon a technicolour one. Grey sky, grey buildings, grey roads, the armed grey military motorbikers escorting our Land Ranger—and grey faces of citizenry? No, people wave to us. The coup seems popular. Traffic is slacker than usual, and we have priority—*wee, wee, whoop*, from the sirens of our outriders—but shops and businesses are functioning.

Checkpoints block access to the Palace and to the Houses of Parliament, and Westminster Bridge is only open to official vehicles. Here was where Wordsworth was inspired to write, "Earth has not anything to show more fair."

Tim is studying me in my very long emerald-green velvet dungarees housing tiers of external buttoned pockets little and large, might come in useful, floppy-neck red chenille sweater, creamy jacket with braid piping—not much time to match costumes except for size. On my feet, the flattest leather shoes I could fit into so as not to stumble or bang my head on low-set obstacles. If I kill myself, I betray Tim. Jock does all the talking from the front, filling me in.

A full-scale coup is a complicated affair. Coordinated seizures of key places, a lot of guns and armour on show, a spate of arrests, control of the media, proclamation of military law, complicity of Chief Constables in metropolitan areas—and society's wheels must still continue turning, networks must carry on functioning.

Armed forces, overstretched and undermanned. No experience of meddling in politics, quite the opposite. Sounding senior officers out, and those sounding out their juniors tentatively, the drawing up of plans—purely hypothetical exercises, of course, a sort of secret and paradoxical morale booster fuelled by a deep suspicion of aliens —and keeping the lid on all the while: this must have taken some finesse and some time, and still seemed like a wet dream. Denbigh bangs the horn, a blaring fart as if by way of comment.

"Magpie on the road—"

There it is, flapping away. An urban magpie. One for sorrow, two for joy, so they say. Can't see a partner bird. If it got into the habit of nipping in to traffic to scavenge discarded burger or whatever, probably it's squashed by now. Tim is my partner, Zandra is my sister. Our outriders have veered, looking back, but Denbigh flashes okay.

Wet dream. But then, because of Cartoo, the fuse is lit—not that Jock or I could be privy right away, though our activities proved a Godsend.

Bye-bye to the permanent government; proclaim a new liberty (not to be enjoyed yet a while), while if possible preventing licence. Crack down after the first lynching of a Mockymen as pro-Humpty sentiment surges. Ban Bliss at once. Users are the last people likely to riot; let families rejoice nationwide. A nation is a living machine with a trillion parts, and suddenly you're steering that machine. Cope with Britain's sudden pariah status, some Ambassadors overseas making the wrong noises though most refraining from comment pending clarification. Cool it on the currency front, suspend stock market trading. Reassure the nation, reassure other nations. No more departures from Hyde Park; it's Independence Day. Tell the Mockymen at the United Nations nothing at all; keep 'em guessing. Announce nothing about Cartoo, of course. Bang on about the evils of Bliss, Britons becoming dummy-slaves. Bang on about Kielder. Trot out old Tories. Britain's Moslems take a welcome lead in supporting the new regime. . . .

And all the while Tim watches the new me, Fuchsia Tree, easily as tall as himself.

"By the bye," says Jock, "did you happen to give Evans my snuff-box before you left Melody?"

"I'm afraid it wasn't to hand."

"Och."

General Abercrombie and his general staff are very busy in Dulwich, though within half an hour the General trundles in to the private office where Denbigh has ensconced Jock, Tim, and me. Five foot ten of burly old soldier with short silvery hair and a contrivedly non-parade-ground gait which conveys an avuncular trustworthy air—just a bit shambly, though purposeful. His bushy white eyebrows bend upward interrogatively and he's so pinkly clean-shaven it looks as if he actually lacks any facial hair anywhere below the slightly bloodshot eyes—not too many hours' sleep recently, though he's visibly in full control and probably runs an electric razor over his face every few hours in the midst of running the country.

"Right, I'm Snowy Abercrombie, and you're Anna Sharman, though I doubt your father will recognize you right off."

Right is a word Snowy Abercombie used quite a lot, as if to emphasize that all is well in the world. He ticks off with topics he already heard of briefly from Denbigh, inviting me to expand before — "Right!" — moving briskly onward.

Food factories: not manna but mass murder in the long run, global problem, we'll need to treat it as such, spread the word quietly — coordination's the key. The Original, Olav as grail, Zandra supposedly awaiting amputation: Denbigh is making arrangements for Olav's well-being, somewhere in the countryside. We'll be watching out for *foreign* Mockymen arriving from abroad looking for him. Heathrow, Dover, all points of entry, arrest newcomers if we can spot them. Plenty of exercise and amusements for Frisvold, don't want him to get depressed. New bodies for old: don't want 'em, it's unnatural, divisive, one life is enough for anyone sensible. Paying full attention to being alive while you're alive's the ticket. Got that crystal? Hand it over.

Which Jock does. Outside, so much is going on. Armoured personnel carriers revving, comings and goings, communications dishes. The rest of the building is buzzing.

"Your testimony, Miss Sharman: that'll be needed, and very publicly too, in another fortnight or so when things sort out. Broadcast to the nation and satellited to the world. Best place for you meanwhile is at home with your father in an easily controllable village, well protected, along with your boyfriend, getting to know each other anew, so to speak, but we'll videotape preliminary material here and now while it's fresh in your mind, right?"

"I'd rather keep busy than go home, Sir." Back home I may kill myself. What, with Tim nearby? With Daddy nearby?

"You've been busy enough. Jock — if I may? — your whole outfit needs a shake-up. Re-gearing. Sorting out. Bit of purging. New loyalties. I'm putting you in charge of that whole shebang, right?"

I break in. "With respect, Sir—"

"Miss Sharman, do call me Snowy while we're in private. I respect you, very much. Deserve the Victoria Cross, you do."

"I was going to say that I'm well qualified to help Jock do that job."

"I don't disagree, but we can't have you in a risk position, right? In any case, until you step into the limelight, who are you? Where did you come from? It'll be lively enough at your father's, not out of touch at all. Army Intel will give you a thorough grilling there, though not with a bag over your head." So I *will* be kept occupied. "In a while you can get back in saddle with real authority if you want to, right? Now you really must excuse me—"

So it has come to this. I have been videotaped for over an hour and now, preceded by a topless Land Ranger mounted with a heavy machine gun, this Roller with armoured glass—that greenish gleam —and armoured bodywork will carry me and Tim off not to Middlesex Square as I slightly imagined—what could I tell Barnabas except something that might drive him wild, and what further business do I have with Olav?—nor to Hampstead neither to unwind with Sibelius, oh Anna lent me her flat for a while, I'm called Anna too, isn't that odd?—but to Withyhope, where Daddy is different again from the person I thought him to be; but then again I am very different too.

Amidst the military comings and goings, Jock bids goodbye. He's bound for Middlesex Square with Denbigh, prior to becoming the new broom of Intelligence.

"What will you tell Barnabas?"

"Nothing about you or Zandra, of course—just that Olav is being relocated as a precaution."

"And when the days will pass and Zandra doesn't return?"

"While there's ignorance, lass, there's hope. Put off today's sorrow till the morrow."

"I want to know—"

If a certain package arrives. Not at Hyde Park—soon the last of our own couriers will all have returned and none will replace them. But in Paris or Dublin, say, to be delivered by dummy to our embassy. And then the next day another similar package.

"Yes?"

"I want to know if anything happens . . . that I need to know."

"I think I follow you." And he may prefer to misunderstand me.

After Tim and I climb into the back of the Roller, weirdly like bride and groom setting off on honeymoon, of a sudden it comes to me.

"Tim, my old body: is it in a morgue?"

"No, it was buried fairly promptly."

"Were you there?"

"Sleeping Beauty Squad saw to it. It isn't in a cemetery, you understand. There wasn't a ceremony or anything."

"A hole in the ground? The same as Robert was threatened with? What happened to *his* body?"

"Buried too—not in the same hole, not in the same place, rest assured. That wouldn't have been right at all." What will Daddy think of this? But I'm still alive, I'm not the body in the hole. I *will* be a body in a grave in Withyhope churchyard before too long.

Our driver's voice comes via intercom. "*Shall I set off?*"

"Go go go," I tell him. He's tasked, we're rolling, if hardly into the main action.

Chapter 29

Somewhere near Reading Tim finally says, "Well, it *did* happen, didn't it?"

Me in a dolly-dummy, quite. I know what he means. It's as if he has been talking to me for a while, though only inside his own head.

"Will you marry me?" he asks of a sudden.

From one extreme to another! Grand gesture—he really is a romantic. Our driver can hear none of this.

The afterglow of Pha is still with me. That's another problem.

"Tim, there's something I ought to tell you . . ." And I do.

"Well, line of duty," is his view. "Can't call that being unfaithful, not that I've any right to! Anyway, you were an Ivoryman *bloke* at the time. So don't go cooking up pretexts, Anna Sharman. Unless it's something deeper, something that really stands in the way. Or unless you're using this to let me down lightly?"

"I just don't know, Tim. Maybe you ought to call me Fuchsia and see how that sounds. Someone else's name. Someone I've stolen."

"For heaven's sake don't feel guilty about that. I want you."

"Mocky-Anna."

"No: Anna, *you.*"

"I'm not teasing, and I'm not fishing. I value you very much,

Tim. Yet I look at myself and I think that this is Zandra who came back." If only, if only. What am I saying to him?

"Your face is different, your hair's quite different, you don't have any scars. Are you proposing you should offer yourself to Barnabas as a substitute? I don't think you'd be on the same wavelength, frankly."

"It's just that . . . I have this body, she's black, she's tall."

"*You* are black, *you* are tall. Not she."

"And if the Original carries out his threat, whether I know about it happening or not . . . I don't think I can go to bed with you, Tim. How can I make love, knowing that her body is maybe being dismembered?" How can I go to bed with him at all, then kill myself?

"Oh you'd feel out of joint." Gallows humour. "Look, I'm happy to wait, Anna. Months. A year. Years, so long as we're together—and I mean *together*, not suffocatingly of course, you'll be working again in a while, but not just being friends. More than that—being true partners. If you will. If you want to."

"That's so sweet. Living together in abstinence: won't it be very frustrating?"

"I don't know yet." And that's honest. "Mightn't even arise. You've only been back a few hours. You're reacting to incredible experiences. If it does arise," and he nudges me gently with the back of his hand, the first actual touch between us, "we could always keep a big blunt sword in bed between us. Isn't that how they used to do it? You're the historian. Vow of chivalry."

"I think chivalry consisted more in putting somebody else's wife on a pedestal as a sort of erotic saint, then buzzing off on a crusade looting and raping in her honour. But that *is* gallant of you."

"Can we hold hands for a while?"

"Yes, Tim, we can." It's the least I can do. And what is the most?

To tell yourself too glibly that you will kill yourself is perhaps the ultimate dishonesty.

When we stop at motorway services, armed police officers are waiting to watch over bikes and limo and usher us to toilets and restaurant, where for my first meal as the new me I devour chicken curry. From the looks I receive I must be a VIP.

As we eat I tell Tim about Mary of Morogoro, which quite surprises him, though he summons a grin.

"So in a manner of speaking you already have a grown-up black daughter! There's nothing like forward planning. Do you want your Mary to come to England?"

"I hardly think she would want to, or would fit in. Oh she might want to, not knowing what's involved, but . . ."

The ache grips my heart again: Zandra, abandoned among aliens, all alone.

Tim knows when to let me be silent.

It's well after dark when we enter Withyhope after passing through a checkpoint consisting of police cars; the village is sealed off except to residents. The Cider Press pub looks busy—people must be puzzling what on Earth is happening down the lane which an armoured car guards. Waved on, we proceed. A couple of large caravans and a communications van are stationed beyond our house as well as several Land Rangers. A few soldiers wearing nightgoggles are out on patrol. Others guard our door and garden.

In the lounge Daddy is seated, and Sergeant Woods and another officer I don't know and a chubby balding bespectacled chap perhaps of Bangladeshi origin dressed in a dark suit—and also Cartoo, unchained, though still in pyjamas and a dressing gown and carpet slippers. Coffee cups stand around.

"Tim!" exclaims Daddy, half rising, cardigan-clad though with his regimental tie smartly knotted. "And—my God." He sinks back again, agape. "You. It is you, isn't it? Or am I barmy?"

"I'm your very own Anna, Daddy."

"Good grief, where did you get that voice? From Jock?"

"Same place I got the body."

"What happened to your *other* body, Anna?"

"Sorry, Daddy, it got shot."

"Christ." He seems a bit poleaxed. "I should have been told. No, maybe I shouldn't have been. . . ! *Who shot you?*"

"Robert the butler. Things went rather wrong."

"My God. But if you were shot—"

"Jock got the transfer crystal to me in time."

Daddy stares. "You're . . . splendid. You truly are. Were you hoping to give me a heart attack?"

The Asian chap is all eyes as Daddy struggles up and advances to embrace me, hesitating only momentarily: "Do you have anything fragile in any of these pockets?"

"Not a thing. Not yet."

"Hmm, ought to be a medal in every one." Now he hugs me fulsomely. "Good job I'm an old man, or this might be misconstrued. I suppose Tim here would sort me out."

"It is his daughter," I hear. "It is the agent. It is amazing . . ."

"I think we should be on our way," says the unknown officer to the British Bangladeshi. "Family reunion."

A reunion with Cartoo, likewise.

"Have my friends come?" he asks, once he realizes who I am.

"No, To-mees betrayed Pha and Shi." It's odd not to lilt and flute at him. "To-mees was studying the three of you on behalf of an Original. The Original let you escape so that you could be examined after the takeover, to find out how being in one of our bodies for years affected you."

"To-mees . . ."

"He wasn't true."

"You are mocking me."

"I was fairly pissed off, myself."

"Not understand. *Not understand.*"

"I played the game of food with them."

"You could not."

"Junior version." Then things became rather more mature. "I vowed that you would be treated very well, Cartoo, and I mean to keep my promise."

"I am well. I can look through windows. I can walk outside."

That's a definite up on the cellar, now that there's no need to hide his presence; nor need for a chain, with armed soldiers on the lookout.

"Things will only get better, Cartoo."

"To-mees, he was our friend."

"And now I'm your friend. If you like, you can teach me and Tim the full food game." We could play using chocolates, though I don't wish to put on weight, nor I suppose does Tim.

"I must be kept here for a long time before you understand the adult game. I think you are too busy."

"Not for the next couple of weeks."

The nuke plan is out of Jock's hands now. Mine too; I'm no longer responsible. Hundreds of people are going to die on Melody and Passion in one incandescent moment. Too quickly even to know that it's happening, or will there be time for half a thought? I don't think there will be time for any thought at all. This, instead of millions, billions of people dying.

Can this method of severing the links with the star-worlds conceivably be kept secret so that relatives of all the foreign couriers suppose they are simply marooned, but still alive? Forming a couple of inadvertent little human colonies? I think it will be rather obvious that ultimate measures were taken. After my testimony is broadcast, will I seem villain as well as heroine?

Oh Zandra, oh Pha.

I can't share with Tim, not yet. I need to be alone in my own old bedroom, just as in my dream I'm alone in my sanctuary. Cartoo has been promoted to the spare bedroom, and he will suffer no dip in circumstances on my account. Blessedly Tim volunteers of his own accord to sleep in the lounge.

"Be cosier than a billet in one of the caravans, and I'll be on hand. If I may, Sir, I'll bring the camp bed up from the cellar."

Which causes Daddy to raise an eyebrow. "But I thought . . . This isn't because Anna's . . . different, is it?"

"No way. Absolutely not."

"Why then, for goodness sake?"

"Daddy, it's because Zandra—the courier who took me, the woman who saved my life—she's . . . The Original threatened to cut off her limbs—and I could save her if I took Olav Frisvold to Melody but of course we aren't going to do anything of the sort, and it's essential not to do anything of the sort, but that means that Zandra . . ."

I'm crying. Fuchsia Tree is shedding tears.

Daddy squints at Tim, but Tim is holding back. I can see Tim's desire to comfort me and more. Too easy to take me in his arms though, too opportune. The sword is between us. If he sweeps it aside he'll be exploiting weakness. Daddy doesn't know what to do.

It is Cartoo, Mocky-Billy, who touches me, stroking my wet cheek while crooning phrases of Ivoryspeak which I no longer understand, then starting to shed tears as well, imitating me.

When I wake in the morning and stretch, I bump my heels against the blanketed foot of the bed. I'll need to go shopping for a new outfit in Hereford. Will that involve an armed escort? Tim will be my armed escort.

Arms, legs, Zandra . . . I think therefore I grieve. Last night in dreams I was happy: complex colourful sensual scenic dreams now dispersed almost beyond recall, leaving only a flavour behind, of richness and freedom, freedom especially from any sense of guilt, Bliss-dreams you might almost say. Pha seems further from me now as though she remains behind in a dream, and is the dream itself, or part of it, from which I now awake, as the world also awakes outside, cold soldiers returning from foxtrotting in the fields and up and down the lane, others going on duty.

When I look out, there's snow—just a light dusting, enough to sprinkle garden and lane and vehicles with icing sugar which will melt or be trampled soon enough, though at the moment all is crisp and pristine. I will bathe this strange younger body of mine, exploring and discovering it, as Tim would wish to, were it not for my grief. Will a hot bath begin the process of healing and reconciliation? Hardly! For the cuts have not yet been inflicted on Zandra far away.

Tony remains at Kielder, catering to the new influx of former government and security internees who might more sensibly be dispersed in many different places rather than concentrated like some opposition in internal exile—however, manpower is stretched fairly thin.

On the international scene, assorted Islamic republics quickly recognize the new British government, which seems unfortunate to me, hinting as this does at an unprecedented mysterious unholy alliance. Wheelchair-bound and one-eyed, Hugh Ellison appears on TV—pre-scripted and pre-recorded, I'm sure—to endorse the new regime, not with a hammering diatribe but with an appeal to the soul of a nation newly purified in the eyes of Jesus, of Allah, of Guru Nanak. Let there be a new brotherly spirituality and turning away from false idols sent to tempt us. This may account for the support from religious countries.

At home General Abercrombie is more of a popular hero than perhaps he expected, for the moment at least. On TV he makes much of a parallel with Cromwell's Commonwealth—behold, Britain has acted in this manner previously in our history, though certainly he does not hint at declaring us a republic. On the contrary, the Palace is apparently supportive, as are all right-thinking traditionalists and persons of privilege who have been in the political wilderness for years.

At the United Nations a Mockymen spokesdummy announces that Britain has suffered a collective mind-malady. Unless the British madness is healed they may need to reevaluate the assistance given gladly to the whole world. The starmen want intervention.

Yet who is supposed to conduct this therapeutic police action, and how? And for what adequate cause? If our country wishes to act as Little England once again we are merely cutting off our own noses. America's libertarian religious right clamours in praise of the British example, stymieing the federal government with threats of secession by a swathe of states. Europe remains extremely cautious, especially after a fundamentalist revolution unexpectedly erupts in Turkey leading to bloody civil war, shades of the bad old days before the interstellar entente, and an almighty distraction compared with the lack of bloodshed in Britain. Any European military coalition will need to cope with the chaos on the eastern flank. Big Brazil and Bigger China are calling for normalization in Britain —China especially has much to lose if Mockymen goodies cease globally—but both are thousands of miles away.

So time ticks by. Another day, and another.

Jock phones to tell me of successes and assorted problems in "cleansing the stables" at Centre Point and at Vauxhall Bridge. When I resume work, supposing that I wish to, I can become deputy director of Combined Intelligence, and director as soon as Jock gladly retires, though at the moment he's on an adrenalin high and thoroughly enjoying himself. It remains unprovable whether the referendum was actually rigged by some spooks at Cheltenham. A lot of data auto-deleted itself. Questioning of personnel continues. It may be advantageous to announce that the referendum was cleverly massaged, but on the other hand General Abercrombie is making a big thing of openness and honesty. A commission of enquiry could be the ticket. Might take a year to report.

Jane Morris—Oxford Jane—has resumed journalism with a rush as campaigner for the ex-Humpties of Kielder. In the *Guardian* and on the web her *Kielder Years* lambastes the lost time and the grinding boredom and frustration of internment, not that any shocking brutalities were suffered, and she campaigns for compensation by penal confiscation of assets from those people responsible, which seems to me like pettiness, and compensation too for the families of dummies on account of psychological trauma, which is slightly absurd when the state must continuing sustaining the dummies till the day they die decades from now—but Jane also calls for a research programme into some way of reanimating dummies. Censorship being patchy, especially as regards the web, she fingered me by name as the MAL minion who dished her, apparently assuming that I'm in Kielder myself these days. I hope she'll have a different attitude after I go public and she realizes the truth, unless the lost years have twisted her.

Since I came home with Tim, Sergeant Matt Woods has been spending his nights in one of the caravans. When Tim and I go for an afternoon walk down the lane through the fields to Morgan's Wood where I used to roam as a child, the Sergeant and another

armed soldier tag along behind as my protectors, not that I am likely
to need their intervention—we rarely see another soul—but my
safety must be guaranteed. They don't intrude. I would like to take
Cartoo with us on these outings, but since he is less of a known
quantity he must stay confined to house and garden. I have taught
him chess instead of us trying to master the food game, and when
we are absent he practises problems, black to play and mate in
three, and so on. On the board of real life there are millions of
pieces. Milly has been moved from under the mountain back to
Middlesex Square. I gather that Barnabas wanted this, though I do
not suppose that Milly, bereft of Robert, behaves quite as before—
while for his part Barnabas must be realizing that maybe he too is
bereft.

Amidst pasture and some apple orchards, a sharp dip in the land
is home mainly to beeches and hawthorns. By a pool is the ruin of
a little medieval chapel. I'm wearing a long black coat with huge
lapels and collar turned high against a keen breeze, and am looking
like a pilgrim perhaps.

"Does this remind you a bit—?"

"Of Ravensdene?" Tim leaps on to a low section of wall and
walks along, mounting higher and higher as if climbing steps. Just
at this moment my phone warbles.

"Anna?" It's Jock's voice, cut by a sizzle, drops of water hitting a
hot hob.

"I'm here, Jock, what is it?"

"I can't hear—" sizzle. Because of the dip we're in. "—Zandra—"

Galvanized, I start upslope as fast as I can, phone to my face.
"Don't ring off, Jock!"

And Tim cries out in startlement, "Wooooo—" He's toppling—
as is a chunk of stonework. He manages to land upright but immediately buckles sideways. He's down and writhing. Must have
twisted his foot. Can't be seriously hurt, can't possibly be, I can't just
leave him.

"Take cover down there—!"

Pistol and automatic rifle raised, the sergeant and the other
soldier are scanning for a possible assassin who has picked Tim off,
and now Woods comes bounding down the slope to protect me
from nothing, nothing at all—unless he's correct and from higher
up he spotted an intruder armed with a silenced gun, Tim can't
really be *wounded*, can he?

"I'll call back, Jock, can you hear me?" Pocket the phone, get to
Tim's side. Through clenched teeth he's swearing:

"Bugger bugger, you told me not to show off, bugger fuck—answer the phone!" No he hasn't been hit, no bullet, no intruder. "It's ricked, bloody hell, don't think it's broken—never mind me, the phone!"

"Take cover, get down—!"

"It's all right, he slipped, he twisted his ankle!"

Woods looks disinclined to believe me till I fairly scream at him, *"Stop!"* And then he stands, sweeping his pistol to and fro, checking all around.

"The phone, Anna."

"I can't from down here. Matt, will you help Tim!" And I'm off and away.

Up top, I call back to Jock.

Only just catching him before he rushes off—for Lionel Evans phoned from Hyde Park: Zandra's there, she came through, she's back on Earth.

She's in shock, her right hand is missing, been amputated. The Original did carry out his threat. Or began to. She's back, though, alive. Mutilated but safe, in London, in the Hyde Park medical wing.

"How, Jock?"

He doesn't know yet.

"Does she have passengers?"

He doesn't know that either.

I have to go to London.

Absolutely not. I'm to stay where I am, safe and sound. She may be a trap of some sort, swayed by the crystal the way she was once before. He'll tell me as soon as he has news. Wanted me to know right away, though.

Glory, glory. Well maybe and maybe not? No, *definitely*: glory hallelujah. Apart from her hand, parted from her. I must rush back to tell Tim.

I don't need to kill myself now. I'm free, finally free.

Jock phones three hours later as dusk deepens to night outside Come-Back Cottage. Tim is stretched out on the sofa, glass of malt beside him rather than a lager, foot and ankle bound by a medic, not broken but a muscle torn, and it was a slow limp back for him, holding on to me.

And soon we all know . . .

That To-mees acted truly after all, or more exactly he acted soon after Zandra's right hand was removed at the Original's say-so by his anatomy specialist using a numbing salve and a nano-machine that neatly separated hand from arm while she whimpered in revulsion, and after the specialist departed from the Bunch-o'-Grapes but before the severed part could be sent packaged to the transit station to be courier-carried, not to Londonoo any longer but perhaps to Paree or Brooseloo.

That To-mees seized a pacifier and stunned Monitors like a person possessed, not that Zandra could understand what he fluted about even if she was in a fit mental state, which evidently *he* was not; and almost immediately he was off and away—up above he must have pacified the Original himself, Two-Stunner To-mees by now. When he returned he was wearing new ribbons.

Next thing, he was freeing Pha and Shi from the thrones where they were tethered to witness punishment, and handing them stunners taken from those he stunned, and freeing Zandra too, and all was warble and trill; and Pha and Shi were soon wearing ribbons stripped from two Monitors.

Then they descended to the underground vehicle park and were off on balloon wheels to the transit station, Zandra coping the best she could as sensation returned to her stump, unscratchable itches and ant-bites, the surgeon not having had prior experience of human anatomy.

At the transit station To-mees left the two supposed Monitors with Zandra in one of the little dummy-dorms, returning soon after with another crystal for her to use. Pha and Shi went into Zandra— not To-mees, though. He must shepherd Zandra to departure and command her despatch to Londonoo; or so she inferred, understanding nothing of what was said.

What To-mees would do afterwards was moot.

His motives must await the downloading of Pha and Shi.

Into two women dummies.

Pha, Pha . . .

"You'll be seeing Pha again, won't you?" Tim says from the sofa.

Cartoo, sitting on the camp bed, cannot contain himself: "Yes yes yes."

"I'm talking to you, Anna."

It's true. Pha in a human body: will the magic linger? What sort of woman will she be? She might even be the girl who resembled a younger sister of mine. That could be very confusing in a menage of three. Might Tim go to bed with her in lieu of me, while on alternate nights I sleep with Pha? Will we all sleep together? I'm free of my curse, aren't I? For Zandra is free.

"Things may become complicated, Tim, but they ought to be interesting."

Is Pha's arrival a different sort of sword placed between us, at least for the moment? Horrid to think this, but frankly thank goodness Tim fell off the wall and incapacitated himself for a while.

It's the next day now, and Jock calls again. Zandra is free of her pair of passengers. They will go to a safe house, which will not be ours — eggs in different baskets. Your rural roof's been fixed then, Jock? So it has, he allows. Photos of the new Pha and Shi are being scan-sent to the com-van, for Cartoo to see, and me too.

Already Pha, breathing anew, has explained that To-mees experienced a great disillusionment when Zandra's right hand was truly cut off.

To begin with, To-mees had believed that the Original had genuinely severed himself. To-mees had never previously been upstairs, to learn otherwise—and so he was mentally in the Original's thrall. That amputation of dummy limbs was awe-inspiring, a redoubtable act of devotion to Su-loo-la. Like mystics squatting up a pole for forty years. Hearing my negotiations with the Original, To-mees realized that the self-dissection was a sham, a techno conjuring trick. This, To-mees could cope with, since . . . I suppose you might say that at least the spirit was willing even if the flesh was weak. But to use the way of enlightenment as a coercive penalty upon *someone else*—this was utterly devaluing. Worse, that an *alien* —Zandra—might perhaps achieve Su-loo-la by this means . . . The bottom fell out of To-mees's world.

To-mees flipped.

The ribbons of an Original could not be obtained from any public ribbon-printer but To-mees had stolen those of the Original. So when he arrived at the transit station properly beribboned, he could only be an Original and an Original must be obeyed. Display of ribbons was how he finessed another crystal from the technical department; and how he ensured Zandra's departure, even if Londonoo was now supposed to be a no-go destination.

As to what he would do after ordering Zandra despatched, why, fairly soon the Monitors in the Bunch-o'-Grapes would revive from their stunning and contact the Hoo-hoo House. To-mees would not dream of ordering himself to be transmitted to Earth. The pain, the hideous pain of it. He intended to hurry to the airport and, showing his ribbons, commandeer a smart voice-controlled flying machine, to take him to the Wilderness of Way-woo. Supposedly a tribe of free and natural Ivorymen persisted. Why they should offer shelter to a body-thief, supposing they existed and supposing he found them, was problematic.

Scarcely have I finished telling Tim and Cartoo and Daddy than Matt Woods arrives from the com-van bearing a couple of colour prints, the mug shots of Pha and Shi, each labelled.

Pha is in the body of a chubby-cheeked, freckly lass haloed with red curls. Bonny and cuddly she looks. Shi is blond, crewcut, blue-eyed, with thin lips, long thin nose, bony rather than bonny, though with undeniable presence.

"Look, Cartoo, look. This is Pha. This is Shi. Look, Tim."

Tim, of course, lingers longest on Pha. "Hmm, looks sweet, doesn't see?"

"These are good faces?" asks Cartoo.

"Best the dating agency could come up with," is Tim's retort, which quite confuses Cartoo.

I need to phone Middlesex Square.

"Barnabas, it's Anna Sharman. Can I speak to Zandra?"

"Well, she can still hold a phone." Zandra doesn't actually need to hold one physically, but his barbed comment is understandable. Is it a petty jibe, considering all that is involved, or is he forewarning me?

"I can't come to you in person, Barnabas. Jock won't let me loose yet. How is she?"

"Could say it's a miracle she came back at all. Hand's a fair exchange for a miracle, you might say. You never bloody well warned her so she could prepare her mind! They just started doing that to her, and how much were they going to do? She had no idea, no more than a rabbit in a lab."

"I didn't tell her because I thought it was a pretend threat, not something real."

"Oh really?"

"If I had thought it was real, how would telling her have helped?"

"Not helped *you*, maybe, darling."

"Barnabas, I was sick thinking about it." Yes, I was pledging myself to celibacy. And death. "She would have been so worried."

"She would have been able to prepare her mind, not be a rabbit. How do you think we faced transit? How do you think we scarred ourselves? You don't understand us."

"Please let me talk to her."

"Talking redeems everything, is that it?"

"Please."

"For your peace of mind?"

"So that I can apologize."

"From a safe distance—or for all I know just round the corner in a car out of sight, hey, I bet that's it."

"I told you, I can't be there with you, and that's true. I'm miles away."

But the next voice I hear is Zandra's.

"Guess what, Anna Sharman? I'm thinking of visiting No Short Cuts." She sounds very haute, though with a tremulous flutter beneath. "I might start a trend."

"Zandra, you saved my life and you saved Cartoo's friends. Thank you so much."

"I didn't save them—it simply happened to me."

"You're the only other human being to have seen an alien planet."

"Much of it I saw. Big deal."

"Oh it's a very big deal. As soon as everything sorts out, you can become famous."

"Zandra Wilde, hostage of Melody. You're in a black girl's body now, right? Tall girl, I hear. How will the viewers tell us apart?"

Aside from us looking quite different, of course.

"Maybe," yes, risk it, "you wave your stump."

It sounds as if she is choking—until laughter comes welling up, slightly hysterical but laughter none the less.

"What you hear," she says, more calmly, "is the sound of one hand clapping."

"That," take another risk, "is a good sound—it's the sound of being human. And human is what we'll carry on being. We shall not be mockied."

"You can say that again, and you probably will. Oh shit . . . we'll talk again." With which, she rings off.

Now we will need to wait a while until others do our dirty deed for us, for the common good.

FUTURE

Chapter 30

The power of will is the key, according to Olav Frisvold. Meaning the key to his own reincarnation.

But what of the power of Will and Shall?

New outlook, new viewpoint, new way of speaking.

Maybe because strange nanos escape from food factories due to inept interference and lack of Mockymen expertise. Maybe because Bliss mutates viruslike in the bloodstreams of former users. Maybe because Jane's crusade for the awakening of the dummies succeeds — the research project unlocks the suspended persons by means of re-engineered Bliss and Laevo-dihydroxy-phenylalanine.

Where are the Selves of the dummies? Locked in a moment before the Now, out of synch, registering in curled-up inner dimensions. According to Yukio Horiuchi, Japan's Einstein, time and energy being twins, and as waves of energy are flowing through time, an undertow returning constantly to its origin, pressure of time against anti-time curling up those micro-dimensions, information-dense.

Maybe because of a shift in mentality as radical as the dawn of language itself, with rogue Bliss as catalyst.

Thinking not being something we "put into words" but on the contrary words being in Darwinian competition to utter themselves, giving rise to our thoughts and therefore to our Selves. Words competing for expression in the individual and in society. Word willing the personal and the social world.

Newspeech begins as youth-jargon world wide, spreads like wildfire in many languages, past becoming present, the demise of was and were and has been, past now vividly present, I fly to Ravensdene with Tim, I am shot by Robert, say so and know these events almost as if new.

The present enriching with becoming-ness, with serene bright enlightenment, paying so much more constant attention, sun shining this morning, birds singing, me sipping this coffee, talking to my comp, comp copying my words to screen, foot itching not-itching now, motes in the air and spider on the ceiling, like my acid trip in Oxford but lucid and sense of time intact.

Being me, being here in Cwmbach Cottage with Tim and our daughter Jane-Zandra downstairs, Jayzee for short, affectionately Crazy Jayzee who sees more than I ever saw, apart from her mother witnessing alien world, alien sun. Daddy dies but always still being here. Pha and Shi and Cartoo travelling in Australia, so-called dreamtime land, and the young being lucidly aware in their dreams nowadays. Mary of Morogoro comes to England, and I do not take her under my wing but Zandra does, her own long-lost child restored fully grown, and Barnabas takes Mary under the wing of his angel.

Olav Frisvold née Jamie being founder-leader of the Rebirth Foundation, offering meditation crystals for personal empowerment and memory enhancement to older people being awkward with newspeech — new mutating words emerging making new meanings often beyond me too, particularly our new future tense, our prophetic tense, of self-command and of bidding events to be so, let it be, almost foretelling.

As Self dawns in ancestral animals long ago, surprising them into awareness, so now being at a threshold, beyond which as yet inexpressible, for me though not perhaps for Jayzee.

Three thousand copies of this book have been printed by the Maple-Vail Book Manufacturing Group, Binghamton, NY, for Golden Gryphon Press, Urbana, IL. The typeset is Electra, printed on 55# Sebago. Typesetting by The Composing Room, Inc., Kimberly, WI.